KU-757-283

RED JOAN

Jennie Rooney

WINDSOR
PARAGON

First published 2013
by Chatto & Windus
This Large Print edition published 2013
by AudioGO Ltd
by arrangement with
The Random House Group Ltd

Hardcover   ISBN: 978 1 4713 5507 3
Softcover   ISBN: 978 1 4713 5508 0

Copyright © Jennie Rooney 2013

Jennie Rooney has asserted her right under the
Copyright, Designs and Patents Act 1988 to be
identified as the author of this work

All rights reserved.

British Library Cataloguing in Publication Data available

Printed and bound in Great Britain by TJ International Limited

RED JOAN

For Mark

'Oh dear. I thought I got away with it.'

Melita Norwood, aged eighty-seven, the KGB's longest-serving British spy, speaking to a reporter from *The Times* upon being unmasked in September 1999

Sidcup
January, 2005

Sunday, 11.17 a.m.

She knows the cause of death without needing to be told.

The hand-delivered note from the solicitor is brief and unemotional, enclosing details of the funeral arrangements on Friday along with a copy of an obituary from the *Daily Telegraph*. The obituary describes Sir William Mitchell's early life in Sherborne, Dorset, where he contracted polio at the age of eight (she had not known that), made a miraculous recovery, and then proved himself particularly adept at Latin and ancient Greek at school. He went on to read Modern and Medieval Languages at Cambridge, was drafted into the Special Operations Executive during the war, and later rose to a high position in the Foreign Office, advising the British and Commonwealth governments on intelligence matters and gaining a number of honorary doctorates from various universities along the way. Apparently he was never happier than when walking in the Scottish hills with his wife, now deceased. She had not known that either.

What she had already known was this: that he would appear to die peacefully in his sleep.

She puts the article and letter on the table in front of her, her breath coming in short, sharp bursts. There is mud under her fingernails as well as on her apron, leaving smudged marks on the cream-coloured envelope. The three terracotta pots on the kitchen table are as she left them, each half-filled with patted-down soil around the geranium

3

stem cuttings snipped from her neighbour's front garden that morning, but they seem somehow changed by the interruption, no longer delicate and victorious at having survived the English winter into January, but straggly and ill-gotten.

She thinks of the silver necklace William gave her sixty years ago, identical to the ones both he and Rupert wore: the engraved St Christopher's charm depicting the ragged saint carrying Jesus on his shoulders across a stormy sea. She had not known what the charm concealed, having mistaken its significance for something else. There was no sign of the needle tip infused with curare, a substance chosen for its untraceable qualities, which relaxes the muscles so effectively that the lungs stop moving almost instantaneously. Death by asphyxiation. So motionless that it passes for peaceful. She would not have accepted this gift from William if she had known what it was, but by the time she read the instructions, it was too late to give it back. He had arranged it that way. He wanted her to have the option too. Just in case.

Is this what has happened? Did they finally come for him, after all these years? If they did, it can only mean that there is some new evidence, something irrefutable, to have made him believe it was not worth trying to defend himself and his reputation. Better to die than to risk the possibility of his knighthood being stripped from him, of having to endure the public recriminations and shame such revelations would bring, along with the inevitable criminal trial. And why should he endure such humiliation? His wife is dead; he has no children. Nothing to stop him.

No son to protect, as she has.

The obituary is accompanied by a picture of William as a young man, his features clear and unblemished, just as he was the last time she saw him. His eyes are directed straight at the camera, a slight smile playing on his lips as if he knows something he shouldn't. She imagines that, to the rest of the world, the mistiness of the black-and-white image might appear glamorous and full of pathos, a picture of youth in a bygone age. But to Joan it is like looking at a ghost.

*　　　*　　　*

They come for her later that morning. Joan is watching from her bedroom window as a long black car turns into the quiet suburban street of pebble-dashed terraces where she has lived ever since moving back to England from Australia after her husband's death fifteen years earlier. The car is out of place in this part of south-east London. She observes the man and woman as they step out and glance about them, absorbing their surroundings. The woman is wearing high heels and a smart camel-coloured mackintosh, and the man is carrying a briefcase. They stand next to each other, conferring, facing across the road towards her house.

Goosebumps rise on her arms and neck. For some reason, she had always thought they would come for her at night. She did not imagine a day like this, cold and bright and perfectly still. She watches as they cross the road and push open her front gate. Perhaps she is being paranoid. They could be anyone. Social workers or meals-on-wheels salespeople. She has sent such people away before.

The knock is loud and staccato; official-sounding. 'Open up. Security Services.'

She steps back quickly, her heart stuttering as she lets the curtain fall in front of her. Too old to run. She wonders what they would do if she does not answer the door. Would they break it down? Or just trust that she is not in, and come back again tomorrow? She could stay here until they've gone, and then she could . . . She stops. Could what? Where could she go for any length of time without arousing suspicion? And what would she say to her son about where she was?

Another knock, louder this time.

Joan clasps her hands across her stomach as the thought occurs to her that they might try to find her at her son's house if they do not find her here. Her neck feels hot at the prospect of one of Nick's boys answering the door, muddy-haired and careless in his football kit, calling out that some people have come about Granny. If Nick saw these two, in their smart clothes and black car, he would think they had come to inform him of his mother's death, and Joan feels a stab of guilt to imagine his shock at this news.

And then a greater, more terrible shock as he learns that no, this is not what they've come to tell him.

And which of those would be worse?

It is a tickling, stealthy creep of a thought, so bold and yet so soft as it insinuates itself in her mind, and she feels a cold spasm of fear run its sharp finger down her back. Yes, she can see why William might have thought it better to kill himself. She could do it right now, take the St Christopher's medal from her bedside drawer and push it open to reveal the needle tip, and then she could settle herself into bed one last time and she would never have to face them. It would be over, finished, and when they found her she would appear just as peaceful as William had, just as innocent. How easy it would be.

But easier for whom?

For one thing, the presence of curare in her bloodstream might now be traceable, even if it had not been sixty years ago, and would be revealed by an autopsy. Or it might not work, it might be too old, it might only half work. And, traceable or not, they might still push ahead regardless with whatever investigations they had begun. Nick would be left to face the accusations alone, and quite suddenly Joan knows with absolute certainty that, in such circumstances, he would not rest until he had cleared his mother's name from whatever charge they brought against her. He is a barrister, and fiercely protective by nature. He would defend her with his last breath if he believed it was the right thing to do. It would all seem too far-fetched, too out of character, to square with the mother he has known all his life.

In the reflection of the glass, she observes the man and woman walk back down the path and stand on the pavement to look up at the windows of the house before turning away. She draws back further. She can hardly believe it is happening. Not now. Not after all these years. There is the click of one car door opening and slamming shut, and then the other one. They are getting back into the car, either to wait for her there or to drive to Nick's house. She does not know which.

This is not how it was supposed to end. A sudden memory of herself as a young woman comes to her with a jolt; a bright Technicolor image of a life which, from this distance, she cannot really believe was ever hers. It seems so removed from the quiet way she lives now, where the only things filling her week are watercolour classes on Tuesday afternoons and ballroom dancing on Thursdays, punctuated by regular visits from Nick and his family. A calm and contented existence, but not exactly the extraordinary life she had once imagined for herself. But still, this is her life. Her only life. And she has not kept silent for so many years just to have it swept away from her now when she is so close to the end.

She takes a deep breath and walks briskly across the room, no longer caring if she is visible from the street. She must sort this out now, alone. She cannot allow Nick to find out like this. The afternoon sun falls in a white blossom of light through the window above the narrow staircase as she hurriedly descends the stairs to the front door. She unhooks the silver chain and tugs the door across the part of the mat which has a tendency to catch on the underside of the wood, blinking as her eyes adjust to the glare of daylight, and then she steps out onto the doorstep, her heart pounding in her chest. She sees the woman turn around as the car begins to pull away, and for a brief second their eyes meet.

'Wait,' she calls out.

*   *   *

They take her to a large building in a narrow street

8

not far from Westminster Abbey and the Houses of Parliament, a forty-minute drive from Joan's house. They do not speak, except to check she is comfortable and to ask again if she would like to call a legal representative. She tells them that she is quite comfortable, and that no, she does not wish to have a lawyer present. She doesn't need one. They haven't arrested her, have they?

'Not technically, but . . .'

'There, see. I don't need one.'

'This is a matter of state security. I would really advise . . .' The woman hesitates. 'Your son is a barrister, I believe, Mrs Stanley. Would you like us to contact him?'

'No,' Joan says, and her voice is sharp. 'I don't want him disturbed.' A pause. 'I haven't done anything wrong.'

They sit in silence for the rest of the journey, Joan's hands clasped tightly together as if in prayer. But she is not praying. She is thinking. She is making sure she remembers everything so that she cannot be taken by surprise.

When they arrive, her seatbelt is unbuckled for her. She follows the woman, Ms Hart, out of the car, while the man, Mr Adams, walks behind them up the steps to a small wooden door set into a carved stone frame. He does not say anything but reaches forward and holds his pass up against a small black box. The door clicks, and he pushes it open.

Ms Hart leads the way along a narrow corridor. She propels Joan into a square room with a table and three chairs and takes the briefcase from Mr Adams. He does not follow them in but waits outside, and then shuts the door behind them.

9

There are microphones set up on the table and a camera attached to the ceiling in the far corner of the room. A glass window reflects Joan's gaze back at her and she looks away quickly, although not before observing the faint shadow of Mr Adams' presence behind the screen. Ms Hart sits down on one side of the table and gestures that Joan should do the same.

'You're quite certain you don't want a lawyer?'

Joan nods.

'Right.' Ms Hart extracts two files from the briefcase. She places them on the table and pushes the slimmer one across to Joan. 'Let's start with this.'

Joan sits back. She will not touch the file. 'I haven't done anything wrong.'

'Mrs Stanley,' Ms Hart continues, 'I would advise you to cooperate. We have enough evidence to convict. It will only be possible for the Home Secretary to show clemency towards you if there is some sort of confession or an admission of guilt. Information.' She pauses. 'Otherwise you will make it impossible for us to be lenient.'

Joan says nothing. Her arms are folded.

Ms Hart looks down at the shiny floor of the interviewing room, adjusting the position of her briefcase with the immaculate point of her shoe. 'You're being accused of twenty-seven breaches of the Official Secrets Act, which is effectively treason. I'm sure you're aware that this is not a light charge. If you force us to take it to trial, it will carry a maximum sentence of fourteen years.'

Silence. Joan counts the years in her head, each one causing a painful tightening across her chest. She does not move.

Ms Hart glances at the shadow of Mr Adams behind the screen. 'It will be of benefit to you if anything you wish to say in your defence has been recorded before your name is released to the House of Commons on Friday.' She pauses. 'I should tell you now that you'll be expected to make a statement in response.'

Friday. The day of William's funeral. She would not have gone anyway. She steels herself so that when she speaks her voice is quiet and firm. 'I still don't know what you're talking about.'

Ms Hart slips a photograph out of the side pocket of her briefcase and places it on the table between them. Joan glances at it and then looks away again. She recognises it, of course. It is the photograph from the obituary.

Ms Hart places her palms flat on the table and leans forward. 'You knew Sir William Mitchell at Cambridge, I believe. You were undergraduates there at around the same time.'

Joan looks blankly at Ms Hart, neither confirming nor denying.

'We're just trying to build up a picture at this initial stage,' Ms Hart continues. 'Place everything in context.'

'A picture of what?'

'As I'm sure you're aware, Sir William died rather suddenly last week. There was an investigation and several questions remain unanswered as a result.'

Joan frowns, wondering how exactly she might be linked to William. 'I don't know how you think I can help you. I didn't know him all that well.'

Ms Hart raises an eyebrow. 'The case against Sir William is incidental to the case against you,

11

Mrs Stanley. It's your choice. Either we sit in silence until you cooperate, or we can just get on with it.' She waits. 'Let's start with university.'

Joan does not move. Her eyes flick to the screen and then to the locked door behind Ms Hart. It will not end here—she will not let it—but she can see that a degree of cooperation might be worthwhile, and could even buy her a little time to decide how much they know. They must have some evidence for William to have done what he did.

'I did go,' she says at last. 'In 1937.'

Ms Hart nods. 'And what did you read for your degree?'

Joan's vision is suddenly concentrated on Ms Hart's hands, and it takes her a few seconds to realise what is unusual about them. They are suntanned. Suntanned in January, and the thought prompts an unexpected thud of homesickness for Australia. For the first time since her return to England, Joan wishes she had not come back. She should have known it was not safe. She shouldn't have allowed Nick to persuade her.

'Certificate,' she says at last.

'Sorry?'

'Women got certificates, not degrees. Back then.' Another pause. 'I read Natural Sciences.'

'But you specialised in Physics, I believe.'

'Did I?'

'Yes.'

Joan glances at Ms Hart and then looks away again.

'Right.' A pause. 'And why did you want to go? It can't have been a very normal thing to do back then.'

Joan exhales slowly, aware that everything she

12

says must be absolutely consistent. No, it wasn't normal, but the only other options seemed to be getting married, teaching or learning to type and she didn't want to do any of those. She closes her eyes and forces her mind back to the year she first left home, wanting to be absolutely certain of the memory before she speaks, and as she does, she finds that she can still remember the feeling of that year with absolute clarity; the breathless sensation brought on by the knowledge that if she didn't go somewhere and do something then her lungs might actually burst out of her chest. It feels odd to remember it now: such a long-forgotten feeling. She had never felt a sensation quite like it before and she has never felt it since, but, now that she thinks about it, she remembers observing that same static energy fizzing out of her own son when he turned eighteen. Not old but no longer young either. An impressionable age, her mother called it.

*　　*　　*

In the autumn of 1937, Joan leaves home to attend Newnham College, Cambridge. She is eighteen years old and impatient to leave. There is no particular reason for this impatience other than an underlying sense of life happening elsewhere, far removed from the ivy-covered lodge of the girls' public school near St Albans where she has lived all her life. The school is a hearty establishment with special emphasis placed on organised games, which (according to the school's prospectus) will encourage the girls to develop a love of justice, alongside the ability to make prompt decisions and to recognise defeat with good cheer, and Joan is obliged to spend several hours every week charging around the school field dressed in a pinafore and wielding a wooden stick in pursuit of these lofty ideals.

As the headmaster's daughters, Joan and her younger sister are not ordinary pupils—they do not have beds in the dormitory or parts in the school play or tuck boxes arriving through the post—and while her parents insist that this set-up is a privilege, to Joan it seems to be no more than a form of constant surveillance and, in her opinion, is bound to give them both asthma. She knows she should be more grateful, being reminded often enough of how lucky she is that her generation has not been sent off to the trenches, and that she is not obliged to run away from home in order to become a nurse in the Great War as her mother did when she was sixteen but, at the same time, she also feels there is something enticing about that youthful display of self-sufficiency, which only serves to make her feel more restless.

There is a whole world out there that is barely recognisable from the safe, padded vantage point of St Albans. She knows this because she has seen it in her father's limp, in the newsreels at the cinema showing the Welsh collieries and deserted shipyards of the North; in newspapers and books and films; in the pictures of small children in doorways with grubby knees and no shoes. She glimpsed it when the Great Hunger March passed through St Albans a few years previously, a straggling procession of men and women so dirty that their skin seemed to have turned a deep, charcoal grey. Joan remembers how one of the marchers stopped outside the lodge as he left town in the morning, leaning against the garden fence and bent double in a fit of coughing.

'What's the matter with him?' Joan had asked her father. 'Shouldn't we call the doctor?'

Her father shook his head. 'That's coal dust,' he said. 'Nothing you can do about silicosis. Cuts into the lungs and kills the tissue. And he's walking to London with all the rest of them because he wants his job back.'

'Why doesn't he just get a different one?'

Her father had not answered this question immediately. He watched as the man drank the glass of water that Lally had taken out to him, and then struggled to catch up with the rest of the marchers. He turned away from her and limped out of the room, muttering, 'Why indeed?'

He answered this question the following day, interrupting the chaplain just before the recitation of the school prayer in a way that only a headmaster can. He waved a newspaper aloft as he declared to the school that it was a criminal sort of government that refused to acknowledge the reality of life in what they called the 'Special Areas' of Britain. It was either a failure of imagination or wilful blindness, but either way it was a betrayal. He instructed each child and teacher in the school to close their eyes and picture life in the ship-building towns where no ships were being built, to think of the boarded-up shops, the Means Test man declaring that a family's only rug must be sold before any relief could be granted. Imagine the destitution. And then imagine it in winter.

He quoted Ramsay MacDonald, leader of the coalition who was supposed to save the country from economic despair. 'Has anyone,' Ramsay MacDonald was reported to have asked in the

15

House of Commons in response to the marchers' request for an audience, 'who comes to London, either on foot or in first-class carriages, the constitutional right to demand to see me, to take up my time, whether I like it or not?'

The question was rhetorical and its impact was lost on many of the younger schoolgirls, but Joan's father let the words hang in the scuffling silence before folding the newspaper in disgust. 'Our prime minister may not know it, but we have a duty,' he said, frowning at a noise coming from a group of girls in the Upper Fifth, 'to make this poor and hungry world a better place for everyone in it. To be responsible.'

Another pause, longer than the first, so that when her father spoke again his voice boomed into the beamed ceiling of the school hall.

'From each'—she remembers his exact words— 'according to his ability.'

*   *   *

To Joan's disappointment, her abilities seem to be limited to hockey and schoolwork. At first, she was unsure how either of these could be put to practical use in the way her father envisaged, but she suspected that one might be of more use than the other. Her science teacher, Miss Abbott, was the first to suggest she might try for university, and it was on her instigation that Joan applied to read Natural Sciences for the honours certificate at Cambridge; the flat, weather-beaten town where Miss Abbot had once spent her happiest years before the Great War marched in and snatched away the life she had planned.

Joan is excited about going, although it is less the qualification that interests her than the prospect of going somewhere, anywhere. And it is also the prospect of learning things that she would never have the chance of knowing if she didn't go, of attending lectures in the mornings, reading books all afternoon, and spending evenings at the cinema watching Mary Brian and Norma Shearer being whisked away on horseback by Gary Cooper, then copying their hairdos later in case the same thing should ever happen to her.

Of course, she knows that in Cambridge she is unlikely to come across Gary Cooper. There will only be real men, men whose teeth do not glint in the moonlight and who ride bicycles instead of horses but still, endless, bountiful men. Boys, some of them, but even they will be a welcome break from the rippling sea of girls at school. Joan did not mention this to her father or Miss Abbott during the coaching sessions for the interview ('And why do you wish to pursue your academic study at the University of Cambridge?') but now it simmers under the surface of her enthusiasm. She knows that it is a privilege to be going and she is constantly reminded of this fact by both her father and the college scholarship fund but, frankly, she would have gone anywhere.

Joan's father is delighted to see her go. He tells her that it will be a wonderful thing to be educated in the religion of reason. These are his words, not hers, although she knows what he means. They understand each other, Joan and her father, sharing a quiet sort of complicity that is not chatty enough for her mother or Lally. Other people tell Joan how much her younger sister resembles her, that they

17

could be twins if not for the five-year age difference, and while Lally flushes with pleasure at this, Joan considers it to be eye-rollingly stupid, although she has to hide this sentiment from Lally. Her sister's temperament is sweet and wide-eyed, and whereas Joan cannot remember there ever having been a time when she was happy to go shopping for dress material with her mother or make daisy chains in the garden, Lally seems happy to do it. It is only her father who does not see this resemblance and grunts his disagreement when anyone else alludes to it. He is complicit in Joan's plans to escape, and Joan loves him for this more than for anything else.

In contrast, Joan's mother is decidedly ungrateful about the whole enterprise. It is clear that she would like to march into that school and have a strong word with Miss Abbott for condemning Joan to eternal spinsterhood by educating her beyond all prospects of future happiness. It is made clear that she does not intend to let the same thing happen to Lally, oh-ho no. Her second daughter will be kept well away from Miss Abbott.

When Joan suggests that going to university is no worse than running away to become a nurse, her mother shakes her head and insists that the two things are quite different. 'They were unprecedented times, Joanie. You can't imagine it. You can't imagine the sound they made, all those boys being delivered at the hospital door, crying out for their mothers as we unloaded them from carts and wagons and ambulances until they filled the corridors. Such a terrible, terrible time.'

Joan has heard this speech before and knows

better than to say what she really thinks, which is that yes, it does sound terrible, but all times are unprecedented. Surely her times are unprecedented, too. But she also knows that her mother will not actually be able to stop her, and so while some of the other girls from her class will be enrolling in secretarial college in the autumn and others will be getting married and moving into their own homes, Joan is the only one who is going to university.

*   *   *

Before she goes, there is the University Trousseau to arrange; it is a compromise, a tactical diversion, to allow her mother this slant on events. A list of items Joan will need is drawn up between them, and Joan is dispatched to the local department store to obtain great swathes of material so that she can be suitably upholstered before leaving. There must be some sort of tweed ensemble, a navy suit, a knitted outfit for lectures, a pair of chic trousers (chic is her mother's word, indefinable for both of them), three blouses, two belts, two bags (one pretty, one practical), a mackintosh, a simple woollen dress and one smart dance dress. Her mother insists that she should also have a fur coat and she will not be budged on this. It is a huge extravagance, there is no question of buying one: one must be found.

'You've got to look the part, Joanie,' her mother tells her, surrounded by pins and cottons and materials cut into unlikely shapes on the living-room rug, although neither of them knows what the part should look like. They know only that they do not know, which is not quite enough.

No mention is made of purchasing the set texts or the equipment required for science practicals or any of the other things that Joan feels might actually come in handy for the course. University, it seems, is mostly a question of textiles.

*   *   *

During those first few days of living alone in Cambridge, Joan finds that she is amazingly, gloriously happy just to be alive. She loves her new home with its red-bricked Queen Anne architecture, its beautifully manicured lawns and sports field and tennis courts. Physically, she equates this excitement to the feeling in her stomach when she cycles very fast over the hump bridge at the back of Clare College, that sudden rush of giddiness in her stomach, and then the exhilaration of speeding downhill.

She attends lectures in the mornings, leaving her bicycle propped against the railings of the science faculty on Pembroke Street, and then sliding into the back row of the lecture theatre with her satchel under her arm. The days of chaperones are over, but the lecturers still largely ignore the female presence, addressing the audience as 'gentlemen'. They tend to stand directly in front of whatever they have written, mumbling 'square this' and 'subtract that', and then wiping the board down to move on to the next calculation before anyone has had time to work out what they are supposed to be doing but Joan remains undeterred. She regards each lecture as a small dot of knowledge which will one day join to another dot, and then another and another, until she will finally understand at least some of the figures chalked up in minute smudges on the blackboard, and she is hopeful that this will come about before the summer examinations.

Her room at Newnham is on the ground floor of Peile Hall, a relatively new block with modern bathrooms and kitchenettes and a view out over the immaculate gardens. It is as large as the drawing room at home, with a small truckle bed pushed up against one wall and a thick-cushioned sofa against the other, leaving a huge expanse of carpet in the middle where she can practise handstands without the remotest possibility of breaking anything. The kitchenette has a single gas ring upon which she has not yet attempted to cook, preferring to skip breakfast in favour of an apple on the way to lectures, followed by a packed lunch of crusty bread with cheese or boiled ham, and then dinner in Hall, a large, light room with beautiful, corniced ceilings and long, communal tables. Although there is no one she immediately takes to in those first few days, she is not lonely. Everyone is astonishingly friendly, and these dinners are enjoyable, rumbustious affairs. She is not used to this after the cliques and hierarchies of school, and she puts it down to the fact that here, in Cambridge, everyone is a bit of a swot, and so for once there is nothing unusual about her.

*   *   *

On her third night, Joan is awoken by a smart rap on the window, followed by a scrabbling noise on the window ledge outside, as if a very large cat is trying to get into her room. She leans out of bed and pinches the bottom corner of the curtain between her finger and thumb and pulls it back. Her hockey stick is propped up against the wall, and there is something comforting about its proximity. She clears her throat, ready to scream if necessary, and peers out.

Two scarlet high-heeled shoes are standing on her windowsill.

She pulls the curtain a little further back and looks upwards. A girl is half-standing, half-crouching in the shoes, resplendent in a black silk dress and a white scarf, and when she sees the curtain lift she smiles and puts a finger to her lips. She crouches down so that her face is almost level with Joan's.

'Hurry up and let me in,' she mouths through the glass.

Joan hesitates for a moment, and then slides out of bed to undo the catch, and the girl steps through the window frame and into Joan's room. 'My room's on the third floor,' the girl announces, by way of explanation, removing her shoes one at a time before jumping down from the windowsill. 'Darned curfew,' she mutters, massaging her toes where her shoes have been chafing. 'Sorry for getting you up. The laundry window was closed.'

Joan rubs her eyes. 'Don't mention it.'

The girl glances around the room, taking in the heavy green curtains and the sofa with its collection of ill-matched cushions. Her hair and eyes are dark, her cheeks smooth and dusted, and her lips bear a bright slash of red lipstick. Joan is suddenly conscious of how she must look, standing barefoot in her nightie with small strips of muslin tied into her hair. She steps back towards her bed, supposing that this might encourage the girl to go, but the girl does not seem to be in any rush.

'Are you a first year too?'

Joan is surprised by the implication in the question that this girl is also a new arrival. She seems so self-assured, so certain of the rules, that it is hard to believe she hasn't been here for years. 'Yes.'

'English Literature?'

Joan shakes her head. 'Natural Sciences.'

'Ah. I was fooled by your cushion covers.' She pauses. 'I'm reading Languages. More modern than medieval. I say, I don't suppose you've got a dressing gown I could borrow? I don't want to get caught walking around like this. Better to pretend we've been up all night drinking cocoa or something like the rest of them.'

Joan nods and turns away, not wanting to let on that this was, in fact, how she had spent the latter part of her evening before going to bed, that she was one of *them*. She goes to the wardrobe and takes out her dressing gown.

'Is that a mink coat?' the girl asks from behind Joan's shoulder, her voice suddenly curious.

'Hmm, yes, I think so.' Joan gives a small shrug, self-conscious at having such a thing in her wardrobe, procured on indefinite loan from a second cousin who no longer had any use for it, but Joan cannot imagine that she will ever be bold enough to wear it. 'It's a bit hideous, isn't it?'

'Well, it's rather *fin de siècle*,' says the girl with a sideways smile, stepping towards the wardrobe. She reaches out her hand and strokes the coat, and then slips it off its hanger, tilts her head to inspect it, and flings it around her shoulders. 'Although at least it's

23

not Arctic fox. They're everywhere at the moment.'

'Except the Arctic regions.'

The girl gives a short, surprised laugh. She turns around and glances at her back in the mirror. And then she lifts her arms and twirls, so that her silk dress clings to her chest and the mink coat spins out like a flapper outfit: miraculously transformed, made glamorous in a way that Joan has never imagined. So that is how you wear it, Joan thinks. Not draped or buttoned or belted. Just flung.

'I don't think it's hideous,' the girl says. 'It's different.'

Joan smiles. She expects that it is different because it was made so long ago that its cut is no longer recognisable. But there is something rich about it as it spins and flares, something luxuriant and soft which she can't help but admire as the girl discards it on Joan's bed. She must remember to thank her mother properly for finding it in her next letter. 'I suppose it's not so bad,' Joan concedes. 'I'm just not used to it yet.'

'I'll bring your dressing gown back tomorrow,' the girl says, tiptoeing to the door and turning the handle. She peers out to check that the corridor is empty, and then looks back to nod towards the pair of scarlet stilettos lying discarded in the middle of Joan's room. 'And I'll pick up my shoes then too, if that's all right? They don't make very convincing slippers.'

'Of course.' Joan waits for the girl to close the door behind her. She picks up the fur coat and goes to hang it in her wardrobe, and then she glances at the girl's shoes, so bold against her beige rug. How could anyone walk in those, let alone climb onto a windowsill? Still considering this, she slides her feet

24

into the steep cavities of bright red leather, a close fit but not uncomfortable. She catches a glimpse of herself in the mirror, and for a moment she pauses, no longer sleepy but giddy and precarious, before coming to her senses and taking them off, placing them next to her well-worn, low-heeled brogues, and getting back into bed.

Sunday, 2.39 p.m.

Ms Hart takes a photograph from the file and places it on the table next to the photograph of William. 'Do you recognise this?'

'Oh,' Joan whispers. It is the picture from her undergraduate laboratory pass while she was at Cambridge. She has not seen it for years, and yet it is so familiar to her that it is almost like glancing in a mirror; a tea-coloured and misty mirror, yes, but a mirror all the same. Her face in the photograph is powdered and rouged, and her eyes have a distant look about them, silvery-grey in the black-and-white spectrum. There will have been lipstick on her lips to make them so dark and defined, and they are parted slightly in a smile. How different she looks there from how she looks now. So young and innocent and, well, pretty. She has not used that word to describe herself for years. 'Of course I recognise it.'

'This is the photograph that will accompany the press statement on Friday.'

Joan looks up at her. 'But why will the press want a photograph of me?'

Ms Hart crosses her arms. 'I think you know,

don't you, Mrs Stanley?'

Joan shakes her head, careful to maintain her expression of confusion. She can see the appeal of this photograph to any members of the press who might be interested in the story, if they know as much as William evidently thought they did. A lump rises in her throat, and for the first time, Ms Hart's eyes seem to show a brief flicker of sympathy.

'Where did you get it?' she whispers.

'I'm afraid I can't tell you.'

'Why not?'

'It's classified.' There is a pause. Ms Hart is sitting with her arms crossed. 'What I can tell you depends on how much you tell me.'

'I've got nothing to tell.'

'Now, that's not true, is it?'

Joan feels her heart flutter inside her but she will not drop her gaze. Her voice is louder now. 'I don't know what you think I've done.'

Ms Hart looks down at her notes. She turns back a page, circles something, and then speaks. 'You've said your father was a socialist—'

'I didn't say that,' Joan interrupts.

'You implied it.'

Joan shrugs. She is annoyed with herself for having said something that could be twisted in an attempt to implicate her father in . . . in what? She doesn't know. All she knows is that she must select her words carefully around this woman. 'But I didn't say it.'

'Well? What was he?'

Joan frowns, considering Ms Hart's question. She wants to be sure of representing her father's beliefs correctly, given that he was always very particular about such things. 'He would never have used that word to describe himself. He just believed there was more the government could have done to help people. Politically and socially. My father put a lot of store by institutions. It was in his nature. Public school, university, army officer, headmaster. He thought the government, as an institution, was letting people down.'

'So he wasn't a member of any political organisation?'

'No.'

'And your mother?'

In spite of herself, Joan raises an eyebrow. 'Most definitely not.'

'So you wouldn't say that you were encouraged to take an interest in politics by anyone in particular?'

Joan looks at her and wonders when it changed. When was it decided that taking an interest in politics was something subversive? As she remembers, it was quite normal to be concerned by such things when she was young. Society meant something in those days. It was not like it is now, when the news is filled with nothing but gossip about people who have never done or achieved anything, who don't seem to know the first thing about grammar or the etymology of the word *celebrity*, who appear doll-like and too colourful and yet somehow the same. What sort of society glamorises these people? She knows what her husband would have said: that the rot set in with Mrs Thatcher, and perhaps it did, but she also knows that it happened on the Left too, after all that fuss with the unions in the seventies. There was nothing for anyone to believe in any more, and the

27

realisation of this saddens her, not just for itself but because she recognises it as an old person's thought. Redundant and unnecessary. She shakes her head.

'Please speak up for the recorder,' Ms Hart says, her voice firm and unwavering.

'Nobody encouraged me. Nobody in particular.'

Ms Hart looks at her as if she was expecting a different answer. Her gaze is unblinking. She waits a little longer. 'Fine,' she says at last. 'I believe you were about to tell me about your friendship with Sonya Galich, as she then was. If we're going to be chronological about it, that is.'

Joan shivers. She looks down at her feet, trying to weigh up how much she can tell them against how much they already know.

*　　　*　　　*

As promised, the girl comes to Joan's room the following morning to return the dressing gown. Joan is in the middle of writing an essay on diffraction techniques in the study of atomic particles and does not hear her approaching. When she looks up, she sees the girl leaning against the doorframe, dressed in a blue trouser suit and wool-covered slippers. Her hair is wound up and knotted in a chocolate brown scarf in a manner that Joan imagines her mother would dismiss as 'washerwoman style' but which, on this girl, makes her look as if she has just stepped off a filmset. She produces a thin silver box and flips it open. The silver glints and sparkles in her hand. 'Cigarette?'

Joan smokes occasionally but only in company and never yet in her room. It makes her feel

28

self-conscious in a mildly pleasurable way. She likes the obligatory pout which the act of inhaling requires, the narrowed eyes, the wisps of smoke. It amuses her to think how furious her mother would be if she could see her now, smoking before lunch on a weekday—*Who do you think you are? Some sort of femme fatale?*—but her mother cannot see her, so she shrugs her assent, and the girl takes this as an invitation to come in. She hands a cigarette to Joan, and Joan places it between her lips in what she imagines to be the manner of a femme fatale. The girl strikes a match to light her cigarette, and then holds it out for Joan to do the same. Joan leans forwards, closing her eyes and inhaling gently until the cigarette catches.

There is a brief silence but it is not uncomfortable. The girl glances around the room, amused to see her shoes filed neatly by the door. 'Thanks for last night. Sorry if I startled you.'

Joan grins. 'You did rather.' She goes into the small kitchen to find an ashtray, rummaging through the cupboards above the gas ring and eventually locating the ceramic bowl she once made in a pottery class at school. She taps ash into it as she walks back into the room and places it between them on the desk. 'Where had you been anyway? Anywhere good?'

'I was with my cousin and some of his friends.'

'Is he a student here too?'

'He's at Jesus College. Doing a PhD.'

Joan waits for her to elaborate but she doesn't. Instead, she leans over the desk to read Joan's half-finished essay, her hand resting on her hip as her eyes skim the page, and to Joan's surprise, she realises that she is glad it was her window this girl chose to climb through last night. She likes her self-confidence, her ease. Joan catches sight of the invitation propped up on her bookshelf. 'Are you going to the sherry party this evening?' she asks.

'The tutors' sherry party?' The girl gives a small burst of laughter, and Joan feels faintly embarrassed for having mentioned it. The girl stubs out her cigarette and then turns to look at Joan. 'Only if I can wear your fur coat.'

*   *   *

Her name is Sonya, an exotic, unusual name, which is fitting for a girl who does not walk through life but sails, who floats in and out of rooms without ever seeming to trip or falter. She makes perfectly ordinary people into an audience, even when they don't want to be. They think they are taking part but they aren't. Not really. Not like Sonya. She doesn't have the humble opinion of her own importance that besieges most girls of her age. She seems to know that she is different and doesn't mind it. Even her clothes are different, but not in the same way as Joan's. Joan's are too new, too homemade to look right. When Joan observes herself in the mirror, she looks as if she is dressed in someone else's clothes which don't quite fit. The hemlines are all too long, the waists too slack. It is an uncomfortable thought and she wishes she did not have it, but no matter how much she tells herself that she is grateful for all the effort her mother put into her University Trousseau, the tugging and pinning and late-night stitching, she cannot seem to wriggle out the thought.

Sonya, in contrast, wears what she likes; black

silk dresses in the evenings and, in the daytime, all-in-one trouser suits and odd, mustard-coloured dresses with no shape, no darts or nips or tucks, which on anybody else would look like old sacking tied up with a too-thin belt, but which on Sonya somehow manage to look stylish. Not chic exactly, but deliberate. And then high heels, headscarf, bright red lips. It is almost a statement of anti-fashion, a shrug of contempt towards garters and girdles and primness in the days before dresses were supposed to make statements. Almost anti-fashion, but not quite. Because soon they will all want to look like her.

Sonya comes back to Joan's room that evening while Joan is getting ready for the party and proposes a swap: mascara for mink. Joan protests that she does not want anything in return. Sonya can just borrow the coat. There's no need for bartering. Mascara is unlikely to be the sort of thing she can pull off anyway so she'd rather not wear it.

Sonya waves her objections aside, wafting her back into the room. 'It doesn't need to be pulled off. If you put it on properly, then nobody will know you're wearing it. They'll just be dazzled by how big your eyes suddenly appear. Come here and sit down.' She shows Joan how to apply it, dabbing the cake of black dye with a droplet of water and then brushing the mixture upwards along her eyelashes with a small brush. 'There! What do you think?'

Joan looks at herself in the mirror and has to admit that the transformation is quite amazing. She has used Brilliantine on her eyelashes before but it has never had this effect. Now her eyelashes flick upwards and curl, and if she lowers them and looks slightly upwards as Sonya instructs, they give an involuntary flutter. So this is how it's done, she thinks with delight.

'What did I tell you? You look like Greta Garbo in *Anna Karenina*.' Sonya grins at her, and then turns to Joan's wardrobe to extract the fur coat, her side of the bargain, flinging it dramatically over her shoulders and spinning into the centre of the room.

'You have to be careful with it,' Joan says. 'I'd get into so much trouble if I lost it.'

Sonya laughs. She extracts a headscarf from her bag—crimson with small white flowers—and ties it around her hair. 'Of course I'll be careful. Now get a move on, Garbo. We're going to be late.'

Their shoes clip on the cobbles and the mink coat flutters behind them as they cross the river by The Anchor. There are wolf-whistles from the pub doorway as they run along Silver Street and onto King's Parade, half-mocking but also amused. Joan is not used to so much attention, noting with surprise that just as much of it is directed at her; a reflected radiance. She wonders if this is how it feels to be Sonya. Always looked at, always admired.

The sherry party is held in an old building in the centre of town, a square, wood-panelled room decorated with books and candles, and Joan and Sonya's arrival goes largely unheralded by the huddle of academics talking in the middle of the room. Sonya goes to hang up the fur coat in the cloakroom, and instructs Joan to procure her a drink. Waiting staff in black uniforms with pressed white collars carry silver trays of tiny glasses in which sherry shines and sparkles.

'Dry or medium?' A waiter is standing in front of her.

32

'Oh.' Joan glances at the tray of glasses and then looks back at the waiter. 'I don't know.'

The waiter's expression is stern, but when he sees her confusion he grins and the skin crinkles around his eyes. He leans towards her. 'New here, are you?'

Joan nods.

'Take the dry. Medium is sweeter, but if you say you like dry sherry it sounds as if you know what you're talking about.' He glances across at the huddle of academics and then turns the tray towards her. 'And that's what seems to matter most around here. It's the one on your left.'

Joan smiles gratefully, and selects two glasses from the tray, one for herself and one for Sonya. 'Thank you.'

She sees Sonya come in and waves to attract her attention, and she observes a glance pass between Sonya and the waiter. The waiter bows in acknowledgement, a small movement but a definite indication that he recognises her, and then he turns away to greet the next entrants to the party.

'How do you know him?' Joan asks once he is out of earshot.

Sonya takes a sip of sherry. 'Who, Peter? I met him last night. My cousin knows him from when the waiters went on strike last year. He did some leaflets for them.'

'Why were they striking?'

'Just the usual. Wages, overtime, holiday.'

They are interrupted by one of the tutors, a tall woman with long, grey hair who is intent on persuading Joan to take her zoology course. She has recently had an article accepted by the *Journal of Animal Ecology*, outlining her research on host-finding parasitic insects, and she is intent on relaying the more intricate aspects of this paper to someone, but Joan is too polite to slip away with Sonya once it has become clear that the paper is not a short one. She sees Sonya joining a group of girls from their year with whom Joan had dinner on the first night. She remembers their conversation quite well: horses, boarding school lacrosse games, sailing regattas in the Solent. Their expressions are strained with interest as Sonya speaks, and she sees Sonya laugh politely in return, but she also notices that there is something distant about the way Sonya talks to them, as if she does not quite know how to interact with them. After a few more excruciating minutes of parasite-based conversation, Joan excuses herself from the tutor and slips across the room to join Sonya.

'Thank God you're here,' Sonya whispers, handing her another sherry which she has managed to appropriate from a passing tray. 'Drink this and let's get out of here. There must be something more exciting going on in this town.'

Joan hesitates. 'Let's stay a little longer. I don't want to appear rude.'

Sonya looks at her with barely concealed irritation, but then she shrugs and gives a small half smile. 'All right. One more hour, then we absolutely have to leave.'

They stay until the end, as by the time the hour is up Sonya has found an appreciative audience of language students who are amazed at how well she speaks German, and she is blithe in her acceptance of their compliments. Joan, however, is cornered by a girl she has never met before: Margaret, a Classics undergraduate, who confides in her at great length about a secret engagement with a young man who works on her family's farm, and when she finally escapes from Margaret, there is someone else wanting to tell her about a fascinating piece of research she is conducting on the contact between Reindeer Tungus and Russian Cossacks in north-west Manchuria. Joan tries to appear interested but it is a struggle, and she loses count of the number of tiny glasses of dry sherry she is obliged to drink. When Sonya comes over to claim her, she is relieved to have an excuse to leave.

They walk home arm in arm, both of them giddy from too much alcohol, and giggling at the memory of how the other girls had responded to Sonya's recitations of German poetry. Sonya does an impression of one of the girls. 'Which boarding school did you say you attended in Surrey?'

Joan laughs, even though she is curious to know the answer to this too. Sonya has no trace of a foreign accent, just a lingering drawl that sounds more American than European, but Joan is pretty certain she is not English.

Almost as if Sonya can read her thoughts, she says suddenly: 'I was only there for two years.'

'At boarding school?'

She nods. 'It was in Farnham, in Surrey.' A pause. 'But I was born in Russia.'

There is a silence as Joan absorbs this fact. There is something about the tone of Sonya's voice that makes it clear this is a carefully guarded piece of information. 'Are your parents here in England too?' Joan asks.

Sonya does not look at her, and it takes a few seconds for Joan to work out that this was a tactless question. 'My father was killed a few years after the Revolution. A small uprising. It's okay,' she adds quickly, shaking her head to forestall any sympathy Joan might attempt to offer. 'I never even met him.' She stops. 'And my mother died of pneumonia when I was eight.'

Joan feels suddenly very young. She reaches out and squeezes Sonya's arm. 'I'm so sorry.'

'It's all right. I don't remember very much about her either. I went to live with my uncle and cousin in Leipzig after that.' She grins. 'That's where I learnt to speak German.'

'The cousin you saw last night?'

'Yes. Leo. He sent for me to come here when Uncle Boris moved to Switzerland.' She pauses. 'We're Jewish, you see.'

'Oh,' Joan says again. 'It must have been terrible for you.'

'I don't know. Surrey's not that bad.' She glances at Joan, a sly, sideways glance. 'Besides, I had Leo so I wasn't exactly on my own.'

Joan feels a stab of pity for her, even though she knows better than to voice it out loud. How different it sounds from her own childhood, so easy in comparison, born in the aftermath of a war she would never have to know. Yes, she knows all the stories: that her father served in France as an officer in the trenches, that her mother was a nurse, that they met in the field hospital in the Somme near where her father's left leg is now buried. It is supposed to be a happy story, this account of her parents' first meeting, a tale of hope and salvation. She can picture her mother administering the anaesthetic as the doctor cut into the shattered, shrapnel-flecked flesh of her father's leg, gangrenous and useless, a straight incision this time, revealing the smooth whiteness of his bone,

36

thick as an elephant's tusk. Ah yes, a happy story; Joan's father lying in a hospital trolley as he waited for his wooden leg to be fitted, an old man at the age of twenty-two, with just enough gumption left to reach up and take his nurse's hand and ask her to marry him.

'My mother taught me to play the piano,' Sonya says, breaking in on Joan's thoughts. 'She used to chalk the keys onto the kitchen table and we'd play along to the gramophone. That's my clearest memory of her. She could play anything—Chopin, Shostakovich, Beethoven.' She pauses. 'Or so she said. She sold the piano when I was a baby so I never actually heard her play.'

Joan imagines Sonya's mother: tall, elegant, perhaps a little thinner than Sonya, but other than that, exactly the same. She watches as Sonya places her handbag unsteadily on the cobbles in front of her, and then runs her fingers through her hair, as if this action might restore her sense of composure. She flicks her hair, shaping it into a loose ponytail, and then twists it, piling it up on her head and pinning it expertly into place with a pencil extracted from her pocket. How does she do that? Surely it will not hold. But it does. The dim glow of a nearby street lamp glances off the pile of dark hair, bringing out an array of colours: hints of rust, chocolate, gold. Her skin is splashed with tiny freckles, fading now that the summer is past, but still creamy and healthy-looking. Yes, Joan thinks, Sonya's mother would have been beautiful too.

'What are you doing tomorrow evening?' Sonya asks suddenly as they turn in through the college gates.

'I thought I might go to the fundraiser for the

37

new building.'

Sonya laughs. 'Really? Don't tell me you've been enticed by the raffle.'

'Just the cake sale. Aren't you going?'

'No, and you shouldn't either. I'm going to see some films at the Town Hall with my cousin.' She pauses and looks at Joan, and her expression is scrutinising but also curious. 'Why don't you come along? I think you'll like them.'

Sunday, 4.08 p.m.

Cambridge, 12 October 1937

To: The Chief Constable
Sir,

I beg to report that at 7.30 p.m. on the 12th inst. with Detective Constable BRIGSTOCKE, I went to the Town Hall, Cambridge, where we witnessed the exhibition of two films by KINO entitled The Factory Lights and If War Should Come.

The meeting took place under the auspices of no particular organisation, but there was undoubtedly a Communist Party flavour to it.

The former film, The Factory Lights, depicted a number of scenes purporting to have happened during the Revolution in Russia, and the second If War Should Come showed the Soviets' fighting services in action against an imaginary enemy. In neither film was there anything to which objection could be taken, although these films are under consideration for re-categorisation as banned material in line with previous films distributed by

KINO.

The audience numbered approximately 300–350,
the majority of whom were strangers to me.

I am, Sir, your obedient servant,
J.W. Denton

*   *   *

Joan is tired. It has been a long afternoon and the
light outside has faded. 'How much longer do you
intend to keep me here?'

Ms Hart glances at the clock. She purses her lips.
'There's a lot to get through before Friday.'

Joan looks up at her, suddenly struck by the
thought that if the announcement is delayed
indefinitely, then it might never come to anything.
She might die of natural causes first. 'But why
Friday? It's not set in stone, is it?'

Ms Hart does not look at her. She underlines
something in her notes, and then repeats the action
three times. 'I've already told you that your name
is being released on Friday in the House of
Commons. If you're going to present anything in
your defence, you must say so before then in order
for it to be admissible.'

'But that's what I mean, why Friday? Surely the
agenda in the House of Commons can be changed.'

'No, it can't,' Ms Hart says.

'But—'

'I'll ask you again. Would you like us to call a
lawyer for you? You're perfectly entitled to have
one. There's legal aid—'

Joan interrupts with a shake of her head. She is
acutely aware that any solicitor she calls is likely to
be acquainted with Nick, or will at least know of

39

him. She is not prepared to take that risk. 'No. You don't have to keep asking.'

Ms Hart looks at her, and then glances at the screen behind Joan and raises her shoulders in a small shrug. 'It's my job to ask.' She pauses. 'All right, let's get on.'

'But I would like to know where I'll be sleeping tonight.'

'You'll be allowed home. We'll take you in the car. As I said before, at present you haven't been arrested, but there will be restrictions on your freedom until such time as the Home Secretary has considered your case. You'll be under curfew, of course, and tagged.'

'Tagged? Like a teenage delinquent?'

There is a pause. 'No, Mrs Stanley. Like any person whose whereabouts are of extreme interest to the Security Services. It will only be until Friday.'

'And then?'

'Well, that depends, of course.'

'Of course.' Joan looks down at her hands, resigning herself to the prospect of further questioning but also allowing herself to feel a tiny bit encouraged that she will be allowed home at the end of the day, albeit tagged. Reluctantly she takes the police report handed to her by Ms Hart and peers at it through her reading glasses. There is an advertisement stapled to it, a small square of paper—*See the Mighty Red Army in Action!*—which attempts to entice audiences with promises of mass parachute descents. A KINO Films production, admission 5d, pay on the door.

Ms Hart is watching her closely. 'Were you there?'

'How would I know?' Joan retorts, her voice

40

raised in exasperation. 'This was nearly seventy years ago. You can't possibly expect me to remember whether I was there or not.'

'So you might have gone?'

'I said I don't remember.'

'But you're not denying there was a possibility that this was the sort of event you might have been attracted to.'

Joan opens her mouth and closes it again. 'Everyone went to that sort of thing in those days.' She stops. There is a flush in her cheeks. She does remember this particular film—how could she have forgotten it?—but it is alarming to see that they might know this too. How could they? How could her presence have left a trace? 'I really don't remember. And I don't understand why it's so important.'

Ms Hart looks at Joan. Her expression is concentrated. 'Was that the first time you met him?'

'Who?'

'Leo Galich.'

Oh. The sound of his name is like an explosion in her chest. It has been so long since she heard anyone say it out loud. She is aware of Ms Hart's pen hovering above her notepad, the small red light on the camera in the corner of the room and the unseen presence of Mr Adams behind the glass screen, unmoving, listening.

*   *   *

When they arrive, Joan is surprised by how many people are already thronging into the hall. She and Sonya pay their entry fee and are given small scraps

41

of paper in lieu of tickets, but there is no definite seating system. The lights are set low and young men are carrying benches into the hall from a side storage room. There is a drinks stand at the back with a large metal tea urn and rows of mismatched mugs. It is nothing like the cinema in St Albans, with its velvet seats and feature ceiling that changes from dusky clouds to starry night sky during the course of the programme, and where the whole auditorium is perfumed with Yardley's Lavender. And very different too from the rarefied atmosphere of the fundraising event they passed on their way out, the bazaar stalls in Peile Hall being set up by the girls under the supervision of Miss Strachey, the college Principal, a long, thin, clever woman with short hair and round glasses who would not know what to make of all this confusion.

Joan and Sonya find seats towards the rear of the hall and Sonya goes to get them a drink before the film starts. Left alone, Joan folds her hands on her lap in an attempt to appear relaxed in this strange environment, and she casts her eyes around, trying to guess which one Sonya's cousin might be.

It is several minutes before she spots someone whom she is almost certain must be Leo. He has a shock of dark hair that stands out against the bright whiteness of his collar, and the same translucent, almost golden, skin as Sonya, the same dark brown eyes behind the wire-framed spectacles, the same tall, willowy frame. He is standing just in front of the stage, his hands thrust into his trouser pockets so that his jacket bunches slightly. He is with a group of three other men, and he is listening to one of the others intently, his whole body inclined towards the speaker as if he could not bear to miss a single word, and it is this that makes Joan absolutely convinced that this must be him: he has that same impression of energy, or perhaps enthusiasm, that she finds so appealing in Sonya. She watches him from a distance, absently at first and then more deliberately as he tilts his head in response to the other man's words. How wonderful to be listened to like that, she thinks.

He seems to spot Sonya as she carries the two mugs of tea back to her seat, and he strides towards her. He knows he is being looked at. Not by Joan (although, yes, she is looking at him) but by others in the hall too. Women with handbags clasped on their laps glance up at him as he passes, while a row of girls from the teacher training college in Bedford (she can tell by their textbooks) cross their legs almost in unison, causing a shadow of a smirk to flutter across his face. When he reaches Sonya, they kiss on both cheeks in the European manner. He seems to say something about the fur coat she has borrowed again this evening, running his fingers along the soft arm of it, and Joan waits for Sonya to turn and acknowledge her, but Sonya does not. She says something else and then laughs, spinning away from him and continuing back towards Joan.

'Was that him?' Joan asks once Sonya has squeezed along the pew to her seat, her voice sounding tight and not as casual as she'd like.

'Who?'

'Your cousin.'

Sonya hands the two mugs of tea to Joan while she takes off the fur coat. 'Yes. Pretty, isn't he?'

Joan opens her mouth and closes it again. Yes, she thinks, that is exactly the right description. Admittedly he is not as rugged as Gary Cooper but there is something so smooth about him, so perfectly symmetrical, that it wouldn't be quite enough to call him handsome. 'Is he? I didn't notice.'

'Well, you'll have another chance in a second. He's coming over now.' Sonya leans back, waiting for him to approach. He slips into the pew in front of them and turns to Joan, holding out his hand for her to take.

'You must be Joan,' he says, giving a small bow. 'I've heard all about you.'

Joan feels her cheeks flush and is relieved when Sonya interrupts by batting Leo on the arm with the back of her hand. 'Why do you always insist on bowing like that? Sometimes I wonder if you're not the most middle-class person I've ever known.'

'How many times must I tell you?' Leo says, talking to Sonya but still looking at Joan, 'I am a socialist, not an anarchist. We must keep some decorum.'

There is a sudden burst of noise as the volume of the sound amplifiers is turned up too high, and then adjusted back down. The screen flickers. 'Oh look, Leo, it's starting.' Sonya tugs at his arm, impatient for him to move out of the way.

Leo glances at her and nods, but instead of moving out of the way he leans further towards Joan so that Sonya is momentarily excluded from the conversation. His sudden proximity, the nearness of him, causes her to wonder if she is having a small heart attack. 'I hope you find it interesting. You must tell me what you think afterwards, if my cousin will allow it.'

'Of course,' she says, managing to compose herself sufficiently to lower her eyes a little so that she can look up at him through her mascara-dusted lashes, but he does not stay to appreciate this performance. Instead he turns to pat Sonya abruptly on the shoulder and then strides back to his place at the front of the hall.

The evening begins with a rendition of 'The Red Flag' which is accompanied by clapping. Once the action begins, it takes Joan a short while to work out that there are actually seven or eight main characters (Joan cannot be altogether certain) played by only three actors with varying degrees of facial hair and accented speech by which they are intended to be distinguishable from one another. It is called *The Factory Lights*, and seems to have a mildly scandalous plot about a woman who is obliged to share a small apartment with two men as a result of a housing shortage in an industrial town in Russia.

Halfway through, the reel runs out and the screen glares white. There is a moment of silence while the second reel is fitted into the projector.

'Well?' Sonya leans in and asks Joan in a loud whisper.

Joan hesitates. What is there to say about it? That it's the worst film she's ever seen and she much prefers *Bright Eyes*? That she hopes Gary Cooper will turn up in the second half? 'It's interesting.'

Sonya laughs. 'That's what my uncle taught me to say when I didn't like something.'

Joan starts to protest, but just then the music blares to announce the start of the second half and Sonya sits back, seemingly unconcerned by Joan's response. But what else could she have said? There is no romance, no adventure. She knows she cannot

45

say this to Leo if he comes over to seek her opinion at the end as promised. She must find something more substantial to say to him, something insightful and intelligent.

The second film is shorter and follows almost immediately from the first after another reel change. It begins with a Red Army air drop over Germany in which hundreds of men parachute from aeroplanes like flying ants, and then use sticks to invade a series of German tanks, battering down their opponents with a violence that causes Joan to look away. Near the end of the film, one character turns to another and says: 'It's not really fair, is it, this battle?'

'What do you mean?' the other says. 'That we have sticks and they have tanks?'

The first man shakes his head, and the music softens, pauses, and then builds up gently behind him as he speaks. 'Would you hit a blind man? We may not have tanks, but at least we know what we're fighting for.'

The camera sweeps backwards as the two men embrace, and there is a burst of percussion to accompany the rush of credits which confirms Joan's suspicions that the acting company was understaffed, and the audience breaks into applause. Joan joins in, not wishing to appear impolite.

There is a buzz of conversation around them as everyone discusses various aspects of the films. What was intended by this scene or that? Was the flower on the factory floor a metaphor for hope or for crushed individualism? Joan listens, and feels chided by these overheard conversations. She did not even notice the flower. She turns to Sonya. 'I'm not sure I understood all the references.'

Sonya laughs. 'It's always like that to begin with. It'll be easier next time,' she adds, casting around for Leo. She spots him standing at the front of the room, talking to a slender girl in a black coat wearing a pillbox hat over her blonde curls.

'Who's he talking to?'

Sonya narrows her eyes in an amused smile. 'So you did notice this time?'

Joan flushes and shakes her head to protest. 'I was just . . . I meant, I didn't think we should interrupt if—'

'It's all right. I'm only teasing. I don't know who she is.' She buttons the fur coat up at the throat and then flicks it out over her shoulders so that it flows out like a cape. It is wildly inappropriate for the occasion but nobody seems to notice. Perhaps it is the headscarf that tones it down, giving it a touch of the Siberian to counter all that mink glamour. 'Nobody important, don't worry.'

'I didn't mean—'

Sonya waves her hand to dismiss Joan's protestations. 'Come on. Let's get out of here before Leo corners us. I'm hungry.'

*   *   *

Joan doesn't mention this excursion when she writes home the following morning. She thinks of mentioning it to her father who would undoubtedly be interested, but it would be odd to send a letter addressed only to him, and she is wary of inciting her mother's suspicions, Soviet propaganda films being likely to fall into the category of things that would garner disapproval. She writes instead of other news, of hockey games and her part in the

47

Freshers' play, and mentions how pleased her supervisor had been with her first essay. She writes a separate note to Lally in which she draws a picture of the college kitten and adopts a mock-serious tone—'I hope the newts in the school pond are quite well'—and then she folds them into an envelope to post on her way to the science faculty.

She is already late for her first lecture. The pavements are busy today, thronging with people. Everything is breezy and bright. Three girls whom Joan recognises from the sherry party are sitting on a bench on the wide part of the bridge on Silver Street as Joan hurries past, each of them knitting purple scarves. KNIT FOR SPAIN, the banner above them reads. The girls are talking and laughing as they knit and Joan slows her pace a little, thinking that perhaps this is something she might do. She knows that the British government has declared itself officially neutral in Spain, but it cannot be a bad thing to send scarves and socks to people who need them, even if it is against government policy. An older man stops to drop some coins into their collection tin.

As she walks on, she hears someone call out her name and she looks around, taking a step out to the side and into the road as she does so. And then, so quickly that she does not have time to register the exact order of events, there is a pummelling against the side of her body, as if someone is punching her in the stomach and sides, and then her arms are up around her head and the road is jolting beneath her as her body crumples to the ground.

'Another step, young lady, and you'd have been done for.'

The voice is close to her head and there is

48

something familiar about the accent even though it is hard to place. She feels a hand on her neck, and allows herself to be shuffled up to a sitting position. The concrete wall of the bridge on the far side of the pavement is dazzlingly white and her body feels sore. She looks at her rescuer, and realises why his voice is so familiar. It is Leo. Up close, he is even more beautiful than she remembers.

'What happened?' she asks.

'You stepped out in front of a bicycle.' He grins. 'The cyclist probably came off worse though.'

'Oh no!' she exclaims, glancing around. A little way down the road she sees a pale-haired man tugging a bicycle over to the kerb. He is rubbing his head with one hand and holding a cloth cap in the other. He straightens his jacket, unwinds his scarf and then reties it. The chain is dangling from the back wheel of his bike and the handlebars are no longer properly aligned.

'Is he hurt?'

The man turns and nods at Leo, who makes an apologetic gesture with his hands in response.

'He's all right.' Leo grins. He picks up her satchel and then holds out his hand to her. 'Come on, then.'

Joan hesitates. She takes hold of Leo's proffered hand and allows him to help her to her feet. Her legs feel weak and shaky, and there is a fizz of heat along her spine. She holds his hand for a little longer than necessary, and then she looks him up and down and smiles.

*   *   *

He accompanies her to the science faculty. It is only

a short walk along the narrow pavement next to Queen's College and then a shortcut along Botolph Lane. Joan's body is still stinging from the impact and her head feels light, but on the whole, she considers that she hasn't come off too badly. 'I'm sorry for causing such a fuss,' she says as they start to walk. 'I don't know why I stepped out without looking.'

Leo looks at her, his eyes narrowing a little as he does. 'Well, if I hadn't called out to you it would never have happened. And I wanted to find you anyway. I only turned away for a minute yesterday and when I looked back you'd both vanished. Like two pumpkins in a fairy tale.'

Joan laughs. 'Or princesses,' she corrects him, surprised that Leo would make a reference like that. He seems too serious to be interested in fairy tales, too distracted by those heavy red books he is carrying under his arm to have much time for fanciful narratives.

But it turns out that Leo Galich has a thing about fairy tales. He likes them. He tells her that they remind him of home, of the clear mirrored lake beside his family's old summer house in Russia before they moved to Germany, of the wide fields spread out like a floor under the great ceiling of sky. Grain and birdsong and too-hot summers followed by knee-deep winters. It is impossible to be Russian, he tells her, and not have a thing about fairy tales.

'Communism,' he continues, after a long period of unspoken thought, 'now there's a fairy tale. The whole of the Russian revolution was built on a fairy tale.'

'I thought it was because of the war. And not

enough bread.'

Leo hesitates at this interruption, and she notices the crooked whiteness of his teeth as he replies. 'That as well.'

'So those heavy books you're carrying are just a decoy, are they?' Joan asks. 'They look serious but they're really full of pumpkins and princesses.'

Leo frowns and then sees that she is joking and gives a short laugh of surprise. He looks at her, his head tilted as he seems to appraise her. 'Sonya said you were different from the others,' he says at last, breaking the silence.

'Did she?' Joan asks, flattered to hear this indirect compliment.

He nods, and gestures towards the books he is carrying. 'They're documents of numbers actually. Not very interesting reading, unless you know what you're looking for.'

'And what are you looking for?'

He glances at her. 'Proof.'

'Proof?'

'That it works.'

'Communism?'

'Yes. Or at least, that the Soviet system works.'

Joan looks up at him in surprise. 'And does it?'

'Put it this way, Soviet Russia is the only state in the world to offer full employment. There are no pockets of chronic unemployment like you find in Jarrow or South Wales. The British government claims that unemployment is nothing more than a minor blip in the system, a temporary malfunction of the markets. But that's not true.'

He stops, taking Joan's arm and turning her to look at him. She feels the warmth of his fingers against her skin, and she has to bite her lip to force

51

herself to concentrate on what he is saying. 'Well, if it's not that, what is it caused by?'

Leo nods, evidently pleased with the question. 'Short-sightedness. Marx showed years ago that unemployment is an inevitable by-product of capitalism, but it suits the government to allow it to happen. It's a way of allowing the market to right itself without them having to make any effort.'

'So do you think Britain should be doing what America's doing? A sort of British New Deal with public works projects?'

Leo shakes his head. He taps the books under his arm. 'If a society is properly planned and organised there will never be any unemployment. Every person will be able to contribute. No waste, no surplus. I mean, just look at the figures. Industrial production in the USSR is six and a half times greater this year than it was in 1928. Capital accumulation is nine times as great. The numbers are little short of miraculous. And it's all because the whole Soviet system was planned in advance on an industrial scale.' He grins. 'It works. It's a fairy tale.'

Joan glances up at him, wondering how Stalin fits into this picture of social perfection. 'And no fairy tale would be complete without a wolf. Is that it?'

'That's a separate point. The wolf isn't really necessary to the story. The system just has to be shown to work first.'

'So he could be left out of the sequel?'

Leo smiles although his expression does not give anything away. 'Potentially, yes,' he says, and then falls silent. They are approaching the science faculty now, and the sudden awkwardness that has arisen is alleviated by the sound of an aeroplane droning above them. They both glance upwards, but the noise is too loud for conversation.

Leo looks at Joan and grins. 'Do you know the Russian word for aeroplane?' he asks once it has passed.

'No.'

'*Samolet*. It means 'magic carpet'. Don't you think that's a wonderful description?'

Joan smiles. As he speaks she gazes up at him, noticing that the bright skin around his eyes appears almost luminous, and for a brief moment she finds herself wondering if his whole body glows like that.

Monday, 8.42 a.m.

There is a knock at the front door of the house, a pause, and then another knock. Joan's eyelids are heavy and her neck twinges painfully as she tries to sit up. She sees that it is light outside, which means she must have slept through the night, uninterrupted. How many years has it been since she last managed that? She presses her palms against her eyes and holds them there, as if by blocking out the light for long enough she might be able to force the memories back inside and erase yesterday entirely.

Another knock. She reaches for her glasses, holds them up to her eyes, and glances at the digital clock next to her bed. They are early. She should have set her alarm.

She lifts her head and pushes herself into a seated position. Her body aches as she moves, her

53

joints stiff and swollen. She is still wearing her clothes from the day before, not having had the energy to change for bed after being escorted home the previous evening by Ms Hart and Mr Adams. Her bus pass and passport were confiscated and the electronic tag was fitted to her ankle, and she had been too tired to protest that such precautions were unnecessary. She has been placed under curfew in the evenings and is expected to cooperate with daily questioning by MI5 until further notice. Or, more specifically, until her name is released to the House of Commons on Friday.

And then what?

She does not want to think about this. Not now. Not yet. She must stay strong for the day which lies ahead. She must not let anything slip.

There is another ring at the door, and then an impatient knock.

She slides her feet into the pair of sheepskin boots bought for her by Nick's wife, which are apparently fashionable as well as comfortable, and pulls her dressing gown on over her clothes. It is cold, and she would like it to be fully apparent that she has just woken up. She will need a few more minutes to get herself together before the questioning begins again. They are interviewing her at home today, having agreed to bring their equipment to the house as a concession to her age, even though she insisted that she was perfectly well enough to travel if they wouldn't mind picking her up from the end of the road as she doesn't want the neighbours gossiping. Or she could get the bus, only then there's the question of her bus pass.

But they had insisted on coming to the house, and now she supposes that it could actually work in

54

her favour. It would certainly be less disconcerting to be able to see Mr Adams' face, rather than know that he is watching her from behind a dark screen. Her only concern is what people might think of all this coming and going with briefcases and cameras. Not because she cares what anyone thinks, but because someone might think to alert Nick, and she doesn't want that.

She runs a brush lightly through her hair. She catches a glimpse of herself in the mirror and puts the brush down. There is no benefit in making herself look any better than she feels. 'I don't know what you're talking about,' she whispers to her reflection, her eyes sad and unblinking, her brow furrowed in confusion; practising. She takes a deep breath and turns away, ready now to descend the stairs and open the door, but before she has crossed the landing she hears a key slip into the lock, turn, and the latch click open.

'Mum?' a voice calls. 'Mum? Are you there?'

Joan feels her breath catch in her throat. Nick. Oh God. What is he doing here? For one thing, he is not allowed in. It is one of the Home Secretary's conditions: all visitors must be vetted before entering. But this is not Joan's main concern. He must not be here when they arrive. He cannot find out what is going on.

Joan walks to the top of the stairs, her legs suddenly weak and unsteady, and she peers over the bannister. Nick is standing in the hallway, wiping his feet on the mat and frowning. He is forty-nine years old, tall and slim with a crop of silver hair. He used to have a beard but when he took silk he decided it would add gravitas to his appearance in court to be clean-shaven, and so he shaved it off, and Joan agrees that he was right. It does make him look more serious. Nicholas Stanley, QC. She has heard him present himself in such a manner before, and each time she feels a shiver of pride at what her son has achieved.

Just pretend, Joan thinks. Pretend nothing is happening. Act normal. Maybe MI5 will be late and he will already have left before they arrive. Perhaps it's just a routine visit, Nick being conscientious in this regard, calling in on her every so often just to check, especially if he has not seen her over the weekend. To check what, he does not say: that she is eating properly, that the house is clean, that she has not dropped dead on the bathmat. The normal catalogue of concerns regarding eighty-five-year-old women. They are not long visits. If she can just get him out of the house quickly enough . . .

'There you are.' He looks up, taking off his overcoat to reveal his usual courtroom attire of black suit and smart black shoes. 'Are you okay? I've just had the strangest phone call.'

Joan feels her heart cramp. He knows! 'Oh?' she says, trying to make her voice light, as if she could not possibly know what he is going to say next.

'It was Keith, one of the solicitors at the Crown Prosecution Service. He heard a rumour.' He stops and runs his hand through his hair. He is jumpy and agitated. 'I'm sorry. I shouldn't even be telling you this. I just wanted to warn you in case anyone came round. I wouldn't want you to be shocked.'

Joan looks down at her feet. She wants to be downstairs, on solid ground, not hovering at the top of the stairs. She grasps the bannister, and descends slowly, deliberately, while her son continues to talk.

'It's probably just a case of mistaken identity but

we need to get it cleared up. This rumour, I mean. And then we might even have a case for libel, depending on how far it's gone. But we'll think about that later. It may be easier to drop it.'

At the bottom of the stairs Joan hesitates, reaching out to put her arms around her son. She wants to feel the warmth of him, the strength of him. She doesn't know what to say. She wonders what she would say if she didn't already know. What would be the convincing thing to do? She crinkles her forehead as if confused. 'What rumour?' she whispers.

'It's ridiculous.' He bends to take off his shoes, just as she always made him do when he was a boy.

Joan turns away from him and starts to walk towards the kitchen. How does this Keith fellow know anything? They said they weren't going to tell anyone. Not yet.

The kettle, she thinks. She must fill the kettle. And then she must make toast. She needs to settle her stomach.

He follows her to the kitchen in paisley-patterned socks where Joan's three potted geraniums remain untouched next to the ashtray bearing the charred remains of the solicitor's letter and William's obituary. She picks up the plant pots and moves them to the windowsill, placing them in a neat line, and then she tips the blackened pieces of paper from the ashtray into the bin. 'He said they've found two old Soviet spies. They started questioning the first one last week, but he died rather suddenly. Probably suicide, Keith said, but it's impossible to force an autopsy when there's no actual proof of any wrongdoing. Or no admissible proof.'

She takes a cloth and wipes the soil and ash from the table. There is mud on the floor too but she cannot think about that now. Her hands shake as she takes the butter out of the fridge. She does not want to think about William. She knows she has never mentioned their connection to Nick, even though he had become quite a public figure in the last few decades and Nick would have been interested. There is no reason for Nick to suspect that she might have any connection with him.

'Of course, they asked his brother to authorise an autopsy but he refused. The families generally do. Said he should be allowed to rest in peace. So that's why . . .'

Joan blocks Nick's voice out of her head and turns on the grill. She has never got the hang of that toaster. Why have a toaster when you have a grill anyway?

'Mum, are you listening? The Home Office is preparing a case against the second spy now. They're hoping this will prove their suspicions about the first one—the one who died—so they can get their autopsy.'

Jam. A knife. Fill the kettle. Teabags in the teapot.

'I know it's ridiculous,' Nick continues. 'He said he couldn't really tell me anything, but he said your name had come up. Linked to your war work, when you were a secretary.'

Slice the bread. Be firm and decisive. Lay it on the rack. Don't turn around. Don't let him see.

'Mum, are you listening?'

Slide the bread under the grill. That smell. How she would miss that smell if . . .

She feels Nick's hand on her shoulder. Her body

is being turned away from the grill, slowly, slowly, until she is facing her son. The water in the kettle is bubbling furiously and her hands shake as he takes hold of them and squeezes them tightly together.

'Mum,' he says. 'They think it's you.'

There is a silence. For a brief moment, Joan is reminded of Nick as a seven-year-old boy, marching home from school to announce the incredible piece of information he had heard that day of where babies came from. She remembers the look of horror on his face as Joan verified that yes, this was indeed true, and she also remembers the terrible feeling this revelation aroused in her because it meant that the time had come. They had agreed that they would never lie to him about where he came from, that they would tell him as soon as he asked. So when Nick pressed his finger against Joan's stomach and asked if he came from in there, Joan had known that she would have to take her little boy onto her knee and hug him tightly, and tell him that there was another mummy out there who loved him very much, but that other mummy had been too young to keep him, and so they had chosen him, chosen him above all others, because as soon as they had seen him they had known he was the most perfect thing they had ever seen.

Joan remembers Nick's small face, open-mouthed and furrowed, as he took in this piece of information. And she remembers the phone call from school the following morning requesting her to come and collect him because he had punched a boy in the face and would not say sorry. She had held Nick while he cried, until finally he confessed that he had punched the boy for laughing at him because he didn't have a real mother.

Joan had regretted telling him then, thinking that perhaps they should have waited until he was eighteen as advised by the adoption agency, although this had seemed deceitful somehow. She had wondered if there might have been a gentler way of phrasing it, if her husband would have done it better. She does not know. Perhaps. But whenever she does think of this moment, there is always one aspect of it she remembers with absolute clarity: that last gasp of innocence as Nick's finger was pressed into her stomach, his face questioning, and the breath of time just before she answered the question, when it was still possible that she could have told her cherished little boy something different, something easy; that yes, he was all theirs, and yes, he had come from in there.

She looks at him now. 'I know,' she whispers.

'What do you mean?'

'They were here yesterday. They'll be here again today.'

'Who?'

'MI5.'

Nick's mouth drops open.

'I've been put under a Control Order. Technically, you shouldn't be here without permission.'

'You're under a Control Order? Why? They're for terrorists about to be deported, not for you.' He puts his arms around her. 'Why didn't you tell me?'

Joan cannot speak. Her body seems to melt with sorrow and she clings to her son, pressing her face into his shoulder so that she doesn't have to look at him when she speaks. 'I didn't want to bother you.'

Nick sighs, exasperated, but he keeps hold of her, shaking his head and stroking her back as Joan had done so many times for him when he was a boy, and which he now does for his own sons. 'Oh Mum, what is it with your generation that you all think it's some sort of favour not to bother people?' He stops. 'I don't understand why you didn't ask for help. It's what I do. It's my job. You must have been so scared.'

Joan nods.

'Right then.' Nick releases her gently, and takes his BlackBerry out of his coat pocket, as if he intends to sort it all out there and then on that odd little contraption. 'We need to make a plan. First of all, we need to see evidence. They can't keep you effectively imprisoned here without providing at least a sufficient amount of evidence for you to understand the charges against you. And when they can't provide it'—Nick snorts derisively at this and continues typing on his phone—'then we'll think about compensation.'

And there it is again: that brief pause in time between one thing and another, in which Joan can only look at Nick and wish with all her heart that this moment might be suspended indefinitely, held in time for ever.

But it cannot. She knows it cannot. There is the sound of a car pulling up outside, doors opening and then slamming shut, smart heels clipping up the path. Bang on time.

Nick starts at the noise. 'Are they here?' He strides to the window and pulls back the curtain. 'Is that them?'

'Please, Nick. Please go.' Joan's voice is perilously loud in her own head. She cannot allow him to stay. She has to protect him from this. 'You can slip out the back and I won't even have to tell them you were here. I'll call you later once it's all sorted out.'

Nick turns to her and shakes his head. He steps forward and places his hand on Joan's shoulder. 'Don't be silly, Mum. I'm not going anywhere until that Control Order has been removed and they've promised they're never coming back.'

'But aren't you expected in court today?'

'I've just emailed Chambers now. They'll send one of the juniors to cover for me.'

'Please, Nick,' Joan whispers, her voice suddenly unsteady. 'Please go. I'll be fine.'

'No.'

*   *   *

What a bad sign it is to get the *Cambridge Book of Romantic Verse* out of the college library. Joan sneaks it up to her room, hiding it under her physics textbook, so that she can read it in bed after cocoa, the only time when she feels it is acceptable to spend a little time wallowing. She has seen Leo a few times since the incident with the bicycle, but each of these times has been casual and unplanned so she has taken to dressing more carefully for science practicals than is strictly appropriate and keeping her powder compact in the breast pocket of her lab coat, just in case. He tends to drop in when he has finished his work for the day, which could be at any time from lunchtime onwards, and on each occasion Joan has found herself rushing to finish so that she might walk home with him and listen to his most recent thoughts on planned economies while also observing the smoothness of the skin around his eyes and the perfect, almost unnatural, definition of his lips.

He tells her: 'It's not that Stalin wants to *control* the economy. The nuances are all wrong. A better translation is that the economy is being *steered*.'

And: 'The stakes are too high in the USSR for anything to go wrong. There's no room for trial and error. Poor countries can only bet on certainties.'

And: 'Variety is a luxury for the rich. To provide an abundance of one thing for one set of people while at the same time failing to provide sufficient food and warmth for others is a gross miscalculation of planning.'

And: 'An unplanned economy is a slow, inefficient system. No individual acting alone can reap enough reward to justify the risks of expansion. Yes, it happens. But not often. And not quickly enough to make the leap from feudalism to industrialisation in one generation.'

His manner on these occasions is intense, deliberate, and it is this quality that convinces Joan that Leo Galich is by far the most intelligent man she has ever met.

The poems are silly, she knows that. She has never been one for poetry. She considers that there is something unsatisfactory about it, and finds herself wondering why hopeless love must always be rendered in rhyme. In her opinion, there is more romance in science than in poetry—in knowing that bodies will always move towards each other in space, in the relentless certainty of pi and in the possibility of iterating algorithms in daisy petals— than there is in all the love poetry in that heavy, dark-brown book which she will keep under her bed until it must be returned to the library. But still, she is a student. She is eighteen years old. The poetry is inevitable.

She does not mention these talks with Leo to Sonya. It is not that she intends to be secretive but she is not yet ready to share them with anyone who might be able to see how much she enjoys listening to him. She can imagine Sonya's expression if she were to let on, the sharp burst of laughter which would accompany any confession of this nature. These moments are too delicate, too precious, to withstand such an onslaught. Besides this, she could not bear the thought that Sonya might tell Leo, and that the two of them would laugh about it together, maybe even with the blonde girl in the pillbox hat whom Leo has never mentioned and whom Joan hasn't seen since the films, but who occasionally appears in Joan's dreams as a pretty yet menacing presence.

Today Leo is waiting outside the science faculty when she comes out of morning lectures. 'I was wondering if you were free for lunch?' he asks, holding up a small shopping bag to indicate that he has brought food with him.

Joan smiles, not wanting to appear overly delighted at the prospect, but at the same time flattered by the trouble he must have gone to. 'I'd love to,' she says and then pauses, glancing back at the science faculty. 'I've got to be back by two though. We've got practicals this afternoon.'

He nods. 'Plenty of time.' He turns around and starts to walk, and then looks back. 'Come on. There's something I'd like you to see.'

They walk together through Market Square and then along Rose Crescent to Trinity Street. This side of town is unfamiliar to her, being home to the older, men-only colleges which Joan is only permitted to enter in the company of a man. They are grander and less welcoming than Newnham, but Leo does not allow her to linger. He marches her past the bookshop and the post office, and steers her through the gatehouse of St John's at the end of the street, gesturing that she should wait outside the Porters' Lodge while he goes in to collect a large, iron key. He reappears after a few seconds, and leads her to a small door at the bottom of the chapel tower in the far corner of the cobbled courtyard. The key slots easily into the keyhole, turning the lock with a clunk, and Leo pushes the door open. 'You first,' he says.

Joan steps inside. She blinks, her eyes adjusting to the dimness of the tiny room. There is a small space to stand in, and then a narrow spiral staircase leading up around a stone support. She takes a few steps upwards, past a bird's feather and some encrusted droppings. Further up it is darker still and the staircase narrows until it is impossible to stand square on any step, and when Leo closes the door behind him she has to feel her way up the stairs until she gets into a rhythm. She hears the key turn in the lock, and the sound causes her to jump slightly, although she cannot be sure whether it is caused by the fact that Leo has invited her here on a picnic, or by the fact that she is now locked in a darkened staircase with a man she barely knows and nobody, not a single soul, knows where she is.

There are small slits in the walls as they progress upwards, punctuating the darkness, and after climbing for several minutes Joan stops at one of these gaps to catch her breath. She peers out, seeing the spires of the chapel in the college next door now at eye level, and when she looks down she can see the modern guttering of the college roofs, hidden behind sixteenth-century turrets.

Walking on, they pass a small ledge next to a slate roof and continue upwards, past the bell chamber and the bell-ringing mechanism until finally they come to a tiny wooden door at the top of the stairs. Joan almost expects to see a white rabbit emerge clutching a pocket watch. She draws back the heavy bolt and the door swings open to reveal a flat, square rooftop, cornered by four decorative towers. The sunlight is dazzling in its brightness. Leo has to crouch almost double in order to get through the doorway, and by the time he has stepped outside Joan is already standing at the edge of the roof, leaning against the stone wall which marks its perimeters. Her body feels hot from the exertion, and she unbuttons the cardigan she is wearing over her blouse, and slips it off.

Leo comes to stand next to her, and together they look out across St John's and into Trinity Great Court, its centrepiece fountain looking much smaller from this distance. Behind that is the Wren Library, and then the River Cam, meandering past King's along the Backs towards Newnham. After a moment, Joan turns to Leo and she notices his eyes flick to the small spattering of freckles on her shoulder before meeting her gaze. It is a bold look, and Joan feels her skin tingle.

'There,' he says. 'What do you think?'

'It's beautiful,' she says. 'And so quiet.'

'Yes. It's wonderful, isn't it?'

Joan frowns. She had not been expecting this response. 'I didn't think you'd approve of all this . . .' she pauses, gesturing about her while she searches for the right word, '. . . extravagance.'

'Where did you get that idea?'

Joan laughs. 'Everything about you. Your thesis, those films, all the things you say, the fact that it's not planned. It's all higgledy-piggledy with statues and crests and—'

Leo smiles and shakes his head. 'But that's not the point. Why does everyone think communism is about destruction?' He is looking at her so intently that she can hardly breathe. 'I don't want to tear this down.'

He is so close to her that she could reach out and touch his face, and a tremor runs through her body at the thought of it. 'What do you want then?'

Leo smiles, as if the answer is perfectly obvious. 'I want everyone to have it.'

He sits down and opens up his shopping bag. He takes out two plums, a hunk of bread, some cold ham, a few tomatoes and two bottles of ginger beer. Joan smiles, and sits down next to him. Already she knows that today is going to be different from every other day she has ever known. It is starting now. Life is starting now. She is having a picnic on the roof of a chapel with Leo Galich and the sky is a deep, brilliant blue.

'So,' he says, tearing the bread in two and handing half of it to her, 'why did you choose to read science?'

Joan takes a swig of ginger beer and squints into the sun, considering the question. To say that she chose it because she was good at it does not seem enough. 'Tadpoles,' she says suddenly, and then turns to him with a smile. 'There was a pond in the school garden where I grew up. It was always dirty and smelly but my sister and I used to catch tadpoles to keep in glass jars so we could watch them turn into frogs. I thought it was like a magic trick.' She laughs, unsure why she is compelled to tell him this but she cannot seem to stop. She supposes it is because she wants him to know that she is different from those other Cambridge girls, just as she knows that he is different. She wants him to see *her*, as she is. 'One day, we collected all the frogs from the pond and put them in a bucket to give them a bath. Smelling salts and rose petals and hot water from the kitchen.'

He smiles at her as she speaks, that rare unguarded smile, and slips his hand across to rest gently on her knee. His skin has that same lemony smell of soap and tobacco that Joan remembers from the first time he touched her.

'But when we came out to see how they were getting on, they had all died,' she says, half laughing, half desolate at the memory of so many upturned frogs' bodies. 'Boiled to death. We thought we were giving them such a treat.'

She takes another swig of ginger beer and sees that Leo is looking oddly at her.

'What?' she asks.

'So you chose to read science to make up for killing those frogs?'

'In a way. They made me want to understand things,' she says, more serious now. 'And I like the fact that it's useful.'

'To whom?'

Joan shrugs. 'Everyone, hopefully.'

She feels the heat of Leo's body as he edges a little closer and she decides that if he should attempt to kiss her she will not move away. Yes, she thinks, she will allow it, and the thought makes her fidgety and anxious.

But he does not. Not now. 'There you are then,' he says. 'I knew you were one of us really.'

'What do you mean?'

'Science is the truest form of communism.'

Joan takes a gulp of ginger beer as she absorbs this information, and then follows it up with a bite of bread and ham.

'Its aim is the conscious subordination of self to serve the common purpose of all humanity,' Leo continues, and although his words are grandiose, his tone retains a hint of his earlier playfulness. He smiles at her and she smiles back at him. 'There's nothing individualistic about it, which is a rare quality.'

'I suppose so,' she says, attempting to convey an awareness that her chosen degree subject is indeed a noble occupation, even though she has never seen it in this light until now.

They sit together, eating plums and looking at the view, until Leo glances at his watch and slides his arm away. 'We'd better go back down. You've got to get to your afternoon session.'

Joan feels a small snap in her chest as he begins to clear everything up and wonders whether to tell him that, truly, she doesn't mind missing the experiment. She can catch it up later, or just copy the notes from one of the other girls. But she senses that Leo has somewhere he needs to get to as well, and so she helps him to gather up the remainder of the picnic. She must not be cross with him for being so conscious of the time, she tells herself. She should be glad that he is concerned about her. He goes on ahead while she pauses to take one last look at the city from this new perspective, and he only turns to check she is following him once he has reached the small wooden door.

They walk down in silence, their feet clipping against the stone. The steps are noticeably steep on the descent, but the curve of the wall means that when she puts out her hand to steady herself, she experiences a strange sort of vertigo, as if she is being sucked down a long tunnel, and it only serves to put her more off-balance. It is a relief when the steps widen so that she can walk straight again; less dizzying.

When Leo reaches the bottom of the stairs he stops suddenly, and the abruptness of this movement causes Joan to bump into him. She tries to step away but there is no room, and now they are standing so close to each other that she is certain he must be able to hear the hammering of her heart against her ribcage. In the darkness, he bends forward to kiss her, very gently, a little too gently, on the lips. She closes her eyes and opens her mouth, and as she does she feels the prickle of his skin, the hardness of his teeth, and the edges of her body seem to dissolve momentarily.

'I'm sorry,' he whispers suddenly, shaking his head and turning to unlock the door so that she has no time to protest that she really didn't mind him kissing her, and that he could do it again if he liked. True, it was not the long, impassioned embrace that she had envisaged for her first kiss, but there is an excess of sensation in her mouth as he holds the door open for her, and she cannot stop herself from grinning as they walk back to return the key to the porter.

'See you at the march tomorrow then?' he asks, and although it is not quite the same as asking when he might see her again, she is pleased to have some

70

sort of encouragement. His hand brushes against hers. 'Sonya said she'd invited you. I'd really like you to come.'

*   *   *

The march is on behalf of the Aid-for-Spain campaign. There are about a hundred people gathered in Market Square when Joan and Sonya arrive, tram drivers and shopkeepers and workers from the electronics production plant on the outskirts of the city, alongside students and seamstresses and a few elderly ladies. All the way from Newnham, Joan has been thinking of how best to bring up the subject of Leo, but there is something that prevents her, something that tells her that her friend might not be unequivocally delighted by recent developments, and so she says nothing yet, deciding to wait until there are no distractions and she has thought more carefully about how to word it.

Sonya is carrying a homemade banner and is seemingly unaware of Joan's mental wanderings. When they arrive, she unfurls the banner, each end of which has been sewn to a wooden stick, and she hands one of the sticks to Joan. UNITED AGAINST FASCISM, the banner reads in neat blood-red paint. There is a cheer-leader to encourage the singing of 'La Marseillaise' and 'iAy Carmela!' and even though Joan doesn't know all the words, she hums along as they walk. Sonya's voice rises above the others, her lips parted in strident song as they head along King's Parade to gather outside the Cooperative Hall, but Joan is amused to see that her enthusiasm does not extend

71

to any form of foot-stamping. When this begins, Sonya leans across to Joan behind the banner. 'The stamping isn't obligatory. It's a trade union thing.'

A man in a bus driver's uniform overhears her and turns around, fixing her with a glare. 'It's a protest thing, that's what it is.'

'All the same,' Sonya retorts, 'it's uncouth.'

The man snorts. 'It's none of your business anyway.'

'What isn't?'

'This march. Spain. Why would you care?'

'Spain is everyone's cause,' Sonya says with a shrug.

'Not yours, it's not. You lot are more interested in putting your "r"s in barricades instead of getting your arse on the barricades. If you'll excuse my language.' He nudges the man next to him, who half turns but doesn't seem to appreciate the joke. 'That's a trade union thing too.'

'Comrade,' Sonya says, taking a step towards him so that the banner is pulled taut and Joan has to step forward too in order to keep her balance. 'I have read Lenin in the original Russian. My father died in the Revolution. I don't see why my pronunciation or where I place my arse, as you call it, is any concern of yours.'

The man looks at her, and for a moment he seems to be considering whether to believe her or not, but her accent is more exaggerated than usual and he evidently decides she is telling the truth because a slight redness spreads to his cheeks and his expression softens. 'I'm sorry to hear it,' he says, nodding at her before turning his attention back to the platform.

Sonya gives him a flash of a smile, and Joan

glances from one to the other, suddenly light-headed with this talk of comrades and the sense of having narrowly escaped the bus driver's wrath. Once Joan is sure he is no longer paying them any attention, she leans across to Sonya. 'I thought you said your father died after the Revolution.'

Sonya takes hold of the banner and shakes it where Joan's movement has caused it to slacken. 'He did. It just sounded better.'

'Oh, I see,' Joan says, annoyed with herself for having offended her friend. 'I didn't mean to . . .' She falls silent as a hush descends on the group at the instigation of a man who has taken to a wooden crate to address the crowd. He is wearing brown corduroy trousers, and there is something in his demeanour that marks him down as a student. His English accent is deep and rounded and his expression earnest, especially when he begins with a small recitation of poetry written by one of the fallen comrades from the International Brigade in Spain which makes Joan feel mildly embarrassed on his behalf. Once the poem is over, he launches into his speech, stressing the need to get tinned food over to Spain, and the possibility that if Spain falls to Fascism then France and Britain could be next. Joan casts her eyes around, aware that she is looking for Leo but trying not to let on.

At last, she sees him standing just behind the makeshift platform, all his attention focused on the speaker. He nods occasionally, and claps along with the rest of the crowd when the speech is brought to a close. She watches as the speaker steps down from the platform and shakes Leo's hand, the two of them conferring briefly before Leo steps onto the platform. His eyes fix momentarily on Sonya

73

and he nods in acknowledgement of her presence, before allowing his glance to move to Joan. Her body flickers at the sudden memory of his lips on hers and she has to look away, but when she looks up again he is no longer looking at her. He is at the front of the platform, surveying the crowd. He does not lift his hands or ask for quiet; he simply waits.

'I was born in Russia,' he begins, 'but for the most part I grew up in Germany.' His style is calm and deliberate, as if he knows there is no need for rhetoric in what he is about to say. He will tell them a story and they will listen, not just because it is expected of them, but also because the story is one they need to know.

He tells them about the terrible depression in Germany after the last war, the growing violence on the streets as the decade progressed, tipped over into near-anarchy by the economic crash in 1929. He goes on to describe the Nazi demonstrations at Leipzig University when he was a student in the early 1930s, pointing to a scar on his lower lip and another on his forehead. He tells them how a Reichsbanner pin on his jacket had been spotted at one of these demonstrations, prompting a Stormtrooper to snatch his glasses from his face, smash them underfoot, and then fling him head first into the river.

He pauses, and the crowd rustles a little, shifting in preparation for what comes next. It is a noise she recognises from school assemblies; the sound of people listening, responding, but whereas her mind would occasionally wander during the scholarly prayers and notices, right now Joan finds that she cannot take her eyes from Leo, not for a second, not even when Sonya hisses her name, trying to get

74

her to pull the banner taut, or when the bus driver steps back onto her foot in order to see better. She sees now what it is that Leo has that other people do not, the quality that sets him apart and makes people listen when he speaks: an absolute conviction that what he says is true.

He tells the crowd that the Nazis were voted into power a month after he was flung into that river, and not a single party voted against them. The disgust in his voice as he says this is almost palpable. Joan feels her neck prickle. He joined the Communist Party that same day and it was this affiliation which, not long after, forced him to leave his home and his country at the age of twenty after the Reichstag burnt down, taking with it the last vestiges of democracy still present in Germany, because by then Hitler had turned his sights to battering the communists first, and everyone else after.

'This is fascism,' Leo proclaims as he draws his speech to a close, not raising his voice but seeming to look into the face of each individual member of the crowd. 'And when the time comes, each and every one of you standing here now will have to pick a side. We will all have to choose.'

He steps down from the platform to a wave of applause, and he holds up a hand to acknowledge the response his speech is receiving, but he does not smile. Sonya takes Joan's side of the banner from her and rolls it up, evidently slightly peeved by Joan's inability to hold it as diligently as she would have liked.

'What did you think?' Leo asks, coming over to them and placing his hand on Sonya's shoulder.

Sonya looks at him, and there is something in her

75

expression which reminds Joan that this is not just Leo's story but Sonya's too. 'Very moving,' she says, and her voice is lower than normal. Calmer, perhaps.

'Moving?' He frowns, evidently displeased with this response. 'I wanted it to be rousing.'

Sonya rolls her eyes and hits him lightly on the arm. 'You're such a perfectionist, Leo. Can't you hear them? I'd say they sound pretty roused.'

Leo tilts his head in reluctant agreement, and Sonya is interrupted by one of the young men Joan has seen her with on a few previous occasions. Surreptitiously, Leo slips his hand into Joan's and pulls her aside. 'Have you told Sonya anything?' He pauses. 'About yesterday, I mean.'

Joan shakes her head. 'I was going to but . . .'

'Good,' he whispers. 'Don't. Not yet. I'd rather tell her myself.'

Joan is taken a little by surprise at this, but she decides that, on balance, it's a good sign that he considers it an event important enough to tell Sonya about himself. After all, Leo knows his cousin far better than she does. She glances over to Sonya who is now deep in conversation with the young man (Daniel, maybe), her hand on his arm and her head thrown back in sudden laughter. 'All right,' she says. 'If you'd rather.'

'It's just that Sonya has a . . .' He pauses. 'Well, let's call it a protective streak.'

'Protective?' Joan almost laughs at the thought of this, incredulous that anyone might think Leo is in need of protection. His whole demeanour is so utterly untouchable that she cannot quite believe his heart could ever be in any real danger. Certainly not from someone like her.

Leo does not laugh. He frowns, and looks down to where his fingers are interlaced with Joan's, their hands hidden from view by how close they are obliged to stand because of the push of the dispersing crowd. 'Her mother didn't die of flu, you know.' He pauses. 'Is that what she told you?'

'Pneumonia.'

Leo nods. 'Close enough.'

'Then what was it?'

'She killed herself. Hydrochloric acid.' He unlaces his fingers gently and allows Joan's hand to drop. He checks to see that Sonya is still engrossed in her conversation, which she is. 'A particularly painful way to die.'

'Why?'

Leo glances at her. 'Never explain, never excuse. Isn't that what you English say?'

Joan crinkles her forehead, not quite understanding.

Leo sighs. 'Nobody knows why. Sonya found her when she got home from school. She was only eight. That was when she came to live with us. She didn't sleep for an entire year.'

'Oh.' Joan is silent for a moment. She feels a burning, choking sensation in her throat, and is embarrassed to find that her voice is a little tearful. 'I'm not surprised she's so protective of you in that case.'

Leo looks up at her. 'Of me?' He laughs suddenly and shakes his head as if Joan has said something monumentally silly and naive. And it is, in a way, although she will only know this later. Because Leo has stopped smiling now. 'She's not protective of me,' he whispers, his lips soft against her cheek. 'She's protective of herself.'

Cambridge Borough Police

To: The Chief Constable

Sir,

I have to report that an Aid for Spain march organised by the Town & University Communist Party (advertised in the *Cambridge Daily News*) took place at the Cooperative Hall, Burleigh Street, Cambridge on Saturday 10 October, 1937. There were two speakers who received a great ovation from the hundred or so persons present. They were William MITCHELL of Jesus College, Cambridge, subject of previous reports to MI5, and a second speaker, who came across as deeply anti-fascist as a result of having spent some years in Germany during his youth, although he is not previously known to us.

It was this second speech which interested us most, the speaker using his personal history to inspire the crowd to great effect. We shall have a full identification report prepared on him within the next few days.

Overall, worth keeping an eye on, but I would not recommend taking any further steps against any speakers or attendees at this stage.

Nick takes the piece of paper from Joan's hand. 'What is this?'

'It's a police report of the march your mother has just described,' Mr Adams says. 'It identifies Sir

William Mitchell as the other speaker.'

'I can see that,' Nick snaps, 'but what's the point of it? What has it got to do with us now? You said you were coming to the point.'

Ms Hart looks at him. 'We're building up a picture,' she says. 'As I explained to your mother at the start of this process, we need—'

'But we haven't seen any evidence. All you've shown us so far are police reports that make no mention of her. It's intimidation. They've got nothing to do with her.' He pauses. 'And is there really any need for this camera?'

Ms Hart purses her lips. 'If you wish to make an official complaint then there are avenues available to you.'

'Good. I shall be—'

'Oh no, Nick,' Joan interrupts, even though she knows it will irritate him. There is something heart-breaking about being defended by your own child, no matter how old they are. 'It's fine as it is. Please. Don't make a fuss.'

She knows what he thinks: that he could sort all this out if only Joan would let him, just as he did after her husband died, flying out for the funeral and then refusing to leave Australia without a promise that she would come to visit. His life was in England by then, his friends and his career, and he was getting married in the autumn, and he didn't understand why his mother refused to come. He begged her to attend the wedding, trying to entice her with the fact that he'd invited her sister's children, his cousins whom he had first met at Aunt Lally's funeral not long after he first moved to England, and didn't Joan always say how much she longed to meet her nieces and nephew? Even though, of course, they were adults by then. Older than Nick.

She had told him it was out of the question: that she was too old; that she was scared of flying; that she had been away too long; but it wasn't until he bought her an air ticket as a surprise and told her that he was going to fly out in order to accompany her back to England that she realised how much it meant to him, and so she had been left with no choice. She had to go, even if she was afraid.

Although she was not scared of flying, as she had told Nick. She was afraid of arriving, of having her passport inspected too closely.

And she was also scared that she would never want to go back.

She returned to Australia after Nick's wedding but only stayed long enough to sell up her house and pack her belongings, and then she returned to England. She bought a small house in Sidcup, twenty minutes' drive from Nick and Briony's flat in Blackheath, lulled by how easy it had all seemed during that initial visit. Briony was pregnant by then, and Nick seemed delighted to have her nearby to ask advice on high chairs and prams and breast-feeding, forgetting that this was not something she would have known much about. It was a wonderful time, but at the same time, it was careless.

She should have known. She cannot allow Nick to stand up for her like this. 'It's fine, Nick.'

'Mum,' Nick reprimands. 'Why do you always do this? Why won't you let me look after you?'

Joan raises her hand to stop him and then lowers it, uncertain. She turns to Ms Hart. 'Could we have a moment alone, please? Just Nick and me.'

There is a brief pause while Ms Hart considers the request. Mr Adams is sitting in the corner of the room once more, tending to the video camera which has been set up on a stand with a large microphone attached. He is sitting in Joan's favourite armchair and sipping tea from one of her old Che Guevara mugs, the symbolism of which is unlikely to be lost on him. He lowers the mug. 'That'd be most irregular.'

Nick glares at him. 'This whole thing is irregular. Have you told her what protection she is entitled to? She hasn't even been given a legal representative.'

'She refused. We did offer.'

'You should have insisted.'

Mr Adams hesitates, but then reaches up and pushes a button, causing the red light on the camera to be extinguished. He stands up and gestures to Ms Hart to follow him. 'You've got five minutes,' he says.

Left alone, Joan turns to her son. 'There's something I need to tell you.'

'No, you don't.' He is leaning forward and although he is whispering, his voice is urgent and strict. 'Mum, you don't have to do this. You can tell them as much about this Leo person as you like but it's irrelevant. I know you haven't done anything wrong. It's not a crime to have had a Russian boyfriend at university, although it is a bit weird hearing about it.'

Joan opens her mouth and then closes it again. She cannot say the words.

Nick is looking at her, squeezing her hands in both of his. 'Just tell them that you need to see some proper evidence, something more than this nonsense. Once we've got that then we can set about clearing your name. They'll see they've made a mistake.'

There is a silence.

'You can do that, can't you?'

Joan looks down at her hands. Nick's forehead is furrowed, concerned.

'Or do you want me to say it? I can say it for you if you prefer.'

Slowly, Joan shakes her head. I can't, she wants to say. I can't. But the words will not come.

'Mum?'

*   *   *

Until she has seen it for herself, Joan has no idea quite how much work is involved in belonging to any sort of left-leaning political group. She has no concept of the number of interminable meetings one is obliged to attend, the volume of books which must be read and discussed, argued over, waved aloft for emphasis and then thrown aside in disgust. She knows that both Leo and Sonya seem to spend a lot of time at the meetings, but she has assumed this is because they are enjoyable as well as necessary. She is not prepared for the seriousness that such meetings entail.

The first time she attends, she arrives with Leo. It has been several weeks now since that first kiss and Sonya has been informed, although not in any detail. Joan goes with him because she is intrigued to know what it is that draws him away from her so frequently, even though he warns her that she might not enjoy it. He leads her up a wooden staircase in one of the old courtyards of Jesus

College to a small room on the third floor and pushes open a red-painted wooden door to reveal a fug of cigarette smoke and a collection of perhaps ten people sitting on the floor and talking. Sonya is standing by the window, leaning back against a storm-coloured curtain. She is wearing a clinging blue dress and smoking a cigarette which she lowers from her lips as they enter, her eyes narrowing as she glances from Joan to Leo and back to Joan again, before smiling and holding out her arms in greeting.

'Joan!' she exclaims enthusiastically. 'What are you doing here?'

Leo has taken off his jacket and is proceeding to hang it from the window-latch. 'I brought her. I told you I might.'

Sonya looks at Leo and raises her cigarette to her lips once more, and mutters something in another language, German or Russian, Joan supposes, which causes Leo to respond with an abrupt noise which sounds more like a tut than a word.

Sonya rolls her eyes and exhales a puff of smoke as he turns away, and there is a momentary freeze in time before she smiles and takes Joan's arm. 'Come on,' she says in her old conspiratorial manner, steering Joan across the room and indicating that she should sit on the floor next to Sonya's perch on the window seat.

Joan hesitates, turning back to Leo to check that he does not object to her going off without him, but he is already shaking hands with a fair-haired man whom Joan recognises as William, the other speaker at the Aid for Spain march, and when he notices her waiting for him he merely waves her on.

She feels her neck flush and glances around, hoping nobody observed the gesture. She is relieved that it seems to have gone largely unnoticed, until she turns to Sonya and sees a small wishbone mark furrowing her normally immaculate brow.

Joan recognises the expression. She has seen it before, just occasionally, on the few times she has tried to talk to Sonya about Leo, and the effect is amused, patronising. For a moment, Joan wishes she hadn't come. This is not her place. It is Leo's, and Sonya's. Joan sits down on the cushion next to Sonya's feet. If Leo hadn't informed her otherwise, she would probably think that Sonya is jealous in some way, but Leo has told her that this is a ridiculous suggestion. Sonya is not the jealous type. She is just protective. Whatever that means. Perhaps it would be easier if Sonya were jealous, as at least then Joan would know what to do. She could reassure her and make sure she wasn't feeling left out. She looks up at Sonya who is leaning out of the window to extinguish her cigarette against the brickwork. She flicks it from her fingers, watching its careless descent into the flowerbed below.

'So what happens now?' Joan asks, anxious to break the silence that has arisen between them.

'We wait,' Sonya says abruptly and then softens, leaning towards Joan in a conspiratorial manner until she is so close that Joan can almost taste the tobacco on her breath. She nods towards the man talking to Leo, the one Joan recognises from the march. 'You should keep an eye out for William, by the way. He rather adores Leo.'

Joan frowns, not quite understanding why Sonya is grinning in the manner she is, but aware that this is an attempt at reconciliation, so she does

84

not question her but smiles, grateful and uncomprehending, glancing over to see William slap Leo on the back and then place his other hand on the shoulder of the young man next to him who seems to jump at the touch. 'Who's that?'

'Rupert,' Sonya whispers. 'You'll get used to him.'

Once everyone has arrived and the door has been pushed shut, Leo announces that the object of tonight's meeting is to discuss the reports of the Moscow Trials printed in the British press. He has managed to obtain a transcript of the first trial from his PhD supervisor, and he reads aloud the confession of Zinoviev, the erstwhile leader of Communist International who stood beside Lenin during the 1917 Revolution, and who has now pleaded guilty to the charge of having formed a terrorist organisation to kill Stalin and other members of the Soviet government.

The reading lasts for approximately ten minutes during which nobody seems to breathe. They are all listening intently to Leo. When he finishes, there are murmurs among the group but nobody seems willing to be the first to speak. Joan knows that, as the newcomer, she ought to keep quiet, but she does not understand why nobody is asking the obvious question. She bites her tongue and fidgets until she can keep it in no longer. She coughs, and then asks in a conversational tone: 'So do you think Stalin forced him to say it?'

As soon as the words leave her mouth Joan knows that her question is a mistake. She does not yet know that Stalin is not spoken of in these terms in public, not as a real person who might be, in some way, culpable. Certainly not as a wolf in a fairy tale. This is something she might say to Leo when they are alone, but not in front of this group of people she hardly knows. Leo looks at her and the lamplight reflects harshly off his glasses. She feels the cold glare of his disappointment, and although she is ashamed to have let him down in this manner, she is also irritated by his response. Surely it is a reasonable question to have asked.

'Of course not,' he says. 'These confessions are freely given, and the only people claiming otherwise are members of the Western press whose sole purpose seems to be to discredit the USSR.' He shrugs. 'His execution was entirely necessary to protect and preserve the revolution.'

Leo has never spoken to her in this manner before and Joan feels her pulse quicken with the urge to defend herself. She does not know why nobody else joins in and backs her up. 'But you can see why they say that some of the confessions simply aren't credible.'

'Who says that?'

Joan stares at him, confused, convinced that he knows the answer to this as well as she does. 'The press. Most people in England.'

A pause. Leo does not look at her but places the transcript very carefully onto the floor next to him. 'Then they're playing into the hands of criminals. Anything dubious in the confessions was put there deliberately by enemies of the state who are trying to discredit the government. It's quite simple.'

Joan leans back against the wall, trying not to appear as annoyed as she feels. The discussion continues with a consideration of how far the execution of traitors is justifiable for the preservation of the greater good. How far may badness extend in order that it might become good? And at what point might the greater good overtip the balance? After nearly an hour of discussion around this point, the group breaks for tea and Joan sees that this is a good opportunity to slip out without causing too much fuss. She starts to gather her things together but before she has the chance, Leo comes across and crouches next to her. 'Jo-jo,' he says softly, conciliatorily. 'You mustn't take anything I say here personally, you know.'

Joan sniffs. She is angry with him and wants him to know that she is. Even if he disagrees with her, there is no need to be so abrupt. 'How can I not?'

'If I disagree with you politically, it's simply that. It's constructive argument, that's all. That's what we're doing here. We're finding a way that works. We can't let emotions get in the way of progress.' He pauses, and strokes her cheek gently with his hand. 'That's the whole point of these meetings.'

She gives a reluctant smile. 'I think I prefer you on your own,' she retorts, only half joking.

*   *   *

He is a mystery to her, this man. She has spent so much of her time with him over the past few weeks, and yet there are instances like this when she wonders if she knows him at all. She wishes she could ask Sonya's advice, not simply because she knows him better than anyone but also as a friend. However, every time she thinks she might be able to bring up the subject in the days and weeks following that first meeting, she finds she cannot. She doesn't know why this is, recognising only that it is a bad idea. Leo and Sonya are practically brother and sister. Perhaps it is just too intimate, too personal. Or perhaps it is just that she doesn't like to talk about him, aware of how vulnerable such a confession would make her feel. It is a way of keeping her heart intact.

Because this is what worries her. On the few occasions when she has attempted to extract some sort of declaration of intent from him in relation to his feelings for her, he has simply said that man cannot be guided by emotion over intellect, and each time she has found herself nodding in reluctant agreement. After all, it is what she always thought when she was younger. It is what she thinks now, rationally, being educated in the religion of reason as she is. But then she thinks of the *Cambridge Book of Romantic Verse* hidden under her bed (which reminds her, she must return it before the fine reaches ridiculous proportions) and she knows that she does not really think this at all.

As a consequence of these discussions, she has decided that she will not sleep with him until he has told her he loves her, and that when he does, this declaration must be unprompted and sincere. Leo, however, is unaware of this decision, and so he asks her to stay every time they spend the evening together and every time she refuses. It has created an impasse in their relationship but it is not uncomfortable. If anything, it raises the tension a little. It keeps them both on their toes.

In the end, it is Sonya who brings up the subject first. She comes to Joan's room one morning before breakfast, still dressed from the night before, and wearing Joan's fur coat. When Joan opens the door in answer to her knock, she extracts two eggs from her handbag and holds one out to Joan. 'I brought breakfast. They're soft-boiled.'

'Where have you been?'

'With Daniel.'

Joan frowns. She gets back into bed and pulls the covers up to her neck. It is still early and the room is cold. 'Is he the one with the big nose who was at the march?'

'Roman nose,' Sonya corrects her. 'No, that's Tom. Daniel's the one with the perfect hands. History at Pembroke. Hockey player. I think you met him once.'

'Oh, him. I didn't think you liked him any more.' Joan looks up at her suddenly. 'Did you . . .?'

A mischievous look crosses Sonya's face. She slips into Joan's small kitchen and starts raking through the cupboard above the sink. 'Where are your egg cups then?'

'I don't have any.'

Sonya raises her hands in supplication. 'Why ever not?' She comes back to the bedroom and sits cross-legged on the floor while she peels away the shell to reveal a perfect white oval.

'Have you done it before?' Joan asks tentatively.

'Done what?'

'You know.'

Sonya leans back against the wall. She is still wearing the fur coat, and it is wrapped around her like a luxurious blanket. 'Of course. A few times. I wanted to get it out of the way early.' She glances at Joan. 'Don't tell me you're waiting.'

Joan shakes her head. 'Not on principle. I just haven't . . .'

Sonya smiles. 'I wouldn't hold your breath,' she says.

'What do you mean?'

'Leo's not like other boys. He's so principled. Incorruptible.'

Joan raises an eyebrow at this but she does not correct her, thinking that it would not be fair to tarnish Sonya's unsullied vision of her older cousin.

Sonya watches her, frowning. 'Aren't you going to have your egg?'

'It's too early,' Joan says. 'I'll have it later.'

'Suit yourself.' She takes a delicate bite of egg, taking her time over it as she describes the cocktails she shared with Daniel and how he had asked her as she left if she would have lunch with him and his parents on Sunday. 'He's such a scream,' she says, incredulous that he might think she would want to meet his parents, 'although I don't think he means to be.'

Joan smiles and turns away, lying back against her pillow as Sonya continues to talk. She is content to lie there, not wanting to get up quite yet, and aware of another sensation insinuating itself into her mind, one that she will not share with Sonya: triumph that there is at least one thing she knows about Leo that Sonya doesn't.

*   *   *

Over the next few weeks, Joan attends several other meetings with Leo although she is more careful than she was the first time. She knows that she is an aberration here, being a non-joiner, and so she makes an effort to be polite and acquiescent to avoid saying anything inappropriate.

Tonight the subject is Spain and William is trying to persuade the others that they really ought to go out there and join up with the Republican forces as

90

part of the International Brigade. Rupert is sitting next to him as usual, dressed smartly in a charcoal grey suit and nodding vigorously at everything William says.

'We've already lost so many of our boys out there,' he declares. 'Cornford, Wallis . . .' He grasps for another name.

'. . . Yates . . .' Rupert interjects.

'Yates,' William repeats. 'And endless others,' he adds, his arm encompassing these nameless volunteers in a sweeping gesture. 'We've got to make sure those boys didn't die in vain.'

How childish he sounds, Joan thinks, how dishonest. Here he is, sitting in a room in Cambridge (on the floor, admittedly, but other than that in perfect comfort) with no threat of imminent violence, not a gun to be seen, biscuits being passed around on a plate, and talking as if he is some sort of battle-worn hero.

She is relieved when eventually Leo speaks. 'It's a war. Everyone dies in vain when it comes down to it.'

'Not if we go out and get more of them.'

Leo makes a clicking noise with his tongue. 'It's not a game of cards. You don't win by counting matchsticks.'

Rupert speaks up. 'But William's right. You don't win by ducking out either.'

'Exactly.'

'I didn't realise you were such a pacifist,' Sonya says to Leo, crossing her long dark-stockinged legs and scattering cigarette ash all over the carpet.

Leo shrugs. 'I'm not saying that. I'm just saying I wouldn't choose to go to war. Who would?'

'But I don't think we have a choice. We have to

91

go,' William announces. 'It's our duty. You said it yourself. When it comes to it, we'll have to choose. Fascism will spread across Europe if we don't stop it now. Everyone has to choose.'

'There are other ways of changing the world,' Leo declares.

A snort from William. 'Maybe,' he concedes, 'but none so fast.'

Leo says nothing, but takes a cigarette from his pocket. He lights it, and Joan sees his eyes flick to Sonya's.

'Go on then, Leo,' Sonya says after a moment's hesitation, leaning back and exhaling a slow spiral of smoke. 'I can see you're dying to tell them.'

Everyone looks at Leo. Joan frowns, suddenly aware that Leo is looking away from her, deliberately avoiding her gaze. 'Tell us what?' she asks.

'Oh!' Sonya says, looking at Joan and putting her hand to her mouth as if she has said something she shouldn't, and allowing the wishbone of concern to appear again on her brow. 'Hasn't he told you?'

'Told me what?'

Leo clears his throat. He takes the cigarette from his mouth and holds it between his fingers. 'I'm going to Moscow.'

Joan stares at him. His face is flushed with excitement. The others fidget and cluster for more details but Joan feels her body start to burn. Why has he not told her already? Why wait until now? She clears her throat. 'For how long?'

'Three months. I've been invited to give a lecture at the university, and then I'll be taken on a tour.'

'Where to?' William asks.

'The usual, I imagine. Collective farms, factories,

schools, clinics.'

Joan has a sudden urge to be outside. The air is so close in here, so stuffy. She stands up and walks over to the door.

'Jo-jo, wait.'

It is Leo's voice, but Joan does not wait. She opens the door and steps out into the corridor, not stopping until she is far enough away to feel alone. She puts her hands over her face. Footsteps are coming towards her. Leo. She knows the rhythm of him but she does not turn around. She sniffs and wipes her eyes.

'I was going to tell you,' he says. 'I only found out yesterday for certain. I wanted to find the right moment.'

Joan does not look at him. She takes the cigarette from between his finger and thumb and puts it in her mouth, closing her eyes so that she can concentrate on the sensation of smoke pouring into her throat and lungs and causing her to gulp for oxygen. 'Well, I'm not sure you found it.'

He gives a rueful smile. 'I didn't know Sonya would bring it up.'

'Of course she would.' There is a silence, and then another thought occurs to her. 'And evidently you found the right moment to tell her.'

Leo steps towards her, his hands firm about her waist, holding her perfectly still. 'I'm sorry,' he whispers. 'I was going to tell you.'

'But you didn't.'

There is a pause as he looks away from her. He is so secretive. How she would like to open him up and see right inside him. Turn him upside down and shake him, until all the little secrets have fluttered out, and then he would simply be there in front of her, just him, and she could wrap her arms around him and hold him tightly against her.

As if he can read her mind, he runs his hands up her body and pulls her face towards his, kissing her lips. 'Stay with me tonight, Jo-jo,' he whispers. 'Please. Before I go.'

She looks at him, holding her breath, waiting for him to say the words. Oh, she knows he will not say them. Of course he will not. She knows it is just a question of whether or not she will capitulate.

William opens the door and peers out to look for them. 'Come along, Pooh, come along, Piglet. We're starting again.'

Joan hesitates. Sonya steps out behind William, still sporting her sympathetic expression, and at the sight of her Joan feels her cheeks flush, because it turns out that she, unlike Sonya, is the jealous type. Or at least, this is what she decides the burning feeling must be. She can feel it pulsing in her chest and rising up through her lungs. She is surprised at the strength of it. And she is angry too; angry with Leo for not telling her first, for not knowing that she might not want everyone else to see her reaction, for not understanding how much he means to her. On top of this, she is also angry with Sonya, even though her reasons for this are less clear. She is annoyed that Sonya knew about Leo's trip before she did, yes, but she is also irritated by Sonya's dismissal of the possibility that Leo might want to sleep with her, the implication that she is not good enough for him, that Leo is too incorruptible to want her.

Her blood runs hot inside her. 'No,' she says suddenly, her eyes avoiding Sonya's. 'We're leaving early tonight.'

94

'Are we?' Leo asks.

'Yes.' She slides her arm around him and he responds to her, pulling her body towards his, and as he does, Joan sees Sonya's eyes widen before she turns away, laughing at something behind her in the room; a shrill, too-loud laugh, which echoes through the courtyard as they leave.

At Leo's college gate they have to sneak past the night porter. Joan puts on Leo's overcoat and hat so that she can stride in after him, her feet slightly out-turned in her flat brogues to give her a manly gait. Nobody calls out to them to stop, and they giggle as they run across the courtyard. Outside his door Leo fumbles for his key and when he hurries her inside she is surprised at how neat it is. There are heavy maroon drapes looped up next to the windows and dustless piles of books on the shelves. The cushions on his sofa are neatly aligned and even the counterpane of his bed is smoothed down.

Leo closes the door behind them. He steps towards her, catching her in his arms and pulling her close to him. He kisses her, and the feel of him is more playful than usual, more deliberate, his fingers light on her neck, tickling, teasing. His tongue flicks against her lips and she kisses him back, her arms encircling his body. He tastes of tobacco and biscuits and warm, sugary tea. He moves his hands down her body, over her waist, and then suddenly he is sliding her cotton skirt up her thighs. His hand slips underneath and his fingers find the top of her stockings, gently following the line of silk where it meets her bare flesh. He presses into her and her hands clutch his neck as her body arches towards him.

'I shouldn't be here,' she whispers, suddenly

95

scared of what they are about to do. What has she been thinking? This is too soon, too sudden. Would she even be here if Sonya had not brought up the subject of his trip to Moscow? She does not know. She steps away from him. 'I have to be up early tomorrow morning.'

'You can sleep in the afternoon, can't you?'

'I suppose so.' If he would only say it then it would all be fine. She would not feel so rushed. She holds her breath, shaking her head—no, she is thinking, no—but her feet are slipping out of her shoes, and now she is standing in front of him in her stockinged feet. He is watching her but still she hesitates, waiting for something.

Say it, she thinks. Please say it.

She should leave. What if she gets caught? She would get sent down from university in disgrace. She tries to move further away from him but the muscles in her feet will not obey instructions.

Leo takes a step towards her, his eyes fixed on her, and still she cannot move. She feels her hands twitching at her sides, and then, before she has quite made up her mind what to do, she finds that her fingers are trembling at the small metal clasp on the collar of her blouse, and as it falls open she knows that she is not going anywhere. She cannot. She wants to feel his body on hers, his naked skin against her own. She wants to run her hands along the furrow of his spine, to kiss his neck and his chest and wrap her legs around his waist. She wants him to be hers, utterly corruptible.

And she knows that once it is over she will want to cover herself up, her too-thin body delicate against the bulk of his. He will be grateful. He will look at her and kiss her, and then he will offer her his jacket as he smuggles her out of his room in the morning, and she will wish she could have stayed there for ever.

But she also knows, before any of this has happened, when she is still standing in front of him with her blouse open at the neck and her shoes kicked carelessly aside, that no, even after all of this, he still will not say it.

Monday, 11.52 a.m.

<u>Special Branch report re: Tour of Russia (departure from Hay's Wharf, London)</u>

22 May 1938

The following is a list of passengers, all travelling on return tickets between London and Moscow, who left this port for St Petersburg at 10.15 p.m. today sailing on the steamer *Smolny*, and who are believed to be members of a party of doctors, scientists and economists visiting Moscow on a tour:

. . . GALICH, Leo Borisovich, Jesus College, Cambridge University, Cambs; ticket no. 7941 . . .

GALICH is of Russian nationality and is currently studying for a PhD in economics at Cambridge University. He has recently purchased various books on Soviet economic policy, also some technical engineering works. He is believed at present to be visiting Moscow as part of a British delegation to an economics conference at the university, but if and when he returns his description is:

Born Leningrad, 20 May 1913, height 6ft 2ins, medium build, hair brown, eyes dark, complexion sallow, clean-shaven. Accent: Germanic. Excellent spoken and written English. We have one photograph which is to be found attached.

The photograph of Leo is produced from Ms Hart's slender briefcase and pushed across the table to Joan.

She holds it delicately at the corner while she puts on her reading glasses to squint at it. She has not seen it before. He is dressed in shorts and a white open-necked shirt, long socks and black leather boots. There is a cigarette balancing on his lower lip, smouldering carelessly, the crumbled ends charred and blackened.

Nick stands up and glances at the photograph over her shoulder. 'So that's him, is it?' he asks with a note of curiosity in his voice, in spite of his policy of tactical indifference. 'Comrade Leo. Off to Russia to prepare himself for the revolution.'

'He was only going to a . . .' she stops, the word eluding her for a second, '. . . a conference.'

Nick's face registers surprise at Joan's defensiveness. 'I was joking.'

Ms Hart ignores him, instead looking intently at Joan. 'But he did think the revolution would come, didn't he? He wanted it to happen.'

'Yes, but . . .' Joan says and then stops. 'Lots of people thought it was inevitable back then. If you'd suggested to any of them there wouldn't be a revolution, they'd have said you had your head buried in the sand.'

'Who exactly do you mean by "they"?'

'Well, all of them. Leo, Sonya. The others at the

meetings.'

'William?'

'I don't know. We never spoke about it. Not directly.'

'And you?'

Joan shakes her head. 'I never joined. I was never a member.'

'Of the Party?'

'Of anything.'

'I believe it was Communist International which was their affiliation, was it not?' Mr Adams asks. 'Comintern.'

Joan shrugs but says nothing.

When it is clear that she is not going to expand on this, Mr Adams leans towards her. 'You wouldn't be giving anything away. That was one of the few things we were able to elucidate from Sir William before he died.' He fixes Joan with a stern look. 'You must have been under some pressure to join. So why didn't you?'

A silence.

'Does it matter?' Nick asks eventually, his voice impatient. 'She said she didn't join.'

'Your mother's political beliefs are not irrelevant to this case. It might help her if we can establish—'

'I wasn't convinced enough,' Joan interrupts. 'I didn't agree with everything, and I didn't like the idea of belonging to something that told me what I could think and what I couldn't.' She pauses. 'I might have joined if they hadn't all been so strict, but that's always the way with any sort of club, isn't it? There's always a party line.' She looks at Nick. 'Like that tennis club your father wanted us to join in Sydney. It was the same there.'

Mr Adams' expression is one of mild disbelief.

99

'I don't think joining a tennis club is really comparable.'

Joan's eyes flick to his. 'You didn't meet them.'

Nick inhales sharply. 'But you didn't join the Communist Party, did you? Or Comintern, or any of them?'

Joan looks at her son and sees in his expression that he is not just impatient. He is pleading with her. He thinks she is not taking this seriously enough. 'No,' she whispers.

The furrow in Nick's forehead disappears and he nods his approval before turning to Mr Adams. 'There, see. She didn't join. She wasn't convinced enough. When are you going to realise that you're wasting your time?'

'Because we're not, are we, Mrs Stanley?'

A silence. Joan sits back in her armchair and presses her hand against her forehead. There is a burning sensation behind her eyes, as if the process of recalling such long-ago thoughts and emotions has a physical effect, and the pressure of her hand against her skin is momentarily cooling. No, she didn't join, but that didn't mean she didn't think about it in those early days, especially in the face of the apparent indifference of her fellow students. The Newnham Hockey Team even went on a tour of Germany during the Easter holidays of 1939, in spite of it being quite clear what was happening to the Jews by then, but nobody else in the team raised any objections. It was only Joan who refused to partake in this jaunt to Frankfurt and Wiesbaden, thus putting an end to her hockey career which, truth be told, was stalling anyway, but she was astonished at the lack of support in college for her stance. Nobody else seemed to care all that much.

Except Sonya.

She nearly joined then, but to a certain extent, she didn't join because she didn't have to. As Leo's girlfriend, she held the privileged position of being able to come and go as she pleased without being obliged to adhere to the conventions of the group, calling the others 'comrade' and reading the set texts while never truly saying what she thought. She knew that, while she was sympathetic to many of their ideas, she was not quite able to match their certainty of purpose, their earnest togetherness, and so it was easier for her to remain on the outskirts, not really one of them but accepted all the same.

The second reason she didn't join is more complicated, and is not one that she would have admitted to anyone at the time, or now for that matter. Refusing to join was simply a way of holding a small piece of herself back from Leo, because even then, before anything had really happened, she had somehow known this was necessary. She remembers how she used to feel when she was with him, succumbing to him, moulding herself around him—it was almost physical, that curling sensation across her back— and she found it disconcerting. It was not how she imagined herself to be. Not very scientific. But, then again, she had never been in love before. Perhaps that was just how it was supposed to feel.

'For goodness' sake,' Nick says, breaking impatiently into the silence. 'There's no crime in having had a few leftie friends at university.'

'We're building up a picture—' Ms Hart begins once more, but she is interrupted by Nick, who has turned to Joan, struck by a sudden thought.

101

'Did Dad know about this?' he asks. 'I don't remember either of you ever mentioning politics when I was growing up.'

Joan glances at Ms Hart and then looks down at her hands, folded carefully in her lap. She nods. 'Of course,' she says, her voice calm and level.

Ms Hart makes a note of this. 'I'd have thought, in the circumstances, he'd have wanted to know more.'

'What circumstances?' Nick asks sharply.

'He knew enough,' Joan says quickly. 'He knew all he needed to know. I didn't lie to him, Nick.'

Nick raises an eyebrow. 'I hope not.'

Joan looks back at the photograph of Leo. She doesn't know who took it or at whom he is looking, not at the camera but slightly to the side, but she recognises the expression on his face, his eyes concentrated behind the lenses of his glasses to give the impression that he is listening intently—which he probably is—while also being conscious of the camera, evident in the slight upturn of his lips, allowing just a hint of that unreadable, blameless smile.

*   *   *

He is back! He is back! He is back! She has prayed for this every night, every morning. It is nearly three months since she last saw him and in that time there have been letters, but not what you might call love letters exactly. They are more like inventories in which he lays out his itinerary of factory visits, hospital visits, details about the Moscow underground system, descriptions of nursery schools where all the children have hair cropped in

102

exactly the same style so you can't tell the girls from the boys, lists of collectivised farms . . . The list goes on and on.

The air here is fresher than any I have ever breathed, he writes. *The central question of the modern world—poverty in the midst of plenty—has been solved, although not yet in its entirety as there are still some technical glitches. But it will come.*

There is no mention of the night they spent together in any of his correspondence, although she thinks of it often enough: how he rolled himself on top of her in the morning, raising himself onto his elbows so that his whole body pressed against her. 'Ah, my little comrade-in-arms,' he had said, laughing at his own joke while bending down to kiss her neck, his penis thickening against her thigh. 'Did it hurt much?'

She remembers how she burrowed her face into his neck, breathing in the smell of him, musty and sleepy, and whispered, 'No, not much.' And then she had paused, not knowing if it was the right thing to ask or not: 'Did it hurt you?'

He laughed at this. 'Of course not. Why would it hurt me? Silly girl.'

There was nothing she could say to that, and he had kissed her neck and breasts before getting up and carelessly tossing a shirt over to her to wear while she drank her tea before he smuggled her out of his college. Does that mean he has done it before? she wonders. And if so, with whom? The blonde girl in the pillbox hat? Possibly. Silly of her to imagine he hasn't. He's a man, after all, and he is older than her. She knows it's different for men, biologically, even though the details of this were never covered in science lessons at school; probably it wouldn't hurt them anyway. She doesn't know and she cannot ask, because she does not want him to laugh like that again, and she can't bring herself to mention it to Sonya.

She has worried about this while he has been away, wondering what it had meant, if it meant anything at all, how it would be between them when he got back. Did he think of her? Did he miss her? But she knows not to write such things to him. He would not know what to do with them. He would reprimand her and think her ridiculous, and so she refrains, adopting his letter-writing style in her replies to him: practical, unemotional, fact-based. It is an unsatisfying style, but she supposes that it is better than nothing. At least it means he is thinking of her.

But now he is back, and she can relax because the first thing he does after dropping off his bag is to climb through the window of the linen cupboard at Newnham College and stride along the corridor to her room as if he has absolute permission to be there. Which he doesn't. If they were to be discovered like this, lying together in Joan's narrow bed, the consequences would be disastrous. She knows the rules. If a man must come into your room for whatever reason, it must be with permission from the Head Porter and, in the words of the Senior Mistress of the College, at least one foot of each party must be kept on the floor at all times, a rule which Sonya dismisses as revealing more about the conservative habits of the college authorities than presenting any barriers to copulation, but Joan has not yet plucked up the courage to ask her how exactly this is the case. Perhaps she will find out for herself soon enough.

Joan sits up and tugs the curtain across the window behind them. It is almost dark. The shadows have slunk across the bed and her throat is dry. She gets up, steps over Leo's crumpled jacket on the floor, his boots, his trousers, until she comes to the small washbasin next to the wardrobe. She hears him stir and looks around.

'Jo-jo,' he murmurs, rubbing his eyes and looking up at her. 'It's really you.'

She smiles. 'Of course it's me.' She gulps down the glass of lukewarm water, and then returns to bed, sliding her legs under the sheets, feeling the bristly warmth of his body against her skin. Unexpected, somehow. She had not anticipated this amount of heat to come from Leo.

He rolls towards her and pulls her back down under the covers. 'Do you know what I'd like now?' he asks, his lips on hers and his hands slipping down towards her bottom.

She leans forward to kiss his neck. 'I might have an idea.'

'Roast beef. Potatoes. The lot.'

'Oh,' she says, disappointed. 'And there I was thinking the gnawing sensation in your stomach was desire for me.'

He laughs. 'It is. But I'm hungry too. The food in Russia was as bad as I remember it.'

And so there it is. He is back, and nothing has changed.

They go to a pub on the outskirts of Cambridge and order two roast dinners, playing ping-pong on the cracked green table next to the fireplace until the food arrives. Untypically for a foreigner, Leo approves of English food. He thinks hot buttered toast is the most delightful thing in the world, and he cannot understand why anyone would wish to taint the perfection of this with anything as garish as jam or marmalade or with something as foul as Marmite. But he wants more than toast now. He wants thick-sliced meat, crispy roast potatoes, Yorkshire pudding, stuffing, horseradish, carrots, turnips, pickled cabbage, and he wants all of it to be swimming in hot, thick gravy.

When their plates arrive, she picks out a selection of food from her plate to add to his. 'Have some of mine.'

'Don't you want it?' He does not stop eating while he speaks, but he pushes her offering back towards her.

'No, no. You have it. I can't eat all of it anyway. And you look hungry.'

He grins, and then spears some of her extra Yorkshire pudding onto his fork. 'I am. Thanks, Jo-jo. My sweet little comrade.'

There it is, his old name for her, still there. She smiles. 'What were you eating out there anyway?'

'Oh, you know. This and that.'

What does that mean? She wants to know, she really does. She cannot imagine what he might have eaten.

'More than most of the population anyway, that's for sure.'

Joan frowns. 'I thought you said . . .'

He waves his fork. 'I did. The problem *is* solved, theoretically.' He glances back over his shoulder and then leans forward conspiratorially. 'But I mentioned technical glitches, didn't I?'

Joan nods.

'Well,' he says, and then pauses, seemingly trying to decide whether to confide in Joan or not. 'You must promise never to mention this to anyone.'

'Of course I won't mention it.'

'No, I mean it. You have to promise.'

Joan looks at him. She does not understand what could be so important but she sees that he wants her to say the words. 'I promise,' she says.

He nods. 'They took me out to the countryside to see what collectivisation meant in practice for the majority of peasants. Most of the farms were pretty well run, but the food production figures they were submitting just didn't seem to me to add up.' He pauses and takes a sip of beer. 'I mentioned this to one of the economists at the university, Grigori Fyodorovich. To be honest, I pestered him about it, and even got my thesis out to go through the figures with him until eventually he cracked.' He pauses. 'He told me something that he made me promise I would never link back to him. And I made him that promise. That's why you must never tell anyone. It's not my secret, or yours. It's his.'

'I understand.'

'You remember the statistics I'm using in my thesis?'

'The comparisons with 1928?'

'Exactly. Well, it turns out they are too good to be true. Grigori Fyodorovich told me that the 1928 figures come from the weight of the grain after it has been harvested and bagged. The Barn Yield, as it's known.'

Joan frowns, confused. 'Well, how else would they weigh it?'

'The way they do now. The Biological Yield. They estimate the amount of grain in the field before it has been harvested and they use those figures.'

'So they're lying?'

'No,' Leo whispers sharply. 'Not lying.' He hesitates, and his expression softens a little. 'Misleading, perhaps. There are many people who would like the Soviet system to fail, so naturally they're cautious about releasing statistics which could be exploited by their enemies.'

Joan allows this information to filter through her mind before responding. 'But you'll publish this information, won't you?'

Leo twists his fork in his hand. 'I don't know. I haven't decided yet.' He pauses. 'I will if it comes to war and these figures aren't corrected.'

'Why? What difference would that make?'

'The Soviet Union relied heavily on aid from America during the last war and they will do again if Hitler targets Russia as he is bound to do.'

'And?'

'It's quite simple, Jo-jo. If the official figures are used, it will make America or Britain or whoever is in a position to provide aid think that there are more reserves in the country than there actually are. Russia would be left to starve.'

'Don't you think people have the right to know the truth anyway, even if there isn't a war?'

Leo looks at her. 'I think everyone has the right to live in a fair society. And if fudging a few figures achieves that aim then I'd say it's justifiable, wouldn't you?'

Joan says nothing. There is something about the strength of his conviction which makes his logic hard to dispute. She watches him as he dips a roast potato in gravy before transferring it to his mouth and then smiles. There were frequent occasions during the three months he was away when she had almost forgotten what he looked like, when she wished she had a photograph of him, something still and steady to help her remember. Perhaps one of him looking just as he does right now, holding his beer in one hand and his fork in the other; distracted, frowning, close enough for her to reach out and touch. Or maybe a gentler pose, him asleep in her arms as he was this afternoon, or perhaps as he was the first time she saw him, standing at the front of the stage and talking to his serious-looking comrades, his hands thrust into his pockets so that his jacket bunched up over his slender hips.

But even now, when he is sitting right in front of her, she finds that he will not stay still in her mind, that his face will not be still, and she realises that it is this quality in him which makes him so hard to remember accurately: the way his face slips from one expression to another in just a fraction of a second, leaving his features unchanged yet somehow transformed, like a barely noticeable flicker of paper in the animation booklets of her childhood. Yes, there it is: she can see it happening now, that infinitesimal shift in his eyes as he notices her watching him.

'But remember, whatever happens, you must never tell anyone,' he whispers.

She leans over and kisses him on the cheek. 'I promise.'

Monday, 2.13 p.m.

The Times, **24 August 1939**

From Our Special Correspondent, MOSCOW

Herr von Ribbentrop, having signed the German–Russian Non-Aggression Pact, spent this morning sightseeing and then left by air for Germany. The terms of the Pact, published here this morning, with smiling photographs of M. Stalin, M. Molotov, and Herr von Ribbentrop, show that Russia has abandoned the policy of the Peace Front.

That being so, the continued presence of the British and French military missions is superfluous and the draft Three-Power Pact so laboriously negotiated is so much waste paper. The newspapers lay stress on the value of the Pact as a contribution to peace. The Peace Front is nowhere mentioned.

Differences of ideology and political system, they say, ought not to and cannot stand in the way of the establishment and strengthening of good neighbourly relations between the Soviet Union and Germany.

Late August, and the newspapers are full of war and Chamberlain. Joan is waiting for Sonya in a café in town, having come up to Newnham early to catch up on some reading before term starts. Under more amenable circumstances, she would say that she loves this time of year: the silvery colours of the morning sky, the tracks of dew across the fields,

110

the long, warm evenings with their trails of pink cloud. But this year is different. There are lines of men smoking cigarettes outside the café, and women pushing perambulators along the cobbles, everybody rushing, rushing, with the sense of something about to start.

Joan orders a coffee, and then wishes she had opted for a weak tea, but she does not really want anything. She knows she ought to eat something but the thought of food makes her whole body feel giddy and waterlogged. She can feel her brain swishing in her head, a light film of sweat clinging to her skin. The waitress is brisk and efficient, dressed all in black except for a mildly offensive bonnet on her head, white cotton edged with lace and tied under her chin. She looks young from a distance, but when she brings the coffee over to the table Joan can see the pores of her skin, an older lady's pores, and she feels sorry for her that she is forced to wear the bonnet. The air smells of bacon fat and warm milk, of grease-smudged aprons left in an old bucket to soak.

Oh God, she thinks, here it comes, a wave of it washing over her, pummelling her whole body with its force, and she has to run to the bathroom to avoid vomiting all over the linoleum floor.

Sonya arrives five minutes later. She is wearing a cape covered in a red tulip pattern, and she has coloured her hair with henna so that it is a deep, rich brown. Even the dullness of the café cannot dim the gleam of her as she comes in and throws herself down opposite Joan in the booth. 'What's the matter with you?' she asks, before Joan can even say hello. 'You look terrible.'

Joan manages a wry smile. 'Thanks.'

111

Sonya looks at her, narrowing her eyes.

'It's just a bug,' Joan says. 'It'll pass.'

'If you say so. What's this you're drinking then?' she asks. 'Hot chocolate?'

'Coffee,' Joan says, offering it to Sonya as she cannot stomach any more.

Sonya declines. 'You can keep your bug to yourself. I'll get my own.'

She gestures to the waitress that she will have the same thing. There is a pause while the two women—yes, Joan supposes, we are no longer girls—look at each other.

'Leo didn't show up at the meeting last night,' Sonya remarks.

'Oh.' Joan glances at her. 'Have you seen him? Has he said anything about me?'

Sonya slips her arms out of her cape and folds it next to her on the bench. 'I take it he's still not talking to you then?'

Joan shakes her head. 'I don't know why he's taking it so personally.'

'He'll come round,' Sonya says, her voice sticky with sympathy. 'It's obvious that it's just a tactical move by Stalin. Any fool can see Hitler's got his eye on Russia next, once Poland's submitted, and Britain and France haven't exactly been offering much in the way of support. He's just buying time.' She pauses. 'And we need time.'

Joan lowers her head. It feels heavy and her eyes hurt. 'Not *we*,' she whispers. '*They*. We're no longer on the same side.'

'That sort of comment is exactly why Leo's cross with you.'

'I know but he needs to understand that we're in Britain. I'm British. When I say "we", I mean the

112

British and their allies.'

'But that's Leo's whole point. Nationhood is a false distinction.'

'Evidently it's not to Stalin. He's put himself on Hitler's side. He's chosen.' Joan takes a sip of her coffee and immediately regrets it. The taste is nauseating. She pushes it away and breathes shallowly through her mouth, trying to control the retch which threatens to rise up from her stomach. 'That's why Leo's cross. Not because of me. He's just taking it out on me because I'm here and Stalin's not.'

'It's a huge shock for him.' Sonya takes out her silver cigarette case, not opening it but rotating it in her hands so that it reflects the velvety pink of her fingernails. 'For us.' She glances at Joan. 'Are you all right?'

A gulp of air. 'I'm fine.'

Sonya observes her for a moment and then selects a cigarette. She lights it, sucks at it, and then exhales a small stream of smoke. 'It was a horrible time, when Leo left us in Germany.'

'I know.'

Sonya purses her lips. 'But you don't know, do you? You don't understand.' Her tone is dismissive, patronising. 'How could you?'

Joan leans back into her seat. She closes her eyes and wishes Sonya would stop being so aggressive, so competitive. Of course she doesn't know exactly, but she has tried to imagine it based on what Leo has told her. She knows they both think it is her lack of understanding that holds her back from joining officially. She brushes a strand of hair from her cheek.

'It's not a bug, is it?' Sonya says suddenly. She is

scrutinising Joan's stomach, watching how her hand rests delicately against it.

Joan drops her hand. 'Oh Sonya,' she whispers. 'I don't know. I haven't been to a doctor yet.'

'Is there any need? How late are you?'

There are tears now, threatening to rise up. 'Five weeks,' she whispers.

Sonya hesitates. 'Leo?'

'Yes.'

'Have you told him?'

Joan shakes her head.

'Good. That's a relief. You mustn't.'

'Really? But I want to. I was just waiting until I was sure. And until he stopped being so angry with everything.'

Sonya laughs. 'Jo-jo-jo-jo. What on earth is it you think he's going to say? Do you think he'll go all gooey over this and ask you to marry him?'

There is a silence. There is a certain quality Joan recognises in herself which makes her susceptible to these daydreams even though she professes not to want them. Weakness, she supposes Leo might call it, but she would not call it that. She is curious. She likes to imagine what might happen, how her life might change if she were to tell Leo, if they were to have this baby now, together. Although it would mean delaying her studies, which would displease her father and Miss Abbott, and she cannot even guess what her mother's reaction would be.

Sonya is looking at her and shaking her head. 'Oh God, come on, Joan. Surely you don't really believe that. He's got a war to fight, in case you hadn't noticed.'

Joan frowns at her. 'But we're not at war. Chamberlain said—'

114

'Rot,' Sonya interrupts. 'You will be soon, whatever anyone says. And anyway, I wasn't talking about Britain's war against Hitler. I'm talking about Leo's own war. The Struggle.' She opens her cigarette case again and tips out a pile of cigarettes, flicking one across the table to Joan and then taking a thin scrap of cigarette paper from the bottom of the tin. She writes something on the paper and then slides it across the table.

Joan takes it. 'What's this?'

'An address.'

'I can see that.' Joan reads it again and then, quite suddenly, she breathes out. 'Oh.' She feels another wave of nausea build and break inside her. She looks up at Sonya. 'I can't do that. I couldn't. And anyway, it's illegal. I could go to prison for it.'

Sonya laughs. 'Of course you wouldn't.' She adjusts the sleeves of her dress, absently rolling back the cuffs to display her delicate wrists, and then leans forward, cupping her hands around Joan's as she speaks. 'Everybody does it,' she says gently. 'They just don't talk about it.'

'Really?' Joan hesitates over the next question, but then blurts it out: 'Have you?'

Sonya looks at her. 'No,' she says. 'There are ways, you know. And I've been lucky so far.' She sits back and smiles at Joan, comforting, encouraging. 'But I would if I had to.'

Joan cannot speak. She feels a strange sort of inertia invade her body, a heaviness that seems to float into every pore.

'Of course,' Sonya is saying now, her voice seeming to come from a great distance, although she is only there, an arm's stretch away, 'it's your decision.'

*   *   *

Sonya knows the way. Number 41, down here on the left. She walks faster than Joan, a few steps ahead. 'You're doing the right thing,' Sonya tells her as they turn in through the front gate. 'And Leo would be grateful if he knew. He'd respect you for it. Not,' she adds, 'that I think you should tell him.'

The house is small and poky. It has a green-washed front wall and a brown door. The colour of vomit, Joan thinks. Sonya rings the bell and they are shown into a dark hallway. There is a crucifix on the wall and a portrait of the Virgin Mary. Joan looks away, staring down at the thin rug covering the uneven floorboards.

'How many weeks is it?' a voice asks from the top of the stairs.

'Five and a half weeks late,' Joan whispers, and Sonya has to repeat it for her because she cannot speak loudly enough for the woman to hear. She is so scared, so sick, so sorry. Her hand is on her stomach again.

'Come on then. Up you come.' The woman holds the door of a room open at the top of the stairs. There is a bed covered in starched, white sheets, and the smell of disinfectant on the woman's hands is strong and causes Joan to retch.

The woman gestures towards a ceramic mixing bowl perched next to the bed. 'If you're going to be sick I'd appreciate it if you could aim for that,' she says, not looking at Joan but taking a towel from the top of a pile in the corner of the room, and dunking it in a basin. Her manner is brisk, matter-of-fact. She has seen all this before. 'Now take off

116

your clothes and jump on the bed.'

Oh, it is cold in here. It is deathly, icily cold. Joan takes off her skirt and stockings, and then hesitates. She looks at Sonya, but Sonya is standing with her hands on her hips, observing the woman's preparations.

'And your knickers,' the woman says, not looking at her but somehow knowing that Joan would have left them on. 'No point being a prissy now.'

Joan takes them off. Every atom of her body is quivering with the desire to leap up and run back down those dark horrible stairs and out of the front door. How did she get here? She sits on the bed for a few seconds and then stands up again. The air is cold against her naked flesh.

'Lie down.'

'I can't,' she says in a whisper. Her limbs move awkwardly, as if she has lost her coordination along with her clothing.

The woman doesn't turn around but continues with her preparations.

'There now,' Sonya says, her voice low and soothing as she steps a little closer to Joan. 'You know you're doing the right thing.'

'Am I?'

Sonya looks at her and nods, and her eyes are so desperate, so sad, that Joan could almost believe that Sonya is suffering more from this than she is. She sits back on the bed. Leo would be grateful if he knew. This is just the wrong time for him. And there are her studies to think of. Her whole body shakes as she lifts her legs up and lies down on her back, her forearms crossed over her lower body in a self-conscious attempt to cover herself up. There is no need for him to ever know. Things can just go back to the way they were.

The woman dries her hands on a towel, looking at the top of Joan's legs. 'No, like this,' she says, adjusting Joan's shoulders and hips so that she is twisted on her side. Her fingers are icy against Joan's skin.

Joan feels Sonya's hand on her arm. She has a sudden, desperate need for something kind, something warm, but Sonya's hand is cool and clammy. She wants to cry out to Sonya to stop touching her, to make the woman stop, to take that tube away from her—what is she doing with that tube?—to stop, oh ow!—to leave her be. There is a terrible stabbing pain in her stomach, a snapping and cracking and sucking, and she wants to curl her body up into a ball. She can feel the woman's hair brushing her thighs, and Sonya's breath on her cheek as she whispers to her—'there now, there now, nearly done'—and she has to push out every thought she has ever had so that she is thinking of nothing at all, not of Leo or her mother or anything else which might have once comforted her. She closes her eyes so that all she can see is blackness, because she does not want to see the bright red blood spreading so quickly on the sheets, nor does she want to remember the woman's hair, lank and greasy and sad to look at, or the crucifix nailed into the wall above the bed, or the smell of rubber and blood and the feel of half-dried towels itching against her skin. Her head is pushing against the wooden headboard and she is hot now, so hot that her whole body is shivering, her teeth chattering in her head, and still Sonya is holding her hand, squeezing, squeezing, until the pain in her knuckles threatens to distract from the other pain and tears

118

are drumming against her eyelids, and she wants to cry out—stop touching me!—but she does not, cannot, and still Sonya does not let go.

Tuesday, 5.09 a.m.

Joan rubs her eyes. It is early, not yet dawn, and it has been an uneasy night. A siege-like rattle of droplets slants against her bedroom window, trapping her, drowning her, keeping her from sleep. The electronic tag rubs against her ankle, too large for her thin bones. She reaches down to touch it, her fingers light against the mechanism. She could almost slip her foot out of it. What would they do, she wonders, if she made a break for it? Would they follow her, track her down? What has she told them in any case? Nothing really. Nothing relevant.

She could take the bus to the station and then the train to Dover. She could be there in time for the first ferry. It seems almost possible until she remembers that her bus pass and passport have been confiscated.

Small things, not insurmountable.

A taxi then, to somewhere in England. She could ask one of Lally's children if she might stay for a while. Not the girls. They would be too inquisitive. The boy, maybe. Samuel.

She closes her eyes. It is a stupid, desperate idea. Samuel is no longer the little boy whose photograph is still in her purse along with pictures of Lally's girls, and the old, faded one of Lally in a punt in Cambridge during the war. He would be fifty-four now, five years older than Nick, with a wife and

119

children of his own. She cannot simply turn up and expect him to harbour her indefinitely. He would probably telephone Nick as soon as she went to the bathroom, concerned that his odd black-sheep aunt was turning senile, if Nick hadn't already called him first. They are not close, Nick and his cousins, but they are dutiful about keeping in touch, all of them keen to make up for the stilted, long-distance relationship their mothers had maintained until Lally's death; two women who were, or so they were told, once inseparable.

But even if Samuel did agree to hide her for a few days, they would be sure to find her sooner or later—probably sooner—so it wouldn't do any good. It would only alarm Nick and make her appear more guilty.

Although of what? They still haven't told her exactly.

She turns over and feels a shiver of fear scrape across her stomach. There is nothing she can do, except, of course . . .

But she will not do that. She cannot. She must remain strong. She must not let anything slip.

She thinks of her room in Newnham during the days following her visit to the woman's house, the ceiling above her bed, the light flooding in from the window. So many memories dredged up from nowhere, jostling with each other for her attention. She remembers lying perfectly still, immoveable, shivering, trying not to think of anything at all, trying not to think of Leo, while at the same time praying for him to visit, wondering if she could have been more sympathetic to his anger over Stalin's treaty with Hitler, hoping it might not all be over between them. Certainly not allowing herself to think of the tiny thing she thought she had glimpsed in the woman's house, impossibly small and which appeared in her dreams as a poor, sorrowful soul with too-large eyes and golden skin.

She has a sudden memory of Sonya bringing mugs of warm milk and blankets to her room, reading out loud to her in Russian as a practice for her end-of-term language tests.

'Have you seen Leo?' she would ask every time Sonya came in, causing Sonya to smile at her and tip her head, not quite a yes but not quite a no either.

'Just rest,' she would whisper. 'Don't worry about him.'

And another memory of Sonya arriving with armfuls of hydrangea, pink and white and blue, harvested during the night from the college flower beds at Newnham, and filling jam jar after jam jar with these beautiful, delicate bursts of colour so that the whole room seemed to be brimming with gemstones when she made her announcement.

*   *   *

'I'm leaving for Switzerland tomorrow. I need to get out before the war starts.'

'Why?'

'I'm not British like you. I have a Russian passport. If I stay and Britain ends up fighting against the Soviets, I could be deported or interned.'

Joan tries to turn over, manoeuvring herself away from the windowsill of flowers so that she can face Sonya. She struggles upright and although the movement exhausts her, she is adamant that Sonya

121

is being unnecessarily dramatic. It is something of which Leo often accuses her, and Joan can see that there is a measure of truth in it. 'They wouldn't do that. You've been here for years.' Her voice is weaker than she intends, breathier. A sudden shooting pain in her stomach causes her to cry out and clench her eyes shut until the shock of it has passed.

Sonya takes her hand and squeezes it, bringing it up to her lips for a quick kiss. 'I'm not willing to take that risk. And who knows? Maybe I'll meet an Englishman out there and marry him. Then I'll have a nice clean British passport like you.'

Joan smiles weakly. 'Maybe.'

'Besides, it'll be good for Uncle Boris to have some company for a while. He has been rather neglected these past few years. He always liked to have young people around.'

At the mention of Uncle Boris, Joan feels a pulse of alarm breaking through the hot fog of her delirium. She has not seen Leo for over a week now, not since she had tried to talk to him after her conversation in the café with Sonya. It had been a final attempt to tell him everything, as she believed that, in spite of what Sonya said, she owed it to him to tell him. Yet when she went to find him the next day, she found that he was still angry with her, with Stalin, with anyone who tried to reason with him. He told her that nothing else in the world mattered now that the revolution had been betrayed. Nothing. Joan had placed her hand on his arm when he said this and he had shaken her off, not quite looking at her. He was not unkind to her exactly, just distracted, careless. Perhaps if he had known . . .

But he had not known. She had not told him. She had left quite suddenly after he shook her off, tears brimming in her eyes, and Leo had not come after her. It was Sonya who came to find her later that day when she heard that Joan had been to see him, Sonya who seemed to know exactly where she would be and that she would have spent the afternoon sobbing desolately into her pillow, who brought her a small supper of bread and cheese, along with some sharp-tasting apples from the college gardens, and who whispered gently in her ear that she would take her to see the woman the following day. She wouldn't have to go alone.

And now it is Sonya who is protecting her, keeping Leo away from her until she feels better and everything can go back to the way it was. 'Is Leo going too?'

Sonya stands up from the bed and walks to the window. 'Leo? No. He won't come.'

Joan hears this with a mixture of relief and concern. Relief that he is not going and she will have the chance to make things up with him and concern that he might actually be imprisoned if what Sonya says is true. Anti-Russian sentiment would be bound to increase once the war actually starts. 'Why not?' she asks.

Sonya sighs, and Joan can tell that Sonya is annoyed with him for not going with her. 'Some nonsense about his thesis. He needs to be here so that he can have access to the documents he needs.' She rolls her eyes. 'Apparently it will cost millions of Soviets their lives if Leo doesn't finish his PhD. I didn't realise how deluded he was. He's so self-important. I don't know who he thinks has told him that he is the only person who can save the

123

revolution.'

'Grigori Fy-something,' Joan murmurs, sinking back into the pillow. Her head is hot and clammy. She can feel her stomach burning. She should not have sat up for so long. 'He said it would only matter if it came to war.'

Sonya does not answer immediately. She steps towards her and takes her hand once more. 'Who?' she asks gently.

Joan shakes her head in delirious response. What was it he told her? 'A man he met in Moscow. He showed him that the grain figures were lying . . .' she corrects herself, '. . . misleading.'

Sonya doesn't move. Her hand feels suddenly cold. 'Lying?'

Oh God. Joan remembers now. He had made her promise and she had done so, easily, casually, as if there were no question. She covers her eyes with her hand, trying to block out the glare of daylight. How she wishes there was a way of taking her words back, of unsaying them, of scrubbing them out. The pain in her stomach causes her to gasp, only this time it does not stop as it has before. It twists and tugs. 'Misleading,' she repeats. 'He told me not to tell anyone. Please. Please don't tell Leo I told you.'

'About this Grigori Fy-something?'

'Yes,' she whispers.

Sonya does not move for a long time. Even her breathing seems to slow and then stop altogether. She bends down next to Joan's bed and strokes her hair. 'Of course I won't tell. You don't have to worry.' She leans forward and kisses Joan's cheek, and at that moment Joan can feel the soft beat of Sonya's heart through her thin cotton blouse. 'By

124

the way, I brought this for you.'

Joan's eyes flicker. She sees that Sonya is holding something in her arms, a silk dress of iridescent blue which she is placing on the sheet next to Joan's pillow. 'I want you to have it,' Sonya continues, 'to remember me while I'm away. I always thought it looked better on you anyway.'

'Dear Sonya,' Joan whispers, tears coming to her eyes as she feels a sudden rush of guilt for having worried even momentarily that Sonya was not to be trusted with a secret. 'Whatever will I do without you?'

'You'll write to me, of course. I'm relying on you to tell me everything.'

Tuesday 8.38 a.m.

The small red light of the surveillance camera flashes deliberatively in the corner of her bedroom. Joan rolls over, turning away from it. The rain outside is gentle now, pattering and peaceful. She knows that she needs to get up and prepare herself. MI5 will be here soon, and Nick too, and they will not want to waste any time in getting on with the questioning. They are anxious to get through everything by Friday, almost as if they expect to lose her as they lost William.

Is that it? Is that what they are scared of?

She pulls on her dressing gown and slippers and goes downstairs to the kitchen. She fills the kettle and cuts a slice of bread from the loaf she bought on Saturday. Was that really only three days ago? She feels time slipping beneath her, the past suddenly so clear and sharply defined in comparison with the fuzziness of the present. She sits down quite suddenly.

In the stillness, she remembers the cavernous sound of the corridors in the empty, unfilled days after Sonya had gone to Switzerland, the unnatural calm of her life as she convalesced. Mornings as quiet as sand, punctuated by the bursts of colour in the jam jars along her windowsill.

She thinks of her reunion with Leo once she was well again; her secret remaining unknown between them, something to be forgotten and ignored so that their lives could carry on as before. She remembers the fervour with which he clung to the idea that Stalin's pact with Hitler was indeed a tactical manoeuvre to buy the Soviets more time, just as Sonya had said, and how jubilant he was at the dawning realisation that his thesis really would be useful to the revolution now that war was bound to come. She remembers how hard he worked during those early months of the war, how pale he became with studying late into the night. And she remembers how it felt to know that his gaze was on her once again, his hands in her hair and his lips on her skin, such attention all the more necessary after having been withdrawn for so many weeks.

A car. Footsteps on the path. The sounds are familiar now.

Joan stands up and places the slice of bread under the grill.

She waits. The knock comes five seconds later, as she knew it would.

She flicks the switch of the kettle. She knows she should not keep them waiting, and yet she does. Just for a moment. Because she finds that if she

126

closes her eyes now, she can still recall the scent of those flowers on her windowsill, heady and sweet, smelling of cut grass and honey.

*   *   *

When it comes the war seems to take place somewhere else, not in Cambridge, although even in this relatively untouched town there are gas masks and ration cards and no new gloves for the winter. And such a long winter! Joan has never had chilblains before but she gets them on her fingers this year which she considers apt, chilblains being the sort of thing one ought to get during a war. She decides to give up her fingerless gloves in favour of homemade mittens until the spring arrives, and she knits a thick cardigan for herself, just in case this winter should, in fact, last for ever.

At first, there is a sense of waiting for things to happen. Everybody knows that this war will be different from the last, yet nobody is quite sure of the manner in which it will be different. Aeroplanes, certainly, but it seems somehow impractical to think of fighting a war for territory up in the sky.

A scheme is concocted to dig trenches in the Newnham garden to shelter the members of the college in the event of an air raid. This scheme stalls slightly when two Saxon skeletons are discovered in a flowerbed and are excavated with toothbrushes and tiny spades, but once this excitement has dissipated, the project is taken up again in earnest. The idea is that the whole college should be able to disperse into the trenches at the blow of a whistle, and Joan takes her turn at digging

127

along with the other girls on her corridor. A fire brigade is formed which appears to consist of nearly the entire college, and there are air-raid drills, fire-watching patrols and stirrup pump practices to attend, along with cold night-time excursions to the trenches. The gardens are turned into giant vegetable patches and beehives are trundled in to make honey.

There are rarely any meetings to attend now, what with most of the contingent being signed up or sent away in some capacity. The town seems to be full of evacuees and army men, along with some members of the government who are temporarily housed in the university for the duration of the war. The talk among those who are left is mostly about the war effort which, at this early stage, appears to be a collective heave of nothing specific. And Joan wants to do something specific. She wants to make an effort.

Well-spoken ladies in brass-buttoned uniforms come to visit, hoping to persuade the girls to stay at Cambridge to finish their studies and then to join the services, or to teach, or do some other job of a useful nature. After much discussion, Joan decides that she will join the Women's Royal Naval Service, or perhaps the female attachment to the Air Force, and she is excited by the prospect.

Leo's response to this is brusque. 'Well, that's a waste of an education. You should be more grateful for what you've had.'

'You sound like my father.'

'He's right. What's the point in all the work you've done and all the teaching you've benefitted from if you're just going to throw it away on running messages or driving a canteen hither and thither?'

Joan feels a small flutter of affection for him. 'Hither and thither?' she asks.

'Is that wrong?'

'No, no. It's right, technically. It's just that you wouldn't say it in this sort of conversation. It's a bit literary.'

He smiles. 'I'll bear that in mind.' He coughs. 'But I stand by what I said. There's nothing noble or heroic in doing things below your value.'

'Soviet value theory, is it?' Joan mumbles.

'Yes, and it's correct. Not everyone is capable of doing what you can do. Not everyone has your opportunities and your brain. You should leave the jobs they can do for them and you should do the hardest thing you are capable of. People need to push themselves. That's how society will progress.'

Joan sighs. 'But the civil service is so drab and boring. I don't want to be stuck in thick tights and sensible shoes. The Wrens have those natty little hats and I like the idea of sleeping in dormitories and going on excursions. It sounds fun.'

'This is war. It's not supposed to be a summer camp. And anyway, you don't like joining things. You always say that.'

'I suppose so. But this is different.' She leans in closer. 'Don't you think you'd like me in that nice little uniform?'

Leo does not flinch. He shakes his head. 'I can't believe you're even taking that into consideration.'

'No. Yes. I just thought . . .' She stops, feeling chided. She knows he has a point and there is a lot she could do with the science she has learnt. She just doesn't want to miss out. This is her chance to be self-sufficient and practical, to demonstrate that she does have those qualities she always suspected herself of having, and she doesn't want to waste this chance by sitting in an office. These are her unprecedented times. She might end up with a degree—or, more precisely, a University Certificate—but what sort of scientific research post could she realistically hope for which might use that knowledge? They'd be more likely to want secretarial college graduates to support their male colleagues than her.

Leo frowns. 'Let me ask around among the other postgrads. Someone is bound to come up with something more suitable for you.'

And so that is how it is left. Leo will sort something out for her, and in the meantime Joan will finish her degree and Leo his thesis. Joan has a lot of work to catch up on, partly as a result of being hopelessly unprepared by science lessons at school to partake in the sophisticated experiments required at university, and partly because of other distractions. Already she knows she will have to work non-stop during the Easter vacation to get through all the reading.

She wishes Sonya were around to distract her from her work, but Sonya has turned out to be a poor letter writer, and while Joan keeps her promise to tell her everything she is missing, Sonya does not write to Joan for almost eight months. When a letter finally arrives, it is accompanied by a beautifully wrapped bar of the nicest chocolate Joan has ever tasted. Joan is delighted with it and eats it slowly, one square at a time, placing it on her tongue and letting it soften and melt before reluctantly swallowing it.

The accompanying letter doesn't say much, but it

does mention that she has met a man, 'a darling pinko', she calls him, who is teaching her all sorts of new tricks. He is from Worcestershire and called Jamie and has (*What did I tell you, Jo-jo?*) a British passport, and he lived in Shanghai before Switzerland, so he is almost the most exotic man she has ever met.

I hope you're keeping an eye on that cousin of mine, she writes. *I'm surprised he hasn't been interned yet after what happened in Poland. I can't imagine the benefits to Russia went unnoticed in England. Send him my love, will you?*

Joan reads this part of the letter out loud to Leo and then stops, but he does not look up from his work. 'What I don't understand is why she doesn't write to you herself?'

Leo's shoulders stiffen. It is a small movement but Joan does not miss it. His pen stops moving but he does not turn around.

'Leo?' Joan feels a sudden lurch in her stomach. Why does she always fear the worst? 'What is it?'

'Sonya and I had a . . .' He pauses, searching for the word.

'A fight?' Joan offers.

He turns the page of the book in front of him. His hands fidget a little as the page springs up again and he attempts to press it flat. 'Clash,' he says eventually, turning to look at Joan. 'We had a bit of a clash while you were ill.'

'Because she wanted you to go to Switzerland with her?'

Leo presses his lips together. 'That was part of it. Not all of it.' For a moment it looks as though he is going to tell her more, but then his eyes become glassy and she knows that this subject, like so many

131

others, is not open to her. She hates it when he is like this. Even though she tells herself that his reluctance to tell her everything is only natural after the life he has had, she still feels angry with him that he does not want to share everything. Perhaps Sonya was right. Perhaps she doesn't understand him enough. But still, why has he not mentioned this until now? Why must this be a secret? He turns back to the desk and picks up his fountain pen, and then he begins to scratch a list of numbers onto the paper in front of him. 'Have you seen my supervisor's book? The orange one?'

'It's over there.' Joan points to the chair where he left it the previous evening, where he always leaves his books, and does not take her eyes from him as he stands up from his desk and goes over to pick it up. 'Well, she sends her love to you anyway,' she adds, not ready to let the subject drop quite yet.

Leo nods. 'Please say I send her my best wishes.' He pauses. 'Tell her I'll write soon.' And then he bends down, kisses Joan on the top of the head, and walks out of the room.

Tuesday, 10.41 a.m.

Ms Hart takes a letter from her briefcase and hands it to Joan. 'This is from Leo's file,' she says. 'He seems to have managed to convince someone that he'd lost interest in the cause by the time the war started.'

Joan does not lift her eyes from the piece of paper.

'Would you say that was true?' Ms Hart asks.

132

Silence.

Ms Hart's voice is gently persuasive. 'I'm just asking your opinion, Mrs Stanley. Would you have said that Leo's dedication, faith, whatever you want to call it, wavered at this point?'

'Leo wasn't a very expressive person. I don't know what he thought, and I wouldn't like to speak for him.'

'But how did it appear to you?'

Nick interrupts. 'Who are you questioning here? My mother? Or this Leo person?'

Neither Ms Hart nor Mr Adams look at Nick.

'I would say,' Joan begins tentatively, 'that his viewpoint changed slightly as a result of the pact.' She pauses. 'But I wouldn't have said he wavered.' She looks up. 'Leo wasn't the type to waver.'

22 March 1940
Leo GALICH has been interned, apparently at the instigation of Sir Alexander Hoyle.

Personally, I think we shall have to decide on a policy with regard to aliens with socialist leanings. If we accepted them in the first place, and if we have no evidence that they abused the hospitality we have shown them by engaging in extreme political activities, there does not seem to be any justification for interning them.

As far as we are concerned, GALICH is a borderline case. We have been presented with evidence by one of GALICH's tutors at Cambridge who declares himself a dyed-in-the-wool Tory. He believes that GALICH's interest in communism stems from witnessing the rise of Hitler during his early years in Leipzig but, like so many of his type, the Nazi–Soviet Pact has done for any misguided

133

sense of loyalty he may have felt towards Stalin.

There does not seem to be anything in his activities to which we could properly take exception beyond youthful exuberance, but it would be more satisfactory if he could find employment in his own sphere of usefulness in one of the Overseas Dominions to keep him out of harm's way. We will ask the Special Branch to pursue this actively.

In my opinion, our policy should be to intern alien communists only when we have evidence that they are in touch with the Communist Party of Great Britain. Any very drastic change of policy should be taken only when it is quite clear that the communists are on the side of Hitler in the war against Great Britain.

In the spring of 1940 the bombing starts—not just in London, Birmingham, Gateshead, Glasgow, but also to a lesser extent in Cambridge—and there is a round-up of enemy aliens. Leo is arrested and marched off to the police station, along with a significant proportion of the science faculty.

'Look after my papers, Jo-jo,' he instructs as he is taken away. 'And can you hand-deliver my thesis to my supervisor and collect it once he's read it? Keep it safe for me.'

'I will,' she says. Her eyes fill with tears and, although she knows that she needs to be brave and there are far worse places he could be sent during wartime than a camp out of the line of fire, she still wishes he did not have to go. Or at least, that he would be less prosaic about his departure. It could be years before they see each other again and she wants something more from him than this. Something to hold on to while he is away.

134

Say it, she thinks. Please say it.

But he does not. He might think it. She is certain that somewhere inside him he does think it, or at least feel it, but he does not say it. He frowns as he pulls on his jacket and pats his pockets to check he has his keys, cigarettes, gloves. 'Don't forget,' he says.

'I won't.'

The policeman puts his head back around the door. 'Come on.'

Leo nods and turns to leave.

'Leo.'

'Yes?'

Her voice is small and hopeful. 'I'll miss you.'

'Of course.' He takes a step towards her and kisses her quickly, too quickly for her to be ready for it and leaving only the lingering scratch of his stubble against her lips. 'I'll miss you too, Jo-jo.'

He is sent to an internment camp on the Isle of Man, and thence to Canada on board a ship flying a swastika flag to indicate that it is transporting German prisoners of war alongside the British internees, most of whom are Jewish and have spent the last five years trying to avoid being trapped in enclosed spaces. However, it is seen as a way of keeping the ship afloat, and the voyage passes without incident.

Leo writes to her from Quebec, reporting that the camp is clean and bright and the air smells of pine needles. There are huge portions of food served up in the canteen, and he has been asked to deliver a series of lectures about Soviet Planning to the discussion group he and his comrades have formed to keep their minds active. Joan can imagine Leo at the camp, assuming his position as

135

unofficial leader as if he would expect nothing else, just as he always did back home.

Although he would not say he is enjoying it exactly, there is no evidence of any bitterness or resentment in his letters, and it is a relief to Joan to know that he is not unhappy. Once again, she takes comfort from the fact that the frequency and length of his letters must at least indicate that he thinks of her often, but she wishes he would say something, anything, a bit . . . well . . . softer.

She does not mention this in her letters back to him. It seems such a small thing to complain about when there are so many terrible things happening across Europe. Later, she will think that one of the reasons for Leo's attitude towards Britain ('an unheroic nation' he will call it, once it is all over) was because he missed those early, dreadful months of the Blitz during which German planes droned over the country every night and the earth shuddered and flashed under the weight of bombardment. He did not stand on the roof as part of the Newnham Fire Brigade as Joan did to watch the fires burning themselves out along Vicarage Terrace, nor did he see the smoking piles of rubble that sometimes littered the streets near the station in the mornings, the photographs of funeral carriages in the newspapers, the pictures of mansion blocks of flats blown open like dolls' houses, women sitting tight-lipped on buses, determinedly not looking out of the windows and smiling at the conductor as she—they were nearly always women in those days—clipped the tickets. And everywhere, in every crack and pore, the tireless, clinging dust.

Joan does not mention any of this either. It is not

136

done to complain, so instead she tells him about the books she is reading, the films she has been to see, the essays and experiments she is working on for her finals. She mentions dances and dressing-up parties and taking fifteen-year-old Lally punting on the Cam when she came to visit by herself for the first time. She tells him about the craze for skating on Mill Pond when it freezes over during Lent Term, and about cycling out to Lingay Fen with some of the other girls from college to practise on the much bigger, smoother rink where the All-England Championships used to take place before the war.

She does not tell him that her greatest enjoyment is her weekly hot bath, how she fills the tub with metallic-tasting water from an array of kettles and saucepans, and holds her breath while she submerges her whole body so that the world around her becomes muffled and muted. She does not tell him that lying naked in warm water is the only substitute she can find for the warmth of his body next to her own, for his arms, his smell, the comforting weight of him, and how, for a brief moment, it allows her to forget the terrible empty ache in her stomach.

*   *   *

Final examinations come and go. The undergraduette protests outside Senate House on results day are muted this year, seeing as the country is in the throes of pulling together and there are far worse things happening in the world than women not being allowed degrees. But still, it exists as a minor gripe, a rumbling of discontent, and there are assurances that surely, *surely*, after this second war, they will have to relent and allow women to be admitted fully into the university.

Not long after this, a letter arrives from the Metals Research Facility in Cambridge summoning Joan to report for an interview the following Monday. Leo has told her to expect this, having learnt something of the project from a fellow internee at the Canadian camp whom Leo has persuaded to recommend Joan for the post. Apparently, Joan is the perfect candidate, according to Leo, although he is not very forthcoming on the matter of what the job actually entails, and nor is the letter of summons. She knows only that it is essential to the war effort, that it is not a research post but still requires detailed scientific knowledge, and that even her Physics tutor has been approached by her future employers to enquire if she is up to the task.

On Monday morning she takes her time, unfurling the rollers from her hair with more care than usual and putting on her best woollen suit, navy blue and a little patched, but brightened up with peacock blue buttons which she hopes will draw attention away from the faded fabric. She looks for her smartest shoes, charcoal grey with a sharp heel, and then remembers that she lent them to Sonya last year and has not used them since. Sonya's room has been untouched since she went away, the war having left several college rooms empty, and she has to borrow a spare set of keys from the porter to retrieve them.

When she enters, the first thing she notices is that Sonya's bed still has the same sheets on it and the pillows are stacked up against the small wooden

138

headboard as if she has just got up and gone out for the day. A glass stands next to the bed, its insides smudged where the water has evaporated. Joan goes to the wardrobe. Her shoes are exactly where she remembers seeing them last, tucked to the side of the bottom shelf. She reaches in to pull them out and, as she does, she is struck by the faint scent of a long-remembered smell. Lemony soap and tobacco. She sees a light blue shirt crumpled into the shelf above her shoes. She takes it out, the cotton soft against her fingers, and she holds it up to her nose and breathes in the scent of it. It is unmistakeable, that smell. She closes her eyes and for a moment she is somewhere else, and it takes a while for the question that is burning in the back of her mind to form itself into words.

How, she wonders, did one of Leo's worn shirts end up in Sonya's cupboard?

Joan holds the shirt away and frowns, puzzled. Leo is normally so careful with his things; everything folded and in its place, quite the opposite of Sonya. He would never bundle it up like that.

The answer comes to her in the form of a sudden sickness in her stomach. No, she thinks, not that, and for a moment she is disgusted with herself that she has even allowed such an unkind, sordid thought to enter her head. What is wrong with her? When did she become so—she cannot think of the right word—corrupted?

Quickly, she stuffs the shirt back into the cupboard, picks up the shoes and closes the door behind her. The lock slips back into the catch so that the room will be left undisturbed once more, either until Sonya returns or the college decide they

139

cannot hold it for her any longer, and then she hurries down the corridor to her own room. Five minutes until she needs to leave. Her shoes still need to be polished, her hair brushed and clipped back. Why must she always be late for everything?

She has been to these laboratories before as an undergraduate, but never into the secure section where she goes now. She is told to report to reception where she is to wait for Professor Max Davis, the director of the Research Facility.

She sees him before he sees her, stopping at one desk and then another to ask questions and nodding his approval to whatever answers are given. She has heard his name mentioned in the science department before, always spoken with a degree of awe, as if his scientific precision is a near-beatific gift. But, in the flesh, he appears younger than she anticipated, perhaps thirty, and dressed in a slim-fitting suit with an eager expression on his face when he talks to the other scientists. He glances up at her and nods, indicating that he will be with her in a moment. He is good-looking, in a conventional sort of way, with dark brown hair that curls up from his head in tufts even though he has attempted to pomade it into place. He looks like the sort of man who used to enjoy a good game of chess during his schooldays, or perhaps ping-pong. When he meets her in the draughty reception room he seems to spring across the room at her, insisting as he shakes her hand that she call him Max rather than Professor or anything of that nature.

'How was your journey?'

Joan smiles, thinking that the ten-minute walk from Newnham to the laboratories could hardly pass for a journey. 'Uneventful.'

'How very un-English of you. Most people would say that uneventful passed for good.'

Joan smiles.

'Ah-ha, but of course. Must be your scientific outlook. Step one of the interview passed with flying colours.' He grins. 'Let me take you to my office, and we can have a look in at the lab on the way.'

There is a long red-tiled corridor of swing doors with square, white-washed rooms to either side which are visible from the corridor through large screens. The building smells of disinfectant and polished glass. It is a clean, light smell, accentuated by the sense of industry present in each of the rooms.

Max is reading from a wad of papers as they walk. 'It says here,' he says suddenly, 'that you liked to attend communist marches, talks, that sort of thing while you were a student.'

Joan does not break her stride as she looks up at him. 'Oh yes,' she says, answering directly as she has planned. It was Leo's advice, of course, to think about how she would tackle this question if it should ever arise. She had guessed that this job would require security clearance given that it is classed as a war job, and had decided in advance that she would admit some interest in the cause if asked, hoping to explain it away as youthful optimism mixed with academic interest. She knows that any attempt to evade or deny would only make her blush and look guilty. 'Yes, I was rather interested in that sort of thing,' she says. 'Intellectually.'

'And now?'

'Now? Well, times have changed since then.' She

141

will not look away. Not yet.

He nods, and for a moment Joan wonders if he is going to confess to a similar leaning. 'Well, I suppose the Nazi–Soviet pact saw to a lot of that.' He pauses. 'Bad idea, in my opinion, but I suppose Russia came out of the first war terribly hard, poor buggers.'

Not a confession then. But Max is seemingly unfazed by what has just passed, and his reaction is considered, almost sympathetic, Joan thinks. They turn a corner and he bounces ahead of her to push open a wooden door, holding it with his arm outstretched along the width of the door so that she can pass through.

'Here we are,' he says, leading her into a smaller office and gesturing towards a chair on one side of the desk while he sits down on the other side, looking directly at her now. 'But still,' he continues, 'try everything once, eh?'

He is testing her now. His eyes are deep blue, sea-blue. She feels a faint burn in her cheeks but she knows she must continue. She must pretend to herself that she is a normal young woman who has never met Leo or Sonya, who was interested in peace marches for a brief while but has no interest in political movements. She must convince herself that she is not sympathetic to the cause, that she thinks communists are brutal and vicious and in need of a good haircut rather than hopeful idealists, and she hears the required note of outrage slip into her voice. It is, she realises as she speaks, her mother's voice, firm yet reprimanding. 'I wouldn't say I went that far.'

'No, no. Of course not. I didn't mean to imply . . .' He coughs, looking down at his papers and

142

swiftly reordering them. 'Now, I see you have a Certificate from Cambridge. Natural Sciences, Upper Second in Part I, First Class in Part II.' He nods, as if this is the first time he has seen her results. 'Not bad.'

Joan nods. 'Yes, Professor. Specialising in theoretical physics.'

'Max,' he corrects her. 'We're going to be working with the Yanks here, so you must call me Max.' He pauses. 'I have it on good authority from your tutor at Cambridge that you'll be interested in our work here.' He looks at her and lowers the papers onto the desk. 'Do you know what that work is?'

Joan shakes her head. 'I wasn't told anything. I just got a letter . . .' She goes to take it from her bag but Max waves his hand to indicate that this is unnecessary.

'No need, no need,' he says. 'We recruit on a recommendation-only basis. You'll see why.' He pauses. 'Have you heard of Tube Alloys?'

Joan frowns. Has she? She shakes her head, trying to hide her disappointment that the science will be materials-based. 'I could probably take a guess though.'

'Go ahead.'

'Well, I would assume it was a project aimed at developing non-corrosive metals for oil drills, gas pipes, or something like that. But I don't really know how it fits in with the war. Armaments? Aerial equipment?'

Max nods. 'Nearly. It's a bit more complicated than that, but it's a good start. Sounds fascinating, doesn't it?'

Not really, Joan thinks, and there is a brief,

awkward moment before she realises that he is joking. 'I don't understand. Is that not what it is?'

'It's a code name. Nobody is allowed to know what we are doing in Tube Alloys. Even some members of the War Cabinet don't know.'

Joan feels a small shiver of fear creep along her spine. 'And what about me? Am I allowed to know?'

'That depends.' Max reaches down and opens a drawer in the bottom of his desk. He takes out a brown envelope which he slides to her across the desk. 'Before we go any further, I need you to sign this.'

'What is it?'

'It's an undertaking that binds you, if you sign it, to keep quiet. You won't be able to tell your family or friends anything about what you're doing here.' He looks directly at her. 'You understand what that means. It means you can't even tell your boyfriend what you've been doing all day.'

Joan returns the look, refusing to flinch. She remembers Leo's insistence in his letters that she must deny any relationship with him, if asked. It is for her own good, he tells her. She steels herself against the memory of him. 'I don't have a boyfriend.'

Max shifts slightly in his chair. 'Ah, well. It was just a figure of speech . . .' He tails off. The morning sun floods the room, catching the edge of the mirror and sending a sliver of rainbow-coloured light along the side of his face and down onto his collar as if he has been dipped in a delicate shimmer of oil. 'Anyway,' he continues, 'the point is that you don't have to decide immediately. I want you to think about it. Take it away, read it, spend some time mulling it over. I want you to understand all the implications of signing it before you do anything.'

Joan takes the envelope and slits it open. She pulls out the sheaf of papers and looks at them. There is a covering note clipped to a carbon paper copy of the Official Secrets Act.

'You can't tell me anything more about it?'

'I'm afraid I've told you all I can.'

Joan nods. Evidently whatever work is done by this sub-division of the laboratory is hugely significant or, at least, is thought to be. She wonders if Leo already knows what it is. No, of course not. How could he possibly know? But still, she worries about herself, about her capacity for discretion. Can she keep her job a secret? What would she tell her parents if they asked what she did?

But then she remembers her earlier visit to the woman's house, the feel of Sonya's hand in her own, and how she had kept the trauma of it a secret from Leo, from everybody, just as Sonya told her to, speaking only of her 'illness' while she pushed the memory of that day down, down, burying it deep inside her until she could feel it crumpling and weakening like a ball of bright blue silk.

'Take a day or two,' Max says, 'there's no rush. It can be hard to carry a burden like this around. Believe me. If you don't think you can do it, it doesn't matter. We can find another post for you somewhere else.'

She knows why she kept that day a secret. She did it for Leo, so that he would not be disappointed in her, tied to her. And now she imagines Leo's disappointment if she refuses this job he has arranged for her, and in this moment she knows

145

what she must do. After all, it is what she has always expected of herself: that she is loyal, trustworthy, that she would make sacrifices for her country if called upon to do so. It is just that she had not anticipated that it would ever really be required.

She takes a deep breath. 'Do you have a pen?'

Tuesday, 2.27 p.m.

Section 1(1) Official Secrets Act 1911 and 1920:
1(1) If any person for any purpose prejudicial to the safety or interests of the State:

(a) approaches, inspects, passes over or is in the neighbourhood of, or enters any prohibited place within the meaning of this Act; or
(b) makes any sketch, plan, model, or note which is calculated to be or might be or is intended to be directly or indirectly useful to an enemy; or
(c) obtains, collects, records, or publishes, or communicates to any other person any secret official code word, or pass word, or any sketch, plan, model, article, or note, or other document or information which is calculated to be or might be or is intended to be directly or indirectly useful to an enemy;

he shall be guilty of felony . . .

Mr Adams holds the file up to the camera so that the document can be recorded, and then readjusts the lens to focus it once more on Joan. The day has brightened into a cold, yellow afternoon, and Joan feels a stirring of hunger. She wishes she had been able to eat the sandwich Nick made for her when they stopped for lunch, but he insisted on spreading avocado across the bread instead of butter. She had asked him not to but he insisted that she'd like it, even though she told him that she'd really much prefer butter. Avocado doesn't agree with her. It never has, although she doesn't expect Nick to remember that, but she doesn't remind him of this fact as she knows it will only prompt another lecture on vitamins and carbohydrates—vits and carbs, he calls them—and she is too tired for that. Why can he not just eat normally, as she does? What's wrong with piccalilli?

'May I see it?' Nick reaches out to take the file from Ms Hart. He glances at the signature on the bottom of the form, his expression registering a flicker of uncertainty before resetting itself into his usual expression of outrage that any of this is happening at all. He places the file on the coffee table. 'Well, I don't see that as particularly significant.' He takes a sip of water. 'I'd have thought it was pretty standard practice to require everyone working on anything remotely connected with the war to sign this.'

Joan feels tears rising at the back of her throat. Her arms twitch slightly, betraying her desire to reach out to her son, to tell him that she doesn't deserve such kindness.

Nick doesn't see Joan's gesture but Ms Hart does, and for a brief second Joan wonders if this is as far as she can go. She has spent a lifetime running away from this moment—never explaining, never excusing—and now she worries she might not

147

have the strength to carry on. She is too old, too tired.

'And did you intend to adhere to it when you signed it?'

In spite of her exhaustion, there is something in Ms Hart's tone of voice that causes Joan to bristle slightly; an ember of fire catching inside her. She glances at Nick and knows that she must keep going. She must protect her son, as she has always done, even if he might not know it. She raises her eyebrows as if affronted. 'Of course I did.'

'But you understand why I ask.'

*   *   *

Her title is stated on her security pass: Personal Assistant to the Director of the Metals Research Facility in Cambridge. How dull that sounds. How disappointing to be using her science only in order to spell the elements in the periodic table. And no hat to be worn at a jaunty angle, no uniform with a tight waist and a bright collar to be flaunted around town while practising her American-style chewing-gum walk. But still, at least she is out there doing something at last, making an effort and earning her own money.

Apart from Max, there are ten others in the department. Of these, nine are men, leaving one other woman, Karen, whose domain covers both switchboard and reception, and over which she is demonstrably territorial. At first glance, she has the air of an old-fashioned schoolmarm, neat and buttoned-up with reading glasses perpetually perched on the end of her nose, but this appearance is misleading as she turns out to be an untapped source of information about everyone in the laboratory. She is forty and a widow, with two sons both away in the RAF, and while not exactly unfriendly, she gives the impression of being bored and a little lonely. Gradually, Joan finds that various tasks which were once Karen's—the morning tea run, stocking the biscuit tin—have been permanently delegated to her, but the upside of this is that Karen shares her nuggets of gossip more freely with Joan than with any of the others, and in this way Joan comes to know more about the people working in the laboratory than she does about most of her friends and relations.

The men are all scientists or technicians. The two most senior scientists on the project are Donald, Max's official deputy, who is never to be seen without his maroon beret and white laboratory coat, and Arthur, a tall, straight-nosed Oxford don who shared a dormitory with Max when they were schoolboys together at Marlborough. The rest of the team are keen scientific types, mostly foreign, and they are set to work on specifically delineated aspects of the project, as it is deemed sensible to restrict the number of people with access to the overall, high-level plans. 'Especially,' she is told in a whisper by Karen, 'the foreign element.'

The mood at the laboratory is one of urgency. From what Joan can gather, they are making some form of weapon. She does not imagine that it is a large weapon, given the size of the operations warehouse where construction is said to take place. There is not enough space, nor are there enough people, for anything very large to be built. Max gives her just enough information to do the work required of her, but he is not particularly expansive.

149

Most of the time, he works on theoretical research in his office with the door closed, but he will occasionally meet with researchers from Birmingham where the other main laboratory is located. This is all Joan knows. She would not go so far as to say that she is disappointed in her lack of involvement, but she will admit that she had hoped for something a little more exciting.

A security guard checks her bag on the way in and the way out; Henry, an old, whiskery man with whom Joan has a brief chat every morning, and who gropes around apologetically in her bag every afternoon, feeling the cloth of the zipped compartment and checking her lipstick and powder compact and glasses case. What is he looking for? she wonders, as he relaxes, smiles, and nods her on her way. Stolen typewriter tape? Stamps? Envelopes?

After a month of making tea and performing general tasks, Max calls her into his office and announces that her probation period has officially ended, and so it is time they had a serious talk. Joan perches on the edge of the wooden chair opposite his desk, wondering if his stern expression is anything to do with her typing speed—she has never been very fast but, she argues in her head, she is accurate—or her occasional lateness. She braces herself, waiting.

At first she thinks she has not heard him correctly. 'The Prime Minister is coming here?' she repeats, her notebook half open on her knee.

Max nods.

'Here?'

'Yes.' Max grins at her, and for a brief moment Joan wonders if there is something else in the smile, a sort of curiosity, and it flashes through her mind that the one person Karen has not told her much about is Max. She must ask her later. She imagines suddenly, oddly, how he might look when he is asleep, and thinks that there is something endearingly boyish about him. She shakes the thought from her mind, hoping it is not evident in her face.

'Tomorrow?'

'Yes.'

'Is it a secret or are the others allowed to know?'

'Nobody outside the laboratory can be told. Everyone here is allowed to know, but only Donald, Arthur and I will be at the meeting. We can't have everyone coming, although the Prime Minister wants to meet them all, shake their hands, that sort of thing. I've put Karen on sentry duty to arrange everything. But only the four of us will be at the meeting, along with the PM and anyone he decides to bring.'

'Four? I thought you said it was just you, Donald and Arthur?'

Max grins. 'I want you to be there too.'

'Me? What can I do? I know less than anyone here.' Joan is surprised at how excited she feels about the prospect of this official visit, even if the thought of actually speaking to the Prime Minister fills her with a slight dread. She feels—what?—starstruck.

Max smiles. 'That's why I thought it would be useful to include you. It's time you started being more involved. There was a reason why I wanted a science graduate to fill your position. And . . .' he looks embarrassed, '. . . we need someone to make the tea and generally smooth things over by looking

151

pretty.'

Joan tries not to blush at this obtuse and unexpected burst of flattery. It is not what she expects from Max, who is normally unwaveringly correct. She attempts a wry smile. 'All the essentials then, I see.'

'But I also think it'll help you to learn more about what we're doing here. I assume you learnt a thing or two about atoms during your time at Cambridge?'

'Of course.'

'Good,' Max prompts, gesturing with his arm that he wants her to expand on this answer.

And so she does, haltingly at first, describing in scientific terms the internal structure of an atom, the nucleus of protons and neutrons orbited by a whirl of electrons. It surprises her to find that she has missed thinking in this way. She has noted the wooden plaque in the entrance of the laboratories, declaring that it was in this very building in Cambridge, in 1932, that the atom was first split, and so she describes this process too; how it is possible to bombard the nucleus of an atom with neutrons so that the energy in the nucleus is redistributed, causing another particle to be emitted and leaving behind a slightly different substance from the original one.

Max nods. 'Exactly.' He presses his fingertips together, which Joan recognises as the gesture of an academic, a theorist. 'And are there any exceptions to this rule?'

'Uranium, I think.'

'And what happens with uranium?'

'It splits in two, releasing energy. But it releases two or three neutrons, not just one.' Joan has read

152

about this in an academic paper for her third-year exams, published just before the war but only introduced to the syllabus as she was about to leave.

'And?'

Joan frowns. 'What do you mean?'

'You're a physicist. So tell me, what are the implications of this? What could you do with that information?'

'I don't remember anything else being mentioned in the paper.' She frowns. 'But I suppose, if you had enough uranium atoms in isolation and you split one of them, then splitting just one would release enough neutrons to split more, and then those in turn could be used to bombard other particles.'

Max nods. 'A self-sustaining chain reaction. And then?'

'It would produce increasing amounts of energy.'

'Yes. Enormous amounts. A new source of power entirely.' Max pauses, as if waiting for Joan to answer a question he has not yet asked. 'So what else could it be used for?'

There is a silence as the implications of Max's question creep up on her. 'An explosion?' she ventures.

'Not just an explosion.' He pauses. 'A super-bomb. A war-ending bomb.'

Joan stares at him. 'Can it be done?'

'Why not? It's possible in theory, although there are still unresolved problems, principally regarding uranium supply.' He pauses. 'But the crucial thing is that it does seem to be possible, and if it is we can't let the Germans get there first.'

'How do you know they're trying?'

Max smiles. 'The first uranium discoveries were made four years ago. Do you know how many

153

papers the Germans have published on this subject since then?'

Joan shakes her head slowly.

'None. Not a single one. Complete radio silence. So I'd say there's a ninety-nine per cent chance they're working on this too.' Max pauses. He picks up a file and hands it to Joan. 'I'd like you to read over these summaries. I need a basic diagram drawn up for tomorrow, not necessarily to scale but large enough to put up on the wall and get the idea across. There are some sketches in here you can use as a template.' He grins. 'How are you at drawing?'

*   *   *

Joan starts with the basics. Initially her drawing takes the shape of a badly proportioned fish. A large fish, perhaps a shark or a tuna. She draws a circle in the middle of the fish's body and splits it in two with a line, the divided core hiding beneath the place where the fins would be, and then she shades this circle with her pencil. The shading represents the critical mass of uranium, the unstable element, not yet unified. If Joan were given to metaphor, she might describe the uranium particles as elbowing one another, jostling for position on the starting line. But Joan is not given to metaphor. It is a simple, scientific process.

But there will be no explosion yet.

The explosion starts with the addition of TNT, which Joan adds into the diagram by enclosing the circle of uranium inside an outer square of yellow explosive, still contained within the fish's stomach. She colours this carefully, not allowing any of it to spill into the core as there can be no easy mingling of substances. When the TNT is activated, it will fire the two halves of the core together to create a critical mass. This explosion will be big in itself, but not huge. At this stage it is not astronomical so much as economical. It will work as a highly efficient multiplier of energy.

The astronomy will occur a millisecond later, when the detonation activates the neutron source, which Joan colours in blue, firing neutrons at the critical mass of uranium. This is where the real explosion happens. This is what Max describes in his papers as the genius of the invention: that having found a substance so unstable that it is ready to burst at the smallest nudge, the trillions of nuclei are pressed together into a critical mass and from then on the reaction is uncontrolled and self-sustaining, catastrophic; an enormous, white-hot burst of energy. It is a process of numbers, of chain reactions. It will be so quick that it will appear instantaneous, a sudden explosion of heat and neutrons and light, as if God himself has pulled his knees into his chest, curled up into a ball and flung himself at the earth.

Joan labels the diagram, sketches in the main design features of the tail, and shades the outer casing in grey. She will not think about the possibilities of what she has drawn. She understands the science, or most of it. Her limitations are merely a question of scale.

*　　　*　　　*

The Prime Minister arrives promptly at 2 p.m., seated in the passenger seat of a dark green car that sits incongruously on the narrow street outside the laboratory. At first he looks so like the photographs and yet so different that Joan wonders if it is not perhaps an impersonator trying a bit too hard. Surely he doesn't always have that cigar in his mouth? She observes him shaking hands with Max and Donald and Arthur and still she is not sure. It is only when he takes her hand in his, smiling plumply out of the side of his mouth so that his face seems to flatten and he booms in that particular clipped voice she knows so well from the wireless: 'Ah, my dear young lady. Who's a man got to ask to get a decent cup of tea around here?'

Now that, thinks Joan, is either a bloody good impression or it's really him.

She feels her face grow hot. 'Milk and sugar?'

He nods slowly, evidently amused by something. 'I've heard that's how it's done.'

She leaves the line-up to make tea in the kitchen and finds that her hands are shaking a little. The visiting party progresses through the laboratory and into Max's office. Joan places the large brown teapot on a tray with some biscuits, sugar and a jug of milk. It is heavy in her arms as she walks slowly along the corridor, pushing the door open with her back and trying to place it on a side table without producing too much of a rattle. She pours the tea and hands it around while Max begins his explanation.

Her diagram is tacked up on the wall behind Max and he is referring to it with a pointer while also gesticulating towards various equations chalked up on the blackboard next to it. Joan's attention drifts as Max speaks, her eyes drawn to Churchill's presence in the room, the watch-chain slung across his waistcoat, the deep frown in his forehead.

'What a curious drawing,' he interrupts. 'Is this actually how it's envisaged to look?'

Max glances apologetically at Joan. 'I think it's an extremely good approximation,' he says. 'Although simplified, of course.'

'Harrumph,' Churchill says approvingly.

Joan flushes. She puts down the plate of biscuits and scrutinises her drawing from across the room. She has seen smaller versions of her fish-shaped drawing dropping from the skies in the past few months. She has seen unexploded ones roped off among the broken-windowed rubble of Cambridge, policemen holding back the crowds as they cluster and crane to see what all the fuss is about, as if a ferocious yet exotic animal has escaped from the zoo. In outline, it's familiar enough.

Max is holding up a graph, inviting his audience to take a closer look. 'Initially, it was thought that several tons of uranium 235 would be required to generate any sort of explosion,' he explains, 'as these are the sort of figures we're used to. And that would be almost impossible to generate, given that approximately 99.3 per cent of all natural uranium comes in 238 form.' He takes a breath. 'But recent calculations have revised the estimated amount needed quite dramatically. We know now that a significant explosion would require a critical mass of only a few pounds.' He cups his hands to demonstrate the amount. 'About the size of a small pineapple.'

Churchill coughs. 'You do understand what you're making here, Professor?'

Max stops. He blinks. 'Yes, sir. Of course I do.'

'And do you ever wonder how we will be judged

157

by future generations?'

'I do, sir.'

Churchill sits back in his chair and takes out a box of matches. He removes one, lights it, and then takes a cigar from his pocket, the end of which he holds in the centre of the flame. 'And do you sleep at night?'

Max gives a half smile. 'I haven't slept for years,' he says.

'Ah, you're one of those. I know that feeling well.' Churchill turns his attention to the cigar, putting it into his mouth and puffing at it until it catches.

Max clears his throat, evidently put out of his stride by the question.

'I didn't mean to alarm you,' Churchill continues in a perfectly enunciated drawl. 'I'm merely checking that this thing is not being built by a monster. If you told me you slept soundly every night without a moment's thought for the end product, then I'm afraid I would probably return to London with your letter of resignation in my pocket.'

Max smiles nervously. 'There are other uses for this research,' he says. 'I like to think that it will do some good in the world. After the war.'

Churchill looks at him. 'Perhaps. I hope so. But for now we must accept that we cannot control how history will judge us, unless we write it ourselves, of course, but we can consider whether we would be judged more for not making this thing than for making it. And I am willing to bank on the former.'

'I believe the idea is that it exists as a deterrent.'

Churchill nods. 'Yes, indeed. But a deterrent against whom?'

'The Germans, naturally.'

A snort this time. 'For now,' he says, and his voice is gruff, low, 'although it's the Yanks we need to worry about.'

Max frowns. 'But they're on our side. We're working with them on this.'

'True.' Churchill takes a deep inhalation from his cigar and then turns to the window to exhale, giving the impression that he is talking to no one in particular. 'But we've got to have one of these buggers over here,' he continues, and his voice is quiet now, considered, 'because if we don't the Yanks will control everything once this is all over. We've got to have one, and we've got to have the bloody Union Jack on top of it.'

Joan hears this exchange but does not really take it in. She has been looking at the figures on Max's chalkboard and now she is staring at the picture, her face suddenly ashen. Max rustles his notes, coughs, and resumes his explanation of how, exactly, this invention can transfer such a huge amount of energy from one source to another, and how once it starts it can continue to do this on and on, creating energy at an inhuman speed.

And there it is at last: the hint of metaphor that she can no longer hold back from exploding in her brain; the word that she has pushed back and back and back, not really wanting to think of what it is they are creating here.

Because it's not just the speed that's inhuman, is it?

Tuesday, 4.02 p.m.

Ms Hart is outside talking to someone on her mobile phone, and Mr Adams has gone to the shops to buy more coffee. The video camera has been switched off during the break. Nick is standing at the window, looking out across the darkening front garden to the road. He is shaking his head, still thrown by this most recent revelation.

'I can't believe I never knew,' he says at last. 'My own mother, working on the atomic bomb. I'd never have thought . . .' He stops. 'You've never even hinted at it. I remember asking what you did during the war and you fobbed me off with your secretary story.'

'But I was a secretary.'

Nick narrows his eyes at her. 'Maybe, but not *just* a secretary, as you told me.'

'I couldn't have told you any more than that. It was still classified. I'd signed the Official Secrets Act.'

'As if that would have mattered by then. The bomb wasn't exactly a secret once everyone knew about it. I learnt about it in school for God's sake.' He stops and turns to look at Joan. 'And you never told me that you met Winston Churchill. Even when I did that school project on him.' He gives a sudden burst of incredulous laughter. 'I mean, who meets Winston Churchill and then never mentions it again?'

Joan leans forward, wanting to reach out to him but retreating when she sees his expression. 'Nobody said what they did during the war. They

160

were different times.'

'I know. I'm not angry that you didn't tell me. It's just such a shock. You never let on that you ever did anything like that. Not once. I feel as if I don't know who you are.'

Joan looks at him. Does he not think she could say the same about him, or anyone for that matter? Although of course, she would never say such a thing. And perhaps the comparison isn't fair. He has always done so well at everything, been so good, that she has worried on occasion that he has done too well. Don't they say that about adopted children, that they think they need to be perfect to make up for the fact that they were once given away? Nick dismissed this theory as pop psychology the one time she tried to broach it with him. 'I'm still me, Nick,' she says softly. 'I'm still your mum.'

He shakes his head, and Joan sees for the first time that he is hurt. His eyes are unnaturally shiny and he is avoiding her gaze. She feels her heart burn.

'But you're not who *I* thought you were. When anyone asks me what you did, or what you liked, I always said you were a librarian at my school and that you and Dad liked playing tennis, and I thought that was the truth. I thought that was all there was to know.'

'It is,' she whispers. 'Or it was by then.'

'But instead you actually spent years working on something which was so utterly . . .' he searches for the right word, '. . . evil. And I never knew.' He pauses, and then shakes his head. 'How could you? Why didn't you just refuse once you knew what it was?'

Joan casts her eyes down. 'It may seem evil now,

161

but it wasn't so black-and-white back then. We had to get there first, ahead of Germany.'

'But they were nowhere near. Surely that was obvious, even at the time. All their theoretical physicists were Jews and had emigrated or been imprisoned. They were pretty much starting from scratch.'

'How could we have known that for sure? We couldn't take the risk. And besides, we thought we were doing something worthwhile.'

Nick rolls his eyes. 'Oh, come on. You can't expect me to believe that.'

'But it's true. That's how we saw it.'

'A super-bomb? How can that ever be worthwhile?'

Joan shakes her head. 'Not the bomb. The science of it.' She remembers this very clearly, the shared belief among the scientists involved in the project that after the war there would be incalculable benefits from their discoveries, not just in energy sources, but potentially in medicine too. Until that moment, nuclear physics had never been an applied science in the way that biology and chemistry were, and there was a sense of excitement about the seemingly limitless possibilities this implied. Joan does not expect Nick to understand this. Nobody else does. There is such a haze of history separating the past from the present, such a terrible barrier of knowledge, that it is almost impossible to describe the bright light of idealism from such a distance. 'I have wanted to tell you before now,' she says at last, 'but it was so long ago.' She pauses. 'And I didn't think you'd believe me.'

'That's not much of an excuse. I might even have been impressed. I knew you'd been to Cambridge but I hadn't ever really thought about how unusual that must have been at the time. I always saw you as, well, just a mum.' He pauses, pressing his knuckles into his palm. 'I wish you'd told me.'

'It was in the past. Your father and I . . .' she sighs. 'Well, he didn't want it mentioned, and nor did I really. I promised him.'

Nick acknowledges this point with an incline of his head, but he does not soften. 'So he did know, then?'

Joan nods. 'Yes, he knew,' she says hesitantly. 'That's why we moved to Australia.'

'But I thought you met on the boat going over to Australia.'

'Well, we knew each other before then but we decided it would be easier if we pretended . . .'

Nick makes an exasperated noise. 'I don't believe this. Is anything you've ever told me actually true?'

'Everything I've told you that relates to you is true, I promise.'

There is a pause while Nick considers this qualification. 'How can you say that *this* doesn't relate to me?'

'We'd agreed not to talk about it. I'd made your father a promise. It was a new start. You were a new start.'

She has told Nick this part before, that he was a new start for them, but she has never gone into the details of it: how much she had longed for him, dreamt of him, ached for him, before their application for adoption was approved. She has always believed that knowing how much he was wanted would be too much of a burden for him, and so she has held it back, the hope and anguish of those years when they first arrived in Australia,

163

before the doctor finally confirmed that no, there was no chance of a baby from Joan's damaged womb, and had they thought about adoption?

This had prompted another long process, and an uncertain one, being told repeatedly that there was something not quite right about their papers although the irregularity was never specified. They were bypassed again and again, until one day Joan received a letter saying that their application had been successful and would they please come to the Royal Victoria Hospital in three months' time to collect their baby.

She will never forget the assault of emotion that hit her when she first picked him up in her arms and felt Nick's soft, tiny hand close around her finger. Nothing could have prepared her for this. She remembers it as a magical time; the milky, dewy smell of him, the way his eyes changed from blue to a deeper, richer colour, almost green for a while, and then finally hazel, as astonishing as a leaf in autumn. She recalls marvelling at his tiny peachy head, his little feet, thinking how light he was, how delicate, so different from the golden-skinned little boy she had once imagined for herself and yet, at the same time, so perfect. A new start.

But now Nick is standing in front of her with his arms crossed, his initial disbelief having turned to cynicism. 'I still think you could have told me.'

Joan's voice is almost a whisper. 'Like I said, nobody talked about what they did during the war. We all knew we weren't allowed to. I didn't even tell my family.'

Nick looks at her. 'But Leo knew, didn't he?'

Joan blinks. She knows that nothing has been proven. She doesn't have to say anything. 'No,' she says, but the hesitation is too long.

Extract from the 'Organisation of Tube Alloys'

14 April 1941

The objectives of the Tube Alloys project are two-fold: firstly the manufacture of the most formidable military weapon yet conceived, and, secondly, the release of atomic energy for power purposes.

The scientific background of this work was well known before the war, and nothing is more certain than that the same subjects are being industriously pursued in Germany. There is, therefore, a race against time between the Allies and the Axis powers to be the first to possess the military weapon. Whatever may be the prospect of success in a reasonable time, it is clear that the subject must be pursued with the utmost speed, regardless of cost.

*   *   *

Joan's billet is in a rooming house for single women run by Mrs Landsman, situated in the rather unglamorous location of Mill Road. She goes to visit her parents as often as she can now that there is less to occupy her time in Cambridge with so many people having been sent away or posted elsewhere. Her mother has joined the Women's Voluntary Service and is helping to run a mobile canteen until she is forced to stop after a huge metal vat is dropped on her foot in the kitchen. Her foot will recover, the doctor says, but for now she winces when she puts any weight on it, struggling with the crutches as she catches and clips them against the furniture.

On top of this, Joan's father seems to have aged enormously in the three years since Joan left home. He retired the previous year, but rather than improving his health by giving him the opportunity to rest, this enforced inactivity only seems to have accelerated his decline. His hair, once thick and white, is thinner, and his dark eyebrows stand out more clearly against his new pallor. Even his eyes seem to have lost some of their colour. When he takes off his suit jacket and loosens his collar at the dining table, his fingers shake a little and his mouthfuls are small and laboriously chewed.

'How's Lally?' Joan asks, wanting to distract herself from the sudden, alarming hint of her parents' impermanence.

'Gadding about with soldiers,' Joan's father says, pushing his half-chewed mouthful into his cheek and grimacing.

'She's not *gadding*, Robert. She's working a few days a week at the Jewish house for the German children.'

'Refugees,' Joan's father corrects her.

'Yes, exactly. That's what I meant. Shame she couldn't be here today though.' Joan's mother pushes the potatoes towards Joan, encouraging her to take another one. 'You must make more of an effort to see her, you know. She had such a lovely time in Cambridge with you.'

Joan does not look up but takes a potato and deposits it on her plate. 'So did I, but it's hard when I work six days a week. I'll invite her again, I promise.'

'Once the war is over,' her mother says.

Her father shakes his head. 'It's not going to be over as soon as you think.'

'Of course it will. Have faith.'

Her father snorts with a mixture of contempt and amusement, a noise which Joan recognises as heralding the start of one of the good-natured yet vehement discussions she remembers so well from her childhood in which argument is treated as a form of sport. 'I don't see how that will help us win the war.'

'Because we're on the right side. Morally right.' Her mother spears a carrot with her fork. 'And that has to count for something. It's just common sense.'

Under normal circumstances, such a comment would have prompted Joan's father to denounce his wife as utterly nonsensical, and he would have taken delight in arguing with her as loquaciously as he could. But today he is too tired to argue, just as he has been on the last few occasions Joan has seen him, and instead he simply laughs and sits back, closing his eyes.

Joan stands up, thinking that she needs to find out if her father has seen a doctor. 'Let me take those dishes out.'

'It's his heart,' Joan's mother confides once they are in the kitchen and out of earshot. 'He's been told to rest and to stop smoking, but there's not much chance of that.'

'He's not that old, Mum.'

Her mother takes her arm and squeezes it while Joan fills the basin with soapy water. 'He's not young. Anyway, we're fine really. How about you? Met any nice young men I should know about? Or are we still moping about that darned Russian?'

That darned Russian is still in Canada. Yes, she tells her mother, she writes to him every week, and no, there are no young men to rival him in her affections. But she is not moping. She is enjoying her job, not just the work but also the money and the independence it brings. She likes the closeness of the laboratory, the sense of urgency and excitement. On top of that, she likes the sociability of it, the endless rounds of dinners and drinking games in the evenings that Karen encourages her to attend. There are long games of poker after blackout, lubricated by crates of sherry and whisky brought up from the basement of the laboratories. Max rarely participates in these, being obliged to keep his distance as the most senior scientist among them, but most of the others are regular attendees and they are fun, odd nights at which the subject of research is studiously avoided, very unlike the earnest discussions of her undergraduate days. She does not tell her mother about these evenings, knowing that she would disapprove, but all in all, Joan does not consider that she has enough time to mope, especially with Leo out of harm's way, which is more than most men of his age can say at the moment.

In fact, the only one of the old Cambridge group still around is William. He is posted close enough to Cambridge to be able to visit, and he gets in touch whenever he has some time off. When she gets home from her visit to her parents' house that evening, she finds him waiting on the doorstep of her lodgings. 'Oh,' she says, suddenly remembering that they had made plans to go to the cinema that night. 'It's tonight, isn't it?'

He grins, leans forward and kisses her on the cheek. 'You haven't forgotten, have you? I've already bought the tickets.'

'Of course not,' she says, fixing a smile on her face. 'What are we going to see?'

'*How Green Was My Valley.*'

'How green was your what?'

He starts to explain that this is the title of the film, but Joan interrupts. 'I was joking.'

'Oh, right. Yes.'

Joan's feelings towards William are ambivalent. She finds it irritating when he attempts to be charming, as he frequently does. It seems too deliberate, too forced, and yet somehow he manages to get away with it. In general, people seem to like him because he quotes *Winnie-the-Pooh* at inappropriate moments and is rich enough to have a perpetually carefree demeanour, and it is a source of mild irritation to her to know that this will be enough for him to have a successful career in the Foreign Office whenever he decides he'd like to, just as his father did before him.

But still, she likes to see him as a reminder of earlier times, of Leo.

The film is set during the strikes in the Welsh mining villages of the Rhondda valley, a long film in which food is carried in beautifully made wicker baskets and little Huw Morgan's eyes gleam from his coal-dusted face over a screeching classical score, reminding her of the columns of coal miners she once saw marching through St Albans.

The evening is warm and musky as they walk back across Parkers' Piece to Joan's lodgings.

169

William holds out his arm for her to take and she slips her hand into the crook of it, although she does not want to. It seems too familiar, too tactile.

'Well? Did you enjoy it, Jo-jo?'

Joan flinches. Only Leo calls her Jo-jo and William knows that. Well, maybe Sonya too. He is probably just trying to be friendly.

'It was sad,' she says. 'And a bit American. Everyone was too pretty. There wasn't enough genuine grime.'

William laughs. 'I think the director did originally intend to film it in Wales but the war got in the way.'

'It has a habit of that,' Joan murmurs.

'It'll get in the way for the Yanks too, soon. Roosevelt wants to join in. It's just the American public who are reluctant.'

'I'd have thought that would be enough to stop him.'

'This war's not like the last one. They can't expect to remain out of it just because they're surrounded by oceans. Something will happen to bring them in.'

Joan glances at him sceptically but says nothing. How can he always speak with such assurance? What is it that makes him so confident of his own opinion?

William casts a sidelong glance in her direction. 'Anyway, how are things with you? Enjoying your job?'

'Yes. Very much.'

'What is it you're working on again? I don't think you've told me.'

'It's research.'

'Yes, I know that. What sort of research?'

170

Joan punches him on the arm. 'You know I can't tell you that.'

'Careless talk, blah, blah blah. I've seen the posters. But I'm still interested.'

'Well, I can't tell you because I don't know. I'm just a secretary. They don't tell me anything.'

'And you don't read, you just type. Is that it?'

'Exactly.'

William purses his lips and looks at her. 'But it must be nice to know you're contributing to the war effort.' He thinks about this for a moment and then grins suddenly. 'How about lunch tomorrow? Or dinner? I haven't got all that much to do, and a chap's got to make the most of his leave these days. They keep talking about sending us off somewhere.'

Why? she thinks. What do you want from me? We're not comfortable together. 'I can't,' she says, trying to look disappointed.

'Why not?' William asks. 'I'll come to meet you at the laboratory. You could just tell them you're popping out for lunch. Or I could meet you after work.'

Joan laughs. 'I'm a secretary,' she tells him. 'I'm not allowed to pop anywhere for lunch. Besides, there's no time. I don't finish until after seven and I have too much to do to go out at lunchtime.'

'Your boss must like you then.'

'Why do you say that?'

'If he didn't like you, he wouldn't give you so much to do. He wouldn't want you around.'

Joan nods. She would concede that there is a certain complicity between her and Max, a calmness in their little corner of the laboratory, even if there is usually a door between them. She likes the way he asks how she is every morning, and the way he thanks her for his morning cup of tea, which is more than most of them do, and he seems grateful and apologetic at the same time. 'I suppose so,' she agrees. 'Why are you interested in all this anyway? It's boring.'

'Not for me it isn't. I'm going to be sent away any day now. It's nice to know how to imagine everything back home.'

She cringes slightly. 'William,' she says. 'I don't want you to get the wrong idea.'

'The wrong idea about what?'

'Well . . .' she pauses, 'about us.'

He laughs and squeezes her arm. 'Don't be silly, Jo-jo. I know. We're friends. That's all. I know it's Leo you're waiting for.'

'I'm not waiting,' she corrects him, but then she looks up at him and allows him to see the blush rising in her cheeks.

'Of course you're not,' he says. 'And besides, I thought you knew.'

'Knew what?'

'About me.'

They are walking down her road now, a row of tightly packed Victorian houses, larger from the inside than they appear from the pavement, with cellars and attics. Joan looks at him and frowns. She cannot think what he means. 'What about you?'

He looks at her, astonished. 'You mean you actually don't know?'

Joan tries to keep the exasperation out of her voice. 'Know what?'

William waves his arm, as if to brush her question aside. 'Ask Leo next time you see him.'

'Fine,' Joan says, irritated that he will not just tell her. 'I will. Well, anyway, here we are. Thank you for walking me home.'

'Don't mention it.' William leans forward and kisses her wetly on the cheek. She feels the imprint of his lips lingering on her skin. He smiles, stands back and salutes in a ridiculously overdramatic manner while Joan rummages in her bag for her key. She wants to wipe the kiss off, but she knows she should wait until she is inside before she does so. She finds her key, smiles, and offers an embarrassed salute in return from the porch as she steps inside.

Tuesday, 6.13 p.m.

'So would you have said that William—Sir William—knew what you were doing at the laboratory?' Ms Hart asks. She is leaning forwards in her chair, her voice betraying a hint of breathlessness. A glance is exchanged between Mr Adams and Ms Hart, and it is clear that this question is something they have planned.

'William?' Joan asks, crinkling her eyes as if confused.

Ms Hart doesn't flinch. 'Yes, William.'

There is a pause, and quite suddenly Joan realises what they are getting at. She remembers what Nick said when he first came to warn her, that they want her to incriminate William, here, now, while there is still time to issue a warrant for an autopsy. Before his body is cremated on Friday. But she has made a promise. She shakes her head, thinking of the St Christopher's charm necklace hidden in the drawer next to her bed, slipped casually to her the last time she saw him so many years ago. 'No,' she says. Her voice is clipped and sure. 'He didn't know anything. He was just mildly inquisitive, and a bit of a tease.'

Ms Hart frowns. 'So you wouldn't say he was deliberately trying to extract information from you?'

'No.'

'And he never made any sort of approach to you?'

'No.'

'Remember that anything you later wish to rely on in court—'

Joan interrupts, not wishing to hear this again. 'I know.'

The Times, 23 June 1941

FULL AID FOR RUSSIA: PRIME MINISTER'S DECLARATION OF BRITISH POLICY

Mr Churchill said:

'At four o'clock this morning, Hitler attacked and invaded Russia. All his usual formalities of perfidy were observed with scrupulous technique. A non-aggression treaty had been solemnly signed, and was in force between the two countries. No complaint had been made of its non-fulfilment. Under its cloak of false confidence, the German armies drew up an immense strength along a line which stretched from the White Sea to the Black Sea, and their air fleets and armoured divisions slowly and

174

methodically took up their positions. Then suddenly, without declaration of war, without even an ultimatum, the German bombs rained down from the sky on the Russian cities.

No one has been a more persistent opponent of communism than I have been for the past twenty-five years. I will unsay no word that I have spoken about it, but all this fades away before the spectacle that is now unfolding.

We have but one aim and one single irrevocable purpose. We are resolved to destroy Hitler and every vestige of the Nazi regime. From this nothing will turn us. Any man or State who fights against Hitler will have our aid. That is our policy and that is our declaration.
It follows, therefore, that we shall give whatever help we can to Russia and to the Russian people. We have offered to the government of Soviet Russia any technical or economic assistance which is in our power and which is likely to be of service to them.'

This speech by Winston Churchill was broadcast in Russian from station GRV last night.

Joan's room in the billet is small and low-ceilinged. It smells of stale tobacco and there is no hot water in the mornings. There are flowers on the dressing table, freshly picked and messy, and the bed is covered in a pink eiderdown. It is Sunday afternoon and Joan is sitting on the bed, waiting, the mattress springs sagging beneath her. She rolls over onto her stomach and unlatches the window so that she can lean out and see into the box garden below. A row

175

of blue ceramic pots sprout lamb's lettuce in great, composted clumps. The paving flags are cracked and moss-furred, and the faint scent of thyme and rosemary is detectable above the damp of the wallpaper. The arched hump of the Anderson shelter rises up from the earth at the bottom of the garden, and in the next-door garden three girls are skipping with an old piece of rope. Joan knows the game, and she watches the pattern of the children's feet; sun, shade, sun, shade.

She picks up the postcard and reads it again.

To my little comrade, he writes. *Now don't get too excited. I'm coming home* (Home! she thinks. Does he mean me? Am I home? Or does he just mean England?) *but it's only for a short visit. I have been commandeered to take up a research post at the University of Montreal for the duration of the war, and I'm coming back to retrieve my papers. I presume you still have them. I'll be in touch when I get to England. Don't write to me here. I won't get it if you do.*
Yours fraternally,
Leo

The postcard is small and battered, and the picture on the front depicts a moose on a snowy mountainside. Brusque as ever, but she has read it over and over again since its arrival two weeks ago. She wraps the sheets tightly around herself, and for a brief moment she imagines they are his arms enfolding her, warming her. Her heart beats faster, the memory of him spreading through her whole body. She closes her eyes and imagines his face,

176

those serious dark eyes and perfect lips.

But no, it is the same every time. The image will not stay still. It falters and fades and refuses to come back. Joan sits up and puts the postcard back on the small wooden table next to her bed. He will be here soon. She must be ready for him in every sense, ready to ensure that she lets nothing slip about the project as he is bound to ask. It crosses her mind once again that he might already know from his friend in the camp, but then she dismisses the thought as impossible, remembering that Max had told her even some of the War Cabinet hadn't yet been told about it.

She has told Mrs Landsman that her cousin will be coming to visit, opting for this story because young men are not generally permitted to stay overnight but exceptions can occasionally be made for family members. She remembers the fracas that once ensued from the discovery of a man in another girl's room in the early hours of the morning, the girl being denounced as a Jezebel while having her belongings flung from the wardrobe into an open trunk in front of the entire house, and Joan does not wish to become the next subject of such scrutiny. Hence they will be cousins, for the time being.

There is a knock downstairs at the front door. She hears it open, and then a man's voice followed by footsteps coming up the stairs. Joan's breath sticks in her throat. She has imagined this moment so many times: opening the bedroom door, taking him by the hand, pulling him inside. She stands up and flattens down her bright blue dress—the one Sonya gave her—as she walks slowly across the room to the door, and puts her hand on the handle.

The sound of the children's game outside is suddenly much louder, faster. Joan can hear the slapping of feet against the hard, hot grass. The singing has become a rising chant, and the skipping game is furious, rhythmic, a whirl of noise and sound and light, and then there is Leo, stepping into her room without so much as hugging her, taking off his shoes and folding his jacket neatly on top of them, and then he is turning, picking her up, taking two strides across the room and diving them both onto the bed, causing the mattress to creak and groan under the sudden weight of them, and although she knows she must tell him that they need to be quiet or Mrs Landsman will throw them out onto the street, she finds that she no longer cares and instead she is falling with him. Down and down and down.

*   *   *

'It's not difficult. Just call Lally and tell her you're sick so you can't possibly go to dinner with her. She can't expect you to drop everything just because she unilaterally decides to come and visit you.'

He is lying on his back. Her head is resting on his chest and his arms are wrapped around her. She knows she has to get up for work but right now it does not seem possible to untangle her body from his. Lying like this, their feet are exactly level, and her big toe is clasped between two of his so that they seem to fit together perfectly.

'She didn't. I invited her ages ago. And she's already bought her train ticket.' Joan hesitates. 'I wanted her to come so if I cancel now it'd put her off ever coming again.'

178

Leo is silent, evidently unimpressed by the argument. 'You can't help it if you're ill.'

'And what if she finds out I wasn't really ill?'

'Then you'll have to tell her you were love-sick.'

'Is that what I am?'

'What?'

She can hardly say the words. 'Love-sick.'

'Yes,' he says abruptly, not looking at her. 'And I'm little-comrade-sick. That's a far worse affliction.'

His words are like a stab to the ribs, and yet they are not without feeling. She does not think she is being naive to believe, just a little, that he does love her really, and that her desire for him to declare his love in the stilted, old-fashioned manner she wants to hear so much is more ridiculous than his refusal to say it. Perhaps this is his way of saying it. They are words, after all. Words to store up and keep wrapped around her heart while he is away.

She forces herself to smile. 'Aren't you funny?'

'I know.' He clasps her toe tighter with his, and then leans forward to whisper to her. 'Please.'

He does not usually beg. All right, this isn't begging. And the situation is different. He is not here for long and she cannot skip work, so it has to be this evening. Surely it is not a bad thing to tell this small lie to her sister in the circumstances.

'I still don't really see why I can't tell Lally the truth. I think she'd understand.'

'You shouldn't be seen with me,' he says. 'It's just easier not to mention it to anyone at all, then you won't forget.'

Joan forces herself to laugh even though she is momentarily confused by the seriousness of his tone. 'You're not actually dangerous, you know. It

179

was just a routine internment. You said so yourself.'

'Just a routine internment?' he repeats.

'Wasn't it?'

'Put it this way, if I had been doing my thesis on the pollination habits of bees I don't think they'd have thought I was enough of a threat to send me to Canada.'

'Oh.'

'But that's irrelevant now. At least I'm out and I can be of some help once I pick up my papers.' He turns to her and kisses her. 'Thanks for keeping them safe, Jo-jo.'

The room is dim, pinkish in the morning light, and filled with shimmering shadows. Leo is nuzzling into her neck. If this were a film, there would be music now, cigarettes and a softening of the light. There are none of these things, but there is something luxurious about this moment, a sense of time pausing, like the breath of wind on a leaf just before it snaps off and floats to earth.

Her body shifts, allowing his arm to slip around her so that his hand rests lightly on her lower back. 'All right,' she whispers. 'I'll phone her from work but I won't mention you. Let's meet in the restaurant at seven.'

*   *   *

'Can't you just tell me the basics? I only want to know what you're doing.' The restaurant is made up of rows of dark wood-panelled booths with red tablecloths. There is a low hum of chatter, and a long bar down the centre of the room decorated with glasses hanging from their handles above glittering bottles of liquor allows their conversation

180

to be shielded from general view. Leo is holding her hand across the table and Joan smiles to think how anyone glancing in their direction might think what a nice couple they make, how close they seem, how intent on each other.

Joan shakes her head. It is the same conversation she has had with William, over and over again, and her answer is always the same. 'I'm not telling you anything. It's the rules.'

'But why should it be a secret? I thought transparency was the West's pride and joy.'

'There's a war on, in case *you* hadn't noticed.'

'And I'm on your side, in case *you* hadn't noticed. Even Winston Churchill says so.' If Leo is disconcerted by her refusal to tell him everything, he does not show it. He picks up the menu and glances at the wine list, most of which is crossed through where stocks have run out and cannot be replenished. 'Red?' he asks.

Joan glances at the menu. There are no prices listed but she knows it will be expensive. 'Can you afford it?'

'Special occasion.' He does not look at her as he says this but turns around, lifting his hand to call the waiter over.

He orders a claret and they wait while the two wine glasses are solemnly set out on the table in front of them, and the wine is opened and poured into Leo's glass first, swirled, sniffed, approved, and then into Joan's.

'So,' Leo says when the waiter is out of earshot. 'I guess it's time I came clean about a few things.' He takes his napkin and shakes it open, laying it smoothly across his lap. 'First things first. I told you I left the Party, didn't I?'

'William told me. You didn't.'

Leo nods. 'Well, whoever. It's not quite true in any case. I was asked to leave.'

'How could they? You were interned for them—'

'No.' Leo's expression is stern. 'I wasn't interned for them. It was for my own beliefs. And I wasn't expelled either. It was suggested to me that I temporarily renounce my membership.'

'Suggested by whom?'

He does not look up. The waiter reappears with a plate of doughy white bread, and there is a lull as it is set out. Leo orders venison and mash for both of them.

'But I haven't decided what I want yet.'

Leo waves his hand dismissively. 'You'll like it. It's the best thing on the menu.'

'In your opinion.'

'Yes.'

The waiter leaves. Leo continues where he left off. 'Instructed by Comintern. I can be more useful, you see, if I'm not officially associated with them. I can continue to work on my thesis at the University of Montreal and not be viewed as a security risk.' He glances at her. 'Any questions so far?'

Yes, she has one glaring question but she does not know how to ask it because he has just imparted the information so casually that she feels she will look silly if she asks exactly what he means by being 'useful'. But she is not sure she wants to know the answer to this question and so she starts with an easier one. 'Did you tell William to take me out to the cinema?'

Leo takes a piece of bread and lays it on his plate. 'Yes.'

'But you know I don't like him.'

'I wanted to make sure you were in the right place.' He grins. 'He says you're impermeable.'

'I am,' Joan says, although the realisation that this is the source of William's interest causes her to flinch, remembering how she had mistaken this interest for something else. 'That reminds me. There was something he said I should ask you. About him.'

'Yes?'

'I said I didn't want him to get the wrong idea about us going out to the cinema . . .' She stops, embarrassed by the smile slowly spreading across Leo's face. 'What? That's exactly how he reacted too.'

'Oh Jo-jo, how do you manage to stay so innocent?' Leo leans towards her and whispers across the table. 'William's not interested in girls.'

Joan looks at him quizzically. 'What do you mean? Is he . . .?' She stops. She does not know how to phrase it. Describing him as a homosexual seems too much like a condition to be an appropriate description. She has a sudden recollection of seeing Rupert with his hand resting on William's arm at one of the meetings, not just for a moment, but for an entire meeting. 'And Rupert too?'

'Ah, my sweet little comrade. Give her enough time and she'll get there in the end.'

Joan looks away, irritated by his patronising tone. 'I just hadn't thought about it.' She considers this for a moment before filing it away at the back of her mind. 'Anyway, you were saying you wanted to make sure I was in the right place. The right place for what?'

'That's the second thing. I need your help. That's

183

why I'm here.'

Joan glances up at him. She feels her face flaring hot and then cold. 'I thought you were here—'

'Yes, yes, I know,' he interrupts. 'To collect my papers.'

Is it possible that he doesn't realise how much his words hurt her? Her whole body prickles with the sting of them. 'I meant, I thought you came back because you wanted to see me,' she whispers. 'I could have just posted your papers, after all.'

'Well, that's the third thing.' His expression changes when he says this, a hint of affection flickering across the surface of it and then disappearing just as quickly. 'How could I go for so long without seeing my little comrade?'

Joan smiles but she is suddenly unconvinced. Her mind scuttles, aware of a certain unease insinuating itself into the conversation.

'So will you help?' He is looking at her now, his expression serious. 'We need designs, documents, research.'

She narrows her eyes to look at him more closely. 'How did you know?'

'Know what?'

'About the . . .' she looks around and covers her mouth with her hand before continuing, '. . . about the project?'

'It doesn't matter. The point is Churchill promised in the House of Commons that all technological advances would be shared between Britain and the USSR. He's not keeping that promise.' He sits back. 'This isn't about you. Your feelings are irrelevant here. This is about saving the Revolution. It's about saving the world. Sharing what you know about the project with Russia is the only way to ensure that we're in with a chance. It's as simple as that.'

Joan stares at him. Surely he is not asking what she thinks he is. He can't be. 'You want me to smuggle the research out? You want me to steal?'

'Not steal,' he says in a softer voice, as if he can hear what she is thinking. 'Replicate. Share.'

Joan doesn't move. She can't believe he is asking her to do this. The thought flashes across her mind that this is why he has written to her all this time, because he had plans for her. Because he thinks he can persuade her to do whatever he asks.

She shakes this thought from her head. Surely not, she thinks. Nobody can be that cynical, that forward-thinking.

His hand is on hers across the table, his voice quiet and urgent. 'Don't you see, Jo-jo? This is your chance to *do* something for the world, to make a difference.'

'I didn't know you were so . . .' She stops. She was going to say she didn't know he was so committed to the cause that he would actually do something like this, but she realises as she is about to say it that, if she did not know this, it was through her own stupidity. He has always been quite open about how much it means to him, so why does it come as a surprise to have it confirmed? Did she just never really believe he meant what he said? She sees that he is still waiting for an answer. 'No, Leo,' she whispers. 'I won't do it.'

Leo's expression is one of studied patience. 'We've been through this before, Jo-jo. Being loyal to a country is a false loyalty. It doesn't mean anything. You know that. Vertical divisions between countries only exist in the imagination. It's the horizontal divisions that count. And as members of the international proletariat, we must defend and help the Soviet state by any means possible.'

Joan shakes her head as he speaks. She knows it is part of his charm, this ability to persuade people that they want to think like him, that they should see the world exactly as he sees it. 'Don't,' she says. 'I'm not at one of your rallies now. It's not my fault my hands aren't worn down by years at the Soviet coalface. I didn't choose to be born in St Albans but I don't see why my loyalties should be any less legitimate than yours.'

'This isn't about where you were born. There are no sides any longer, not once this thing exists. This isn't the sort of weapon only one *side* should have. A whole nation can be destroyed in a single swoop. It's inhumane.'

His persistence is astounding. Surely he must have known she would not do this. She is too honest, too loyal. If he does not know this about her, how can he know her at all? She looks up at him. 'There must be a reason why Churchill isn't sharing it with Stalin. Perhaps he is, for all we know.'

This is the wrong thing to say. She knows this as she says it, and she sees Leo's expression harden but, for the first time, she doesn't care.

'Don't you see? Churchill *wants* the Germans in Moscow. There are thirty thousand Russians dying on the Eastern Front every week and it's the only thing keeping Hitler out of Downing Street.'

Joan looks down. 'I'm sorry, Leo. I won't do it.'

Leo shakes his head. 'I expected more from you, Jo-jo. I thought you, of all people, would be able to

186

see that there's more to loyalty than being true to an arbitrary place or state.'

Joan feels her chest swell and her eyes burn but she does not move. 'Stalin didn't think so when he signed the pact.'

Leo leans forward, his hands pressed flat against the table and his expression suddenly hard and unreadable. She knows she has scratched a nerve. 'That was tactical.'

'If you say so.'

'I do.'

There is a pause. 'Anyway,' she says, 'I'd have thought the Soviets would be developing their own weapons?'

'They are. But it's taking too long. They're starting from a disadvantage.' He sighs and reaches once more across the table. 'Please, Jo-jo. Don't you see? You're in a unique position here to change the history of the world.'

Joan crosses her arms across her chest. 'Why must you always be so dramatic? You're worse than Sonya.'

'Because it's the truth.'

'Well, I won't do it. You shouldn't have asked. I wish you hadn't.'

Leo sighs. He sees that the matter is, for the moment, closed between them. The waiter brings their dinner and they eat in silence, the meat tender and perfectly done, the mash creamy and light.

'Nice, isn't it?' he says, his voice flat in an unenthusiastic attempt to change the subject.

'It's all right.' Joan will not allow him the satisfaction of thinking she is enjoying it. The taste is bitter, metallic, and quite suddenly she knows that this is it. This is the end, right now. She swallows a mouthful of food, feeling the lump of it in her throat. Her chest feels tight and constricted. 'I'm not very hungry,' she says in a voice which is intended to be both strong and offhand at the same time.

Leo looks at her, and then picks up his fork, reaches over, and swipes half the venison from her plate. Joan's mouth drops open but Leo does not flinch. 'Couldn't let it go to waste.'

The waiter returns to refill their wine glasses, pouring the luxurious blood-red swirls of liquid into the silence. When he has gone, Leo raises his glass. He clears his throat in a conciliatory manner. 'A toast, anyway.'

Joan shakes her head. How can he ask this of her and then, when she refuses, just carry on as if it was a perfectly reasonable request? As if nothing has happened. Why does he not even apologise when he sees how much he has upset her?

She wants to stand up, spin on her heel and fling the door of the restaurant shut behind her so that the window cracks and shatters. She wants to make a scene. She wants him to run after her, catching her in his arms and kissing her in a blaze of sunlight like a princess in a fairy tale, and declare that he loves her and has loved her all along. She wants to force the words out of him.

There is a pounding, aching silence. Joan raises her eyes to meet his and, in that moment, she realises it is hopeless. It always has been. For over a year she has waited for him, dreamt of him, written to him, and in all that time he has never once told her he loves her because—the reason is suddenly glaringly, blindingly obvious—he does not. Or not enough. Not in the way she wants. He is not

188

interested in love. Emotion without intellect, he has called it before. Why did she not see it then? How can she have been so blind? She realises now that he will never hold her in his arms and kiss her like a princess in a fairy tale because that is not Leo's kind of fairy tale. His fairy tales are fields of spun gold, full of barn yields and statistics.

Joan raises her glass numbly, suddenly stricken with the knowledge that he has not come to see her because he loves her but to persuade her to do this for The Struggle. Because he thinks, because they all think, that she will do anything he asks.

'To the future,' Leo says.

Joan shakes her head. Her chest aches as she holds out her glass to his. She had not known it could hurt this much. 'I'm not going to change my mind.'

'Oh, come on, Jo-jo.'

She wants to put her face in her hands and sob. She shakes her head. She will not cry. Not yet. She will later—she will lie on her bed and curl herself into a ball and her body will be racked with the strength of her despair—but she will not cry in front of him. 'To the past,' she murmurs.

'Ah no,' he says, and Joan registers the familiar flash of his lenses as he smiles at her. 'There's the difference between us. I don't feel like this is the end. You'll come round. I know it.'

'No, Leo.' Joan is adamant. 'I won't do it. You shouldn't have asked.'

She lifts her glass to his and they drink, silently, their eyes locked on one another. And then a single spot of red wine spills onto her dress.

189

Tuesday, 7.32 p.m.

In the bathroom of her house, away from the questioning and alone for just a brief moment, Joan turns on the cold tap. The shock of icy water against her skin makes her shiver. It is almost like being touched, and the sensation awakens an old hunger in her, one to which she has lately grown accustomed. Until her husband died, she had not realised how much it mattered, to touch and be touched, but right now, she misses the physical comfort of his arms around her, the smell of his skin, the habit he had of tapping his spoon against his bowl between mouthfuls of cornflakes. She thinks of his body filled with tubes as he lay in his hospital bed the day before he died, reaching for her hand and smiling, telling her that he'd be right as rain tomorrow.

It shouldn't have been as much of a shock as it was. She had known he was ill. She just hadn't thought it would come so soon. She hadn't expected to be left so abruptly, to be cut adrift with nobody to talk to, nobody who knew what she *meant* about anything, always having to explain herself and never quite being able to.

She remembers suddenly that it is Tuesday, and that normally she would have spent the afternoon in her watercolour class at the church hall, putting the final touches to her snow scene in preparation for the exhibition her class is planning for the end of the month. She likes her classmates, the seams of their faces reflecting her own. It is a comfort to know that they are all in it together, this business of

190

being old, complicit in their unspoken agreement to make the best of what they have left and not be too morbid about it.

Their exhibition is to be called 'Snow: a Study of White on White', which they had thought rather amusing at the time but which now strikes Joan as slightly pretentious. What would they say if they knew? She feels a tremor along her spine as she imagines them reading about her in the evening newspaper on Friday, fear turning to horror as she imagines how they might react if they were ever to see her again. She could not go back. It wouldn't be fair. She thinks of her unfinished snow scene lying discarded in the corner of the room while the others are framed for the exhibition, eventually being thrown away once it is clear she will not be coming back for it.

But then again, the third day of interviewing is nearly over and they still haven't got anything to bring against her. Perhaps . . .?

No. She cannot allow herself to get hopeful. They must know more than they are letting on, or why else would William have done what he did? They're just holding back so that her confession is not forced, giving her space to implicate William as well as herself.

She glances at the shelf above the washbasin, and observes her stash of blood pressure pills, thyroid pills and vitamins which she keeps in view so that she does not forget to take them. The accoutrements of managed decline. Aspirin, calcium supplements, zinc. Has she taken any of these since it all began? She cannot remember. The days are rolling and fading into one another and into so many other long-forgotten days. She picks up the thyroid tablets to take one, and at the same time she notices a small tinted bottle of sleeping pills at the back of the shelf—it is full when she shakes it—and her heart shivers inside her. Quickly, she replaces the packet of thyroid tablets in front of the pill bottle. She knows she cannot think like that.

Her lipstick and mascara lie untouched next to her toothbrush, and for a moment Joan allows herself to be distracted by them, thinking that she must remember where they are when she is getting ready to give her statement to the press on Friday. *Always rouge, always darken, always pat*, Sonya used to say. *No situation was ever made worse by looking pretty*. Is that what Sonya would do if this was happening to her instead of Joan? Would she dress herself in fur, throw her hands in the air and deny everything?

Just thinking about Sonya makes Joan feel suddenly numb. She wonders, as she has often done, if Sonya ever made it back to Russia as she planned. And if she did, was she happy there? Is she still alive? Joan turns off the tap and scrutinises her reflection in the mirror, her eyes ice-blue against her pale skin. What a terribly lonely thing it is to grow old. She is not sure she would recommend it to anyone; outliving everyone she ever cared about, her husband, her sister, her friends; watching them fall away one by one, a slow closing-down of life and laughter.

Except for Nick, of course, and his family.

She has experienced loneliness before, although never like this. Never solitariness. She remembers those long days after Leo went back to Canada, when she lay on her bed and sobbed, allowing herself to weep as she never had before and never

192

would again. She had hoped he might come to see her again after that last argument and beg her forgiveness, but he had not. The day of his departure to Canada came and went without any communication from him, and she had spent the next week feeling sick and hopelessly, deathly cold.

The war had continued to drag on in its dreary, terrifying manner; busy, restless years of sleepless nights and long hours at the laboratory, punctuated by tea dances and raffles and early-to-bed curfews. She did not write to Leo and he did not write to her, and Sonya's letters also dried up at around the same time, although Joan continued writing to her for a little while before deciding that there was no point. It was clear that Sonya had been informed of the rift between Joan and Leo and had chosen a side, and it astonished Joan to see how easily it could all unravel.

In time, however, Joan began to feel as if she might not be dying after all. It came to be a relief that she did not hear from either of them as it meant she didn't need to think of them so often. She began to pay more attention to her work, and even started to make plans to go back into academia after the war, perhaps as a research student in Cambridge, or even as a teacher. Sonya's decision to cut her off no longer upset her as it had done at the time, as Joan came to accept that she had always known, right from the start of her relationship with Leo, that if it ever came down to a simple choice, she would be the one to be cast off. It was to be expected. They were family after all.

That might even have been the end of it if Sonya had not come home when she did, turning up in the late spring of 1944 with Jamie, the young man Joan had read about in her early letters (*He's so clean, Jo-jo! And such a lovely head of hair!*), having married him in Geneva and persuaded him to come and live with her in a farmhouse in Ely. When they met, Sonya introduced Joan to him as her best friend, startling Joan because, while this might once have been the case, it was no longer true. And yet there was something in Sonya's tone of voice which Joan recognised as an appeal to her of some sort, to stand by her, to not be cross with her for ignoring her for so long and for choosing Leo over her, and so Joan had simply laughed and nodded and squeezed her friend's arm. After this the lie seemed to stick, and their old friendship was resumed as if Sonya had never been away, although Joan was more careful this time, aware now of how easily she might be cut adrift.

When Sonya came to Cambridge to remove her belongings from her old room in Newnham, it was Joan who helped her pack up everything. They managed to fit most of her things into a single trunk, and one of the porters helped them lug it to Jamie's car. It was a warm, sunny day, one of the last sunny days of the year, and when she looks back on it, Joan remembers that it was marred only by her sudden recollection of the shirt she found in Sonya's cupboard after Sonya had gone. Leo's shirt. She knows that if she had not accompanied Sonya to pack up her room she might never have brought up the subject, and even now she cringes to remember how she broached it with Sonya. She couldn't help it. How suspicious she must have seemed. How unkind.

It was just as they were about to leave. Joan had gone to the wardrobe and pulled the discarded shirt from the shelf with an accusatory flourish. It no longer held any trace of Leo, but gave off a musty odour. 'Whose is this?' she had asked, holding the shirt up to the light and putting her hand on her hip.

Sonya had simply glanced at the shirt and shrugged, turning back to the trunk that she was unpacking in an attempt to re-pack more efficiently. Her face remained utterly expressionless, as if Joan was holding up a ragged dishcloth. 'I don't know.'

'Don't you think it looks like Leo's?'

'It looks like a shirt. And you look like Miss Strachey when you stand like that.'

'But Leo wore ones just like this,' Joan persisted, ignoring her remark.

Even now, after all these years, she couldn't have explained exactly what she thought Sonya would say. It was only a shirt, after all. It was just that she had been so certain when she first smelt it, so sure, that she couldn't push from her mind the belief that there was something odd about it that she couldn't put her finger on. Come to think of it, why had Sonya not made a joke of a man's shirt being found in her cupboard as she would normally have done, or taken it as an opportunity to reminisce over which of her young men it might have belonged to?

'But aren't you even curious? Why would a shirt like Leo's—'

'Oh come on, Jo-jo. Why are you being so peculiar?' Her face broke into a smile. 'I haven't been in this room for years. How can I possibly remember whose it is?'

'But you were just going to leave it there.'

'I can't be taking other men's shirts back to my

marital home. My husband would want an explanation.' She raised her eyebrows at Joan and her face broke into a sudden, bright laugh, so familiar that Joan started to laugh too, and she found herself stuffing the shirt back into the cupboard and following Sonya outside to the car, no longer sure why she had been so adamant that an explanation was required. They had driven into town and the rest of the day had passed in a luxurious haze of sun and long walks and iced tea with slices of lemon.

'Just like old times,' Sonya declared before she left, squeezing Joan's arm and then kissing her abruptly on the cheek.

The subject of the shirt was not brought up between them again, and after a while Joan became convinced that she had been mistaken. She did not like to think of it, not just because she was ashamed of how she had acted, but also because it was uncomfortable to recall those earlier suspicions. Once again, it was Sonya with whom she drank cocoa on the rare nights she was not working at the laboratory, Sonya whose clothes she borrowed to go to the cinema with unsuitably earnest young men, Sonya who fixed her hair when she bleached it for too long and it turned green instead of blonde, Sonya who was her dearest, greatest friend. And Sonya who, when she found out that Joan was being sent to the University of Montreal on a research trip that summer, was the first to hear about it.

The trip to Canada was, according to Max, an opportunity for the British research plant to combine its results with the Montreal laboratory, and for the two sections to work on a strategy for future collaboration. Not to be mentioned to a single soul. Joan did not need to be told this. She knew it already. She knew which particular aspects of the project the Canadians were working on, and she knew how important this trip could be for the project. She also knew that there were dangers in crossing the Atlantic at this stage of the war, and that Max had left instructions on how his work should be continued if they did not make it back, but she was not put off by the danger. So many people were facing far greater dangers than this. These were unprecedented times, after all. On top of this, she still believed, along with the rest of them at the laboratory, that they were working against Germany, that their project would act as a deterrent, that it was a safe, clever thing that was worth the risk of an Atlantic crossing. And so of course she would not have told a soul. Why would Max even think he had to tell her?

When Joan mentioned the trip, Sonya merely exhaled smoke through her nose, and tilted her head to look at Joan with a hint of mischievousness in her eyes. 'Will you see Leo when you go over there?'

'No,' Joan said, trying to appear shocked at the very thought, as if it had not even crossed her mind.

'Really?' Sonya said, looking away with a slight smile twitching on her lips.

'How's his thesis going anyway?'

Sonya glanced sideways at Joan. 'Now why would you be interested in that?'

Joan shrugged. 'I heard so much about it. And it was important, wasn't it?'

'Well, it depends who you ask. If you ask him, you'd think he'd invented a cure for cancer.'

'So he's finished it?'

Sonya nodded, although her eyes betrayed some degree of irritation. 'He's advising the American and Canadian governments on Russian aid.'

'But that's wonderful. It's what he wanted.'

Sonya took a deep inhalation of smoke and shook her head. 'There is such a thing as pride, Jo-jo. The Soviet Empire doesn't need American help.' She paused. 'Leo thinks they're going to be grateful, but . . .' She stopped, deciding against whatever it was she was about to say. 'Anyway, so it's just you and Max going on this trip?'

'Uh-huh.'

Sonya smiled, a slow, spreading smile.

'What's so funny?'

'Well, you know how you could really annoy Leo . . .' she said, nodding at Joan in that knowing and mildly patronising manner that Joan remembered from those late-night meetings at university, '. . . if you wanted to.'

'I don't want to.'

Sonya took out her lipstick and brushed it lightly across the plump part of her lower lip, and then pressed her lips together so that when she grinned again her whole mouth had turned bright red. 'Fair enough.'

Joan sighs. 'All right then. How?'

'Oh, come on, Jo-jo, it's obvious. You've got to sleep with Max.'

'But he's married.'

'Ah yes, my dear, but otherwise you're going to turn up and see Leo—'

'I'm not going to see him.'

Sonya shook her head. 'It's inevitable. He won't be able to resist finding you once he discovers you're coming to his university, and he'll just wrap

198

you around his little finger again. The only way around it is to sleep with someone else first. Preferably someone like Max.'

'How do you know what Max is like?'

Sonya lowered her cigarette. 'Because if he were ugly, you'd have told me by now.' She paused, considering this theory further. 'Besides, you must miss it a little bit. Don't you?'

'Miss what?'

'You know what.' Sonya looked at her. 'Sex.'

Joan remembers how she had been shocked by this question. It was one of the qualities she admired in her friend, that she would say things no one else would dare to say. She had a talent for it.

'Sometimes,' she whispered, and she knew as she said it that it was true, and that she would not have said it to anybody else in the whole world but Sonya. 'But it's not personal. I just miss the feeling of it, the . . .' She stopped, uncertain of the word. 'The comfort of it.'

Sonya had smiled at this confession. 'There you are then. And besides, what else are you going to be doing for all those days cooped up on a boat to Canada? You might as well.'

'Well, I thought I'd be conventional and take a book or two.'

Sonya lowered her eyes and looked up at Joan through her eyelashes, just as she had once taught Joan to do. 'Oh Jo-jo. Will I never grind that streak out of you? Anyway, do as you please. I know which I'd rather do.'

*   *   *

There is a knock on the bathroom door.

199

'Time to resume.' Mr Adams' voice is abrupt and impatient.

Joan jumps at the interruption and realises that she is crying. She is standing in front of the mirror in the bathroom, her hands numbed by the cold water, and tears are pooling in her eyes. She is glad that Mr Adams cannot see her. It would not do for them to see how easily she can break under the strain of their questioning. She must not let them see how tiring it is to remember everything in such vivid detail. She must be stronger than this, if not for herself, then at least for Nick.

She reaches for a towel and dries her hands. Her hair is thin and white, and her skin appears papery in the dimming light. It has been so long, she thinks, since she was *held* by anyone. And yes, she does miss it, but who is there to tell now?

She wonders once more about Sonya, if she is still alive, if she ever thinks of her, if she is standing alone in a bathroom somewhere, running her fingers along the surface of her skin, observing how it flakes and sags, and wondering how she ever got so old.

*　　　*　　　*

The boat leaves at dusk. It is large and grey and decked out with civilian flags. There is a contingent of orphans being sent to Quebec where the boat docks, the children being crocodiled into bunks away from the rest of the passengers, dangling teddy bears and blankets along the planked decks. Joan and Max have cabins on the same corridor; second class, but not adjoining. The boat is not due to leave for another hour or so, but already it feels full.

Max puffs to the top of the stairs and edges sideways along the deck towards her, their two suitcases knocking against the wooden railings. 'What have you got in here?' he asks, not stopping but grimacing his face into an expression of mock despair.

Joan grins. 'All my warm things. And some books.'

'We're only going to be away for five weeks.'

'Exactly. Five weeks. And Canada's supposed to be cold.'

'Not in July.'

'It's always cold in the mountains. I've seen it on postcards.'

Max rolls his eyes and picks up the cases again. 'All right, all right. I'll leave it in your room for you. See you at dinner?'

'Are you not staying for the big send-off?' she calls after him.

He turns at the door leading to the cabins and shakes his head. 'I've never liked goodbyes.'

After he has gone, Joan remains standing on the deck. Already the shore looks untouchable, transient, even though the ropes are still attached and a platoon of soldiers is waiting to board, black-booted and loaded with duffel bags. The clouds on the horizon are inky blue, spun through with fading silver sunlight. She thinks of Leo leaving from this same port and feels a rising sense of sickness at the thought of seeing him again. Her fingers are cold and her lips dry in the sea air, and she finds with a tangle of annoyance that Sonya is right. Even the thought of being near him makes her suddenly aware of her heart's frantic activity in her body and she knows she must not make any attempt to see him. It would be just as it was and she would have to be strong all over again, and the thought makes her feel heavy and tired.

She retreats to her cabin and changes into a light cotton dress. The lighting in the cabin is dim and flattering as she pins up her hair, and she hesitates for a moment over whether or not to wear make-up. She is most certainly not going to sleep with Max—why should it make any difference to her whether Sonya would or wouldn't?—and so she doesn't want Max to think she is a floozy by turning up for dinner in lipstick and rouge. She slips on her shoes and turns to leave, and as she does, she catches a glimpse of herself in the mirror. Mousey-English, Sonya might call her if she saw her going down to dinner like this. She hesitates, and then steps back towards the dressing table. Perhaps it is foolish to think that Max will even notice whether she is wearing make-up or not. What the hell, she thinks. She'll wear lipstick if she wants to. She is going to dine at the Captain's Table and drink wine and listen to swing music and forget about everything just for a short while. What does it matter?

Max is already in the dining room when she arrives. He stands up when he sees her coming and pulls out her chair. 'I pinched a bread roll for you.'

'How gallant.' She sits down next to him and smoothes her napkin over her knees. He is watching her, smiling in an odd manner which she puts down to the fact that they have never been alone together like this before. 'So do you think we'll see any bears in Canada?' she asks, wanting to

202

break the silence.

'Of course we won't. They don't roam the streets. Not down in the cities. We'd have to go up into the mountains to see a bear.'

'Oh. That's disappointing. I've always wanted to see one.'

Max leans back in his chair, holding his champagne glass, and grins. 'I'm not sure they're quite as cuddly as you think. Or did you see them on your postcards too?'

'What postcards?' Her reply is too quick.

'The ones you mentioned before with the snowy mountains.'

'Oh, those.' She breathes out slowly. 'No. Only mooses.'

The dining room is opulent while also being safety conscious. Its tables and chairs are screwed to the floor and decorated with starched tablecloths and silver napkin rings, and there is a pile of life-jackets next to the stage reflected in the glass chandelier above. A woman in a glittering evening gown glides past. There are sailors in blue and white uniforms with ribbons on their hats, a double bass leaning grandly against its stand, drums and a dark-wood piano. There is a shout from the kitchen and then a sudden billow of smoke visible behind the portholes of the black swing doors.

To begin with, Joan and Max talk mainly about work; safe, unremarkable topics. The focus of the trip is to ensure the cooperation of each country's scientific organisations, specifically in the area of electromagnetic separation, but it is also to allow them to assess the suitability of the plant, and the possibility of moving some of the UK operations across to Canada. 'It's a question of space,' Max informs her while they wait for dinner to be served. 'The only site in Britain which would be big enough to house all the operations is Billingham, but the accommodation there is terrible and, frankly, it'd be hard to find a less suitable place geographically than Billingham.'

'Where's Billingham?'

'Teesside. It's just too far from the other research sites to be feasible. And even if it were suitable, I wouldn't be able to convince everyone already working on the project to move there.'

'It's closer than Canada.'

He acknowledges this point with a tilt of his head. 'That's different.'

They talk like this until the first course arrives: smoked salmon with a dill garnish, shipped over from Canada on the outward journey and stored in ice. Joan grins as the waiter lurches away from them, his sea-legs not quite up to the task. She was not expecting this level of luxury.

'Have I told you my sister's called Joan?' Max asks suddenly. He leans forward and squeezes a quarter of lemon across Joan's salmon, and then does the same to his own. 'And I've never met a Joan I don't like.'

Joan smiles, momentarily distracted from the plate of food in front of her. How strange the human mind is, she thinks. Unknowable and unpredictable, its thoughts whizzing like electrons inside an atom. Invisible to the human eye. 'I used to want to be called Margery,' she replies. 'I thought it sounded more glamorous than Joan.'

Max laughs, and it is a surprisingly nice laugh, deep and infectious. 'You may be right. But I still like it. It suits you.' He looks straight into her eyes as he says this, and Joan feels a tingling in her neck because she has a sudden sense that she has never really been looked at quite like this before. It is a nice feeling, but also an unnerving one, the sense of being utterly transparent. Even Leo had never managed that. She had always been too much on her guard with him, too aware of her own vulnerability.

After the salmon comes a main course of beef cooked in butter and perfectly tender. They drink their champagne, Max quickly, Joan slowly. Joan has never had champagne before and she does not intend to waste it. She wants to remember how it tastes: the flavours fizzing on her tongue, sugary explosions of tiny pink snowdrops.

Max drains his glass, leans back and stretches his arms above his head, and then he slumps, relaxed, in his chair. 'Ah, I could get used to this.'

Joan nods in agreement. 'Shame about the U-boats though. If not for the constant possibility of being violently sunk, it'd feel like we were on a luxury cruise.'

'No, no, this is better. At least we're going somewhere. Cruises are awful. They're full of people who use "cruise" as a verb. *Do you cruise often?* That sort of thing.'

'Oh.' Joan smiles. 'And do you?'

'Do I what?'

'Cruise often.'

'No. Only on my honeymoon.' He grins. 'It was terrible.'

Max does not mention his wife very often, but Joan knows from Karen, as keeper of the switchboard, that relations between them are civil at best. When he refers to her at all, it is never by name but only by title. Joan knows that her name is Flora, but only because Karen has told her. With Max, it is always 'my wife'. There is something distant about this, and there is even now, as he turns away to watch three young men in dark suits and thin bowties step onto the stage. There is the thrum of a double bass being moved, a quick flourish with a brush on the snare drum, a tinkle of piano keys. The bassist plucks a chord and adjusts his tuning. There is a countdown, and then a flare of jazz piano and bass and drums.

Max turns back to Joan but now he has to shout to make himself heard. 'Her choice. I wanted to go to Cornwall.'

Coffee is served from large silver pots, and as the band lapses into gentle swinging tunes, they continue to sit at the table and talk, not about work or science but about their childhoods, their families, prompting a discussion on whether it would be preferable to lose an arm or a leg, if you had to choose between the two. Joan listens as Max describes a visit to a farm when he was a child, and how his sister tried to make a herd of goats line up so she could feed them one at a time from a bag of broken biscuits. She hears how they crowded her, bleating and butting, but she remained determined to boss them into shape even when in mortal danger of being trampled, and she was only saved by a courageous passer-by who kindly reached into the mêlée of goats and lifted her out.

'She's the headmistress of a girls' school now,' he says. 'It suits her.'

He tells her that he was sent to boarding school at the age of seven, that he came from Dundee originally, although you wouldn't know it from his accent, that his family had once been related to an earl of somewhere Joan hadn't heard of and wouldn't like to have to spell, but there had been disinheritances along the line so now there was no inheritance left to speak of. There is a family tartan and a hunting lodge in the Borders.

No, Joan thinks. Nothing to speak of.

Max grins, as if he can read her mind. 'It's cold and bleak,' he tells her. 'You really wouldn't like it. Believe me.'

She gazes beyond Max's shoulder, out through the small, round porthole behind him where the moonlight breaks upon the water, cut up into hundreds of tiny shards of light. She imagines a wood-panelled living room with paintings on the wall of lochs and mountains, and old vases with sprigs of lavender on the sideboard. She pictures a log fire, crystal glasses, a tartan rug. Max takes a cigarette out of his pocket and balances it lightly between his lips.

She realises now that she is thinking about those lips.

I wouldn't be so sure about that, she thinks, and then looks away, hoping that he has not seen the flicker of the thought across her face.

*   *   *

The voyage passes more quickly than Joan had anticipated, her tattered library copy of *Now, Voyager* remaining unopened throughout the six days at sea, even though she takes it out with her every morning, intending to get started. There just never seems to be a chance to read it. She and Max do crosswords together and take walks on the deck,

207

and when they are not doing either of these things they seem to be eating, occasionally being sick, or just talking. It is an odd sort of complicity, as if they have been thrown together on an exotic holiday without really knowing each other. She can imagine the expression on Sonya's face if she were to tell her that she hasn't touched either of the books she brought with her, intrigued at first, then exasperated when she finds out that they have been doing crosswords instead.

After dinner on the last evening, the music is halted for the announcement that land has been sighted. There is applause from some of the tables and a fresh burst of music, but Max frowns and bends forward, studying the swirl of coffee in the bottom of his cup.

'That's a shame,' he murmurs, still not looking up. 'I was starting to think this might go on for ever.'

There is a pause. They both know that once they walk off the boat, things will be back to the way they were before, and there will no longer be hours to spare for puzzles and walks and lengthy dinners. Joan takes a gulp of red wine. She has drunk more than she usually would and she can feel a slight giddiness rising to her head. She glances at Max. 'I think your wife might have something to say about that.'

He shrugs. 'I don't think she would.' He pauses. 'She lives in London, and I live in Cambridge. We don't see much of each other as it is.'

Joan has heard this already from Karen but she decides to pretend not to know. She does not fully understand why she does this. It is instinct, she supposes, which makes her lower her eyes and say:

'I'm sorry to hear it.'

'Don't be. We married when we were very young. Our parents wanted us to. It was expected of us. I didn't have the gumption to go against their wishes.' His voice is unbearably sad.

'Did you love her when you married her?'

He rolls his eyes. 'Only a woman would ask that question.'

'Have many women asked it before?'

He shifts his glance from hers. 'No. Not really.'

'Well? Did you love her?'

'I was eighteen.' He looks at her. 'Yes. No. I don't know. I don't think so.'

'Did she love you?'

'I think she thought I was dashing, or something like that. I could have told her then that I was never cut out to dash for long. She wishes I worked in the City like all her friends' husbands. Or was an officer in the army. She hates this scientist thing. It embarrasses her in front of her crowd.' They fall silent, and then Max asks, 'How about you, if you don't mind me asking? I find it hard to imagine you don't have a whole host of suitors trying to marry you. Are none of them up to the task?'

Joan sighs. She thinks of Leo, of his eyes in the restaurant on that last night, hard and glittering and unknowable. She pushes this thought away, down, down. She will not think of him, not now. 'There was one once. I loved him, I suppose, and I think he loved me back, although he never said it. I thought I would marry him.'

'And?'

'He never asked.'

Max picks up the bottle of red wine—the second one they've had that night—and pours the remnants into her glass and then his, not saying anything. 'Well, for what it's worth, he sounds like an idiot,' he says, although he does not look at her as he says it. Just then, a young man in a sailor's uniform taps Max on the shoulder. He says something to Max, who laughs and leans towards Joan.

'This young chap would like to know if I'll allow you to dance with him.'

Joan glances up at the sailor. He must be at least five years younger than her, Lally's age, perhaps nineteen or twenty, with bright blue eyes and a look of—how can she describe it?—extreme cleanliness, as Sonya might say. He gives the impression of gleaming, of having been ironed and polished before being sent out. She grins and looks back at Max. 'And will you allow it?'

He reddens a little. 'It's not my choice. It's yours.'

She looks at him and sees, quite suddenly, that he is anxious she might say yes. There is a sudden flutter of desire in her chest and she finds herself wondering what it would be like to kiss him, really kiss him, with her arms around him and his hands in her hair. She takes a deep breath. 'Then tell him that no, you absolutely won't allow it.'

He turns back to the sailor who is entirely nonplussed by this response, and grins at Joan before wheeling away to a neighbouring table which appears to be hosting a surplus of women.

'How did he take it?'

'I expect he'll recover.' Max pauses. 'Of course, I had to make something up. I couldn't just reject him outright.'

Joan smiles. 'So what did you say?'

Max leans a little closer, his eyes fixed on hers, and for a brief moment Joan finds that the pulsing of her heart is almost painful in her chest. 'I said I wanted you for myself.'

He holds out his hand and Joan takes it, standing up and following him onto the dance floor, both of them swaying a little as they walk with the combination of wine and the movement of the boat. His arms feel strong and comfortable as he twirls her, spins her, and suddenly they are dancing, and Joan feels her body moving in time with his, glittering in the bright lights of the stage and the yellowed glow of the horizon. His fingers brush against the silk of her dress, Sonya's dress, which she has saved for the last night of the voyage because it is the best one she has. She remembers Leo once telling her that it matched her eyes, and when she thinks about it, she realises that this is the most romantic thing he ever said to her. Why did she put up with that? All those years and he never once told her he loved her, not even just to make her happy.

The music changes, slowing a little, and they stop, breathless, smiling at each other. She readjusts her hand on Max's shoulder so that she is closer to him now, as if by accident. Can she do this? Is it wrong? Will she regret it in the morning? She suddenly realises that all she has to do now is look up at him through her eyelashes the way Sonya has taught her, and everything will change between them. She thinks she knows why she is doing this. She is doing it to make herself strong. And she is doing it—she will admit this to herself now—because she wants to. She lifts her eyes, slowly, slowly, and then they are kissing, just as Joan had

211

known they would, and although at first it crosses her mind that she should not have started this, within a couple of seconds she is glad that she has done so, because it is the best, most perfect kiss she has ever known. She feels a quickening of her heart, her lungs. Max's hands slip down her body and he holds her gently by the waist.

Joan lifts her cheek to his. 'Come to my cabin.'

Max looks at her. 'Really? Are you sure?'

She nods.

'I don't want to cause any . . .' He hesitates, searching for an appropriately vague expression. 'I don't want to cause any bother.'

She grins up at him and laces her fingers into his, suddenly bold. 'I think I might rather enjoy a bit of bothering from you.'

Tuesday, 8.09 p.m.

Max is right. There are no bears in Quebec and it is scorchingly, blindingly hot. The city is light and still, with colourful pyramids of fruit stacked up in grocers' windows. A scent of freshly baked bread and pollen hangs over the streets. Was it ever like this in England before the war? Joan does not remember. She does not think she has ever seen such colour in all her life.

They are put up in an elegant hotel by the waterfront, and are joined for dinner on the first night by Taylor Scott, the new head of the atomic energy plant at Chalk River. He used to be assistant director of the theoretical research section at the University of Montreal, but has now been promoted to lead the new plant and will be more involved in experimentation than previously. It crosses Joan's mind that Taylor Scott might know Leo from his time at the university, and is immediately irritated that she has allowed herself to think of him.

Taylor Scott is a tall, thin man, with wire spectacles and a deep Canadian accent. He is dressed in a brown jacket and grey flannels, both of which are in need of pressing. They look borrowed, as if they are meant for someone bulkier. In that respect, he is much like many of the other scientists to whom Joan has grown accustomed at the laboratory, only his voice is louder and his shirt whiter.

'They've just got in one of those new spin-washer machines at the plant,' he announces, undoing his cuffs and rolling up his bright white sleeves. 'It's incredible.'

Joan imagines he is saying this for her, based on the supposition that all women are bound to be interested in laundry. 'Oh?'

'Incredible things,' he continues. 'The physics of them is quite remarkable.' He shakes his head. 'Quite remarkable.'

Joan glances at Max and raises her eyebrows, but Max's face remains expressionless. This is how he has been ever since their arrival in Canada, polite but cautious. Apart from his earlier whispered warning that Taylor Scott is well known for being a terrible bore but a brilliant physicist, there have been few other moments of normal communication between them and the presence of this slow-talking Canadian has only made him more reserved. Indeed, there have been moments since they arrived in Quebec when she wonders if it really happened, if Max really came back to the cabin with her and took off her clothes, piece by piece, unbuttoning her dress and lifting her slip over her head, and then sliding his fingers under the line of her stockings so that they could be carefully rolled down and lifted from her feet in a shimmering web of silk. She remembers the colour of his skin under his clothes, oyster-shell pink, and not at all like Leo's dark, tanned body, how he kissed her neck and then slept all night with his arm (which was heavier than you'd think) draped across her hip-bone, how they awoke in the morning with a start, both of them jumping in the air at the shock of finding the other next to them, and then giggling like children. She does not remember ever having laughed like that with Leo. She suspects that Max would be easy to love in a way that Leo never was, but then she catches the thought and crumples it up, berating herself for having allowed it to arise at all.

They eat fish and drink strong gin and tonics while Taylor lists the reasons why the Montreal laboratory at the university has not been as successful as it might have been. 'The bloody Yanks just won't share,' Taylor says in a heated whisper. 'They've got it into their heads that we want Russia in on the project.'

'There is an argument for that,' Max says absently, his main focus being the huge white plate of food in front of him. 'It will only make them more paranoid if we keep it as a secret.'

Taylor looks at him, and a shadow of a frown passes across his face. 'I wouldn't let the others hear you say that.'

Max looks up. 'What? No, of course not. I just meant that we won't be at war for ever. There are longer term implications . . .' He tails off, turning his attention back to the dish of sole Veronique cooked in an exquisite buttery sauce of pre-war richness.

'The Americans are looking for any excuse to shut us down. They were even talking about cancelling the Canadian project at one point. We have three hundred guys working like crazy on the theoretical side, but we can't try it out because they won't send us enough materials. It's impossible to build a reactor on that kind of budget.'

Max leans across to Joan while Taylor continues to talk and places his hand on her arm. 'Do you have the agenda for the trip?' he asks, and Joan nods, reaching into her bag to extract a sheaf of papers. He takes them from her and scribbles on the top sheet while Taylor is speaking. Taylor isn't saying anything of any interest, nothing they don't already know, but Max seems to be paying an inordinate amount of attention. He looks up from his notes only occasionally, frowning at some aspect of internal politics or other that Taylor has just mentioned, or to take a mouthful of food. After their plates have been cleared away Taylor excuses himself, and for a moment Joan and Max are left alone. Max does not look at her but instead pushes a piece of paper across the table in her direction. It is the agenda, but it has been so thoroughly scribbled upon that it is no longer readable.

'Am I right?' he asks.

Bode's Law, he has scrawled on the paper, and then a diagram of the sun, Mercury, Pluto, and then a circle with arrows dissecting each other at right angles, below which there is a series of numbers. *Centrifugal force of mass (m) rotating at angular speed (w) at distance (x) from the centre: $m + w^2$. So if the speed is v, then $w = v/x$, hence the centrifugal force is* . . . There is a complicated sum written out at the bottom.

She frowns. It seems to make sense to her but she is not quite sure. 'What is it?'

He grins. 'It's a spin-washer.'

There is a pause. And then she bursts into laughter.

*   *   *

The next morning they are driven twelve hours north-west up the Ottawa River to the new Chalk River plant in the depths of Ontario. The car journey is hot and sticky, and they stop on the hilly outskirts of Montreal for lunch, beef sandwiches with melted cheese, which Joan regrets as soon as she has finished for the greasy, sickly feeling left in her stomach. From this height it is impossible to see a single person down in the criss-cross of the city, but Joan feels suddenly and terrifyingly visible, as if Leo needs only to glance up in order to see her, an ant under a magnifying glass. She turns away and walks back to the car to wait for the others to finish, sitting in Max's vacant seat and leaning her head against his jacket. She closes her eyes and waits. No, she will not think of him.

The Chalk River atomic research plant is set within an area of pristine greenness, surrounded by pines and aspens and fir-covered hills which house a piercing chorus of cicadas. The ground is hot underfoot even though it is evening by the time

216

they arrive, and the full glare of the sun has tipped below the horizon. They are shown to their respective bungalows, small log cabins painted in army green and set out along muddy, duckboard paths above which electricity wires cluster, indicating a hasty, haphazard set-up. There are several larger buildings made of corrugated iron in which the machinery is housed, and there is only one brick house, an old school building from before the war, shared between the administrative and theoretical divisions of the plant, and in which Taylor Scott's wife and children have taken up residence on the top floor.

The days at Chalk River are full, mainly consisting of eighteen-hour shifts with no let-up until Sundays. Joan and Max will be staying here for three weeks, but during that time they are obliged to become fully acquainted with every aspect of the plant. Max is to work closely with Alan Kierl, a quiet, colourless physicist who is in charge of developing samples of uranium 235 and another artificial fissionable isotope, uranium 233, while Joan is to assist with the smaller tasks: copying, filing, taking notes.

In the evenings, a large communal meal is served in Taylor Scott's house, everyone filing into a huge room which was once the school dining hall. There is a long wooden table running down the centre of the room, and the conversation is mainly to do with science and chess. Even after the wine has been poured, there is no let-up in seriousness. Tonight, Joan is sitting beside Max, who is questioning Kierl on whether he thinks the 233 isotope is likely to be suitable. Kierl's answers are, as ever, short and precise, not expansive enough to be classed as conversational. Max has complained about this before, frustrated with his slow progress in getting what he needs from Kierl, who does not offer information so much as have it extracted from him.

After the soup starter has been cleared away, Kierl excuses himself, saying that he needs to retrieve his notes in order to answer one of Max's questions, and Max turns to Joan with an exaggerated sigh. 'He's exhausting,' Max whispers. 'I don't know why he won't just talk normally. He only responds if I ask him a direct question, but then occasionally he inundates me. That's why he's gone off to get his notes.'

Joan grins. 'He's like one of those slot machines.'

'In what sense?'

'You pay a penny to get any sort of movement, and occasionally you get a windfall.'

Max looks at her for a moment and then starts to laugh, which sets Joan off, and soon they are both giggling just as they did on the boat, coughing and snorting and trying to pretend they're not laughing, even though it wasn't a particularly funny observation. Certainly not this funny. Taylor Scott frowns at them, and Max manages to resume his serious expression once Kierl has returned with the file, but Joan can see his eyes glistening.

She sits back, trying to suppress the sudden surge of guilt mingled with attraction which she feels whenever she is with him. She cannot seem to push the thought of him out of her head, the memory of her fingers reaching out to unbutton his shirt, slowly, slowly, and then tugging at the knot of his tie (the same one he is wearing now) and pulling it off over his head. Her body burns to think of it. But at the same time she also feels guilty, because he is

218

married (even if it is unhappily), and she should not have encouraged him, whatever Sonya might have said. It had just seemed so natural. So inevitable.

On previous evenings, the men have stayed behind after dinner to smoke and drink whisky upstairs in Taylor Scott's drawing room, and Joan has walked back along the duckboards to her bungalow alone, but tonight Max refuses a cigar and declares that he needs to sleep. Instead, he leaves with Joan and they walk together, both of them slightly dizzy with wine. She gets the sense that he has left early in order to be with her.

This is dangerous, she thinks. She glances up at Max. He is frowning, quiet, and she knows he feels it too. It is starting now. Something irreparable is starting now.

'Joan,' he says, and then stops. He is holding his breath.

'Yes?'

'I want to tell you something.'

Joan turns to look at him. Her whole body is tingling. She waits for him to speak, but he doesn't say anything and quite suddenly she realises that he is not going to say what she thought he would. He is going to tell her it was all a mistake, that things have to go back to the way they were. 'It's okay,' she whispers, her voice painful in her throat. 'You don't have to say anything. It was my fault.' She tries to breathe more slowly. 'I'm sorry. I promise I won't tell anyone what happened.'

'No,' he says quickly. 'That's not it.'

'What then?'

'I want to tell you . . .' He stops. 'I love you.'

The declaration is so unexpected that at first Joan thinks he cannot mean it. Is he teasing her?

She hits him lightly on the chest. 'Don't be silly,' she says.

'I'm not being silly. I've loved you ever since you said you wished your name was Margery. I remember the exact second.'

'That is silly,' she says, laughing and lifting her hand to his chest. 'Although it was the crosswords that did it for me.'

She moves towards him and kisses him on the lips. She waits. She kisses him again. Bold, yet light. She stands in front of him and waits for him to kiss her back, only he does not. Something isn't quite right. His hands remain by his sides and he appears sad and resigned.

She steps away from him, suddenly hot with embarrassment. 'I'm sorry. I thought you meant you wanted . . . oh God.' She turns towards her bungalow and starts to walk, half marching, half trotting, her eyes suddenly smarting at her own foolishness. She hears him start to jog after her but she does not stop to allow him to catch up. How did she misinterpret him so enormously? But didn't he say he loved her? She doesn't understand and she doesn't want to. She wants simply to be inside her small hut with the door closed so that she can't make any more blunders like this. Why didn't he stop her when he saw she was going to kiss him? Why did he just let her carry on like that?

Gently, he catches her hand and swings her round to look at him. 'You weren't listening properly,' he says. 'I love you. I can't stop thinking about you. It's been like this for weeks now. I want to be with you all the time. I want to . . .' he raises his hands in a gesture of despair and for a moment it seems that he is going to say something outlandishly romantic, '. . . *talk* to you. For ever.'

Joan smiles, although she still does not quite follow his logic.

His look now is desperate. 'That's why I don't want to have an affair with you. Not like this. Do you see? I love you.'

He takes her other hand in his and there it is again: a rising sense of panic that something is starting now. Something dangerous. Because she realises that what he has just said is probably the most romantic thing anyone will ever say to her. 'Yes,' she whispers. 'I think I do understand.'

'You deserve more than that. And maybe, one day . . .' He stops, leaving the sentence unfinished, hanging in the air between them. And then, very slowly, he leans forward so that Joan feels the lightest graze of his lips against hers, and for that brief moment before they turn into their separate bungalows, it feels like the saddest way of one person touching another it is possible to imagine.

＊   ＊   ＊

And that is it. Nothing more is said on the matter. It is not awkward between them as Joan fears, but peaceful. He is so open, so unwaveringly kind, that it is impossible to maintain any feelings of affront. And more than that, he is careful with her. He makes coffee for her and brings her lunch from the canteen, and he installs a radio in her bungalow so that she can listen to music in the mornings. Perhaps this is what it means to be loved, she thinks, and she allows herself the luxury of holding this thought for just a moment before banishing it.

They work together diligently and finish ahead of

221

schedule, and it is decided that they will stop in Montreal for a night on the way back to Quebec. Taylor Scott arranges for them to stay with his colleague, Professor Marsh, who will show them around the theoretical department at the university before they sail home, and he is quite insistent that they do not refuse the invitation.

'We're being shown around the university?' Joan repeats, having only been informed of this aspect of the itinerary once they are packed and ready to leave their bungalows.

Taylor nods and continues, explaining that their visit will be purely political, a bit of a waste of time, but necessary to keep everything ticking along between the two Canadian departments. There is still tension over which department does what and how the funding should be split, so in the interests of diplomacy they should make a token visit to the other side.

Joan feels hot. She takes off her cardigan and bends down to unzip her suitcase so that she can slip it into the side pocket, aware that she will not need it for the car journey. She is relieved for the distraction, not wanting anyone to see the flush of her cheeks. How she hates her own weakness. She is being silly, of course. It is highly unlikely that she will bump into Leo in such a large place. His department is probably located in a different part of the university, possibly even in an entirely different part of the city. There is no reason to feel scared; no reason for her fingers to tremble like this.

Kierl is watching her when she stands up again. 'Let me take your case for you.' He lifts Joan's case and struggles to the car with it.

Max puts his case on top of Joan's in the back of the car and then rolls up his sleeves to prepare for the drive. 'We'll only spend the morning at the university. We could do some sightseeing in the afternoon, if you like? What would you recommend, Kierl? Anything we ought to see in Montreal?'

A long pause while Kierl frowns, trying to muster up a response. 'You could walk up Mount Royal,' he says at last. 'It's nice up there.' He looks at Joan and offers a sharp sort of smile which Joan supposes is his attempt at a farewell gesture, and then he turns sharply and walks away.

Max watches him go, shrugs and gets into the car. 'Odd chap.' He looks at Joan, and for a moment a smile flickers across his face. 'I'm all out of pennies now.'

*   *   *

They arrive at Professor Marsh's house late at night after the long drive from Chalk River and Joan is put up in the attic room. It is a child's room, decorated with pictures of mountains and horses, and Joan falls into a restless, fitful sleep. At first, she dreams of the sea, stretching out along the horizon, blue from a distance and wide, and she is walking along the deck with Max, but he spins away from her so that when she looks for him again he has gone, and the sea is closer now, colder. The spray is not blue but colourless. And suddenly, the figure beside her is not Max but Leo, and Joan finds that, for the first time since he left, she can picture him exactly: his perfectly drawn lips and illuminated expression as he explains statistics to

223

her, his lemon-soap and tobacco smell, his expression as he leans across a restaurant table and swipes a cut of venison from her plate; and when she wakes up she finds that she is sobbing as she did when he left, crying and squeezing her hands into two tight balls so that her nails leave little crescent-shaped marks where they press into her soft skin. Crying because he had not loved her as she thought he did, because she had not even realised what love meant until Max stood outside her bungalow and told her that he couldn't stop thinking about her and wanted to talk to her for ever, and then kissed her so gently that she thought her heart might break.

*   *   *

In the morning, she dresses carefully before going downstairs for breakfast, dabbing face powder onto her cheeks and applying a light lipstick. She hopes that by pretending to be perfectly all right she might be able to convince herself that this is the case. They will only be at the university for a few hours. That's all. A few hours and then home again.

Max is in the front passenger seat of Professor Marsh's car and the heat of the day is already evident. 'You look tired,' he says, turning around to glance at Joan.

Joan smiles nervously, suddenly horrified at the thought he might have heard her sobbing from the upstairs room. How ridiculous she would have sounded. 'I suppose I am rather.' She undoes the latch of the car window and pushes it open, and as the car moves faster she closes her eyes and feels the freshness of the breeze against her skin, lifting

224

her hair from where it prickles against her neck and dislodging the hairclip that she had put in so carefully that morning.

She excuses herself when they arrive, wanting to sort out her hair before the meeting, and she is encouraged to find she has the ladies' lavatory to herself. She is in a cubicle when she hears someone else enter the room. The footsteps on the tiled floor cause her to hesitate. It is a rhythm she recognises.

No. It can't be. Not in a ladies' lavatory.

The footsteps stop as the person seems to glance along the row of cubicles to check which ones are taken. She knows there are four empty cubicles to choose from, and yet the footsteps do not move away. They simply turn, shuffle a little, and then turn back. The tread of the shoes is too heavy, too flat, for a woman. She sees the tips of two brown shoes facing her.

It can't be him. Surely not.

Her body feels suddenly itchy and too hot.

'Jo-jo?' a voice whispers.

The breath catches in her throat. What is he doing in here? How did he know where she would be? She feels a sudden burning sensation in her chest, and realises that it is not anger or fear or any of the other emotions she expected to feel when she saw him again. It is sadness. No, she thinks. No, you don't. Her hands shake as she flushes the lavatory. She has not yet combed her hair and she runs her fingers quickly through it. She takes a deep breath, slides back the bolt on the door, and steps out.

'My little comrade,' he says, kissing her drily on the cheek, not heeding the fact that she does not sink into him but stiffens a little and draws away. His old name for her does not have the softening effect she had feared it might. 'How are you?'

'Very well.' She tries to be brisk as she steps around him to the washbasin. The oddness of the situation makes it easier to cope with Leo's nearness. 'How did you know where I was? Why didn't you just leave a message instead of lurking out there like that?'

Leo shrugs. 'It's better if nobody sees us talking to each other. I'm known here. My work is known.' He hands her a towel. 'Here.'

'Thanks.' Joan dries her hands, turning away from him and trying to quell the confusion of feelings inside her. She takes a comb out of her bag, her fingers trembling, and she runs it through her hair. She sees him watching her, and realises that her old guardedness has returned. It is a shock how unfamiliar this feeling has become. She had always assumed it was normal to feel like this in any relationship, but she is no longer so sure. She clips her hair back into place and turns to him, slipping the comb inside her bag. 'So how do I look?'

Leo frowns. 'Combed,' he says. She remembers this from before: description is the closest he will come to any sort of comment on her appearance. He flicks a cigarette out of his silver tin. 'Smoke?'

Joan takes it. She places the nub of it in her mouth, allowing him to shield the tip with his hand as he lights it so that his hand brushes against her cheek. He smells different today, and she is relieved. No trace of lemon.

'So you're here on a research trip?'

She nods. 'Uh huh.'

'Dare I ask?' He gives her a slow smile. He must know the effect of that smile. It must work on others as it does on her.

226

'Same old research. And the answer's still no.'
She wonders how many other women there have
been since she last saw him, and for a moment she
is grateful to Sonya for having put the idea of Max
into her head. How does she always seem to know
these things?

'All right, all right. I won't ask.' And he doesn't.
He goes to the window and unlatches it, shoving it
open to reveal a concrete yard, empty except for a
few bins. He leans out, looking first one way and
then another, flicking cigarette ash as he does. He
turns back to her. 'Listen, Jo-jo. I came because I
had to see you. I thought you might have . . .' he
hesitates, '. . . changed your mind. You've still got
the chance, you know.'

'No,' she whispers. 'I've already told you I won't
do it.' She pauses. 'Is that the only reason you
wanted to see me? Have you got nothing else to
say?' Her voice betrays her feelings more than she
would wish, but she is no longer willing to hide her
anger. Of course she is cross with him after the way
things were left between them and she wants him to
acknowledge it.

Leo's expression is pained. 'Of course not, Jo-jo.
I think about you—' He stops.

'Is that it? You think about me?'

'I think about you a lot.' He puts out his hand to
touch her face, and she does not move away. He
runs his finger gently along her cheek before letting
his hand drop. 'You're my little comrade. You
always will be.'

Joan feels her heart quicken, but will not allow
herself to believe him. She is not as gullible as he
thinks. 'Not any more.'

'I know you agree with me really. You think the

same as I do. The bomb should be shared. The Russians should be allowed to know.'

Joan opens her mouth and then closes it again, annoyed by his refusal to see their history together as something separate from his politics. She wants to push him away, both hands on his chest, and make him understand that she will not be persuaded. 'No, I don't,' she whispers.

Leo is undeterred. 'We're supposed to be allies,' he continues. 'If they don't share it now, what happens after the war?'

'How should I know?' Joan snaps. 'I can't see into the future. We're making this now so that Hitler doesn't get there first.'

'But you're not going to drop it on Hitler, are you?'

'Of course not. It's a deterrent.'

Leo smiles. 'Oh, Jo-jo. Always so trusting, aren't you?'

Joan glares at him although she feels herself to be wrong-footed. 'But it's true.'

He takes her by the shoulders. 'What I meant was that you're not going to drop it on Hitler because this bomb is not a bullet. It's made for . . .' he pauses, pretending to calculate something in his head. 'You probably know this better than I do. How many people live in a city, on average? How many babies, mothers, fathers, brothers, sisters—'

'But that's why it's a deterrent,' Joan whispers, exasperated.

Leo sighs and shakes his head. 'I really thought you were braver than this.'

Only he doesn't say *really*. He says *veally*. And Joan knows that there was a time when this would have made her heart melt just a little. 'Don't. It

228

won't work.'

'Fine. Write to me, if you change your mind. In fact, tell Sonya next time you see her.'

Joan does not reply. She does not trust herself to speak. There are tears brimming, pulsing, behind her eyes. 'I have to go. They're waiting for me.' She blinks and turns towards the door and, for a moment, she believes his hesitation is because he is summoning up the courage to say something he has never said before, to catch her in his arms and kiss her properly, in which case she is certain that she would push him away. She absolutely would. But he does not. After a few seconds, he merely whispers: 'You go out first. I'll follow you in five minutes.'

'I thought you were going to climb out of the window.'

Leo gives a small snort of surprise. 'Don't be ridiculous. I'm a research fellow. I work for the government. I can't be seen clambering out of windows in the science department. I'll follow you out.' She turns to leave but he takes hold of her wrist. 'I know you'll come round, Jo-jo. I know you better than you think.'

She shakes her head. 'No, you don't.'

'I know you can do it. You just won't because you're scared.'

'That's not the only reason. But yes, of course I'd be scared.'

Leo's grip tightens around her wrist. 'Then you're scared of the wrong thing. It's far more dangerous to the world if it's kept from us. The West hates communism. They'd do anything to destroy it, whatever the cost, and now they can. Russia needs a bomb for her own protection.'

Joan shakes her head. 'I can't, Leo. I'm under

oath.' She pauses. 'And I won't.'

He does not drop his gaze from hers but he releases her wrist, and then takes a step away from her. 'You'll come around, Jo-jo,' he says quietly.

'No.' She walks to the door and opens it, glancing back only briefly to witness him stubbing out his cigarette on the windowsill and flicking it outside. Her whole body trembles as she steps into the corridor, closing the door behind her. How long has she been in there? What on earth will Max think she has been doing?

She hurries down the corridor and as she gets to the meeting-room door Max flings it open. 'What happened to you? I was beginning to think you'd drowned.' He sniffs. 'Have you been smoking in the toilet?'

'I was just . . .' Joan falters. She feels dizzy, as if teetering on the edge of a great precipice. Max looks at her, his expression turning from incredulous to amused and then softening into something else entirely. He holds out his hand to her. It is a small gesture, nothing much, but to Joan it feels like a hand reaching over a cliff, offering to tug her up. She takes his hand and squeezes it.

'It doesn't matter. We're about to start.'

Wednesday, 9.03 a.m.

'Preparing Exhibit A,' Ms Hart announces for the video recorder.

'Can't we just wrap this up now?' Nick asks. 'She's already told you everything you need to hear. We went through it all yesterday. They asked and

230

she said no. Twice.'

Ms Hart ignores Nick. She takes a thin document out of her folder and Joan registers a flicker of triumph in the movement. It is happening now. They're producing their trump card. She can see it in Mr Adams' expression and in Ms Hart's eagerness.

Joan stands up. She needs to see the document before Nick does. She needs to know what it is.

'Please sit down.' Ms Hart's voice is loud and stern. 'I'm passing Exhibit A to the accused,' she announces, directing her voice towards the microphone and holding the piece of paper out to Joan.

She takes it and holds it against her chest, shielding it from view while she puts on her reading glasses. She has to squint to make out the words. The document is dated 2 September 1945 and is rather laboriously entitled *Fluctuations in the Efficiency of a Diffusion Plant, Parts I–IV*. Nick stands up and goes to read over her shoulder but Joan quickly folds the paper over.

'Well?' Ms Hart asks.

'Well what?'

'Do you recognise it? Does it mean anything to you?'

Joan is silent for a moment. 'No,' she says at last.

Ms Hart acts as if she has not heard Joan's response. She picks up the file and points to the document. 'This report was produced by the Cambridge division of Tube Alloys in 1945. It was classified material at the time. And somehow it found its way to a KGB file in Moscow, attributed to Agent Lotto.'

'Who's Agent Lotto?' Nick asks.

Joan does not look up, but she feels Ms Hart's eyes scrutinising her response. 'We have identified this intelligence as having originated from you,' Ms Hart continues. 'It's come to us rather late, smuggled out of the country by an ex-KGB operative who brought these to the British Security Services as a condition of our assistance in enabling his defection. He copied out hundreds of files by hand and hid them under the floorboards of his dacha in the countryside outside Moscow. Dedicated, wouldn't you say?'

Silence. Joan's lungs pulse inside her.

'And by a stroke of luck, yours was one of them. Agent Lotto. There is plenty here to ensure a conviction. Enough, certainly.'

Joan opens her mouth to deny it but then changes her mind. Never excuse, never explain; Leo's long-ago words echo in her mind, offering a dim glimmer of hope. 'Surely there must be some question over the reliability of documents taken from a KGB defector.'

'We trust him,' Mr Adams interjects. 'Absolutely.'

'But it's not admissible as evidence, is it? You couldn't use this in court, even if you did know who Agent Lotto was.' Joan indicates the document she is holding, and tries to appear dismissive. 'It doesn't even say much. You can't build a bomb from this.'

She glances at Nick hoping for some verification of this point, but Nick is not looking at her. He has taken the folder from Ms Hart and his eyes are scanning the index of documents.

Ms Hart does not flinch. 'That's not the point. It was classified material. And it's not the only one. As you can see, there's plenty more where that

232

came from.' Ms Hart indicates the file in Nick's hands. 'There are four more folders just like that, all attributed to Agent Lotto.'

'But Agent Lotto could be anyone. It could be twenty different people.' Joan makes another silent appeal to Nick, wanting him to say something, anything, but he does not look at her. He is turning the pages of the file now, slowly and deliberately, the sudden pallor of his face contrasting with the flush of his neck.

'I've told you already. Our source is completely reliable. We know for a fact that there are identical copies of these files stored in the KGB archives.' There is a pause. Ms Hart stands up and gestures to Mr Adams to do the same. 'Coffee?'

'Right. Yes.'

'We'll resume in thirty minutes, and when we do I'll ask you again if you recognise the document you're holding. I would advise you to think carefully about your answer.'

Mr Adams switches off the video recorder and follows Ms Hart outside, shutting the door behind him.

There is a clock on the mantelpiece and Joan can hear the soft whirr of time passing. She pulls her cardigan more tightly around her. She understands now why William did what he did. He must have thought he didn't stand a chance. There is such a weight of evidence in this one file alone. She thinks of Ms Hart's declaration at the beginning, that the charges carry a maximum of fourteen years in prison. Her mind is drawn to the sleeping tablets in the bathroom, and she imagines herself swallowing one handful after another, and the thought is almost comforting.

She closes her eyes. She knows she cannot do that. She hears Nick turning the pages of the file. She could still insist that she has never seen these documents before. After all, she has not admitted to anything. Not really. But if she does try to deny it, what next? Presumably they would take her to court and put her on trial, opening up her whole life to public scrutiny. She would have to stand in the dock and continue to deny everything, even when presented with exhibit after exhibit such as the one she has just seen. There would be a judge and a jury, witnesses, policemen, journalists.

And Nick would have to watch. Would he defend her, she wonders, if it came to it? Would he stand beside her, as he has done for so many others in his career, and speak on her behalf? Of course he would, if he believed it was the right thing to do. But would he do it if he believed Joan had done what they say she has?

She does not know. And, in any case, it is too much to ask. She can imagine the headlines if they made the link between her and Nick. *QC's mother revealed as a Soviet spy.* It would be the end of his career. It is her duty to protect her son, not the other way round, and as she sees it, there is only one way to avoid a long, drawn-out trial with all the media attention it would inevitably attract.

'You did this, didn't you?' Nick whispers. 'You did this.'

'Shhh,' Joan says, her hands patting the air in front of her in a nervous gesture. Her whole body is clenched with fear.

'I don't believe it.' His voice is suddenly tight, and the beam of his gaze is like a bright white searchlight falling coldly across Joan's chest. 'I

234

don't believe it. How could you?'

She looks down at the carpet. She still cannot say the words. She has a sudden thought that if she could only explain her reasons, then maybe he would understand and it wouldn't seem such a terrible thing to have done. At least it would be explicable.

'Why? Why would you do it?' His face is incredulous now as the enormity of the accusation sinks in. The flush of his neck has risen to his face and Joan sees that there are tears glistening in his eyes. Real tears this time, not just a hint of them as there was before.

Joan looks away. How to explain it? She has a theory that everyone has a certain view of themselves, of what they would do and what they would not do in any given circumstance, and it is the combination of these choices that makes up a personality. Take Nick, for instance. What if he had been drafted into the German army in 1942, stationed in Auschwitz—terrible to think of it—and told that all he had to do was flick this switch on, wait perhaps twenty minutes, and then switch it off again? Oh yes, he's a brave man. Braver than most. Joan can imagine his outrage if she were to suggest this. He'd say that he would have stood up against them, sacrificing himself if need be, adding himself to the list.

And maybe he would have sacrificed himself. People did. Some people. But most didn't.

So how about we introduce a few ambiguities. What if doing it meant that his boys would be kept safe—Joan can picture them both—with their shocks of blond-brown hair and big breathless smiles, plasterings of mud on their little knees. Not enough? His mother, old and in need of care. His wife Briony? A cousin? A second cousin?

Too remote?

Okay, so maybe he'd be less certain now, but he'd still be adamant that a loophole could be found. Maybe—ah-ha—maybe he would have done it just until he found that loophole. Perhaps he would offer a moment of kindness to some of the people in that camp, extra rations, conversation, a smile of encouragement, and he might start to tell himself that this made up in some small way for the flicking of that switch. A gasp of humanity in this cold, bleak forest where even the birds refuse to sing. He might have found that he could turn off the guilt he felt, tune it out.

What did Milgram call this? The Perils of Obedience. Something like that.

Because whatever else that experiment showed, it also showed that it can be hard to hold onto the things you thought you knew about yourself, the things that seem so definite when there is nothing there to test them. Real life is not that simple. There are endless ambiguities. Impossible to be certain of the things you would do and the things you would not do.

'Why?' he asks again. His expression is pleading, vulnerable, as if he is willing his mother to tell him something other than what he believes, to proclaim that of course she has never seen any of the documents in the file before and it's all a huge misunderstanding, and that she has a committee meeting to get to. Behind his shoulder is a row of old school photographs, brought over from Australia by Joan and now a source of amusement to his sons whenever they come to visit. The frames are dusty and tired-looking, but the boy grinning out from the pictures is young and optimistic and full of energy, growing older picture by picture, smarter and more confident each year. There is one of Nick leaving school, one at his graduation, his nose burnt from having spent the previous day at a students' march in Sydney, one of him being called to the Bar in London, dressed in a wig and gown and looking mildly embarrassed. Tell me, Joan thinks, tell me you wouldn't have done the same in my position.

But she will not say this. Because the only way you can tell the absolute truth is to tell it fast and tell it straight. Never excuse, never explain. Leo was right.

Joan looks up at her son, wishing with every cell of her body that there was something else she could say right now. But there isn't, and so, very softly, she whispers a single word. 'Hiroshima.'

*   *   *

The first test of the atomic bomb takes place in America during the height of summer in 1945, not long after the conclusion of hostilities in Europe. It explodes just before dawn into a cloudless sky, and even from twenty miles away the light it produces is astounding, a ball of energy hovering above the plain, dwarfing the distant mountains and mushrooming smoke into the night sky.

'They've done it,' Max announces that afternoon after the news has been cabled to him and he has called everyone into his room for a meeting. 'The Yanks have done it.'

It is no surprise that the Americans have got

there first, but the response to the news in the laboratory is a collective gasp. Not surprise exactly, but astonishment, or perhaps pride, to discover that it works—it actually works!—and that it is possible, after all, to create power from nothing, or from very little. It is not an exaggeration to say that something new has arrived on the planet, rewriting all the basic precepts of science in the process, and it is an incredible thing to know that they and their American counterparts have brought it into being. It is the Creation story rewritten for modern times. Let there be light! And it is so, at the press of a button. No other process has such efficiency, or such potential. But potential for what?

Joan turns to look outside and sees a thin sheet of cloud wafting across the deep, dark blue of the sky. The light emitted by the explosion is said to be brighter than the sun, but here, in Cambridge, house martins flit from branch to branch in the tree below the window. It seems so peaceful that it is almost incredible to believe that an explosion of such magnitude has taken place just across the ocean. How can something so big leave so little trace? It is not a thought she has had before, not at any time during the war when there were countless air raids and explosions that might have prompted it, and this was just a test bomb. Nobody was actually hurt. No homes were destroyed, no livelihoods erased. So why does this one above all others cause her heart to slow as if it is pulsing treacle?

Donald is the first to address Max. 'What now then?'

Max's expression is still incredulous. 'They'll use it on Japan, I suppose.'

Joan looks up with a start. 'But they won't just drop it on them, will they? I mean, they'd have to be warned. It's supposed to be a deterrent, isn't it?'

He shrugs. 'But we're at war. There's not much opportunity for a chat.'

The curtness of his response surprises Joan. It is not what she expected from him. Gentle, thoughtful Max, who she often catches quietly watching her while she works, who tells her he loves her and then refuses to kiss her because she deserves more than that, who can make her giggle like a child. 'Of course there is,' she says, and her voice is louder than normal. 'They could stage another demonstration and invite Japan, and that would give them the chance to surrender.'

Donald snorts. 'They wouldn't surrender. Not Japan.'

'But they should be given the chance.'

Max looks at her. 'Can you imagine Hitler offering the same to us if Germany had got there first?'

Joan is silent for a moment. 'I suppose not. But that doesn't mean we shouldn't offer it. Hitler was hardly a paragon of fairness.'

'Ha!' The noise comes from Arthur this time.

'But it's all hypothetical anyway,' Max says. 'You can't expect America not to use it now that they have a chance to end the war.'

Joan opens her mouth and then closes it again. She doesn't understand how they can all be so calm about it. Do they not feel the same sense of responsibility as she does? She understands now why this explosion is having such an effect on her. She has not felt responsible for any of those previous raids—or no more responsible than any other citizen of an implicated nation—but she does feel responsible for this. Yes, it would still have happened without her (she has some perspective on the limits of her contribution) but she can't understand how the others can be so detached.

'She's got a point though,' Arthur interjects. 'Now that it's not a secret in America, it's bound to come out that we're making one here.' He pauses. 'Stalin will know. Russia will want one too.'

Donald nods, and then laughs. 'Stalin will be furious.'

'Exactly. They'll have to bring Russia in on it now.'

Max shakes his head. 'I don't think so. We may be allies at the moment, but we won't be once the war is over.'

'But we won't be enemies.'

'That's not the point. The point is that we don't want Stalin having a weapon like this.'

'Why? In case he uses it?'

'Yes.'

'Then what's the difference? We're going to use it against Japan. Why does it matter who's underneath it?' Joan pauses, suddenly aware that she has heard this argument before, only this time she seems to have changed sides. Although what are the sides now? It no longer seems clear.

Arthur sighs. 'But we'd be using it to end a war. To save lives.'

'Not us,' Max corrects him. 'America.'

Joan looks at him, and she feels a spinning sensation inside her, as if a taut spring has suddenly snapped. Karen is smiling, her expression resigned and sad, as if to say that it's useless to argue such things where men are concerned.

240

'Oh, don't get upset,' Donald says eventually. 'Inviting the Japs to a demonstration wouldn't make any difference. They're not the surrendering type. The point is that it works. The science is correct.' He grins. 'Come on, let's have a drink and celebrate. Pub lunch, everyone?'

'I don't see why not,' Max says.

Joan looks away. She cannot seem to quell this rising sense of hysteria. 'But that wasn't the original idea, was it? It was supposed to be a deterrent against Germany. And now it's going to be used against Japan. Then who next?' She opens out her arms. 'You've all done the sums. If twenty kilotons could kill, say a hundred thousand people in Japan, then what next? They retaliate, but they don't stick to kilotons. They go for one megaton . . .'

Arthur snorts at this.

'. . . and that would kill . . .' she pauses, waiting, multiplying in her head, '. . . five million. And then what?'

Max shakes his head, as if this is a ridiculous proposition. It is, but then so was this super-bomb ten years ago, and it exists now. 'That's not going to happen.'

Joan stares at him. She can't believe he is disagreeing with her, that they are all disagreeing with her, that they are going to sit in the pub and eat fish and chips to celebrate this terrible destructive force. Where is their perspective? Until now, she would have said that they all shared the same sense of ambiguity towards this aspect of the project, even Max. Especially Max. But now she is not so sure. She turns to him. 'But how do you *know*?'

241

Three weeks and a day later, a uranium 235 bomb is dropped on the city of Hiroshima. This is how it is reported in the press, as simple, incontrovertible fact. Perhaps it is the case that these words are sufficient, from a purely narrative point of view, to explain the day's events to the rest of the world who were not there and did not see it. But it will never be enough to describe the truth of that day.

Of course, people will try to describe it, but it will be impossible for them to do so. There will be pictures in the newspapers of a brilliant blast of light and a great mushroom cloud hanging over the city as the dust swells and regurgitates, clawing at the earth as it rises. The reports will tell how it was so hot that some people simply vanished, swept off in a swirl of dust and ashes and debris. But there is no language that can really convey the truth of such destruction. The words do not exist. Or if they do, they are incomprehensible because human sympathy cannot absorb that amount of suffering. It is limited by necessity to the extent of its imagination. Beyond that, it's all just numbers.

But the people of Nagasaki are doomed to understand. Three days later, a plutonium bomb hits the city, and Japan surrenders. Joan hears the news at the laboratory with everyone else and feels the stab of responsibility once more in her stomach. She remembers her mother's stories of how the last war ended, a sudden weary silence cutting into the deadlock, the toll of church bells echoing across the battlefield. A terrible war, momentarily redeemed by the civil nature of its ending. Not this indiscriminate rain of ruin. Where is the birdsong this time? Where are the poppies? Where are the people who once lived their small lives in those ill-fated cities? And where next?

Wherever America decides.

All around her, people are talking loudly and laughing. Bottles of champagne and beer are brought up from the cellar where they have been sitting out the war. A conga line forms with Karen at the front, leading the jiggling procession along the main corridor to Max's office and back again. Arthur produces a bin lid and a guitar which suffice to create enough noise to make this terrible occasion feel like a celebration. Which it is, in a sense. The war is over. She should at least try to be pleased. She forces a smile, taking a glass of champagne from Karen and drinking it all in one go. It is sickly sweet.

She feels a hand on her shoulder and she turns sharply. It is Max.

'Dance with me?' he asks, shouting to be heard above the racket and attempting to spin her towards him. His eyes are sparkling.

Joan shakes her head.

'Please. Just one dance.'

She cannot do it. If she really tries, she can just about move along with the others, slipping her hands around Karen's waist and kicking her legs out to the side in time to the music, drinking more champagne when it is forced upon her and talking about how wonderful it is that the war has ended. She can force her mouth to smile and she can push down the giddy, sickening sensation that comes from knowing that they have just been party to a terrible, evil act. But she cannot dance with Max.

He must have known from the start, she thinks.

243

He must have known what they were going to do.

When the drinks run out, they go outside to continue the celebrations. The streets are already teeming with people, everybody singing and whistling. Why does nobody else seem to feel the way she does? Is it that they are not thinking about it? Or just that they don't care?

She realises that nobody will notice if she drops back now, fades away into the crowd and slips off to her lodgings where she will be able to sit upstairs in her room, alone with the knowledge of her own contribution, and nobody will even think to wonder where she is; they will assume that she has found some friends and gone off with them to celebrate. Nobody will miss her, except Max. She knows he will look for her when she has gone, but right now she wants to be alone.

But when she gets home, she finds a telegram waiting for her instructing her to go to her parents' house immediately.

*   *   *

Her father is asleep when she arrives, his pyjama jacket unbuttoned to reveal a creamy white chest, starkly delineated below the ruddy collar line on his neck. The heart attack was not without warning, but the frailty of her father's body, the greyness of his flesh, comes to her as a shock. He looks deflated, as if he has been holding his breath for years and has finally decided to let it all out.

She tiptoes out of the bedroom and goes downstairs to find her mother in the kitchen where she is cooking a casserole. The house smells of soft-fried onions and boiled chicken bones. It is the only

244

solution her mother can see to this problem, that her husband must be comforted from the inside out. She whispers to Joan that she blames herself for not seeing it coming. She should have paid more attention to the clues. She should have made him more cups of tea, more casseroles.

'Of course it wasn't your fault,' Joan tries to reassure her, prising the chopping knife from her mother's hands to prevent her from wielding it in despair. 'He's old. He's not been well for a while but he's on the mend now.'

These are the doctor's words, and Joan is repeating them back to her mother, but she also knows that if anyone should be taking responsibility for not looking after her father enough, it should be her, Joan. She has not visited as often as she should, and although she can almost convince herself that she has an excuse because of the long working hours at the laboratory, she also knows that it is exactly that. It is an excuse. She knows that she does not run for the early morning train she would have to catch to get home on Sundays because she chooses not to, preferring to spend her days off with Sonya in Cambridge, going to dances and drinking cocoa and taking long walks to the pubs in Grantchester.

She looks at her mother now, observing the grey hair falling around her eyes. 'He was just upstairs, clattering about,' she is saying again, although Joan has already heard this twice. 'Said he needed to sort out his old stuff in the attic. Clear it out. He had the wireless on, and then suddenly there was this almighty crash. I went up there but I couldn't get him down . . .' She starts to cry, her hands gripping Joan's. 'I had to leave him in the attic and go to call for the doctor and he had this terrible pain . . .' She indicates her chest. 'I've never seen him in such pain, not even when we took off his leg.'

This is the only time Joan can remember that her mother has referred to the removal of her husband's leg without simply including it as an incidental part of the story of how they met. When she was younger, Joan had sometimes wondered if her parents had known each other at all before they married, but now she realises that the amputation of her father's leg was an act too intimate for them to share with other people, even with her and Lally; it was something they kept as a secret between themselves, the terrible moment of immolation, emasculation, which had stuck them together, and which now threatened to come undone with this sudden faltering of her father's heart.

'Where's Lally?' she asks suddenly.

'She's on her way.' Her mother pauses. She wipes her tears with the back of her sleeve and sniffs, straightening her neck, armouring herself. 'You go upstairs and see if he's awake. I'd better get on with these parsnips.'

'Joanie,' her father says as she enters the room, holding out his hand for her to take. It is rough and sausagey, an old man's hand. She does not remember when she last held it. It must have been when she was a child. Crossing roads. Learning to swim in the river behind the school. She has a vague memory of being swung around by those hands, her shoulders popping in and out and her legs flying faster than the rest of her so that her body seemed to become tangled in mid-air.

'How are you feeling?'

'Been better.' His voice is quiet and cracked, but

246

typically he attempts a smile. He has done up the buttons of his pyjama top now, but it is an imperfect attempt. 'Did I hear right?' he asks, lifting his head from the pillow in a conspiratorial manner. 'Have they dropped another bomb on Japan?'

Joan looks at him. She knows that her mother would not want her to indulge her father with this sort of conversation while he is unwell, but she cannot lie to him. He must have heard it on the wireless before his attack and the thought flashes across her mind that perhaps it was brought on by the shock of hearing it. She nods slowly.

He shakes his head. 'And they told us that ours were the unprecedented times,' he says, echoing his wife.

Joan feels the pressure of his hand increase. How she wishes she could tell him, ask his advice, seek his—is this the word?—forgiveness. He has always been so proud of her, his delight in her scientific progress standing in stark contrast to her mother's disapproval and embarrassment. Would he still be proud if he knew what she had been doing? What would he say if he knew what had been keeping her away for such long stretches of time when really she should have been here, helping out, looking after them, getting married and having babies to make her mother happy?

There was a war on, she thinks defensively. She had no choice.

But her father has not finished. He is looking at her with his grey eyes, and he is squeezing her hand now. 'Your times were supposed to be better than ours.'

'Oh, Dad,' she says, placing her free hand on top of their clasped hands. 'Don't be silly. These are

247

your times too.'

He smiles and shakes his head, and she realises as she says it that the words have cost him enough to say, and he has not intended that she will dispute the tense of them. He does not want anything to do with these times. He has done his part, given all he could, and it was not enough. It is for someone else to do that now. To succeed where he has failed.

Joan brings her father's hand up to her lips and kisses it. She does not usually kiss her father, and it is an unexpected, regal gesture that takes both of them by surprise. She sits by his bedside until her mother comes up with three bowls of casserole on a tray, leaving an extra one warming in the oven for Lally, and they sit together and eat, watching as the sky turns from silvery-grey to a deep, impenetrable blue.

*   *   *

He suffers another heart attack a week later, this one much larger than the first. A telegram arrives for Joan at the laboratory, given to her by Max and written by her mother in the throes of grief so that no attempt is made to soften the blow. PLEASE COME, it reads. FATHER DEAD.

The war is over and most people have lost someone—not quite unprecedented, these times—but until this moment she has never known the wash of emptiness that comes from such finality. To know that she will never speak to him again, never hear his voice or know his thoughts or bury her head in his chest as she used to when she was a child. This knowledge provokes in her the odd sensation that she is disintegrating, that her grief is

248

pooling away into a great ocean of shared sadness.

And now what? she thinks. What happens now?

Max is watching her, looking at her in that way he sometimes does. Slowly, he turns around and closes the door so that they are momentarily alone, and then he takes her in his arms and she feels the solid press of his body against hers. It is familiar and strange all at once. So much has changed since they last touched that she is no longer sure she recognises the person she thought he was. 'I'm sorry,' he whispers. 'I'm sorry about everything.'

Everything? Joan thinks. About my father dying, yes; about your wife, maybe. But *everything*?

'I wish I could come with you and look after you.'

'I'll be fine,' she whispers, and although she appreciates that he is trying to be kind, she finds that she cannot look at him. She knows why not, although she will not explain it to him. It is a silly thought—irrational—although she cannot entirely dismiss it and she feels her heart hardening, darkening, even as she rests her head on his shoulder. Because he led the project here, didn't he? He provided the principal contributions from Britain to the American project in terms of the development of plutonium. If not for him, it might never have happened. Her father might never have had that first heart attack in the attic with the radio on. He might have lived another ten years.

Where does responsibility begin, and where does it end?

*   *   *

Sitting on the train to St Albans, she closes her eyes and remembers her father's voice, deep and clear,

249

his way of glancing at her during her mother and sister's odd conversations, smiling and rolling his eyes just a touch. She remembers how he sat on the back step before her university interview, blackening and polishing her shoes until they shone, how he kissed her on the head in delight when he found out she had got a place. She is dreading the eulogy, when she will have to walk to the altar and deliver the address. Her mother will not want to do it, and Lally is too young, so it will be left to Joan. She will have to block out the terrible truth of what she has done and pretend to be the girl he believed her to be. What would he have thought, if he had known? Would he have been proud of her? From each, he once said, according to his ability. Is this what he meant?

The memory of these words makes her heart stagger. She remembers Churchill's promise in parliament, and the terrible reports of the war on the Eastern Front, the pictures rumoured to be from Stalingrad during the siege. She thinks of Leo, standing in front of the washbasins in Montreal University ladies' lavatory and telling her that she is scared of the wrong thing, and for the first time she understands that he is right. The realisation strikes her with such force that she cannot push it aside. The war is over, and yet she knows that there can be no hope of peace in the future if one side alone has a weapon like this.

She recognises now what he meant when he said she was in a unique position to make things fair. To make the world a safer place. To do her duty, as her father once told her she must.

The countryside flickers past the train window. All she has to do is give the information to Sonya.

That's what Leo implied. Sonya would pass it on to whomsoever requires it, and beyond that . . . At this she falters. Beyond this, Joan cannot imagine. It sounds so simple, so easy. She feels a terrible stab of regret to know that, in order to do this, the person she will have to betray is Max. She knows that, to him, the bomb is not just a thing. It is his life's work. There will be no going back once she has done this. He will never again hold her hands and tell her he loves her and wants to talk to her for ever. There will be no lingering 'maybe' left hanging between them, no hope of another perfect kiss like the one on the boat.

But did he not mislead her too? Did he not lie to her, just a little?

She takes a notebook and pen from her bag. She knows that what she is about to do will be breaking her oath under the Official Secrets Act but she will not think about this. Not now. From memory, she notes down the basic process involved in making an atomic bomb. It would be easier to do this at the laboratory where she has access to the figures, but at this stage she wants to give an outline, to see if they are as interested in the information as Leo believes them to be. She gives details of the difficulties in uranium production and adds various suggestions of how these might be solved, specifically by the use of plutonium. She describes the tamper and the casing used to hold the bomb together while the chain reaction gets started, and the materials to be used at the implosion stage, and she sketches a diagram of the finished product, as yet unbuilt, including its projected dimensions.

Carefully, she rips the pages out of her notebook and folds them into her pocket as the train pulls

251

into the station. She does not want to waste any time for fear that indecision will get the better of her. At the station, she fumbles in her bag for change. She walks to the nearest telephone box, slips a coin into the slot and waits for the operator to pick up. Her stomach is giddy. The connection is made, plainly, calmly, and Joan recites Sonya's extension.

'Putting you through.'

There is a brief pause at the other end of the line, and then a click.

'Hi, it's me,' she says. 'I'm in St Albans. I . . . I need to see you.'

'Oh?' Sonya's voice is soft, musical, as though she is smiling. 'Is it urgent?'

Joan pauses. It is not too late. She could still change her mind. 'Yes, it is rather. I have something for you.'

'I wondered if you would,' Sonya says, not asking what it is but receiving the instructions calmly, as if she has been expecting a call like this. 'Right. I'll borrow Jamie's motor. If I leave now, I can be there by late afternoon.'

A deep breath. In and out. Joan tries to make her voice sound light and breezy, pretending to herself that this arrangement is nothing more than two friends meeting for a natter. 'Meet me in the coffee shop by the cathedral at four thirty.'

She replaces the receiver and feels a shiver of cold running through her. She waits for a moment, her hand resting on the receiver. She could stop it all now. She could call Sonya back and tell her not to come because she has changed her mind. But then she remembers her father's leg, the way he used to hop across the room in the morning before he had strapped the wooden support to his bandaged stump, the noise of it on the bedroom floor. She thinks of her mother's boys crying out for morphine in the hospital, corridors and corridors of them, and the terrible mushrooming swirl of heat and ash in the pictures of Hiroshima, and she clasps her hands together across her body in a sort of prayer. Only it is not a prayer. It is an entreaty, a plea, a promise. It is a wash of conviction that rushes over her chest and causes her to inhale deeply, involuntarily, until her lungs are full of air.

After the flood, a covenant.

Wednesday, 11.42 a.m.

Joan slumps back in her chair. She sees Nick's expression of disbelief.

'No, Mum, no. Stop the tape. She doesn't know what she's saying. She's only saying it because she's scared. She thinks it's what you want to hear.' Nick lunges towards the video recorder, reaching for the stop button. Mr Adams blocks him, extending a solid arm to discourage him from touching anything, and for a moment the two men look at each other, locked in a breathless impasse, until Nick lowers his head and steps back. Turning around, he comes to kneel in front of Joan, his hands on her knees. 'Please, Mum. You don't have to say this. You didn't do it. I know you didn't.'

Joan reaches forward to take his hands. How she wishes she could stand up, take her son in her arms and feel the warmth of him spreading through her body like forgiveness, but she does not dare. 'I'm

253

sorry, Nick,' she whispers. 'I'm so sorry.'

'You have to stop talking,' he urges, and he is whispering now, his lips close to Joan's ear. 'They'll send you to prison for something you didn't do. Do you know what it's like in there? You're eighty-five years old. I need to look after you. I *want* to look after you. How can I do that if you're in prison?'

Joan puts her hand on his. 'I can look after myself.'

'No, you can't.'

Joan looks at him, her darling boy of whom she has always been so proud, who has worked so hard and done so well, who is strong and generous and gentle with her, and she knows she does not deserve him. Her heart breaks to see how much he wants to protect her, convinced that she needs him to do this for her, that she could not cope without him. She understands why he thinks this. It is the role she has always played. But she will not allow him to protect her now, not over this. It is her duty to protect him. She shakes her head, slowly, slowly. 'It's too late,' she whispers. 'They already know.'

*   *   *

All the papers produced by the research team are duplicated and numbered serially and stored in Max's heavy-duty metal cabinet. Joan has always done this in the meeting room at the end of the corridor, and now she agrees with Sonya that she can simply make an extra copy of anything that looks important, one to be filed and the other to be handed to Sonya at their monthly meeting, and then Sonya can pass the information on.

'But to whom?' Joan wants to know when Sonya

describes this stage of the process to her.

Sonya raises an eyebrow. 'I'm not going to give you names.'

'I don't want names. I just mean in general.'

'To a contact at the centre in Moscow.'

'The Lubyanka?' Joan's eyes are wide. She has heard of this place before. It is the headquarters of the Soviet foreign intelligence unit and was frequently mentioned in hushed tones during those early university meetings. She used to picture it as a grey, labyrinthine Soviet building until Leo corrected her, explaining that it was actually quite grand, having been originally built for the All-Russia Insurance Company before the Revolution, and then requisitioned by Lenin to house his secret police. She knows it will not be the same now as it was then, its parquet floors unpolished and its pale green walls grubbied by time, but it is still daunting to imagine. When Leo visited Moscow before the war, he described the building works which were in the process of adding an additional floor to the top of the building to house the ever-expanding police service, covering up the baroque features that had made it such a grand building in the first place. He told her there were prison cells in the basement where enemies of the state were imprisoned and interrogated, and that this was where the old Soviet joke originated that the Lubyanka was the tallest building in Russia because you can see Siberia from the basement. Joan tries to imagine her documents arriving there. 'Will you send them by post?'

Sonya laughs. 'Don't be silly. I'll radio it.'

'Is that safe? Can't people listen in?'

'I'll encrypt it first. I learnt how to do that in

255

Switzerland.' She takes a bite of sandwich and her nose wrinkles ever so slightly at the taste of powdered egg. 'Didn't you know? Jamie was my instructor. That's how we met.'

No, Joan did not know this, but she had often wondered what he did as Sonya had only ever described him as being 'in business'. 'So you radio it to a contact. An agent?'

Sonya shrugs. 'An officer, usually. Although it's not always the same person. They come and go.'

Joan frowns, not understanding. 'Come and go where?'

Sonya sighs and shakes her head. 'Moscow is full of traitors. If someone disappears, you don't ask what happened to them. You just accept the new one.'

'What do you mean, "disappears"? Do you mean they get imprisoned in the basement?'

'To start with.'

'And then what?' She remembers Leo's Soviet joke. 'They get sent to Siberia?'

'If they're lucky.'

'And if they're not?'

Sonya smiles. She puts a finger to the side of her temple and her thumb mimes the act of pulling a trigger.

Joan stares at her.

Sonya laughs. 'It's all right, Jo-jo. It's not going to happen to you. They'd have to get you to Moscow first and they're not going to do that. You're just helping out. You can't betray them because you don't know who they are.'

'But you do.'

Sonya shrugs. 'I do.'

'And they know you.'

She nods.

'So how do you know who you can trust and who you can't?'

Sonya looks at her and smiles. 'I trust myself.'

There is a silence while Joan waits for her to expand on this. 'And?'

'And that's it. The most important rule of the lot. Trust no one.'

'What about Leo?'

Sonya waves the question away, as if it is a ridiculous thing to ask. Of course it is. There is no time to dwell further on this because Sonya has moved on to issue general instructions, telling her that she must learn to be on the lookout for people following her. She should travel by taxi whenever she is carrying classified material, and she should double back on her route every time. Never go directly to any meeting point.

'Why?'

'It's the only way to be sure you're not being followed.'

'Sounds like an expensive way to get around.'

'You'll be reimbursed,' Sonya tells her, 'and more.'

'I don't want money. I'd rather just get the bus.'

Sonya ignores this. 'And if you think you're being tailed, cross the road a few times and see if they follow.'

'And what if they do?'

'Well, then you're in trouble.' Sonya's expression is deadpan when she says this, but then she throws her head back and guffaws with laughter. 'I'm pulling your leg, Jo-jo. You won't be. And we'll always meet in large and busy places, just in case. Department stores, stations, Market Square. If you

257

think someone is following you, then go into a shop where it will be difficult for them to follow without being conspicuous. So if it's a man, go into a lingerie store or a ladies' shoe shop. He'll never follow you. Just remember that every move you make must be in some way accountable and then you'll be fine.'

'So I should buy a pair of stockings every time I think I'm being followed?'

Sonya grins. 'Well, a girl can never have too many.' Her hand reaches out for Joan's and she presses it. 'But this is the important bit. If you think someone is following you and you're coming to meet me, then you must hold your handbag by its strap in your left hand and pretend you don't know me. Not over your shoulder. Not in your right hand. In your left. Then I'll know.'

Joan nods, wide-eyed and suddenly fearful of what she has agreed to do. Is it just Sonya being dramatic? Or does she mean it? 'What if *you* think you're being followed?'

Sonya thinks for a moment. 'If I'm being followed, I'll have a headscarf over my hair. If it's around my neck, then you know we're fine.' She pauses. 'Don't worry, though. These are just precautions. As long as we're careful, there's no reason why anyone would ever suspect us. We have the perfect cover, after all.'

'Have we?'

'Of course we have,' Sonya says, casting a demure glance over in Joan's direction. 'Who'd ever suspect us of doing this sort of thing? We're women.'

*   *   *

Joan stays with her mother for a week after the funeral before returning to the laboratory where her first task is to take a pile of Max's papers down to the meeting room for filing. There are more than usual on account of her absence from work and so she tells him that she will be in the meeting room all morning. The sight of his handwriting on the papers makes her feel mildly ill, the swoops and curves of it now being as familiar to her as her own. She turns the top sheet over.

There is a device for making carbon copies, and the only difference now is that she makes two copies instead of one if she considers the document to be of significance. When she is given something short to type that afternoon, she simply types an extra copy at her desk and folds it into one of the novels she keeps in her handbag, so that she can add it to the growing pile of documents which she has collected in an envelope and stored at the back of a metal filing cabinet in the meeting room.

She puts the small Leica camera given to her by Sonya at the bottom of an old tea tin hidden under a thin layer of metal because occasionally there might be designs or documents that would be better photographed. These films can be slipped into the envelope along with the duplicates while the camera should then be returned to the tea tin, which Joan will refill every Monday morning so as to check that her hiding place is safe. The kitchen is her domain now in any case, and the others rarely trouble her in there. Even Karen wouldn't dare to start messing with the stack of tins at the back of the under-sink cupboards in case she ended up being lumbered with the morning tea round as she

259

was before Joan took it over, so Joan knows her hiding place is safe.

She works harder and more diligently than before. She still chats with Karen and the scientists and technicians, although not quite as much as she once did, and takes care to keep the biscuit tin stocked. Her typing is as slow and immaculate as ever, but something is different about her, although nobody can be quite sure what it is. She dyes her hair darker than normal, almost auburn, and even Max comments on it, telling her that she looks like Joan Crawford.

'Do I?'

'Is that who I mean? The pretty one.'

Joan laughs, but she does not blush as she might once have done. Her hand is no longer there to be brushed against, as if by accident, the way it used to be.

She knows that Max has put the change in her down to her father's death, but Karen pooh-poohs this idea to anyone who will listen. She believes Joan has got herself a young man, and although Joan is embarrassed by this sudden universal interest in her private life, it is a useful cover story. She does not deny it outright and so it is assumed to be true. Karen seems to be genuinely delighted for her, having despaired of Joan ever finding a husband during the four years she has been at the laboratory, and this is matched only by her delight in having a fresh piece of gossip to impart when conversation dries up over morning biscuits.

'Who is he then, this bloke who's stolen your heart?' Donald asks at the Friday night drinks after several weeks of speculation.

Joan flushes. 'Donnie!' she says, mock-bashful.

Max is standing with his back to her, but she can see the side of his face in the mirror, a pinch of colour spreading across his cheeks.

'No, go on. I want to hear all about him.'

Joan takes a sip of her port and lemonade. 'There's nothing to tell.'

'Hmm, well, I don't believe that. But I don't mind if you don't want to tell me.'

Joan laughs. 'I promise I'll tell you when the time's right. Just not now. Not yet.'

'Don't want to jinx it. I understand.' He takes her glass from her. 'Another?'

She shrugs. 'All right then.' She watches him disappear through the crowd to the bar, and turns to look in a small mirror on the wall beside her. A strand of hair has come loose from her hairclip, and as she reaches up to fix it, she sees Max watching her.

Nothing happens straight away, or at least nothing anyone could put a finger on with any certainty. A few seconds pass before he steps forward, turns her to face him, and takes the hairclip from her hand. 'I hope this man, whoever he is, deserves you,' he says gently.

Slowly, carefully, he slides the hairclip back into her hair and then tilts his head to check it is in the right place, and Joan feels a fierce, burning sensation rising up through her body. She watches him turn away and walk out of the pub, leaving his half-finished drink on the table next to her, and she feels lost.

But this is how it has to be. She has made her choice.

*   *   *

261

At the end of the month, she takes a train to Ely as arranged between her and Sonya, a brown envelope tucked under her arm. The envelope is sealed and addressed to a name Joan has taken from the phone directory at the laboratory and has committed to memory in case she is asked. The address is an amalgamation of different addresses for plumbers in the Cambridgeshire area. She sits next to the window with her bag clasped on her lap, waiting for a delayed signal to be put right so they can leave the station. She bends down to adjust her shoes and her head is dizzy when she sits up again at the sight of a policeman at the gates. Suddenly she wishes she had taken a taxi as Sonya instructed.

Please, she thinks. Please hurry up and leave. Her hands are gripping her bag and the fabric of its handle is hot and itchy where it touches her skin. She must keep hold of it in her right hand. Everything is fine. Nobody is following her. She checked this on the way to the station, doubling back on herself and popping into the chemist for a packet of cough drops, an accountable errand saved up for today. A convincing errand. She coughs, and clasps the handle of her bag more tightly.

The compartment is half full, busy with commuters wearing light summer jackets and pale-coloured ties, men who glance at her as they always do when she wears this particular shade of blue, hoping to catch her eye in an absent, questioning sort of way. It is not suspicious, just faintly sexual. Normally she would avert her eyes, but today she finds herself glancing back at these men, observing them, wondering if any of them suspect her. Are there any clues which might give her away? Does

262

she look different from how she did before, when she was just another person going to work through the rubble like everyone else, pulling together, partaking in the war effort and wearing mittens over her chilblains?

A whistle blows at the same moment as the door to the compartment is flung open. A lady in a smart burgundy dress pushes her head into the carriage, looks around, and fixes her eyes on Joan. The woman is hot, breathless, holding a suitcase in one hand while pressing her hat onto her head with the other so that her hair is flattened and messy. Joan feels a squeezing sensation in her stomach.

'Is this train going to Ely?' The woman addresses Joan directly.

Joan's instinct is to avert her eyes but she does not. 'Yes.'

'Wonderful.' The lady steps up into the carriage and slams the door behind her just as the train starts to move. She sits next to Joan even though it is a bit of a squeeze and there is more space further along the bench. Her breath comes in heavy gasps, and she takes off her hat to fan herself. 'Just in the nick of time,' she says, nudging Joan.

Joan nods, smiles and looks away, relieved. Nobody seems to have noticed anything unusual. There are no policemen chasing the train, their clipped heels and whistles echoing through the fug of steam, no detectives in high-collared mackintoshes slipping along the glassy corridor. She knows she does not look suspicious. She looks clean and respectable. Not necessarily a church-goer—who is these days?—but her nails are buffed and clean, her hair is neatly pinned up. Sonya is right. She is the sort of person people choose to sit

263

next to in train carriages. Who would ever suspect?

She feels a small tremor of excitement at what she has begun. She knows that there is nobody else who can do what she is doing, nobody else with the same level of access and knowledge.

Apart from Max, of course.

Is she frightened of getting caught? Yes, of course she is. If she stops to think about what she is doing, she is terrified. If she were caught, she would not tell, and she knows what this would mean for her. 'Come on,' they'd say when they came for her. 'What's a nice girl like you doing mixed up in something like this? Someone must have got you into it. We just need a name.' But she would not give them a name, because the only names she has are Leo and Sonya.

And so she does not think about it, most of the time. Because she knows that once a thing has been done, it can never be undone. There is no going back. This is it.

Wednesday, 12.02 p.m.

Evidence collected for the Prosecution in the case of R vs Kierl, December 1946

Between 1943 and 1946, the defendant had a number of meetings with a man he has described but who has not been identified. These meetings took place in a country road just outside Ottawa, Ontario, except for a few occasions when they met in a café opposite the Central Bus Station. The meetings were usually in the afternoon at weekends and the times were arranged to fit in with the trains from Montreal. The man always arrived and left by train.

He stated that this man was in his opinion an alien, although he spoke good English, this being the language in which his espionage transactions were carried out. He has described him as a slim, athletic man in his early thirties.

The material handed to this unknown contact consisted solely of carbon copies of his own papers, typed by himself or in manuscript and he says he passed on no work prepared by others or by himself in collaboration with others.

Although he has been shown a large number of possible photographs, he has been unable to identify any of them as that of the man in question, and without further information it seems improbable that this contact will be identified.

Nick has not spoken since his outburst. His expression is blank, numbed by shock. He starts now, and holds out his hand towards the file. 'May I see?'

Joan watches her son's eyes as he scans the sheet of paper Ms Hart has given to him. She wishes she could have just a moment alone with him. He is impossible to read when he is like this, withdrawn into himself. If she could only speak to him away from the video recorder and these incessant questions, then she might at least have a chance to explain herself. She wills him to look up at her, just a glance, but his eyes are fixed to the sheet of paper.

'You mentioned that you met Kierl in Canada. Did you have any notion then that he was

265

sympathetic to the Russian cause?'

Joan shakes her head. 'I didn't ever really speak to him. He was a quiet sort of chap. Very highly regarded as a scientist though. I remember that.'

Ms Hart nods, pursing her lips in that head-girl manner she occasionally adopts. 'Well yes, and a very adept spy. He stole actual samples of uranium isotopes which were personally transported to Moscow by the ambassador.'

'I remember.'

'Must have scared you a bit. Lifetime imprisonment.'

The words hang in the air between them.

Joan hesitates. She remembers the headlines plastered across the newspaper stands as she cycled into the laboratories that morning. SPY TIPS OFF! SPY TELLS ALL!

She had braked abruptly, dropping her bike against the pavement so that her bag and umbrella fell out of the basket strapped to her handlebars, and a man stopped to help her gather her things and pull the bike out of the road so that it could rest against a bakery window while she bought a newspaper from the stand. She remembers how her fingers fumbled in her purse for change, clumsy and hot, and she recalls recognising Kierl in the photograph under the screaming headlines. According to the newspaper reports, MI5 and the Canadian police had been informed by President Hoover that there was a leak coming from somewhere in one of the atomic research units, and he had asked both the British and the Canadians to please investigate; Kierl had been decided upon by a process of elimination. Then came the details of his arrest, the tap at his bungalow door, the

266

Canadian police officer asking if he might put a few questions to him.

Ah yes, Joan most certainly remembers reading about that.

Kierl was arrested later that night. The following morning he confessed to the crime of sending information to the Soviet Union. A windfall. There were protests at the time that the sentence was too harsh. He hadn't been giving secrets to an enemy, after all. Russia was an ally at the time. Although, by 1946, this position was a little more ambiguous.

Joan looks at Ms Hart. Her head thrums with exhaustion. There is no let-up from the relentless run of questions. She looks at her watch. Forty-seven hours until her name is released to the House of Commons, and until William's cremation. Forty-eight hours until she has to make her statement to the press. She supposes that this is why they are mentioning Kierl now. To prepare her for what will happen to her.

'Yes,' she says eventually, and her voice is thin and uneven. 'It did scare me a little.'

*   *   *

When she arrives at the laboratory, everyone is already there. They are gathered in Max's room, standing, talking, reading aloud snippets from the newspapers. Donald is shouting something about the blasted Ruskis. Karen is positioned at the door, gesticulating to Donald that he needs to pipe down. Joan drops her bag at the cloakroom and goes in. Max is standing behind the desk, his shirt crumpled and his hair standing up in clumps, his eyes ringed by shadows. Their eyes meet across the room and there is, for a brief moment, a hint of the closeness they have lost, ignited by this reminder of their trip to Canada, before he coughs, looks away, and raises his hands in an attempt to get everyone's attention.

'You all know why we're here,' he says. 'You've all read the papers.' He dips his head and rubs his eyes with the heels of his hands. 'I don't know what to say. I feel . . .' He stops.

'Pissed off?' Donald ventures.

Max nods, but he does not smile. 'That'd be putting it mildly.'

Silence hangs in the room. There is the atmosphere of a siege, of being listened to, which means that nobody quite knows what to say. Eventually Karen speaks. 'Did they come here too? Were we under investigation?'

Max looks up. 'I expect so.' He raises his hands again to calm the chatter this response provokes. 'I think we all need to just get on as normal, as much as we possibly can. There's going to be a bit of press attention and I believe the police are on their way here now, but it will pass. It'll be worse at the laboratories in Brum.'

'Everything's worse in Brum,' Karen interjects from the doorway.

'So we just carry on as if nothing has happened?' Donald asks irritably.

'Well, nothing has happened, as such,' Arthur says. 'They still can't make the bomb based on the information he's given them. We haven't even done it yet.'

'No. But what's the point in making it if they're going to have it too? Stalin will blow us all up before we get the chance to stop him.'

'All right, all right, Donnie. That's enough gloom

268

and doom for today,' Karen calls out. 'Joan, come over here and let's do the tea.'

Max smiles gratefully at Karen. 'Fine, meeting closed then. Motto for the day is to be cooperative when the police turn up, show them we've got nothing to hide, and keep buggering on. I think that's all we can do.' He pauses. 'And be extra vigilant, extra careful. I want cupboards locked, no documents left out overnight, no idle talk. All those war mottos still apply to us.'

'Right, boss.'

There is a palpable release of tension as everybody turns to leave and resume business as normal.

Oh, what an effort it is for Joan to move slowly, to give the impression that she is as stunned as the rest of them (which she is, in a way), and that she has no reason to rush. But it is hard to stop herself from moving fast. She feels giddy and out of control, as if she is careering downhill and the grass is slippery underfoot, too steep to stop. It is almost a reflex, this urge to put her hands out to protect herself. There are so many things she needs to do. Get to the meeting room. Find that brown envelope that she has already addressed to the fictitious plumber and then left, stupidly, carelessly, on the sideboard under a tray, stuffed full of duplicated documents. And then there is the camera, tucked away in the tea tin, just as it always is. Yes, she knows they are unlikely to look in there, but if they did it would be quite a find: a small camera containing a roll of film with close-up snaps of the reactor design.

'Joan, would you mind staying here for a minute?'

269

Her heart stops in her chest. 'I . . . erm . . . have some things to sort out.'

'This won't take a minute.'

She has no choice. She stops, letting the others file past her while her thoughts flit between the envelope of documents and the camera. How can she have got so careless? So reckless? Did she think she was invincible? She waits for everyone else to leave and then closes the door and goes to sit in the chair opposite Max. He is sitting at the desk, idly doodling on a file with his fountain pen.

'So, our friend Kierl was more of a slot-machine than we thought,' he begins, glancing up and giving Joan a rueful half smile before continuing with his doodle. 'That's quite a windfall.'

Up close, his skin is as oyster-shell pale as she remembers. The memory brushes uneasily against her thoughts of the envelope and camera. 'What did you want to ask me?'

He looks up, his mind evidently distracted, because a few seconds pass before he is able to speak. 'I've been asked to submit a report of our thoughts on Kierl in Canada. Any conversations we had with him, any comments he made, any allusions as to his contacts.' He pauses. 'I've done an initial draft which I'd like you to read over.' He pushes a piece of paper across the table to her. 'It doesn't really say anything they don't already know, but just add anything you can think of.'

Joan nods. 'Right.'

'It needs to be finalised as soon as possible so before midday would be ideal. Just think about anything he might have said. I'm not expecting anything dramatic.'

'I hardly spoke to him.'

270

'I know.' Max pauses. His eyes are fixed on the doodle in front of him and he doesn't raise them to meet hers when he speaks. 'There's something else as well.'

Joan takes a shallow breath. 'Yes?'

'I've been given a list of potential suspects identified in Canada who might have been Kierl's contact.' He taps the table with his pen. 'One of the names on it, Leo Galich, was associated with you when you started here. I'm afraid I have to ask: did you see him when we were in Canada?'

Joan's heart freezes in her chest, starting again with an almost painful thump. Does he already know? Is that why he's asking? Could he have spotted Leo following her into the ladies' lavatory? No, she thinks, Max wouldn't have recognised Leo then. Even if he has seen a photograph now, it wouldn't make any difference. Slowly, she shakes her head.

Max is watching her carefully. 'He was the one though, wasn't he?'

Her tongue feels as if it has become swollen with air, a great ball of puffed-out flesh. 'The one what?'

'The one you mentioned on the boat. The one who didn't ask.'

It takes Joan a few seconds to figure out this reference, and when she does the realisation is devastating and sweet all at once. She nods. 'Yes, but it was a long time ago. I'm surprised you remember that.'

Max takes a shallow breath. 'I still think he's an idiot, by the way.'

There is a pause as their eyes meet, and for that moment she wishes with all her heart that she had never got into this in the first place because she is suddenly so unbearably tired and scared that she fears she might weep.

Max seems to see this in her face as his expression registers mild alarm. 'I haven't mentioned Leo Galich in our report,' he says quickly, 'and it doesn't sound like there's any need to. Would you agree?'

Joan nods, grateful that he cannot read her quite as well as she once thought, or that he trusts her enough not to try. 'Thank you,' she whispers. She stands up, feeling the soft burn of Max's eyes still upon her. 'I'll have the report back to you before lunch.'

She hurries from his office to the kitchen and shuts the door behind her. Her heart is pounding. She is not cut out for this. She leans back against the door as she lifts the false bottom of the tin and extracts the camera, slipping it from the palm of her hand into the depths of her handbag. She knows it is not safe there, or not safe enough. She will have time to come up with a better plan later, although she does not know what.

The door handle turns behind her and Joan jumps away from the door.

A voice calls out to her: 'Would you like some help with the tea?'

She jumps and spins around. It is Karen. Of course it is Karen. Who else would it be?

'I'm fine.' Her expression is glassy. She is holding the tin and the kettle is not yet on, and she sees Karen's eyes flick from the tin to the counter. 'Just refilling the tin.' She looks away, and then up again, suddenly aware of the perilousness of her position, of the need to act normal. 'It's rather unsettling, isn't it?'

272

Karen nods. She edges in conspiratorially. 'I don't know if it's all the stress of this, but I'm having terrible cramps today.'

Joan smiles sympathetically, and as she does, she sees that this is it. This is her chance. It's her cover. Sonya was right. She fills the kettle with water and then turns to Karen. 'I'm really sorry to ask,' she begins tentatively, 'but do you have any spare sanitary towels? I've been caught short . . .'

'Of course. I'll leave a box in the lavatory for you.'

*   *   *

The police arrive just before noon. They enter the laboratory quietly, dressed in plain clothes and without any fuss. Joan is in the meeting room with the door closed when she hears unknown voices in the corridor. She does not look up. There is no time. She must finish what she has begun.

She has a system. It is an imperfect system but she can think of no better way of hiding the extra duplicates, seeing as they cannot be destroyed. Not here. Not today. She files them instead with their counterparts, having decided that it would be enough of a defence to claim she had copied a batch of documents twice by mistake the previous day. It is not something she has done before, but nor is it an implausible mistake. To the untrained eye, most of the documents produced by each scientist are very similar to all the others already produced. If spotted, this duplication would no doubt be put down to a lapse in concentration, or even to a presumption of Joan's lack of knowledge. And surely that is not a bad thing.

273

She is moving fast. Her fingers are deft and precise, and the small hairs on the back of her neck are standing up straight. Her handbag is propped up against the table leg, half obscured but still visible. She hears footsteps in the corridor outside the room. They stop, turn around, retrace their steps. Quickly, she slips the papers into their respective files until the envelope on the sideboard is completely empty.

The footsteps come closer again, and this time they do not stop. The door handle turns. 'Sorry to interrupt, miss, but the professor said you were in here.' A policeman is standing in the doorway. 'I need to take some of these files.'

Joan stands aside and gestures for him to take whatever he wishes.

He steps forward and starts to read the labels on each file. He nods and gestures to another policeman to come and collect the ones he has selected, which he does, filling his arms with them and causing him to lean backwards as he walks to counterbalance their weight. He stops when he sees the envelope and puts the files on a table. He picks up the envelope, shakes it, and then peers inside before putting it back down, picking up the files again, and walking out.

When he has gone, the first man turns back to Joan. 'Is that your bag?'

Joan glances down to the bag at her feet. She nods.

'Mind if I take a look?'

'Of course not.' She picks it up and hands it to him. Dampness spreads across her back. He takes her purse and opens it, checking through the scruffy roll of receipts in the rear compartment. He shakes

274

out a neck scarf, a novel, an umbrella, a lipstick. He picks each item up in turn and inspects it, turning it over and running his fingers along any seams capable of concealing anything.

'Apologies, miss,' he says. 'Routine, I'm afraid.'

He opens the bag wider. It is almost empty, except for one item which seems to be wedged against the bottom of the lining. He lifts the bag up and turns it upside down, and then he shakes it until the tiny Leica camera falls out.

Only it is no longer camera-shaped. It is a camera in disguise. It is a camera broken by a stiletto heel in the ladies' bathroom, ground into small pieces, and then hidden inside ten sanitary towels, each one slit open, packed, and then folded neatly, symmetrically, back into its original packaging. The man picks up the box and inspects it, not immediately realising what it is. He frowns as he reads the packaging and then reddens as he realises what it is, apologises, and puts it back in the bag.

*   *   *

That was too close. It was reckless, stupid. She is cycling fast, her cheeks hot and her whole body shaking at the thought of how near they came. She feels as if she has just been pulled back from falling under a train, two hands on her shoulders, yanking her back. She passes the station and carries on along identical roads with their small terraced houses, war-worn and flaky with flowers curling on the windowsills, until she reaches her road and turns in with relief.

There are cars parked on her street which she

doesn't recognise, but then again, why would she? She hardly ever looks. It is only when Sonya reminds her that this is one of the precautions she ought to be taking that it even crosses her mind to look out for them. What should she be looking for in any case? A man in a mackintosh smoking a cigar and looking suspicious?

Just for anything unusual, Sonya tells her. You have to know what is usual in order to spot if something is unusual.

True, but she has not done this. Today she passes eight cars before reaching the red-bricked mansion block of flats at the end of the street, and she concludes that she does not know if she has seen any of them before. Once again she resolves to begin making a proper record of the number plates. Sonya gave her a small ledger for this purpose when she first moved into her new flat, but she has still not quite got around to starting it. She has lived here for over a year now, having moved out of the rooming house on Sonya's insistence not long after she made her decision. In fact, Sonya had even found this new flat for her, telephoning her at work to announce that it was perfectly located with lovely light rooms, high ceilings and a cosy kitchen, and Joan had allowed her to go ahead and secure it on her behalf. True, Sonya did not mention the damp or the lack of central heating or the fact that there was no hot water in the bathroom, but these things were minor gripes really, and Joan did not like to appear ungrateful by mentioning them.

She props her bike against the front fence of the mansion block, opens the door and quickly scans the console table in the hallway for post. There is a gas bill and a letter from her mother, both of them thrown in amongst a pile of circulars and letters for the other inhabitants of the block. She extracts her own, checks the rest of the post, and then runs up the sixty-four stairs to her flat. There are two locks, a deadlock to be opened by a large bronze key, and then a smaller Chubb lock. She reaches down to the deadlock and takes hold of a single strand of dyed dark hair, one of her own, which she pulls delicately through the lock. It is a trick Sonya taught her, to check that the lock has not been tampered with during her absence. She inserts the key, and the deadlock clicks three times before opening. This is due to a fault in the lock: if it is clicked three times when the door is locked, it also requires three clicks before it will release the catch. It doesn't lock the door any tighter but it is an added precaution to supplement the hair.

The flat is in darkness when she enters, just as she left it. The curtains are drawn in an attempt to put intruders off, although she cannot really imagine anyone climbing a drainpipe up to the fourth floor. Joan takes off her coat and hangs it on the peg. She stands at the wooden dresser in the hallway, leaning her head against the side of the mirror. Her heart is still pounding a little too fast. She reaches out to switch on the light in the hallway, and as it flickers to life she sees a man's arm reflected in the mirror, draped lazily over the side of the sofa behind the living-room door.

Joan's stomach contracts. A scream rises in her throat and sticks, so that the only noise she makes is a silent, terrified exhalation. She turns around slowly, slowly. Her hand reaches for the front door but it is too far. Her feet shuffle silently towards it, and she is torn between an urge to run and a desire to know who on earth is sitting in her darkened front room in such silence. The police? MI5? One of Sonya's people?

In the silence, she hears the sound of someone breathing.

She puts out her hand to steady herself, gripping the coat stand and edging backwards into it. Her hand curls defensively around the wooden pole. The hooks at the top of the pole are gratifyingly sharp. She grasps the door handle, and all of a sudden she realises that whoever this is must have known to look for the hair in her lock, as there is no other way into the flat. Who could Sonya have told about this trick? And why would she tell anyone?

And then a voice: 'Don't be scared, my little comrade. It's only me.'

Wednesday, 3.16 p.m.

Joan allows him to stay out of courtesy, because by the time they finish talking and have had something to eat it is late and he has missed the last train back to London. A bed of cushions and blankets is made up for him in the living room, and as she climbs onto a chair to retrieve a spare blanket from the top shelf of her wardrobe, she is disconcerted to discover that his presence is actually comforting to her. It has been a relief to be able to talk openly for a whole evening, not constantly having to hide and dissemble her true feelings, not being obliged to explain anything. Of course, she knows he won't have changed. People don't. He has hurt her so much in the past that she cannot believe she could

278

ever countenance such thoughts again, but she also knows that she is stronger now than she once was. She knows how it should feel to be loved.

She takes the blanket down and steps off the chair. She will not think about this now. It has been a tiring day. A frightening day.

Leo keeps the door of the living room closed while she makes up her hot-water bottle and uses the bathroom. Even when she stands in her nightie and knocks on his door to wish him goodnight, remembering to warn him that there is no hot water in the bathroom so to please help himself to the kettle on the stove, she tells herself that she is relieved he hasn't tried anything. Her hand lingers by the door handle as she thinks this, until she comes to her senses and spins away into her room and proceeds to plait her hair with ferocious care. She jumps into bed and turns her back to the door, to him. It is not that she wants something to happen. She is adamant about this. She is only having these thoughts because he is here now, in her flat, behind a thin panel of wood with damp set into its upper reaches, and her heart will not be still.

She sleeps fitfully, her dreams full of policemen and bursting brown envelopes. It is dawn when finally he comes to her room, pushing the door ajar and standing half-dressed in the dark blue light. He does not make a sound, but she senses his presence and stirs. Her eyelids flicker and for a moment they are back, back at the same old impasse, and she knows what she should do. She should tell him to go away, and then turn around and go back to sleep. She opens her mouth to say exactly this, but then she closes it again because she also knows that there is nothing she would like more than to feel the warmth of another body next to her, protecting her. It is such a lonely thing, having a secret like hers. She wants to be held by someone who can reassure her that she is doing the right thing. That she is safe. And who else could she talk to so openly?

Well, maybe Sonya. But at this precise moment, Sonya will not do.

In the darkness, Leo tilts his head.

And, so slowly that the movement seems almost geological, Joan lifts a corner of her blanket and draws it back.

*   *   *

She catches him watching her as she gets dressed that morning, buttoning up her soft cotton blouse which makes her breasts seem larger than they are—he tells her this too—and shaking out her towel so that it opens before her like a flower before tying up her wet hair in an elaborate turban. He watches her as she lays out the butter for his toast, wafting her hand under the grill to check it is hot enough before filling the kettle with water and putting it on the hob. She picks up the toast by its hot crust, pinching it and throwing it onto the plate next to her.

'Ow!' she says without turning around. 'Do you want jam?'

'Just butter.'

Of course, she thinks. How could she have forgotten?

'Go on then,' she says eventually, placing his toast and tea on the table in front of him.

'Go on what?'

Joan gestures around her. 'This,' she says. 'You coming here. What did you really want?'

He pauses. 'I wanted to see how you were. I was worried about you.'

'Did Sonya send you?'

He frowns. Small golden leaves flutter past the window. 'She doesn't know I'm here yet.'

Joan is uncertain whether to believe him. She wants to know where she stands. 'But she must have told you about my precautions. The hair in the door.'

Leo shrugs. 'I knew what I was looking for.' He glances at Joan. 'Who do you think told Sonya about those tricks in the first place?'

Joan squints at him. 'Could have been Jamie.' She stands up and kisses him on the top of his head while he eats. 'You don't need to worry. I know what I'm doing.'

'So did Kierl. I wanted to warn you about him.'

'Bit late.'

'I know.'

Joan looks at him. 'Did you know Kierl then? Did you warn him?'

Leo closes his eyes and rubs his head. He nods. 'I knew him.'

'Did you . . .?' She is going to say 'recruit' but the word is wrong. It is too formal, in her opinion. It does not describe the process.

'I met him in Montreal at the university.' He takes a sip of tea. 'He fell more easily than you did. Pro-Soviet sympathies, ex-Party member, anger at the exclusion of Russia from the project during the war. He was a sure thing. That's how I knew you were coming to Canada.'

281

'And where we were having our meeting at the university.' Joan pauses. 'They're onto you, you know. You're on a list. Max—Professor Davis, that is—told me.'

Leo nods. 'I know.'

'And? Aren't you scared?'

He laughs. 'They don't have unlimited resources to follow everyone they've ever had slight suspicions about. I'll be fine. And besides, I was working for the government during the war. I'm in the establishment now. It would make them look pretty slack if they hadn't spotted me before so they're hardly going to make much effort to investigate me now. I've just got to keep my nose clean.' He grins. 'Is that the right expression?'

Joan nods but she does not smile.

'Oh Jo-jo, don't frown like that. I've been doing this a lot longer than you have. I came here because I wanted to warn *you*.' He takes hold of her hands and holds them in both of his. 'You need to be careful.'

'I *am* careful,' Joan says with a hint of indignation in her voice, trying to conceal her pleasure at his concern for her.

'More careful then.' He squeezes her hands. 'You're the best they've got now. You're more important than you realise. Your safety is their top priority.'

Joan flinches. 'Don't be silly.' She slips her hands out of his and turns away. She does not like to hear this sort of thing. It does not fit with what she tells herself, that what she is doing is not really that significant. It is how she justifies it, being careful always to make sure that none of the intelligence she passes on is information that she actually seeks out. It is information that is given to her, one way or another; it passes into her knowledge, and then it drops out again. She shares it rather than steals it, which is an important distinction to her. True, her position means that she knows practically everything that goes on at the plant, but once it is *her* knowledge, in *her* head, then it's not technically stealing, is it? She does not want to be considered special or important to any of them. Except, she thinks in a tiny corner of her head, Leo.

'Okay, okay. *I* want you to be careful,' he says.

'I'm always careful. You can ask Sonya. We've had fire drills. We take precautions so that we're safe . . .'

'That's what I mean. Feeling safe is dangerous. Routine is dangerous.' He picks up his mug of tea and takes a sip. 'I'm only saying it because I worry about you. I know how it feels to have a secret.'

Of course he does. Joan knows this. She has tried to imagine how it must have felt for him when he left Germany, leaving his father and Sonya perhaps for good, knowing that he was unlikely to return. Did he hesitate? Joan wonders. Or did he just walk forwards, knowing that there was nothing to gain from looking back? She knows he would dismiss such thoughts as overly sentimental but there is something so grand about this moment, so pitiful, that she cannot help but be drawn to it. She wonders if, put in the same position, she would have had that same capacity for stoicism, for bravery in the face of exile. She cannot imagine it.

But she also knows that this was the moment which yoked him irrevocably to Sonya, forging the bond of which Sonya is so protective, brought into being by that step across the border. She knows he is proud of the fact that he kept his promise to his father, sending for Sonya three years later once he had found a boarding school for her to attend in Surrey and a sympathetic Quaker family to take her in during the holidays. He has told Joan how he arranged to meet Sonya at the docks in Dover, dutifully appearing at the landing stage and searching the crowd for the sorrowful little girl who had arrived at their apartment eight years previously following the sudden death of her mother; a little girl who could not eat without being coaxed and for whom he gave up his bed and slept on a mattress in the living room so that she could sleep in the room overlooking a streetlamp because she was afraid of the dark. And that he did not realise how long he had been away until he saw Sonya step off the boat.

She would have been sixteen then, but Joan can see how he would have imagined her unchanged. She would have given that slight, half-shy wave— the same movement she gives now when she sees someone she knows in the distance—and that he would have held out his arms to embrace his cousin, but the hug which followed would have been awkward and strange because she was no longer the little girl he remembered but a willowy young woman with dark, moist eyes and bright red lips.

It is almost as if he is thinking the same thing, because quite suddenly he looks at Joan and says: 'You mustn't tell Sonya you've seen me. I'll mention it to her when the time's right.'

'Just like the old days, then?'

'Yes.'

Joan turns away from him, irritated by this. Why does she allow him to do this? To stroll back into

284

her life and take up again as if he had never left, as if they had not spent the last four years—is it really that long?—at loggerheads, albeit from a distance. It is a static sort of attraction, hers and Leo's, like cat's fur against a coarse carpet, irritating and repellent but also sparking and sticking.

He looks at her and his eyes are unblinking, so utterly unknowable and yet so vulnerable all at once. She knows he will never look at her as Max did on the boat, and as he still does when he thinks she is not looking. She knows they will never wake up in each other's arms and burst out laughing for no reason at all. But things with Max can never now be put back, and he is not free to love her in any case, so when Leo bends down to kiss her softly on the neck, for a moment she wonders if she could be happy enough with him. She has loved him before. She could love him again, and perhaps things might even be different between them this time after all that has happened.

Leo walks over to the window, and then comes back to where Joan is standing and slips his arms around her waist. His chin rests on her shoulder. 'It's for your own good,' he says. 'Sonya thinks life is a game. She always has.'

'She's not stupid, Leo,' Joan says, teasing, smiling, feeling the warmth of his body against her own. She lifts her face to look at him but he is distracted, his eyes fixed on something outside the window.

'No,' he says eventually, 'she most certainly is not stupid, but she still doesn't seem to realise that there is a difference.'

'What do you mean?'

He lets his arms drop from where they have been

encircling her and he takes a step away, backwards, not quite looking at her again. 'Games have rules.'

Wednesday, 5.40 p.m.

At about 1.20 p.m. on 5 January 1947, Detective Peter Wood of the local constabulary and I went to The Warren, Firdene, Norfolk.

As we entered the house—a squareish stone farmhouse abutting directly onto the road with double gates at the side, giving on to a large farmyard with barn outhouses—we noticed Mr Jamie WILCOX sitting in the lounge reading a newspaper. The door was answered by Mrs Sonya WILCOX who is a somewhat impressive type with curled dark hair, probably dyed, and of rather neat appearance. She acknowledged her identity and we were shown into the lounge, her husband attempting to bow his way out but being prevented from doing so by Detective Wood.

We introduced ourselves, and she immediately asked if our interests lay more with her husband, pushing him forwards. Mr WILCOX looks uncomfortably young even for his thirty-three years, but he was completely overshadowed by his wife who quite dominates the household.

I told them that we possessed information which made it necessary for us to interrogate Mrs WILCOX in connection with her past activities and family connections, and she immediately asked to see our warrant cards so as to be satisfied as to our bona fides. Once this was established, I went straight into the attack and told Mrs WILCOX that we had a vast amount of information in our possession and we required her cooperation to help us clear up ambiguities and to resolve the position surrounding her at the present time.

She made it quite clear from the start of our interview that she did not 'think she could co-operate'. It is fair to say right away that by the stand she took up she tacitly admitted that she had, at one time, worked for Soviet Intelligence. The manner in which she did so was credit to the training she must have received, for every possible piece of cajolery, artifice and guile that could be employed was employed, albeit without any success. She made no denial whatsoever, sheltering always behind the rock of 'non-cooperation'.

It was concluded that Mr WILCOX might turn out to be the weaker vessel, and after a period of interviewing them both together, we released Mrs WILCOX. We broke into Mr WILCOX's taciturnity, but in spite of every possible inducement we did no more than elicit from him that he met Mrs WILCOX in Switzerland in 1940 quite by chance, having previously been introduced through a mutual friend in England, 'bumping into her as one bumps quite readily into people in Marks and Spencer at home.' He had gone to Switzerland as he did not like the state of affairs in England at that time. The more intricate details of their courtship and of their marriage he did not feel at liberty to discuss. When asked if they had any children, he answered, 'No, not really.' When pressed to clarify this response, he said, 'Mrs Wilcox and I have not had any children together.'

After a longish interval Mrs WILCOX returned, still in a non-cooperative frame of mind. It was urged upon her that her refusal to talk might well be a positive disadvantage to some of her connections. They might be, it was said, under some suspicion which could be removed if she were frank. By inference, it was implied that these suspicions might be directed against those near and dear to her—specifically Leo GALICH, her cousin and a pro-Soviet economist who has recently taken up a fellowship post at King's College London—but she preserved a Slav-like indifference to this line of argument.

Towards the end of this second stage of the interrogation, Mrs WILCOX seemed to be psychologically at her lowest ebb. It was pointed out at this stage that there was the clearest possible evidence that the loyalty she felt towards the government of her native country would not be reciprocated should she ever require their help, but in response she merely indicated that her loyalties were to ideals rather than to people.

In conclusion, we got little positive information. She is quite clearly fanatically anti-Fascist and agreed to some extent that she was disappointed with Russian policy in 1939/40, commenting that many people lose their faith in governments but retain their political beliefs, but she would not be drawn on giving anything further away. As a result of this interrogation, we regard ourselves as confirmed in our beliefs even if we are still lacking an explicit confession.

'So they were on to Sonya already,' Nick says.

'Leo too,' Mr Adams adds. 'MI5's file on Leo is quite extensive.'

Joan's eyes flick up, suddenly alert. It has been

an exhausting day. She turns to Mr Adams. 'Can I see it?'

He shakes his head. 'It's classified. You will undoubtedly be entitled to see some of it when this goes to trial, but I can't let you have the file.'

Joan is tempted to ask why not, but she also realises it is pointless to argue with him. He doesn't give the impression of a man open to entreaties. And in any case, she does not need to see the file. None of this is news to her. She was aware of Sonya's interrogation at the time, although it is strange to see it described in such a detached manner.

It was Leo who told her about it. She remembers that he was living in London by then, having secured a teaching fellowship at King's College which enabled him to continue his research on Soviet Planning Policy while also supervising PhD students with similar inclinations to his own. Talent-spotting, he called it. In addition to his university digs, Joan had given him a key to her flat so that he could come and go as he pleased, and he had fallen into the habit of turning up without warning whenever he could get away from his academic duties to spend time with her.

He had come to Cambridge on the evening of MI5's visit to Sonya, having been wired the news by Jamie, and Joan had felt the prickle of sweat on his palms as he gripped her hands in his and told her once again that she was not, under any circumstances, to mention his name to anyone; not to Sonya, not to her mother, not to anyone at all. Their relationship with each other must be untraceable, for Joan's sake.

'I know. We've been through this dozens of

times. I haven't mentioned you to a single person.' She had had to resist the temptation to blurt out how hard it was for her to keep him a secret on top of everything else, but she had known it wouldn't help. Besides, things seemed bad enough just then without her adding to them. 'Anyway, you said you were going to tell Sonya about us.'

Leo flinched. 'I tried.'

'And?'

'She said we shouldn't see each other. She said it would compromise you too much as a source.' He paused. 'And perhaps she's right.'

'No, Leo.' Joan shook her head, her lip suddenly trembling at the thought of not seeing him. At least when she was with him she could relax without worrying about giving herself away. 'Please. I couldn't bear it. I'm so tired. I didn't know it was possible to be this tired. I couldn't carry on without you.'

'Yes, you could, Jo-jo. If you had to.'

'No,' she whispered. 'Please don't go.'

He had stepped forward then and gathered her in his arms. She remembers that his grasp was tight, a little too tight. 'Don't worry. We'll carry on like this. We don't need to tell her for now as long as we're careful. You just have to be aware that people are watching.'

'Watching who?'

She felt Leo's pulse quicken. 'Me.'

'You? They're watching you too? But you said—'

'I know, I know. I didn't think they would.' He shifted his position slightly, loosening his grip on her. 'But they asked Sonya about me. They can't have found anything on me yet though otherwise ... well, otherwise they'd have arrested me. We just have to wait for this Kierl business to blow over. We have to be patient.'

'But what if they followed you here?'

'They didn't.'

'How can you be sure?'

'I checked.'

'But—'

'Jo-jo, listen to me. You can trust me. We're in this together.'

Joan pressed her face into his chest so that her voice was muffled when she spoke. 'And will you still see Sonya?'

'Of course. Our relationship is already known so there's no point in hiding it.'

And what could she say to that? It was true. Their relationship was established and familial. Invincible, Joan thought, and then chastised herself for her own lack of generosity.

She remembers the weight of Leo's arms around her, the pleading sound of her own whispered entreaty. 'Hold me.' How blind she had been then. How blind both of them had been. Scared of the wrong thing entirely.

*   *   *

Joan realises that Mr Adams is addressing her. He is looking at her with an expectant expression. They are all looking at her. Her head feels hot. 'Are we finished for the day?' she asks.

'We're just taking a break.' Mr Adams reaches out and switches off the video recorder. 'We'll resume in thirty minutes.'

'But it's late,' Joan protests. Her throat is dry. 'I'm tired.'

Ms Hart leans forward and puts a sympathetic hand onto the arm of her chair. 'I'm afraid we can't stop yet.' She glances at Mr Adams. 'We have a lot to get through before Friday.'

Mr Adams stands up. 'Exactly. I'm going out for a kebab. Can I get anyone anything?'

Nick shakes his head, ready to decline the offer, but then shrugs. 'All right, yes please.' He pauses, too distracted to think properly. 'I'll have whatever you're having.'

'Anyone else?'

Ms Hart shakes her head. She brought a homemade salad with her that morning, and she goes to eat it in the kitchen, leaving Joan in her armchair and Nick at the window, staring out at the cold, dusky street. The living-room door is open, and although Joan knows that Ms Hart could listen to their conversation if she wanted to, it seems that she is not paying much attention. And why should she? They've got her confession now, and she can't go anywhere with her electronic tag on. All Joan wants is to talk to Nick, to get him to understand. This might be her only chance, but she knows from the shape of his back that he is not feeling sad. He is cross.

Joan looks down at her feet. 'I'm so sorry, Nick.'

A silence. 'For what? For what you did? Or for getting found out?'

Joan's expression is pained. 'For this,' she says. She makes an expansive gesture with her hand, meaning that she is sorry for the amount of his precious time that she has already taken up, for implicating him in the glare of MI5's contempt, for not having told him any of this before, for the trial which is now bound to proceed, for being a bad

292

mother. 'For everything.'

Nick shakes his head. 'Sorry doesn't really cut the mustard here, I'm afraid.'

Joan opens her mouth and then closes it again. She knows this voice. It is his work voice; his my-learned-friend-is-sorely-mistaken voice. It has not been directed at her for years, but now it reminds her of a period during his teenage years when he started calling her by her first name, refusing to call her 'mum' because he wasn't a phoney and Joan wasn't his real mother. He conceded that they could pretend he was her nephew, if Joan preferred, but he wasn't going to live a lie. That was the first time Joan had heard that particular quality in her son's voice. If it hadn't been so painful, Joan might have found this teenage pretension amusing in its dramatic sincerity, but there was nothing funny about it back then. The phase had lasted nearly six months, and she still remembers the stab of those words, the terrible, metallic sting of them, and the way she had tried not to show how much they hurt, not wanting him to feel any sense of responsibility for her feelings. Her husband had wanted to reprimand Nick for being petulant, as he called it, but she had told him he mustn't. Nick would soon grow tired of being angry, and in any case, she knew this was what it meant to be a mother. It is my privilege to care this much, she had told herself back then, sitting on her own in their house in the suburbs of Sydney, the porch door still swinging after Nick's departure. It is my privilege to love him this much.

There is a pause. 'Nick.' Joan hesitates. 'There's something I want to ask you.'

'What?'

293

'Could you . . . I mean, would you speak for me? When this goes to court.'

Silence.

'I'll plead guilty. I'm not asking you to lie for me.'

Nick snorts. 'Of course I can't lie for you. I'd get struck off and we'd both be in jail.' He pauses. 'I suppose your only chance would be to show that there were mitigating circumstances but—'

'Exactly,' Joan interrupts. 'I need someone who understands.'

'What makes you think I understand? I don't. I just don't get it.'

'You would have done, Nick, if you'd been there. You became a barrister because you wanted to fight for justice. It's the same thing.'

His eyes widen. 'No, it's not. I can't believe you would even think—'

'No, I mean that you became a barrister because you cared. You thought you could change things.' A pause. She knows he is listening. 'And so did I. The world was different then. Lots of people thought as I did.'

He raises his hands as if in supplication and then drops them. 'But that's not enough. You can be sympathetic to a cause without giving away your country's biggest secret.'

'But I was in a unique position to change things, to make it fair. I thought it was the right thing to do.'

'Oh, how noble of you.' He shakes his head. 'Don't tell me you haven't even stopped to think about what you actually did? What made you think you had the *right* to do it? That it was up to you to make everything fine and nice and equal. It's not a game of cricket where you can just tell everyone to

294

play nicely.'

Joan feels the tears rising in her throat, choking her, gagging her. 'Nick, please.'

'But that's what I don't understand. What huge, stupendous arrogance made you think that it was up to you? How audacious do you have to be to believe that you can sort out the whole world, and that it has to be done your way?'

'I was only ever trying to do my best.'

'By sending secret information to a murderous dictator?'

Joan shakes her head. 'We didn't know that then.'

'*We*? Who's *we*? The comrades? How can you say that word without blushing? Aren't you ashamed? Haven't you read the news in the last sixty years?'

'Of course I have. I only meant me and Leo and Sonya. All of us. How could we have predicted how it would all turn out? We thought we were doing something good.'

Nick snorts. 'Even now you can't see them for what they were. They were using you.'

'No. Leo loved me. I know he did even if he didn't say it. And Sonya was my dearest, greatest friend.'

'Pfhrrrh,' Nick says.

'So, will you do it for me?'

Silence again.

There are tears now, brimming over and running down Joan's cheeks. 'I'm so scared, Nick. I don't want to go to prison. I don't want to die in prison.'

Nick does not look at her, but Joan knows that he is crying too. He takes a handkerchief from his pocket and presses it into the corners of his eyes, and then he rests his head against the cold windowpane. 'I don't know,' he says, and there is a long pause before he speaks again, selecting his words with such care that when he speaks, Joan feels the precise stab of them. 'I don't know if I can, Joan.'

Wednesday, 6.43 p.m.

Re: Leo GALICH

The detailed movements of the above over the past two days are as follows:

Sunday, 25 May 1947

GALICH left home at 10.55 a.m., bought a single newspaper and went for a walk in Camberwell Green. He then took a bus to Kensington High Street, where he had his shoes cleaned and at 11.55 a.m. he went to the Ballerina for a pot of tea. He reappeared an hour and a half later at 1.30 p.m. to go for a walk in Kensington Gardens and Hyde Park. He met a lady corresponding to the description of his cousin, Sonya WILCOX, at the corner of Cromwell Road and Exhibition Road and proceeded with her to the Serpentine Gallery.

The lady referred to above is described as follows:

Age about twenty-eight; 5'5" in height; auburn hair (seemingly dyed), rather girlish face with red lipstick, wearing a burgundy dress and beret and black high-heeled shoes. She carried a black leather bag and appeared to be pregnant.

At 5.10 p.m., GALICH proceeded by tube to

King's Cross Station accompanied by the aforementioned lady. An argument took place between the two, with the lady crying and the gentleman showing some reluctance to comfort her. Our men were not close enough to hear the nature of this exchange, but the implication was that he believed her to be acting unreasonably and would not concede to her wishes. When finally she was persuaded to board a train to Ely, she kissed him on the lips in what seemed to be a romantic fashion, and although he did not resist, he appeared uncomfortable at the display.

At 6.40 p.m., GALICH appeared alone and walked down Farringdon Road to the Bear Hotel where he dined by himself. Forty minutes later he took a bus to Marble Arch. He went into the foyer of the Odeon there, discovered that the last performance of Caesar and Cleopatra had already begun and was not sold out, bought a ticket, and up to a late hour was observed sitting at the back of the half-empty theatre. After the film had ended, GALICH proceeded by tube to Elephant and Castle and then by bus to Camberwell.

Throughout this day GALICH exercised every caution to discover if he was being followed. When walking, he continually looked over his shoulder, and when he took a bus he waited until late, jumped on, and stood on the platform to see if he could recognise anyone. It seems probable that he did, in fact, spot one of our men.

'Listen carefully. There's a concert at the Royal Albert Hall on Saturday afternoon. Your ticket's at the box office. The others will pick up their own so just collect yours and we'll meet in there.'

'The others?'

'Yes.' He pauses. 'I've told her, Jo-jo. I did it.'

Joan smiles a wide, delighted smile. At last! And about time too. She is twenty-eight years old, for goodness' sake. She shouldn't be creeping around with a secret boyfriend.

'She wasn't happy,' he says, 'but I told her she needed to accept it.'

There are so many things Joan wishes she could say. 'Oh,' she says, trying to make her voice light and airy for the bugs Leo has told her will be listening in to their conversation. 'That's wonderful news.'

'It'll be all four of us this time. I've booked your ticket under the name we agreed, so don't forget. Take a train in the morning when it's busy.'

How she would like to talk to him properly, openly, without all these codes and instructions. She is still smiling, and she hopes it is evident from her voice. 'I can't wait to see you,' she whispers.

Leo gives an awkward cough. 'You too,' he says, and then, 'Jo-jo?'

'Yes?'

'Be careful.'

He rings off. Joan replaces the receiver and waits for a moment. She does not like it when he is like this. It unnerves her. She is pleased he has told Sonya but she also knows that she will not sleep tonight. She knows the sensible thing would be not to see him, of course, to wait until they can be sure he is no longer under any suspicion so that she does not compromise herself by being seen with him, but she needs to see him. She needs his reassurance in order to carry on. She must see it through. It is almost there.

She takes the train to London on Saturday as instructed, arriving at midday with the day-trippers and commuters. King's Cross is full of people in a rush, swarming and jostling and generally creating confusion, and she walks down the steps to the Underground with purpose, aware that Leo wants her to be part of this mass of people so that she is less conspicuous.

There are a few people queuing at the box office when she arrives, and she gives her name as Jean Parks as arranged between her and Leo. Once she has collected her ticket, she walks to a milk bar in South Kensington and orders a ham sandwich and a glass of milk for lunch, and then she sits at a table in the corner of the room which affords her a good view of the entrance and the other customers, and she watches them, envying the ease with which they come and go. They are so relaxed, just as she must have been before this began, although she can barely remember it now. How wonderful it would be to feel like that again.

For a moment, she imagines going to a concert like this with Max, instead of with Leo and Sonya. They might agree to meet here first for a bite to eat, and he would arrive on time, smiling and uncomplicated, ready to draw diagrams of spin-washers on paper napkins to make her laugh, and she feels a sudden weariness descend across her shoulders at the thought that this will never now be possible.

But it never was possible, was it? Besides, she is with Leo. Their relationship is no longer a secret. She reasons that just because they don't say the words doesn't mean they don't feel that way about each other. Comparisons are unfair. They don't work, rationally.

She stands up and walks over to the counter to pay. Nobody looks up. Nobody follows. She opens the door and walks out into the spring sunshine, heading back to the Albert Hall and arriving late as arranged. The foyer throngs with people. Men are dressed smartly in hats and suits and the women wear long dresses and high heels. She can see why Leo would choose to meet here, somewhere dark and busy with all these interconnecting corridors and staircases. She shows her ticket to the usher who indicates her allocated seat with his torch, and she has to step across bags and feet in order to get there.

'So sorry,' she whispers. 'Excuse me. I'm so sorry.'

Her seat is in the middle of a row, near the back of the stalls. She takes out her binoculars and places them on her knee. There is a hush as the lights go down and the pit orchestra begins to tune. Where are they? she wonders. How late are they planning on arriving? She settles into her seat, self-conscious at being on her own but trying to give the appearance of being quite at ease. As the conductor lifts his arm to hush the sound of the orchestra tuning, she sees three people making their way towards her row, having entered the auditorium from the opposite door.

Leo, Jamie, Sonya. She recognises the silhouettes of each of them. She smiles, suddenly overcome with pleasure at the prospect of this evening, of simply being together as if there had never been any complications. Perhaps, just for this evening, they can pretend to be normal.

The conductor of the orchestra calls for silence

as the three latecomers reach their seats. Leo sits noiselessly down next to Joan, the familiar scent of him enveloping her. Jamie leans around Leo to give her a small wave and Sonya blows her an exaggerated kiss. And then she unbuttons her coat.

Joan feels her whole body snap to attention. The swell of Sonya's stomach under her coat is hard and round, protruding lightly from Sonya's wiry frame. It is not huge, perhaps six months, but it is unmistakeable. Joan has to put her hand to her mouth to suppress a gasp, and the thought of that terrible room in Cambridge cracks across her mind. She remembers the woman's hair and Sonya's hand gripping her own too tightly as the bright red blood poured out of her. She pushes the memory from her mind. She must not think about it. She must be happy for her friend. She must hold out her hand and congratulate her, and then kiss Jamie's grinning cheek. 'Oh, Sonya,' she whispers, 'how wonderful!' She has not realised until this moment quite how much the memory of it hurts. It pounds in her stomach.

'Shhhh,' the lady in front of them turns around to whisper, 'it's about to start.'

Sonya raises her eyebrows in amusement and they are forced to sink back into their seats in temporary silence, blocked from each other's vision by Leo and Jamie. Never had Joan imagined she could be so grateful to anyone for shushing her in public. She knows that if that moment had been prolonged any further she would have burst into tears, and she does not want to do that. Not to Sonya, her dearest friend. Not in front of Leo.

The conductor introduces the first piece of music, and while he is speaking, Leo reaches across and takes hold of Joan's hand in the dark. They sit like this for the whole of the first piece, both of them perfectly still. Joan closes her eyes, feeling the calm of the music wash over her, building and rising but never breaking and becoming discordant. She feels sick and dizzy. The sound of applause breaks the spell, causing her to blink.

Leo's lips brush her ear. 'How are you, Jo-jo?'

She forces herself to smile up at him. 'Happy to see you.'

He smiles quickly. He leans towards her and for a moment Joan thinks he might be going to reciprocate with some whispered sweetness, but he doesn't. He has something else to tell her. 'I've got some news.'

'Sonya's expecting,' Joan whispers, wanting to get the moment over with. 'I'm not blind.'

Leo frowns. 'Oh that. Didn't you know?'

'Of course not. I haven't seen her for months and you didn't tell me.'

'No, I suppose I didn't. Well anyway, it's not that.' He pauses. 'I've been invited back to Moscow.'

'Moscow? You didn't mention anything on the phone.'

'I only found out today.' He grins. 'Sonya's just told me.'

He is evidently pleased with this news but Joan feels a sudden grip of fear. 'Does the Party want to see you?' she whispers.

Leo nods. 'Of course. They've invited me.'

'But why did they not just invite you directly instead of through Sonya?'

He shrugs this question away. 'It's quicker like this. They want me to deliver my research at a conference in Moscow next week. There'd be no time to send an invitation through the post.' He beams briefly as he speaks, and Joan feels the hairs rise on her arms and neck.

'But if they were . . . upset with you, they wouldn't have told Sonya, would they? They know she'd warn you. They'd just tell her the same story.'

Leo shakes his head. 'She was adamant. They're very interested in the research. They actually said I might get a medal for it.' The conductor is turning to the audience and holding up his hands. 'And you know how that would irritate Sonya. She wouldn't pass on a message like that if she didn't absolutely have to.'

Joan looks away. Silence is requested once more in the hall for the second piece of music. A chorister steps out of his place in the choir stand and walks forward. He is only young, perhaps eleven or twelve years old, and his eyes are wide with fear. An expectant hush falls upon the crowd. He starts to sing unaccompanied, his voice high and pure, and a series of rising, perfectly held notes cut through the silence of the Albert Hall and seem to slide into the cracks of the building like water into a sponge, filling it with a deep, rich warmth.

Joan closes her eyes, her hand still locked in Leo's. She tells herself she is being silly, but she cannot push from her mind the conviction that something here is not right. She feels a sudden cramp, an irrational impulse which makes her want to cling to Leo, to beg him not to go, to make him tell Sonya that he is grateful for the offer but that he is too busy to attend a conference in Moscow.

The boy's voice rises, higher and higher until it reaches a crescendo of tautness, almost faltering, almost breaking, but not quite, holding perfectly to the note until the conductor lifts his baton for silence. There is not a sound within the auditorium.

The boy grins, big-eyed and golden-skinned under the bright stage lights while the applause rises and fills the hall, and in that moment Joan knows there will never be another moment quite like this and if she doesn't say the words now she may never say them. And she needs to say them. She needs to know how they sound. She leans across to Leo and whispers something in his ear. He turns to her, smiles, and kisses her slowly on the lips, and for that brief moment Joan thinks her heart might actually burst.

Wednesday, 7.35 p.m.

Three weeks after the concert, Joan and Sonya are standing outside the newly built Guildhall in Cambridge town centre, Sonya's hands clasping Joan's. Her protruding belly forces them to stand at an awkward distance from one another, so that when Sonya says the words, she cannot quite lean in close enough to hug Joan, so Joan is forced to see the whole of Sonya's face, her eyes flicking down to the ground and then back up again.

'Shot? What do you mean, shot?' Joan cannot take it in. 'With a gun?'

Sonya nods. 'I'm sorry, Jo-jo. He was declared an enemy of the people and they shot him.'

Shot? She pictures Leo's body, cast forward onto a concrete floor, blood spooling onto the floor beside him. A noise comes out of her then, neither

304

a cry nor a sob but a loud, staccato burst of pain. She slaps her hand over her mouth to stop it but it will not be pushed back. Her whole body seems to crumple.

She does not know if she wants to hear the details gathered by Sonya from her contact in Moscow. She does not want the burden of this terrible knowledge. True, she has often lain awake at night since his departure and feared that something might have happened to him, and she had thought it odd that she hadn't heard from him. She has clasped her hands so tightly together in prayer that the skin around her knuckles has broken where her nails pressed into it, but she has not really been able to picture it. Not until now. And she does not know if she can bear the pain of it.

But she hears it anyway. She will not let Sonya go until she has heard every last detail. And later, when she is alone once more, she imagines the whole scene again and again. It plays in her head, reeling through her mind like a news report, mixing the things Sonya told her with her own imaginings. She imagines Leo arriving in Moscow and going downstairs for dinner in the hotel restaurant on his first night, just as Sonya described. She pictures him coming back to his room to discover the door hanging from the hinges. Tape plastered across the entrance; not official tape, but duct tape. Stepping into the room, he would have seen the light smashed above the bed, the wallpaper torn from the walls and his clothes strewn across the wooden-boarded floor. Even the bed would be slashed across the mattress and pillows. He could have stepped back then, Joan thinks. He could have

305

stepped back and made a run for it, but confusion would have overridden the fear he should have felt. He would have assumed there had been a mistake. Even when he saw the two men sitting at the small table by the window, drinking the bottle of red wine he had brought with him from London and dropping cigarette ash onto the table, he still would not have understood.

'Citizen,' one of the men might have said. 'Please gather your things.'

'I'm a Party member, Comrade.' Joan can imagine this response. He would be confused, but he would still be proud, still loyal. 'What on earth—?' he might say, and then stop, suddenly remembering that he would need his notes for the conference. He would pull open the drawer where he had put them. Empty. 'Where are my notes? And my passport? All my papers?'

The men would glance at each other. 'I'm afraid you are no longer entitled to these documents, Citizen.'

'Why do you keep calling me Citizen? I'm a Party member. I have a card. I've been invited to talk—' And only then might he have faltered, his eyes darting from one man to the other as realisation dawned. He would step back. She can imagine the feeling, his body suddenly heavy as if moving through water. He might turn around to run, and even if he did not see the gun, he would have heard the mechanical tilt of it, and then he would have felt the crack of its handle as it was brought down on the back of his head.

She imagines him waking up with a pounding headache in a small concrete room in the basement of the Lubyanka. The cell would be dark except for

306

the small patch of light coming in through the grate in the door. The rancid odour of the cell would make him retch, and he would vomit into the slop bucket. He would still be wearing his suit but his collar would be caked in dried blood. He might feel about him for his wallet and find that his pockets were empty except for the concert ticket. She imagines him taking it out and staring at it for a brief moment—did he think of her then?—before sliding it back into the breast pocket of his jacket where it would be found untouched, days later. He would have stood up and started hammering on the door, calling for water.

But nobody would come. Nothing would happen. The stench of the cell would be overpoweringly stale. He would not know what time of day it was, or how long he had been there. Impossible to tell in a room with no sunlight, no windows, no lights to be turned on or off, intermittent food and nowhere to wash. His mouth would be dry and sore, and it would hurt to swallow.

At last, the door would be unlocked and pulled open, and the light from the corridor would temporarily blind him so that he could see only the silhouette of a guard standing over him with a baton. Leo would sit up, shielding his face from the light with his arm. 'There's been a mistake. If I could just see someone about it and explain—'

But no. That would never have worked. He's in the system now. She imagines the guard's silence as he takes Leo's arm and hauls him roughly out of the cell and along the too-bright corridor. His limbs would ache at the movement, and his lips would sting with dryness. His whole body would be weak and crumpled, and he would be taken to another,

307

similar room, only this time it would have an electric bulb, and he would be shoved inside.

Still no water.

Sonya told her that the interrogation lasted five days. Joan burns to think of the pain they must have inflicted upon him. She has read about the 'special measures' allowed during interrogations. The broken bones, the dislocations, the bright lights and loud noises. The terror.

After three days, another man was brought into the cell, but Sonya says that she doesn't recognise the name. Leo's co-accused, who was shot a few days after Leo.

Shot? she thinks again. Such a clean, abrupt word.

Joan cannot think who this other man might be, but he enters her dreams at night. She sees a face so badly beaten and bruised that Leo does not recognise him either.

'Do you know this man?'

'No.' The man's mother would barely recognise her own son after what they've done to him. 'I've never seen him before.'

'You're lying.' A wooden stick is brought down onto Leo's left arm, leaving a sharp, sudden pain in his elbow and a dull nausea in his stomach.

'I don't know him,' Leo would still have insisted.

'Are you willing to swear that you have never before met this man? That you have never—'

In Joan's imaginings, Leo does not hear the end of that sentence. It happens every time she pictures this, Sonya's words running hopelessly around in her head. She pictures Leo staring at the man, and there is something in his expression that tells Joan he did know that man, although Joan did not, and that he could remember the particular colour of his eyes, the shape of his head. The few remaining recognisable features of his swollen face. The next blow would have been to Leo's right arm. And then to his back and his ribs and his kidneys. He would have felt his pulse slowing, his heart suddenly unable, or unwilling, to beat as strongly as it had before.

The following morning, Leo was dragged outside and shot in the back of the head.

Joan cannot speak. Her heart pounds in her chest. 'But why?' she whispers.

Sonya shakes her head. 'Who knows? But he has been quite critical of the regime. It did sometimes cross my mind that his research undermined the whole system.'

Joan stares at her. 'You don't believe them, do you? He didn't do anything wrong. You know he didn't. He only published those results to prevent famine during the war.'

Joan's voice is raised, and she feels Sonya put her hands on her shoulders, trying to calm her and quieten her. 'Shhh, Jo-jo, not here. People can hear you.'

But she cannot be quiet. 'He wasn't a traitor. You know he wasn't. It was his whole life. He only ever wanted to make it work.'

Sonya shakes her head and puts her finger to her lips. 'I thought so too,' she whispers, her voice soft and soothing; too calm, Joan will think later. 'But it's like I told you. Trust no one.'

*   *   *

Nick stares at her, disbelief evident in his face. 'Is it

true? Did they actually kill him?'

Joan nods slowly. Her eyes are dry now but there is a pain spreading through her whole body at the memory. She wills herself to think of something peaceful and ordinary—a cloud floating in a bright blue sky—in an attempt to calm her fluttering heart.

'I don't believe this.' He looks at Joan, and for a brief moment Joan detects a flicker of sympathy mixed in with the anger. 'But why?'

'With respect,' Ms Hart interrupts, 'Stalin ordered the execution of millions of people. I don't think he was particularly fussy.' She takes a piece of paper from the file and holds it against her chest. 'However, in this case, the KGB report from Leo's interrogation was included in one of the other files smuggled out by our defector. Would you like to see it?'

Nick sits forward. 'Yes.'

Joan does not speak. It was all so long ago. It can't change anything. It can't bring him back. It can't make his death any less terrible. And it won't make Nick forgive her.

'I can read it out to you,' Ms Hart offers. 'It's only short.'

Joan shakes her head. 'I don't think . . .'

Nick does not seem to notice his mother's objection. 'Yes, just read it out.'

Ms Hart glances at Joan who does not protest this time. 'Fine,' she says. '*Citizen Leo Galich was today found guilty of attempts to undermine the Soviet Empire with his campaign of misinformation in relation to the Soviet agricultural policies and his work with the Canadian government during the Great Patriotic War.*' She pauses. '*His connection to Citizen*

Grigori Fyodorovich—'

At this Joan emits a small cry. Ms Hart glances at Nick and then back to Joan, who is sitting with her hand over her mouth.

Ms Hart looks down and continues to read, her voice louder now. '*His connection to Citizen Grigori Fyodorovich was denied to the bitter end but the evidence we received from Agent Silk is utterly trustworthy, and so for this reason we know for a fact that Citizen Galich is a liar as well as a traitor. He is hereby sentenced to immediate death by firing squad.*'

Joan opens her mouth and closes it again. There is something she desperately needs to ask but her voice is not to be trusted. It breaks and croaks as she tries to speak.

'What is it? What are you trying to say?' Ms Hart asks.

Nick takes the piece of paper from Ms Hart.

'Who's Agent Silk?' Joan whispers, and she notices that the words are somehow joined together when she speaks. She tries to lean forwards while the wave of nausea passes but she finds that she cannot move her body. Or at least, she can move half of it, but the rest seems disjointed and slack. It is stuck, suspended in time.

She hears Ms Hart's voice but, really, she does not need to be told. Sonya. Sonya was the only other person who knew about Grigori Fyodorovich. Sonya must have told them about Leo's encounter with him. But why?

She imagines Leo denying all knowledge of him, even though it would not have saved him anyway. Always so stoic, so brave. The cause above all else. Perhaps he was still convinced that it was a terrible mistake and they would realise they had the wrong

311

man before it was too late, and that he had actually been invited over for a conference. For a medal. If she closes her eyes, she can still remember the beam of his face as he confided his hope of a medal to her, and it is momentarily soothing until, with this, comes an earlier memory of his triumphant return after that first trip to Moscow when he told her what he had learnt and insisted that she must never, ever tell anybody, and Joan is hit by the realisation that when Leo was dragged out to the execution yard all those years ago he must have believed it was she who had betrayed him, because he would not have known who else it could have been.

No, she cries, although her mouth will no longer move, so the cry is inside her head and she does not know if Nick or Ms Hart or Mr Adams with his video recorder can hear it. There is a blackness rising up inside her. She can see it. She can almost touch it. She reaches out to Nick. How to tell him what is happening? My heart, she thinks. Oh, my heart. She feels a stabbing pain in her head, a giddy swirl of light and noise as her heart seems to slump in her chest. And then nothing.

Wednesday, 10.44 p.m.

'She's been lucky.' The voice is deep, young-sounding. 'It was only a small one. It's fortunate you were with her when it happened as if they're left untreated the little ones often lead to much larger ones. But this should leave no lasting damage.'

Small what? thinks Joan. She is lying in a strange bed in a strange room and it is hard to distinguish Nick's voice above the noise. She opens her eyes but the process is laborious and her mind feels strangely detached. Where is she? What is she doing here? For a moment she doesn't remember anything at all. There are flowers by her bedside, a few sprigs of foxglove in a plastic-looking vase. She thinks they must be from Nick. Who else would have given her flowers? She remembers suddenly that he has been cross with her although she cannot think why, and for an instant she believes that perhaps she has been forgiven for whatever it is she has done, and it is a warm, woollen feeling, as if the bandage on the part of her head where she fell is not medicinal but a soft hand, stroking, anointing.

The flowers in the vase remind her of another sick bed many years ago, and with the memory comes the return of awareness, spreading slowly across her brain like congealing blood. She thinks of Leo and her heart thuds inside her.

'Ah, hello there,' says the doctor, noticing that she is awake. He comes to her bedside and leans over. Joan's eyes flicker and she catches a glimpse of him. He is not as young as he sounds. His hair has receded halfway back along his scalp and his eyes look as if he has been awake for hours. 'Now, Joan. Don't worry, you're going to be fine. It was a minor stroke, a transient ischemic attack to give it its proper name, but I've been treating you and you're going to be absolutely fine.'

'A stroke?' Joan whispers. Her mind is numb.

'Just a small one. Nothing to worry about. You may experience a few lingering symptoms but they should clear up in the next few hours.' He stands up straight, wipes his hands on his jacket and looks across at Nick. 'Make sure she doesn't get anxious,' he says. 'Press this button if you need me or one of the nurses. I'll be back in an hour or so to see how she's getting on.'

He leaves, slipping out between the curtains, and Nick watches him go. He turns to Joan and attempts a smile, although it is not his habitual, easy one. 'Well,' he says eventually. 'I thought you were a goner for a moment.'

Joan does not move. 'I'm sorry for giving you a scare,' she whispers, and his expression momentarily softens.

'Don't be sorry. Briony and the boys send their love. They wanted to come in but I told them visits were restricted because . . .' He stops and makes a sweeping, uncertain gesture. 'Well, I haven't told the boys yet.'

Joan nods. She understands. 'Thank you for the flowers,' she whispers.

'What flowers? Oh, those. They're not from me. They're from our friends in MI5.'

'Oh,' she whispers. 'I thought . . .' Stupid of her to think he could be so easily won over. Who is she to expect such forgiveness? What right does she have to expect it?

'They're waiting outside. Maybe they think I'm going to help you stage some sort of getaway.' He laughs at this, a sharp, too-loud laugh, but it is not unkind exactly. Hurt, perhaps.

It tears at Joan's heart to hear it. 'I take it you haven't changed your mind then?' she asks tentatively.

'About what?'

'About being my lawyer.'

314

There is a brief silence. Nick sits down and picks up a magazine which has been left by the previous occupant of the cubicle. 'Let's not talk about this now.' He turns a page of the magazine, tuts, turns another page, tuts again. 'How much of this did Dad know?' he asks suddenly.

Joan closes her eyes. Her head feels fuzzy from the medication.

'I mean, you and he were so close,' Nick goes on. 'I often think of how you two were together, and I've even thought that Briony and I lack something in comparison.' He stops. 'I haven't said this to her. I haven't said it to anyone. It's just that I don't remember you ever snapping at Dad as she does at me. Or him ignoring you when you said something.' He gives a half smile. 'Apparently I do that to her.'

Joan reaches out her hand and holds Nick's arm. She is touched that this is how he remembers his childhood, although she is aware that there was another reason why she would never have snapped at his father, even if she had felt like it, which, in truth, wasn't often; how grateful she was to him; how careful she had always been to try to deserve him. 'Australia was a long way from home,' she says eventually. 'We were all each other had. And I didn't have a high-powered job like you do. It's much easier not to snap when you're not so busy.'

Nick shakes his head, moving his arm slightly so that Joan's hand falls away. 'There was more to it than that. You both laughed at each other's jokes even when they weren't funny. You just seemed so . . .' He stops. 'So happy.'

'Yes,' Joan whispers, thinking of her husband's hand reaching for hers from his hospital bed. Right as rain tomorrow. She feels an ache in her chest.

315

'We were happy.'

There is a pause. Nick leans forward. 'But how much did he know?'

Joan closes her eyes. She cannot speak. 'Enough,' she whispers.

Thursday, 10.00 a.m.

After a depressing hospital breakfast of cold toast and margarine along with a bowl of watery porridge, Joan is informed that she is being discharged. Ms Hart appears at the door when this news is delivered, and it is apparent that she has been there all night, dozing in the corridor outside Joan's room after visiting hours had ended and keeping an eye on things. The nurse has evidently not been told the nature of their relationship, and is talking to Ms Hart as though she is Joan's daughter or some other close relative, explaining what Joan should eat, how many aspirin she should take, while all the time affirming that Joan will be absolutely fine as long as she is properly looked after.

Ms Hart nods, her expression indicating that she is listening intently, but Joan knows that the cause for her concern is not, as the nurse believes, Joan's welfare, but the fact that the announcement in the House of Commons is scheduled for just over twenty-four hours' time and they still haven't got anything on William. Joan asks the nurse to close the door while she gets dressed, and there is a brief moment of confusion before the nurse realises that Joan wants to be alone, and that she also wants the woman who sat up outside her room all night to be

316

taken outside too.

Once Joan is ready to go, the doctor comes in to talk to her. She observes his eyes flick down to the electronic tag on her thin ankle, visible above the slippers she was wearing when the stroke occurred, and which nobody had thought to replace so that she might be more appropriately dressed when she left the hospital. He looks away again, his curiosity unsatisfied but hidden now beneath a veneer of professional calm. He seems to have an idea of who Ms Hart is and why she is being so attentive, but Joan can see in his expression of pity and kindliness that he does not know any of the details. He would not smile at her like that if he knew what she'd done. She wonders if he would recognise her if he saw her picture on the evening news. Possibly. Probably. She feels a throbbing pain in her stomach.

'Rest, rest and rest,' he announces. 'That's all I'm going to prescribe. And aspirin.'

He looks at Ms Hart as he says this, but she is preoccupied with removing the plastic lid from a huge coffee cup without spilling any of the contents, and doesn't appear to be listening.

The doctor coughs and continues: 'There should be no lasting symptoms, but you must come straight in again if you feel anything unusual. Anything at all.' He pauses. 'Are you sure you feel okay?'

Joan looks at him and she knows that she is being given a chance. If she claimed to feel dizzy or light-headed now, he would believe her. She would be allowed to stay here. She could delay the press conference, maybe even delay the statement in the House of Commons, at least until after William's cremation.

317

But she also knows that there is no point in delaying. It will not go away now. And it is what she has always known. Badness deserves to be punished.

Her bones feel like chalk when she stands up, rubbing against each other as she walks to the door. 'I'm fine,' she whispers. 'I'd like to go home now.'

*   *   *

Those first few months after Leo's death pass in a blur for Joan; blank, sleepless passages of time through which she gropes her way, cycling to the laboratory every morning, forgetting her sandwiches, working so hard that she emerges from the building blinking like a new-born rabbit and then cycling home again. Getting out of bed every day feels like stepping into the North Sea on a chilly morning, but without the benefits of any bracing after-effects. She is thinner, smokes too much, drinks sherry on her own when she gets home. The invitations from the young men she used to date are no longer forthcoming. Most of them are now married or have moved away, but Joan is largely indifferent to this lack of romantic interest. She cannot be bothered to attend cinematic outings with men she cannot talk to. How could she possibly talk to anyone when there is nothing she can say? Or nothing true, at least.

There will be things she will later remember about that time. Sitting at the kitchen table and eating burnt toast. Listening to the phone ringing, ringing, and marvelling at how long some people (Sonya, her mum, Lally) will keep holding, still expecting an answer. Why don't they realise I'm not

318

here? she thinks. And she is momentarily irritated by this until she realises that she is there. She is always there. She puts a cigarette in her mouth but she does not light it. She simply holds it. Waiting.

At the laboratory, she continues to make copies of everything but she does not give them to Sonya. She feels Max's eyes on her as she works, and he will occasionally ask her advice on something he is working on, how to phrase something or present it more clearly, but he does not pry. He simply watches.

'Does it not hurt your neck, to type so bent over like that?' he asks one afternoon, when it is just the two of them in the room.

She sits back and rubs her neck. Has she always sat like this, or just recently? 'I suppose it does.'

'Maybe you should get glasses.'

She doesn't look at him. 'They wouldn't suit me. I'd look like a hedgehog.'

There is a pause. Rain falls quietly on the window. How she wishes she could tell him everything. What would he say then?

Probably not this: 'Then get tortoiseshell frames. Hedgehogs always wear wire-rimmed ones.'

She almost laughs.

The copies she makes are filed in a separate folder in Max's office, labelled and left neatly stacked on the shelves. It is habit, she supposes, which keeps her doing this, but she knows that is not the only reason. She does it because she is scared. She is scared they might come for her next. If Leo could be accused of treachery, so could she. So could anyone. She wants to be able to show that she intended to keep on giving the information but was just waiting until it was safe to smuggle it from the laboratory into Sonya's hands.

But when the time comes for her next appointment with Sonya, she does not turn up. Nor does she call to say that she will not be coming. The same happens the next time, and the next. She receives a couple of letters from Sonya which she merely skims and then throws away, and then a card announcing the birth of her and Jamie's baby. There is a photograph enclosed with the card. A baby girl with big round eyes and tiny dimples, named Katya after Sonya's mother. Joan burns the card. She props the photograph up on the mantelpiece and then takes it down again. She puts it in a drawer.

And then there are the stories which appear in the newspapers almost daily, describing how Russia is consolidating its grip on Eastern Europe, buckling down its buffer zone over the war-ridden states, and crushing any glimmer of democratic opposition. The show trials that Joan remembers so vividly from Russia in the 1930s are being repeated in Warsaw, Budapest, Prague, Sofia. Can it still be justified as Leo used to claim the first time it happened? She is no longer sure. Certainly the gleam of heroism attached to the Russian war effort is starting to lose its dazzle. It is becoming opaque and cloudy, and Joan finds these doubts inhibiting. Whereas before she had been comfortable in her belief that sharing these secrets, fulfilling Churchill's promise to share, was the morally decent thing to do, she can no longer hold to this with such certainty.

Quite simply, she wants out. But what is the procedure for leaving? If she tries, will they send for her, just as they sent for Leo? She does not know. She can only withdraw quietly and hope that nobody notices.

Eventually Sonya comes to visit her one Sunday morning, waiting at the front door of the mansion block until one of the other inhabitants lets her in. She leaves her perambulator at the bottom of the staircase and puffs her way up to the fourth floor with Katya in her arms, knocking triumphantly on Joan's door.

Joan is asleep when she arrives, having discovered that she sleeps more easily after dawn than before, and so she has fallen into the habit of making up for lost sleep at the weekends. On hearing the knock, she sits bolt upright. There are various people she thinks it could be, her mother, Lally, Karen, other friends she sees occasionally, but she does not think of any of these people. She cannot say exactly what it is she fears. Two men, dressed in black with low-brimmed hats. Large, physical men who could take her away, just as they took Leo. Or a policeman, short and amiable, with handcuffs clipped to his belt.

Sonya calls out to her. 'It's me, Jo-jo. Are you in?'

Joan breathes out. She pulls on a dressing gown, runs a brush through her hair, and takes the photograph of Katya out of the drawer and props it up once more on the mantelpiece. Then she runs to the door and flings it open. 'How lovely to see you! And hello, Katya.' She chucks the little girl's chin. 'We meet at last!'

The little girl in Sonya's arms smiles, and Joan is astonished to see that she is no longer a baby but a small child, not quite a year old but nearly.

'Jo-jo, you're not dressed.'

'I was asleep.'

'But it's past midday.'

Joan shrugs. 'I was tired.' She steps back so that Sonya and Katya can come in.

Sonya walks into the living room and surveys her surroundings. There is a sofa with a matching armchair, and a ramshackle bookcase along which she runs her finger and then frowns at the dust. She draws back the curtains while Joan goes to the kitchen to make a pot of tea. 'You haven't been coming to our appointments,' Sonya calls out to her from the living room.

Joan does not reply at first. She pours hot water into the teapot and then swirls it slowly. She takes out a tray—mugs, sugar, milk—and carries it slowly into the living room. 'It's not safe,' she says eventually.

'It's just as safe as it was before.'

'But I don't *feel* safe.'

'You know Leo wouldn't have wanted you to stop.'

Joan glances at her. 'How can I know that? After what they did to him . . .' She stops, unwilling to let herself think of it while Sonya is here. She does not want a witness to her grief.

'You told me he believed in the cause. If you believe that, then you must know he wouldn't have wanted you to stop.'

There is something in the phrasing of this which causes Joan to frown. 'Don't you think he did?'

'Of course,' Sonya says, and her voice is high with enthusiasm. 'Not that it matters what I think. It's what you think that counts. And if you believe that, then you must continue.'

'But I'm scared.'

322

'Don't be. There's less to worry about now, you know.'

'In what way?'

Sonya hesitates. 'Now that Leo's gone, I mean.'

Joan stares at her. 'What?'

'MI5 were on to him, Jo-jo. You know that. It was only a matter of time before they found you, especially if you got married.'

'Married? Did he say that?'

Sonya's eyes widen, and then she turns away so that Joan cannot see her face when she answers. 'It's just a figure of speech,' she says lightly.

'No, it's not,' Joan says, although she wonders what she would have said if he had asked. It would have depended, she supposes, on how he phrased the question.

Sonya bends down and picks up Katya. 'But it's irrelevant anyway because he didn't ask, did he?' Katya throws her arms around Sonya's neck and grips her hair with her hands. 'I'm sorry, Jo-jo, that was unkind.' She shakes her head, trying to loosen her daughter's hold. 'All I mean is that you're safer now than you were before. We all are. MI5 are off my back, which means that the KGB are too.'

Joan stares at her. It is the first time she has ever mentioned the KGB by name. 'So you're saying it's all worked out for the best? That Leo's dead so now we can all carry on as normal?'

Sonya puts Katya down again and walks over to Joan at the window. She puts her arms around her. 'Of course that's not what I'm saying. I loved him more than anyone in the whole world. Except Jamie, of course. And Katya. I'm just saying that you're safe. I don't want you to feel vulnerable. But they do ask about you. They want to know why

323

you've stopped.' There is a pause, and then she says: 'You should try not to upset them too much.'

Joan stares at her. 'Why? What would they do? Would they send someone to find me?'

'Not yet, Jo-jo. I'm just warning you. All I've heard is that they're so close to being finished, and the documents you send are so useful. You can leave, I promise, once the project is completed.'

'What do you mean, leave?'

She shrugs. 'I'll make sure they know you're no longer available.'

'Can't you do that now?'

Sonya looks at her and shakes her head. 'Just a bit longer, Jo-jo.'

Joan hesitates.

'Better to play by the rules,' Sonya says, causing Joan to look up suddenly at this echo of Leo's words.

But what are the rules exactly? And how far might they extend? To her? To her family? There is no way of knowing. She knows only that if she stops now they might send someone to find her, just as they sent someone for Leo.

Sonya steps away from Joan and bends down to take something out of her bag. It is a thick, brown envelope. 'They gave me this to give to you.'

'What is it?'

Sonya shrugs. 'Open it and see.'

Joan takes it and puts it on the bookcase. Whatever it is, she does not want it. She does not want anything from them. She sits down on the sofa next to Katya and sees Katya's expression of alarm at her sudden proximity, her big brown eyes turning to gaze imploringly at Sonya, following her every movement. There is something overwhelming

324

about such adoration, something terrifying. Such a lot to live up to. 'Motherhood suits you, you know,' she says eventually, wanting to change the subject. 'I didn't think it would.'

Sonya grins. 'I'm a chameleon. Surely you know that by now.'

Joan smiles. She remembers an earlier time, many years before, when Sonya came twirling into her room at Newnham dressed in a peach-coloured dress on her way to meet one of her young men in Cambridge. 'We are both actresses, you and I,' she had said, and Joan had laughed in surprise at the thought that anyone would ever consider her suited to something as glamorous as acting. But remembering this now, Joan wonders if perhaps Sonya had seen in her the capacity for betrayal even then, and the thought leaves her dizzy.

'Anyway, what news have you got? Any excitement?'

'What sort of excitement are you expecting me to be having?' The tartness in Joan's voice causes Sonya to look at her in surprise but she does not blush. There is something obstinate about her breeziness.

'I don't know,' she says. 'I thought maybe I hadn't heard from you for so long because of some grand romance.' She smiles, her mouth suddenly opening wide in mock astonishment. 'In fact, maybe *that's* the reason you're still in bed at midday?'

Joan shakes her head. 'Don't,' she says.

Sonya leans towards her. She lays a hand gently on Joan's knee. 'You have to forget him now, Jo-jo. He's gone. It's been over a year.'

'Has it?'

Sonya nods. 'And you're no spring chicken.'

Thursday 11.14 a.m.

The video camera and interviewing equipment have been installed in the upstairs bedroom. Joan is sitting in bed, sipping water from a glass. Mr Adams is leaning forward, tapping his pen against his knee as she speaks. 'And what about William?' he asks when she stops.

The mention of William causes her to look up suddenly, and she spills a small splash of water onto the duvet. 'What about him?'

'Did he try to persuade you?'

Joan's glasses dangle from the shoelace around her neck but she will not put them on. She does not want to see properly, as she knows she wouldn't have the courage to carry on if she could see the expression on Nick's face. What would it be? Anger? Disappointment? Outrage? She shakes her head.

'Please speak up for the camera.'

'No.'

'Are you sure?'

'Quite sure.'

'Did you see much of him?'

'I told you, I didn't know him well.' She pauses. 'I saw him now and again.'

'And he made no mention of it?'

'No.'

Mr Adams frowns. 'And did he tell you what he was doing? Did he *allude* to anything?'

Joan hesitates. 'William was always alluding to things. That's just how he spoke. He was full of hot air. I didn't listen to half of what he said.'

326

'I need examples.'

'I don't remember.' She pauses. 'It was seventy years ago.'

'Then think.'

'Now, hold on a minute,' Nick interrupts, his voice sharp and suddenly officious. 'She's just had a stroke. You have to go easier on her.'

'It wasn't a proper stroke,' Joan says, torn between her desire to reassure Nick that she is strong enough to cope with this on her own and her need to appear forgetful in the face of this questioning.

'It was still a stroke.'

Mr Adams takes a deep inhalation. 'We've wasted enough time as it is. If your mother intends to enter a plea for leniency, then we need this information before we present her name to the House of Commons.'

'She has to rest. Look at her. Can't you see she's exhausted?'

Joan shifts a little against the pillows, trying to find a more comfortable position. She puts the glass on the bedside table and pulls the duvet up around her shoulders. Her fingers lace together under the sheets.

'Okay. Let's take a break.' Ms Hart looks at her watch. 'Twenty minutes.'

*　　　*　　　*

Joan closes her eyes. She can hear Nick talking on the phone to his wife outside her bedroom, his voice clipped and stilted. There is too much for him to explain, and she can hear him hesitating as he selects his words with care. How could she have done this to him? It is not what she ever wanted.

She is relieved to have been allowed the break. It is the lying that exhausts her most of all.

But, in any case, she will not give them what they want. She will not tell them that William did try to persuade her too, that he came to the laboratory not long after Sonya's visit and waited for her outside, his grey woollen suit impenetrable and immaculate against the winter sun. She had not seen him since he started his job in the Foreign Office, and she remembers how she felt an unexpected rush of nostalgia at the sight of him, as if someone was pulling the concrete earth from beneath her.

'What are you doing here?'

'Just passing,' he said unconvincingly. 'Can I walk with you?'

'I can't stop you.'

She remembers his habit of closing his fingers over hers and steering her along the pavement, his fingers light yet firm. 'Sonya tells me you've lost interest in the cause.' When she didn't respond, William leant in closer. 'Look, Jo-jo, I haven't come here to force you to do anything you don't want to do. You know you're the best Moscow have got. I'm told that every message coming through from the Centre these days is asking about you, where you've gone, what you're doing.' He paused. 'Do you realise that you're giving up the chance to make the world a safer place? Do you understand what you're doing?'

Joan had not known what to say to that, but she also remembered that she no longer knew what to believe. 'But I'm tired, William. After Leo.' She stops. 'I want out.'

He looked at her and shook his head. 'Don't ruin it because of Leo. You didn't start this because of him. You know it's not right to allow one country, or one power system, to wield all that potential for destruction. It's not safe. So forget Leo. It's not about him.'

'I know it's not,' she had whispered back and it was true, or at least it had been, at the beginning of it all. But she also found that she could no longer think of her actions in such a rational manner. Russia was no longer the distant, faraway place for which she once had such sympathy but could not really imagine. She felt the existence of it now inside her, gripping her stomach with its cold, steel claw, refusing to let her go. 'Don't you miss him, William? You always cared for him, didn't you?'

William hesitates.

'It's okay. I don't mind that you did.'

'Of course I did. And of course I miss him now. But that's why it's so important to carry on. Besides, you're just passing on things that were supposed to be passed on anyway. It's not stealing. It's just sharing.' Leo's words, spoken by William.

'We're not allies now. The war's over. And what if I get caught?'

William continued to steer her forwards. 'You won't get caught. But if anything were to look like it might happen, I can help you. I'll know in advance if you're going to be under suspicion from MI5, and I can always get you out . . .' he waves his hand, '. . . Canada, Australia, anywhere. You just have to ask.'

'How on earth could you do that?'

He shrugged and gave a small, self-satisfied smile. 'I'm quite high up in the Foreign Office these days. For some baffling reason they seem to rather like me. And counter-intelligence is my area. I'd be the first to know.'

Joan raised her eyebrows. Baffling indeed, although she kept this thought to herself. 'Leo always said you were the bright young hope.'

William repositioned his hand on her arm. 'Oh, I don't know about that,' he said, although he looked pleased to hear this praise from Leo. 'It certainly helps, having the—shall we say—*interests* that I do. We're the most committed sort apparently.' He paused while Joan took this in. 'Although I haven't mentioned this to my fiancée yet.'

'Your fiancée? You're getting married?'

William nodded. 'She's one of the secretaries. Lovely thing, my Alice. I rather adore her.'

'But you're—'

William put his finger to his lips to shush her.

'It was suggested to me that I might need to take a wife to put paid to some of the rumours floating around.'

'But what about Rupert? And Alice? Don't you think it's unfair on her?'

Joan remembers how William had tilted his head to the side while he considered this. 'Rupert understands. And I've thought long and hard about Alice,' he said at last, 'and I've come to the conclusion that she must know. I think the old girl understands too. I think she just wants a companion to go walking with her in Scotland, setting traps for heffalumps and such like.'

Joan had shot him a sceptical look when he said this, but William only grinned and she had not known if he was teasing her or not.

'So I'll tell Sonya to expect you, shall I?'

'I don't know,' she said. 'Maybe.'

'Come on, Jo-jo. Just a bit longer. Then we're home and dry and you've done your bit. Saved the revolution. Saved the world from nuclear annihilation by America.' He paused. 'Just remember why you started in the first place. None of that has changed.'

True, Joan had thought. None of that has changed, nor will it ever change. The photographs of that terrible day will be impossible to forget, those images of dust sucking and swirling upwards, and the feel of her father's hand clasped tightly in her own. But by then, something else had shifted inside her. Because she had also found out what happened to people who didn't do as they were asked, and she felt the weight of this knowledge sitting on her chest at night, heavy as an owl.

Joan remembers that she did not answer William at first. But she wasn't stupid. She knew when she was trapped.

'Okay,' she whispered. 'I'll do it.'

Thursday, 12.15 p.m.

The break is over and everyone has congregated in Joan's bedroom. At this time, she would normally be preparing for her ballroom dancing class, but not today. It bothers her that she cannot even call them to apologise that she will be leaving them with an odd number as what reason could she possibly give? If she told them about the stroke they would be bound to turn up after class with flowers as they had done for her dancing partner after his corns were removed, and she couldn't tell them anything else. She couldn't bear to voice it out loud.

'Let's go back to the packet,' Ms Hart begins, her voice calm and deliberate.

Nick snaps to attention. 'What packet?'

'The packet Sonya gave to your mother.'

'Oh that.'

Joan is sitting in bed, propped upright by an array of cushions and pillows. She has not considered this to be a particularly important element of the story, but now she sees that Mr Adams is watching her more intently than before, and he is nodding as if he already knows what she is going to say. 'Well?'

'A thousand pounds,' she whispers.

'A thousand pounds? In 1947?' Nick stands up and walks to the window. 'That must have been worth . . .'

Joan nods. 'A lot.'

Nick presses his head against the window. His whole body slumps against the glass.

Ms Hart glances at Mr Adams and he nods, as if to tell her to keep pressing on with the questions. 'That must have come in handy,' Ms Hart prompts.

Joan shrugs. 'It might have done, if I'd kept it.'

'What did you do with it?'

'I gave it away.' She pauses. 'I didn't want it. I hadn't earned it. So I gave it away.'

'All of it?'

'Yes.'

Mr Adams frowns. 'Why? Didn't you need it? You can't have been earning all that much as a secretary.'

Joan sighs and looks away. There was a medal too, an Order of the Red Banner, but she will not mention this. She remembers the weight of it in her hand, a block of precious metal bearing a red flag partially obscuring a sturdy-looking hammer and sickle, sheathed in golden corn. She had taken it to the riverbank in the fields outside Cambridge and buried it, so that now she could not be sure of where exactly it was. But she had not buried the money. She could not bring herself to do that. The economy had been ripped apart by relentless years of war and had left Britain ragged and hungry. There was not enough to go round. She only did what anyone would have done in her position.

'Whom did you give it to? William? Sonya?'

Joan shakes her head. 'There was a fund for Japanese orphans set up in London,' she says. 'I gave it to them.'

A silence. Nick looks at her. 'I hope you kept the receipt.'

*　　　*　　　*

'I'll meet you outside.' Max says.

'Right, I'll just be a minute.' Already Joan regrets agreeing to go for a drink with him after work. She is not free to do this. He, of all people, is off-limits, out-of-bounds. If she thinks back, she can still recall the list of documents that she gave to Sonya last week. There was a paper outlining the difficulties of multi-point detonation in an explosive device which he had written, a series of graphs describing the comparative critical mass of plutonium as compared with uranium 235, detailed information on the core and an explanation of the need for an initiator.

But it's not stealing, she tells herself. It's sharing. That's all.

She observes her face in the compact mirror she carries around with her, dabbing her cheeks lightly with powder and brushing her lips with lipstick, and noticing that trace of something in her expression (she has observed it before) which makes her want to look away. She knows why she agreed to the drink when he suggested it. Sonya's comments had something to do with it, but the bigger push was the memory of Katya looking up at her. She has been haunted by that expression all week, those dark eyes, so innocent and hopeful and young, reminding her that life is short and that these unprecedented times of hers will not last for ever. So when Max asked if anyone was going for a drink after work on Friday, she had not slunk off as she usually did but had agreed with enthusiasm, and only later did it transpire that it would be just the two of them as everyone else had other plans for the evening. Her fingers fumble as she puts the lipstick back in her bag. She narrows her eyes to scrutinise her appearance and then snaps the case shut with an abrupt click. Too late to turn back now.

As they walk, Max tells her about his mother's heart operation, about his wife's flat in London to which he is never invited, about playing tennis with his sister the previous weekend. Joan laughs as he describes how his sister managed to swing her racquet back to hit herself in her own eye, and that the bruise has now progressed to a fetching smoky blue which she has been trying to disguise with eye shadow. Joan feels her body relax, wanting to respond to him, and she recognises this as a dangerous feeling.

'You don't look like a hedgehog in your glasses, by the way,' he says suddenly, stopping on the pavement. 'I've been meaning to tell you.'

Joan blushes slightly and smiles. 'I do a little.'

Max shakes his head. 'Well, that's because you ignored my advice and bought wire-rimmed ones. But they still make you look just as . . .' he lowers his voice so that any passers-by cannot hear him, but he does not stop, '. . . just as *beautiful* as I thought they would.'

She hears his words and once again, she feels lost, just as she did in Canada when he told her he loved her then refused to kiss her. Why is he doing this? Does he not realise he can't do this? Not now. It's been too long. Too much has happened. And if she stays here now, with him, what next?

She puts her hand up to her mouth, trying to feign surprise. 'Oh, no,' she says. 'I forgot. I'm supposed to be meeting a friend.' She steps away from him. 'I have to go.'

He shakes his head. 'I don't believe you.'

Joan turns and starts to walk away.

He catches her up. 'I don't believe you.'

She looks down at her feet.

'If you really mean it,' he says, 'that's fine. I'll go, and we can pretend this never happened. But I want to hear you say it. I want to hear you say that you're happy with things between us staying as they are. I want to hear you say you don't ever wonder how it could be between us. Because not a day goes by . . .' He tails off, but he is still holding her by her shoulders and searching her face.

It is this that finally undoes her. She raises her eyes to his, and then there it is again, the sensation she had on the boat to Canada that he is truly looking at her. Not just looking, but *seeing* her. She has a sudden spark of fear that he might take her

335

word for it, he might leave and this day would end up being as dull as all the other days of the past few months, the past year, and she finds that the prospect of this happening is absolutely unbearable.

'But you're married. You said you didn't want to have an affair.'

'I don't.'

Joan steps back. 'Then why are you saying this?'

'I've asked her for a divorce.'

'Oh.' She looks at his hand on her shoulder and then back at him. 'I didn't know.'

'Actually, I've been asking her for years, ever since we got back from Canada. She's always refused, but she can't hold out for ever. I've offered her . . .' he raises his hands and shrugs. 'Well, everything. All I've got.' He slips his hand down and laces his fingers into hers. 'I want to be responsible for my own happiness. And that means being with you.'

Joan looks at him. She feels unsteady. Her body is warning her to step away, to wait just a little longer.

'We could go for one drink, I suppose,' she says eventually and her voice comes out a little breathless.

*   *   *

At the pub, Max takes off his tie and undoes his collar button. His hair reverts to its habitual springiness, seeming to know for itself that there is no need for smartness now.

'So,' he says, grinning at her. 'Joan Margery Robson.'

Joan laughs. 'You remember.'

336

'Of course I do. That was the moment I realised I was in serious trouble.' He laughs. 'I remember everything about that boat trip.'

There is a pause, a breath of time held between them. 'So do I.'

They sit in the corner of the pub, their hands occasionally brushing under the table, talking as if they had never stopped. He tells her how excited he is that the project is nearing completion, although he qualifies this by insisting that his interest is purely theoretical. He talks only of the long-term, energy-making possibilities, and is careful to avoid any mention of its explosive qualities. He tells her that it has already transformed energy systems as we know them, and wouldn't that be a wonderful thing to have dedicated their lives to?

Yes, she agrees. It is wonderful. She surprises herself with how smoothly the words fall from her lips as if she has never doubted the truth of them. She feels the powder on her cheeks as a thin layer of disguise, a silken covering to hide the blush of dishonesty as she thinks that you could quite easily say the opposite, that it is a terrible thing to have dedicated any amount of your life to. It alarms her to know how easily she can hold two opposing viewpoints at the same time. Surely it is not normal to feel no sense of contradiction?

No, it is not normal. Of course not. But it is not something she wishes to think about. Not now. Because now his arm is around her, his fingers brushing the bare skin of her neck and her whole body is suddenly tingling with nerves as she is aware of him looking at her, at her eyes, her lips, and she feels a sudden urge to be in bed with him again, holding his naked body in her arms, and the strength of this urge is a shock to her, something unfeminine and animalistic and absolutely necessary.

Back at Joan's flat, Max unbuttons her blouse. He traces his finger along her collarbone and she feels goosebumps breaking out across her skin, and a great flooding sensation in her stomach. She steps out of her skirt so that now there are only Max's clothes to be dealt with. Her impatience makes her clumsy. The buttons on his shirt will not come undone. She fiddles with them until he lets go of her for a second and pulls the shirt over his head and kicks off his trousers, leaving them in a rumpled mess on the floor. And then he is kissing her neck, running his hands all over her body. They tug and whirl each other into the bedroom, breaking apart for a desperate, fleeting second as they fling themselves onto the bed, both of them grinning widely and ridiculously, and she kisses his neck and his chest and feels the weight of his body on top of her, warm and gentle and comforting in the bulk of it. There is no contradiction in this, she thinks.

She buries her face into his shoulder as he presses himself into her, and she wants to cry out but she thinks there must be something shameful about this much pleasure. It overwhelms her. She breathes him in, the hot, rough smell of him, until she has to turn her head away and bite down upon the edge of her pillow so that when finally it happens, she does not make a sound or at least, not a sound that can be heard. The noise happens inside her, a million tiny explosions all over her body, and when Max slackens in her arms and collapses onto the pillow next to her, it amazes her that he does not seem to have heard it. He tugs her towards him and holds her in his arms, peaceful now, his body pressed against her own, their limbs relaxed and entwined. Neither of them says anything. They open their eyes and gaze at each other, red-cheeked and rumple-haired, and there is something calming about the symmetry of this.

They spend the next day together and Max insists on cooking breakfast for her while she takes a bath. After breakfast, he suggests they go to the park for a walk and maybe do a crossword, just like old times on the boat to Canada. When she asks if there is anything else he would rather be doing, he laughs as if this is the most ridiculous suggestion he has ever heard. Joan is not used to this, having grown accustomed to the impression Leo always gave that there was somewhere more important he really ought to be.

'I've waited years for this,' he tells her. 'So if you'll allow me, I'd like to spend the day with you.'

Joan smiles. 'I'd like that too,' she whispers, pulling him towards her and kissing him. 'But I think the crossword can wait.'

*   *   *

And so it begins, tentatively, secretly. She does not have the strength to refuse him, to refuse herself the possibility of such happiness. Surely there is something more complicated to it than this, she thinks, but then again, why should there be?

'I love you, Joanie,' he tells her. 'I've loved you for years.' He says it as though he has thought it up himself, this turn of phrase, to reflect his exact feelings for her, but she knows, everyone knows,

339

that he has not. He looks at her when he says it with a look so certain, so undistorted, that it frightens her. She is not used to this sort of untangled love. She worries that she cannot reciprocate in that same measure of certainty.

But after a while she finds that there is no need to worry. There are so many little things she loves about him: his habit of making lists and ticking things off once he has done them, the way his eyes and mouth seem to be made of perfectly straight lines when he is thinking, that he sleeps on his front holding his pillow beneath him, that he does not snore. And how easily he allows her to see these things, not as if they are secrets to be extracted from him but as if they are things he is happy to share.

She marvels at her own capacity for contradiction. (She will not call it deception. That is too personal.) Is it normal, she wonders, to feel the way she does for Max, to love him and cook for him and peel oranges for him at dinnertime so that he does not get his fingers messy, handing him the segments on a plate with a napkin, while also knowing exactly how much information about his secret project she has already given away?

But then there is the question of his wife. His wife will not let him divorce her, nor will she agree to divorce him. He has offered her everything: the house, money he does not have, any lies she wants to tell, but she will not agree to any of it. It is bad for her reputation, apparently, to either petition him for a divorce on the grounds of his unfaithfulness to her—'people will think I'm unsatisfactory'—or—'good grief'—on the grounds of her unfaithfulness to him.

Ah, Joan thinks, now there's the crux. If this is something he can live with, then surely she is entitled to her own contradiction. Perhaps, when they are lying together in bed and he is telling her he loves her as he winds his fingers through her hair and she is gazing back at those pure sea-blue eyes, perhaps his deception is the worse of the two. Hers is not personal, after all. It is political.

And this is how things seem set to continue. It is a happy, sunlit span of time. Later, Joan will look back at these months and wonder at her own naivety, because she should have known that this sort of thing cannot go on indefinitely.

Thursday, 2.28 p.m.

And then it all seems to happen at once.

First of all, Lally announces that she is getting married the week before Christmas. She has a ring and a dress and a suitor called Jack.

The second thing happens much further away. On the dry grasslands of the Kazakh steppe, a bomb explodes above a village. The houses in the village have been hastily constructed from wood and bricks, and there is something ghostly about the vastness of the place. There is a huge bridge thrown down across the Irtysh River. No roads lead onto or away from the bridge as it is not expected to last. Nobody lives here except animals: sheep and chickens and goats, more than a thousand of them brought to the steppe in petrol-guzzling trucks as part of Stalin and Beria's grand experiment. They scuff about in groups now,

341

pinched-looking and tired and resigned to their fate. The labourers have left so there is no one to feed them. The construction projects are complete, and the men who made them are now rattling back across the steppe towards Siberia, watching the land change from dust to forest.

The hot Kazakh sun will not come up today, or at least, it will come up, but it will not be seen. There is nobody here to see it. Yes, there are people living here and this is known to the research centre, but the inhabitants of these remote villages are not recorded on any official census. No evacuation orders are sent down from the Kremlin, because if they are not official then they do not count. The fallout is uncertain, in any case. Why go to extremes to protect people who may not need protection? Details, details, as Beria might say.

But of this bomb, not a single detail has been neglected. Each of the detonator capsules, the component which guarantees simultaneous explosion of the neutron fuse, explode within 0.2 microseconds of each other. This is as it should be. It guarantees an explosion big enough to rival the Little Boy Hiroshima bomb. The blaze and the roar of the bomb are registered fifty miles away from the test ground. In the report sent back to Moscow, it is concluded that the test has been an enormous success; fifty per cent more effective than anticipated in theoretical trials. It is a bomb to make Stalin proud. It is a bomb to hold up to the West, to say, ah-ha yes, we've got you now. It is a bomb to make everyone stop, hold their breath, keep a finger hovering on the trigger, aiming but not firing, waiting to see who's going to blink first.

* * *

These two events, while differing in magnitude, are both announced in the same issue of *The Times*. On the one hand, the delay is caused by the need for a date to be set for Lally and Jack's wedding, and on the other, the delay is more a symptom of disbelief than anything else. Conservative estimates had put the Soviet bomb project as at least four years behind Britain but now there is incontrovertible evidence that this is not the case. How could they have succeeded so quickly, so suddenly?

Eventually a statement is issued by 10 Downing Street declaring that His Majesty's Government have evidence that in recent weeks an atomic explosion has taken place in the USSR. The left-wing press are mutedly jubilant, claiming that the West can no longer arrogantly continue their programme without finalising some international system of control. This will force their hand. Russia's new power will have to be recognised. Concessions will have to be made.

Joan goes into the small kitchen and locks the door behind her. She leans against the wall, shaking her head slowly, incredulously. Was this because of me? she wonders. Did I do this? She feels a pinch of fear at the enormity of what she has done. It swirls inside her, a terrible giddiness that forces her to steady herself against the tiled wall. She thinks of Hiroshima, of the heat, the bodies, the terrible mushroom cloud of ash above the city, of Leo's words back at the beginning of it all: there are no sides any longer, not once this thing exists.

But she has seen the strength of it. Can Stalin really be trusted with such a weapon? Would he

343

really keep such a powerful thing in reserve and never use it? She is suddenly unsure, and a hot sweat breaks out across her back, a creep of fear at the thought of what an explosion of that magnitude might do in Britain.

How she wishes Leo were here now. She thought that being with Max had cured her, that she had done all her crying for him long ago, but now here she is, standing in the kitchen, squeezing a handkerchief and biting her knuckle to stifle her tears.

Karen knocks on the door. 'Joan? Is that you?'

Joan turns on the tap. She wipes her eyes with her sleeve. She hears Karen's feet shuffle on the tiles outside.

'Are you all right?'

Joan presses cold water into the corners of her eyes. She can't go out like this. 'I'll be fine in a minute,' she says.

Karen pauses. Joan imagines she can hear her face break into a sympathetic smile. 'Take your time. I'll cover for you if anyone comes looking for you. It's a shock for all of us.'

Her kindness makes Joan's heart heavy. If she only knew, Joan thinks. If any of them knew. What would they think of her? Would any of them understand? And Max . . . Oh, she cannot bear to think of it.

'Thank you,' Joan whispers.

She hears Karen's footsteps fading along the corridor. She closes her eyes and clasps her hands together as if in prayer, an involuntary, calming movement. She remembers the despair on her father's face as he lay in bed, his hand limp in her own, and the thought of him makes her strong. It's

344

done, she thinks. We've done it.

And then she thinks: I can stop now.

Later, as more information comes out, the British will say that it was based on the American design. It was not a Soviet design, but a Manhattan Project design. But this is not quite true. The American design has a horizontal reactor running through the middle. The Soviet design does not. And the British design does not. This is not conclusive—in some ways it sounds like simply being one of two obvious options—but there are documents in the archive that suggest the USSR project was heavily influenced by the British design. Impossible, Britain will declare in talks with America, we're tight. But neither of them will believe it. They know there is a leak. And they have to find it.

*   *   *

Max is sitting at the desk with his head in his hands. He has been sitting in this position ever since the announcement was made. Occasionally he will stand up, walk to the window and thud his forehead against it, leaving it there until the glass frosts and clouds under his breath, and then he will sit down again, tap his pen, shuffle his papers, put his head back in his hands. He has not attempted to gather everyone together as he did on the day of Kierl's arrest. He does not seem to have the heart for it this time. He cannot take it in, that his project has been trumped like this.

Even when Joan appears at the door, slipping around it and pushing it shut behind her, Max does not move. She leans against the door to keep it closed. 'They're here.'

He gazes up at her, momentarily mute. There is a long silence. 'Who?'

'The police.'

His head drops to rest on his arms, so that his voice is muffled when he speaks. 'I still can't believe it.'

'They're not in uniform but they're the same ones as before.'

'I didn't mean them.' He sighs, and stands up abruptly, pushing his chair back from his desk. 'I wanted us to succeed. I wanted us to do it first.' He looks at her and then looks away again, almost shy. 'Childish, isn't it?'

'Max, I don't think you understand. The police are here. They want to see you. They have a warrant for your arrest.' She hesitates. 'I told them I thought you were on a telephone call so you've got a minute or two.'

'For God's sake,' he says. 'What do they want from me? Got to keep the bloody Yanks happy, I suppose.'

Joan feels a heart-thud of fear. He doesn't understand, she thinks. He has no idea what's happening to him. She finds herself suddenly caught up in a strange, giddy panic: a combination of anticipation and fear, a swelling across her throat and chest. 'Oh Max,' she whispers. 'I'm sure it'll be fine.'

He looks at her, puzzled. 'What are you talking about? I haven't done anything wrong. We lost the race, that's all.'

Joan nods. 'I know you haven't.' She holds out her hands to him and he takes them in his, pressing them in a manner which seems to be intended to

346

reassure her. He is not taking her seriously. She pulls him towards her. 'But they think you have. They think there's a leak at the top.'

'That's ridiculous. Surely they need some evidence to make that kind of assertion.'

Yes, she thinks. They do. And perhaps they have. But at the same time, she has to hold on to the possibility that there cannot be any real evidence, not yet, as if there was, surely it would be her they would want, not Max? And Sonya would have warned her, wouldn't she? Or William? Didn't William say he would? She can hear footsteps approaching along the corridor and she has to suppress a sudden urge to sweep the door open and hold out her arms in a Messianic surrender—I am finished!—but it is a fleeting thought. She knows she will not, cannot, do it. Not now. Not now that she's got away with it for this long and it is so nearly over. If they take Max for questioning, it will only be temporary. She just needs to trust that they can get through this now, her and Max, and then that'll be it for ever; over.

Max takes a step towards her. They look at each other, enclosed in this moment of time that seems to float and lengthen and Joan feels her lower lip begin to quiver. 'Don't cry,' he whispers. 'It's just routine.'

Joan gulps. Her heart shudders in her chest. The sky outside is scudded with clouds. Max's hands are pushing down into his pockets, his shoulders rounded and hunched. His eyes are closed. There is a sort of resigned weariness about him, as if he knows that he must be stronger than he feels. He glances up, his eyes searching to meet Joan's gaze, and then he leans forward and kisses her softly,

347

gently, on the lips.

'Ready now,' he whispers.

'Are you sure?'

He squints at her, rubs his hand gently over his chin, and nods slowly, decidedly. 'I might as well get it over with. I've never been the running type.'

Interrogation of Max DAVIS by Det. Supt. Minchley

Cambridge Police Station, 24 September 1949

Having reached this stage of the interrogation, I alleged to Max DAVIS that he had been in touch with a Soviet official or a Soviet representative and had passed to that person information bearing upon his work. DAVIS's first response was to open his mouth as though surprised, and then to shake his head quite vigorously and say, 'I don't think so.' I then said to him, 'I am in possession of information which shows that you have been guilty of espionage on behalf of the Soviet Union.' DAVIS again replied, 'I don't think so.' I told him this was an ambiguous reply, and he said, 'I don't understand. Perhaps you will tell me what the evidence is. I have not done any such thing.'

I then told DAVIS that I was not really questioning him about this matter but that I was stating a fact. I should however want to question him about the manner in which he gave the information, how he made the contact and the full extent of his guilt. He repeated that he was quite unable to assist me, and strongly denied that he had ever been responsible for such a leakage. He said that it did not make sense, since he had done all that he could to help win the war. He was

348

perfectly satisfied to be in the vanguard of progress of this new scientific development, and could not think it at all likely that he would have any reason for passing the information. He knew quite well that a decision had been taken to exclude Russia from sharing the information. He thought this was a 'jolly good idea' from a scientific point of view, since the British were well equipped to make all the necessary experiments, and he was not concerned with the political motives underlying this decision.

The interrogation was broken from about 1.30 p.m. until just after 2 p.m., while we had lunch, and I deemed it prudent to allow DAVIS to lunch alone and think about what had been said. Upon his return he had nothing fresh to tell me, and this remained his attitude in spite of the many opportunities I gave him to confess. In addition, I sought to make it quite clear to DAVIS that the decision as to whether he would remain at the laboratory, having regard to the delicate relationship to be maintained with the Americans, was one that the Ministry of Supply was actively considering. I felt quite sure that whatever the Ministry decided, we should advise that a big risk would be taken by the continued employment of DAVIS on this top-secret work under such conditions. Whether the Ministry would take our advice or not would be a matter for them.

He professed to recognise the extremely difficult situation in which we were placed and said that he was so sensible of my inability to produce any evidence against him that he was barely able to restrain himself from thumping the table between us and demanding that the evidence against him be produced. In the absence of any evidence against him, he felt he was utterly unable to help the inquiry. He also made the point that since he was under suspicion he might, upon reflection, think it quite impossible to continue his work at the laboratory in any case, and if he came to that conclusion, he would offer his resignation. He seemed to consider that in this eventuality he would be able to apply for a research post at a university, and while demonstrating frustration at not being able to continue with his work at Cambridge, did not seem to be fully aware of the consequences of these allegations.

I find it extremely difficult to give a conclusive view qua the guilt or innocence of DAVIS. His demeanour during our interview could have been indicative of either condition. If he is innocent, it is surprising that he should receive allegations of this kind so coolly, but perhaps this squares with his mathematical approach to life. It could also be argued that he is a spy of old standing and was prepared for such an interrogation. On the other hand, his flat refusal to cooperate and his occasional bursts of anger might be seen as an indication of innocence.

However, reviewing all the facts in the light of the interrogation, I feel sure that we have selected the right man, unless by chance, someone in the nature of a twin brother was in Canada when he was there and continues to be at Cambridge with him now. Having considered all other scientists at the laboratory who would have had access to the same information, it is difficult to find any candidate for the suspect other than DAVIS himself.

That same afternoon, an official charge is brought

against Professor Maxwell George Davis.

*   *   *

Nick smashes his hand against the windowsill. 'I knew it!'

'Nick, wait.'

Nick does not wait but strides out of the room and down the stairs. The back door opens and then is slammed shut.

There is a pause. 'Could I go outside for a minute?' Joan asks.

Ms Hart glances at Mr Adams. 'I don't know if that's appropriate.'

Mr Adams sits back in his chair. 'None of this is appropriate, but it won't change anything when it comes down to it.' He shrugs, and indicates the recorder which holds the entire roll of evidence. 'Might as well let her go.'

Joan gets out of bed and walks to the door. Her head feels dizzy and she has to clutch the bannister as she descends.

'Five minutes,' Mr Adams barks after her.

Nick turns to face her as she steps out onto the patio. 'It's Dad, isn't it? He worked on the bomb too, and he didn't bother to mention it to me either.' He shakes his head. 'Why did nobody think I'd like to know? I always thought he was too much of an academic to be teaching at that school.'

'But he liked it there. He didn't want to be working on the bomb any more, or have anything to do with it. He liked his long summer holidays and playing tennis in the mornings and living by the sea.' She pauses, and when she speaks again her voice is softer. 'And you, Nick. He adored you.'

'But you let them arrest him. You let them come and arrest him and you didn't even stop them.'

'I thought he'd be fine. There was no evidence against him so I thought they'd just let him go.'

'But you still allowed it to happen.' His neck is flushed with heat. 'You were too cowardly to stand up for him when he needed you.'

Joan opens her mouth to protest but then closes it again.

'Everything you were saying in there, it's all excuses, reasons. You still think you were right, don't you?' Nick's voice cracks as he speaks. 'You've always thought you know best about everything. You've always wanted to control everything.'

'No, Nick, no.'

He waves her away with his hand. 'All my life, you've wanted to control me, to have things your way. I never asked to be so *special*. I used to pray that you'd adopt another child so that it wouldn't all be on me.'

'Oh, Nick.' Joan's stomach feels as though it is full of ice, huge numbing lumps of it, sharp-edged and heavy. 'Of course I thought you were special. I'm your mother.'

'No, you're not,' Nick mutters, but already his shoulders are drooping. He has always been quick to flare up, although the initial burst of anger doesn't usually last for long. His voice is quiet when he speaks again. 'Just tell me one thing. Are you sorry? Do you regret it?'

Joan is silent for a moment. She feels the beating of her heart strongly now, pulsing through her whole body. 'I thought it was the right thing to do. In the circumstances.'

'You thought it was right to spy?'

'I thought the information should have been shared with Russia. After Hiroshima. I thought it needed to be made fair, so that it didn't happen again.'

Nick doesn't move.

'Russia needed it. They had just lost twenty-seven million people during the war. Can you imagine it? Twenty-seven million.' She stops, suddenly aware of how much like her own mother she sounds. 'Everyone was more sympathetic towards them in those days, and everyone believed they would be the next target.' Joan glances at him. 'And besides, there was still hope that it might work.'

'What might? The great experiment?'

'Yes.'

Nick rolls his eyes. 'And now?'

'I still think communism is a good idea.'

'But it doesn't work, does it? Humans are too selfish for it to work.'

'I know. But in theory—'

'No!' he shouts. 'Why can't you just admit you were wrong? That it was the wrong thing to do. That it was bad, Leo was bad, Sonya was bad. That you're ashamed of what you did.'

Joan is silent for a minute. How would you know? she thinks. You didn't see how much they cared, both of them.

'They weren't bad,' she whispers.

'How can you be so naïve? Can't you see anything? Sonya didn't care about you. She betrayed Leo, her own cousin, just to keep you as a source.'

Joan shakes her head. 'No,' she says. 'No. It was

353

a mistake. She didn't mean to.'

But Nick doesn't stop. 'The interrogation proved to her that MI5 were onto him. It was only a matter of time before they worked out he was seeing you, and then your information would dry up too. And she wanted to protect that.'

Joan shakes her head but she does not deny it.

'Who else would it have been?' he continues. 'Maybe she didn't intend for them to shoot him, but it's like Leo said: she was out of her depth. She thought it was all a game.'

Joan feels the ground tip beneath her. 'But she loved him,' she whispers.

'Exactly. But she couldn't have him, could she?'

Joan looks at Nick. No, she thinks. No, no, no. She will not believe it. And yet there is something in the suggestion that makes her wince. The expression on Sonya's face when she told her that he'd been shot, her breeziness over Joan getting on with her life. These things struck her as odd at the time but she had refused to think about them. She had been so determined to hold on a little tighter, wanting to protect their friendship from unravelling, as it had done once before. 'But why would she do something so callous?'

Nick shrugs in an exasperated manner. 'Because she was jealous.'

Jealous? Joan shakes her head, although the word prompts a sudden memory to flash in her mind and then disappear. What was it? Something Jamie said in the Albert Hall? She closes her eyes and tries to summon it up, but her mind is blank, empty. It has gone. 'No,' she says. 'Sonya wasn't the type.'

'For God's sake! Even now, you still think she's

354

some sort of super-human. She's just evil.'

'She's not evil.'

Nick shakes his head. 'And what happened to her then? Did she ever get caught? Oh no, let me guess. She didn't. She got away. She was fine. She just left you to clear up the whole bloody mess.' There is a pause. 'Am I right?'

Somewhere in the distance a police siren wails and fades. Joan shudders. And then, so slightly that the movement is barely perceptible, she nods her head.

Thursday, 4.44 p.m.

There is a stunned silence in the laboratory. Nobody can quite believe that it has happened, that the Russians have beaten them to it and Max—Max!—has been arrested.

'You don't think he did it, do you?' Karen asks.

'Of course he didn't.' Joan's voice is a scrubbed whisper. She turns the wireless on, hoping that the noise of it might calm her, might drown out the terrible thumping of her heart, but it is yet another news report about the Russian bomb. She turns it off again. She stands up. 'I'm going home,' she announces.

Karen raises her eyebrows. 'Don't you think we ought to stay here in case they need us?'

'They'll be able to find us if they need us.' She pulls on her jacket. 'See you tomorrow.'

But Joan will not be coming in tomorrow. She knows that already. At her front door, she pulls the dark strand of hair from the lock and slots her key

355

into it. One, two, three. Undisturbed, for now. She goes straight to the bathroom cabinet and removes the box of sanitary towels in which she has hidden her most recent documents. She no longer leaves them at the laboratory after the previous incident with the police. It is easier to hide them here. Safer. She thinks of tearing the documents out and flushing them down the toilet but she has no faith in the cistern. She imagines them blocking the drains and being dragged out weeks later, incriminating her beyond all possible defence. She takes them to the fireplace and throws them into the hearth. The match will not light. She strikes it four times before it catches and even then it flickers and extinguishes before she can hold it to the paper.

'Damn,' she whispers. She tries again, and this time it catches straight away. She throws it onto the fire, watching as the flame spreads, devouring words and pictures until it burns itself out.

She stuffs a toothbrush and a change of clothes into her travelling bag and then stands perfectly still, her hand pressed to her forehead, and for a brief moment she wonders if she will ever come back here. Is there anything else she needs? No. There are things she might want, but nothing she needs. For a moment she wishes she had kept the money from Russia and then she would have something to work with. She could have made a plan, disappeared for a while until all this has blown over. But go where? she thinks as she unhooks her jacket from behind the door and slings it over her arm. To Canada? Australia? Russia? Her key sticks in the lock on the way out and she has to tug at the door to make it close. Would it be more obvious to run than to stay and stick it out? And what about Max?

She stands at the top of the stairs, suddenly giddy with the thought that Max might already have guessed her involvement. What if they have some real, actual evidence? Perhaps he is holding the evidence in his hands right now, shaking his head, wondering. Max, the only man in all the world with whom her cover is utterly useless, the only one who knows exactly how much she knows, who has taught her everything himself, who tells her that he loves her without the slightest hesitation. Would he tell them if he knew?

She does not know. Impossible to guess how he might react. Impossible to know if they have any evidence at all. The only thing she can be certain of is the knowledge that she has to leave Cambridge. She just needs a little time to think, somewhere to give her a few days' start. And first of all, she needs to see Sonya.

She walks to the station, doubling back on herself to check that nobody is following her. Once there, she buys a ticket to Ely and hurries onto the train. She blinks as it pulls out, dazzled by the brightness of the sun, the green of the countryside. She squeezes her hands together and closes her eyes.

Sonya and Jamie's farmhouse is quiet when she arrives, slightly breathless from the long walk up the lane from the nearest bus stop. The car has gone and there are no signs of tyre tracks on the path. She does not knock at the front door, not wishing to draw attention to herself, but goes around to the back and knocks gently on the glass. Nothing. She presses her nose up to the window and sees plates stacked neatly in the dish-rack with two wine glasses and a child's beaker upside down next to them. There is a newspaper lying open on the table, and Sonya's bright red coat flung over the back of a chair. Joan knocks again, but the sound only echoes and repeats.

She tries the door handle and, to her surprise, it is unlocked. She goes in. She calls out. 'Sonya. Jamie. It's me. Are you here?' She listens. 'Katya?'

Nothing. She goes into the front room. The fire has not been swept and the curtains are open but left untied, as if they have been dragged back in a hurry. She goes upstairs. There are no toothbrushes in the bathroom, no lipsticks by the mirror, no hairbrush by the bed. Joan whirls around. She goes to open the wardrobe and then realises that she should not touch anything.

Gloves. Where are her gloves?

She roots around in her handbag to find them, and her fingers are clumsy as she puts them on. She flings open the wardrobe door. There are gaps and spaces where clothes might once have been. She rakes her gloved hand along them until she comes to something familiar, her mink fur, hanging at the end of the rail. That's where it got to. She always suspected Sonya of having taken it. She slips it off the hanger and folds it over her arm.

As she does so, she notices that it has been concealing a cardboard box at the bottom of the wardrobe. It is small and dusty, but there is something about the box that makes Joan curious. She leans forward and pulls off the lid, unleashing a puff of dust, and revealing a small pile of photographs. Joan feels a quickening of her heart, anxious in case any of them are ones Joan has previously passed to Sonya revealing aspects of the work being done at the laboratory, all to be sent back to Moscow. Surely she wouldn't keep them here? She would have more sense than that.

Cautiously she slips her hand into the box and takes them out. Ah, she thinks, old photographs. Her hands are clumsy in the gloves but she is careful with the delicate paper. She flicks through the pile, just to verify absolutely that there is nothing incriminating, and almost at once a picture of a boy catches her eye. It is Leo as a child. It must be. He is perhaps six years old, skinny, with his head tilted and sunlight flashing from his spectacles, standing under a tree. His features are less pronounced but he still looks so like the man she once loved that her eyes burn. Shot, she thinks, and the word explodes numbly in her mind.

She crouches down on the carpet and flicks through the rest of the photographs. There are not many. In each one, the same boy looks straight at the camera, unsmiling but curious. It is Leo's expression exactly. In some of them, he is standing with a man whom Joan assumes to be Uncle Boris, Leo's father. He looks old. She did not expect him to be so old. She wonders if there will be some of Sonya as a child, but then she remembers that Sonya's childhood was spent elsewhere, and does not sound like the sort of childhood which would lend itself to cheery snapshots. There are numbers scribbled on the backs of the photographs, which at first Joan assumes to be dates. The first photograph reads 30.06.46, which would mean it was taken three and a half years ago. She frowns. Not a date then. Something else.

There is a small pile of larger, more faded

pictures at the bottom of the box, which Joan recognises as having been taken at Cambridge while they were undergraduates. Why has Sonya never shown her these before? She recognises herself in a few of them—such a strange feeling to be transported in time like this—and there are several of the whole group. There is one of William delivering a speech on a stage at one of the marches, and another in which he is kissing Rupert on the mouth, not a chaste, joking kiss, but a proper kiss, two men locked in a passionate embrace. Joan stares at this picture for a few seconds, wondering how it was that she never guessed at the time. Why did nobody ever tell her—Leo or Sonya or someone else—when they all knew anyway and were so accustomed to it that there is even a photograph of it?

She puts the photographs back in the box and replaces it in the corner of the wardrobe. She knows Sonya will not come back. She has gone for good, without even saying goodbye. She must have thought she was in real danger to leave so suddenly that she could not do that, as otherwise, surely, she'd have made some effort to get a message to Joan, even if only to warn her. Wouldn't she?

At this, Joan feels a sudden jolt of fear as she realises that this is it now. She is alone. She is alone and they have taken Max. It's only a matter of time before he realises. And then there will be nobody to turn to, nobody she can ask for help. Except, perhaps, William. She sits perfectly still. She cannot move. Her legs are pulled into her chest and her arms are curled around her knees but she knows she cannot stay here. What if they come for Sonya and they find her here instead? What if someone saw her come in? She stands up and hurries to the bedroom door.

But then a thought occurs to her. She turns back to the wardrobe and extracts a single photograph from the cardboard box. She slips it into the pocket of her fur coat, and as she does she feels a terrible flush of shame at the knowledge of what she might do with it.

For immediate attention:

I am anxious to establish the present whereabouts of a certain Sonya WILCOX née GALICH, her husband, James WILCOX, and their daughter Katherine (a.k.a. Katya) WILCOX of The Warren, Firdene, Norfolk. The aforementioned were the subjects of an interrogation approximately two years ago on 5 October, 1947. We have reason to believe that their house, The Warren, is at present untenanted, and no forwarding instructions have been given for correspondence to be sent on. We also believe that in January of this year Sonya WILCOX mentioned to her neighbour, Mrs FLASK, that she intended to visit her son in Switzerland. We had been unaware of the existence of a son, but Mrs FLASK informed us that he was born in 1940 and is named Tomas, and he lives with his grandfather in Switzerland. It is, of course, possible that she has indeed travelled to Switzerland and not returned.

I should be very grateful if you could make discreet enquiries as to where Mr and Mrs WILCOX have gone, and if possible what her intentions were regarding her future movements.

Yours sincerely

The name is illegible, a blue-inked scrawl across the bottom of the paper.

'Did you ever hear from her again?'

'No,' Joan whispers. 'Never.' She does not look up. She is staring at the piece of paper. 'But I don't understand this. She didn't have a son. She never mentioned—'

Nick groans suddenly and sinks his head into his hands. 'Of course she did.'

'What? Nick?'

He shakes his head but he does not reply. Instead he turns to Ms Hart. 'You knew, didn't you? You knew all of this at the start.'

Ms Hart glances across at Mr Adams, and then back to Nick. She nods. 'It's our job to know these things.'

'This is cruel. Can't you see she's old? This could kill her.'

'What could?' Joan asks.

Mr Adams interrupts. 'With respect, your mother is charged with a very serious offence. If we had told her this earlier, it would have compromised any information she might have chosen to tell us.'

'Told me what earlier?' Joan asks again, and suddenly the room falls silent. Nobody speaks. 'Will someone please tell me what you're all talking about?'

Ms Hart looks at Joan and then at Nick. Her look is questioning.

'Oh, just tell her,' Nick says suddenly. 'She deserves to know.'

Ms Hart's voice is soft. Her hand is on Joan's arm, and even though Joan is listening and listening, straining to understand, and she can see

362

Ms Hart's mouth moving, her mind has thickened so that she cannot hear a single word of it. She feels that same terrible blackness rising within her once more, and she knows she must not let it overwhelm her.

The boy, she thinks. The boy in the photographs. It wasn't Leo. The dates weren't wrong. Uncle Boris had looked old in those pictures because he was old. Not just a great-uncle to the boy but also a grandfather.

'Excuse me,' Joan whispers, putting up her hand. She does not want to hear any more. She does not need to. She allows Nick to help her to her feet as she stands up and walks out. Her body feels light and insubstantial, as if she is simply evaporating. She goes to the bathroom and closes the door, and then she sits on the side of the bath, gripping the washbasin with her hands and trying to hold herself in.

Quite suddenly, the recollection she was unable to find before is there again, flashing in her mind. Jamie, she thinks. Jamie in the Albert Hall, the last time any of them saw Leo. That was it. She remembers now. Oh, the memory of it thuds in her stomach. During the interval, she and Jamie had stayed in their seats while Sonya and Leo went to get tubs of ice cream from the usherette. 'Feels like old times,' Joan had said to Jamie, trying to avoid any prolonged discussion of Sonya's pregnancy. 'Before the war.' And then she had paused. 'Before you too, I suppose.'

Jamie had grimaced at this. 'I can't imagine how that worked.'

'What do you mean?'

He nods towards Leo and Sonya. 'I mean the

three of you. Sonya must have hated it.'

Joan thought for a moment. 'She wasn't jealous, you know. Leo said.'

Jamie snorted with contempt. 'Nonsense. She's just good at pretending. She's jealous now.'

'Is she?'

'Of course she is. They're as thick as thieves, those two. You need to remember that. Nothing and nobody can come between them. You think you can but you can't.'

'They're family. They're practically brother and sister.'

Jamie raised his eyebrows. 'Is that what you call it? They're not like any brother and sister I've ever seen.'

Joan remembers how this had confused her at the time. She recalls how she had looked over to where Leo and Sonya were queuing for ice cream, and had watched as Sonya took Leo's hand and pulled him towards her, placing his palm against her swollen stomach. 'Wait,' Sonya seemed to instruct him, and he did, even though his body was inclined away from hers and he was not looking at her. They stood like this for nearly a minute, until Leo seemed to start in surprise.

'There!' Sonya exclaimed, loud enough for Joan to hear. 'Did you feel it?'

Leo had raised his eyebrows and stepped back, smiling at her and then patting her on the shoulder.

'See,' Joan had whispered to Jamie. 'He's just being brotherly.'

'It's not him, Jo-jo. It's her. She does this every time she sees him. I think she sees it as a sort of substitution because he missed it the other time.'

The other time? Joan had turned to ask him what

he meant but Sonya and Leo had come back over at that point laden with tubs of ice cream, and they had been obliged to change the subject. She had resolved to ask Jamie later after the concert, but there had not been a chance to get a moment alone with him, and then, after Leo died, the conversation had slipped out of her head.

She realises that if this child, Tomas, was born in 1940 as Ms Hart had said, then that would fit exactly with Sonya's sudden departure for Switzerland in the late summer of 1939, and her period of silence at the beginning of 1940 after her and Leo's 'clash', as he put it. Did Sonya know, she wonders, when she took Joan to that horrible woman's house, when she sat by Joan's bedside and nursed her back to health afterwards? Perhaps not. Perhaps that was when she realised that he was not so incorruptible after all. And then the thought strikes her that it must have happened while she was ill.

She remembers Leo's despair over Stalin's pact with Hitler. She can imagine how he might have turned to Sonya then, she being the only one who would really have understood the depth of this betrayal, the only one who had seen what it was like in Germany, how they had suffered, and Leo in particular. Sonya had even warned Joan at the time that she was not being sympathetic enough but Joan had not heeded the warning. She had wanted him to take it in his stride as she had done. She had not understood.

She can imagine how it might have happened. They were not brother and sister; just cousins, yoked together by their past. Sonya might have put her arms around him, comforting and familiar, and

365

he wouldn't have been able to help but feel the smallness of her waist, the nearness of her as she held her face close to his and looked up at him, knowing now that he was not as incorruptible as she had thought.

Joan puts her head in her hands. She cannot believe she has been so blind, so stupid. She remembers the blankness of Sonya's expression when she confronted her about the shirt in her wardrobe. Why had she not pressed her further? Why had she chosen to believe her when she knew she was being lied to? She had known there was something she was not being told, and yet at the same time, she had not wanted to know. Sonya was the only person in the world to whom she thought she could say anything at all, who knew her better than she knew herself. It had seemed too much to lose.

Nick taps on the bathroom door—she recognises the knock—but Joan does not call out for him to come in, nor does she get up. After a pause of a few seconds, he opens the door.

'Are you okay?'

Joan does not answer. She takes the tissue he offers and blows her nose, and then attempts a smile to show that she is grateful for his presence.

He sits next to her on the side of the bath. 'I found something while you were in hospital,' he says, brandishing a small pile of papers.

Joan glances at them but does not ask. All she wants is for her son to sit close to her, to put his hand on her shoulder and tell her that she is not alone, that he will stay with her even though he is angry with her. That he will not desert her.

'I got some help from one of the clerks at

Chambers.' He fans the papers out in his hands and holds them out for Joan to see. 'Marriage certificates for Sonya: one in Zurich in 1953, one in Leipzig in 1957, and one in Russia in 1968. She wasn't easy to find as her name had changed, but we were able to trace someone matching her description through Tomas and Katya. It's impossible to say for certain, but it seems likely that these are her documents. The clerk thinks Jamie ended up in New Zealand.'

Joan looks at them, and sees the pale history of her friend set out in official form. 'So Sonya made it back to Russia,' she murmurs eventually.

He nods, and holds out another piece of paper.

'What's this one?'

'Death certificate. She seems to have died in St Petersburg in 1982. Twenty-three years ago. I thought you'd want to know.'

'Oh.' Joan pushes this one away. She does not want to think about Sonya dying.

'And good riddance,' Nick mutters. 'After all she did to you. And Leo. Leaving you to rot.'

Joan closes her eyes. She knows she should think this too but right now she cannot find it within her. She is too exhausted by her own pain to hate Sonya as well. She might have done once, for the abortion, for having Leo's baby in secret, for betraying him, but really, what else did she expect? Her mother killed herself by drinking hydrochloric acid. She came from a hard, ruthless place. Is it any wonder she ended up the way she did? Who else was going to look after her?

Nick moves closer to her, not too close, but close enough to lower his voice. 'Look, I've been thinking. I'm still . . . well . . . angry is putting it mildly.' He pauses. 'Disappointed, too. I'm not sure that things will ever go back to normal. Between us, I mean.' Another silence. 'But I've thought about it long and hard and I've decided that I will help you, but you have to do as I say.'

He waits for Joan to respond, and when she doesn't he places his hand firmly between them on the side of the bath. 'Tell them it was Sonya,' he says. 'Tell them she did everything. You can work out the logistics later, but it's pretty clear from what you've said that she manipulated you into doing what you did. We can just say you were confused in your original confession, and then everything could be worked to show that Sonya stole the documents from you and radioed them to Russia. It could work to your advantage, actually, that you were so used to being manipulated that you thought you should admit to it.'

Joan shakes her head. 'That won't work.'

'But it might. And tell them that you think William killed himself because he was guilty. Tell them something he did, so they can at least issue a warrant for a full toxicology report on his body to prove it. That's all they want to hear. You just have to give them what they want.'

'They want me.'

'No, they don't. They just want someone. They practically told you at the beginning that there was room for leniency if they got what they needed.' He turns to her, his voice low and urgent. 'Don't you see? It's embarrassing for MI5 that you weren't found before. Even now, they didn't actually find you. They were *told* about you. They had a Russian spy sitting under their noses at the top of the atomic project, slipping secrets to Russia for nearly five years, and it seems that nobody ever thought to run a proper check on you. And do you know why?'

Joan's brain feels fuzzy. 'No.'

'Would there have been the same laxity in the security checks if a man with a science degree from Cambridge had been in the same role as you?'

'I suppose not.'

Nick smiles for the first time in what seems like days. 'Exactly. So that only adds to the embarrassment. Not only did they not check up on you, but the reason they didn't was because you're female.'

Joan rests her head in her hands. 'I still don't see how this would help me.'

'It helps you because, politically, it would be better for them if you were innocent. So tell them something they want to hear, something that makes them look better. Let them have William. He's dead anyway, isn't he? And tell them that Sonya tricked you. They tracked her down, didn't they?'

'But if I deny it, they'll still take me to court. There'd have to be a trial.'

'Maybe.' Nick's voice betrays a hint of his growing impatience. 'You'd just have to stick to your story then, wouldn't you?' He pauses. 'It's your only chance.'

Joan looks down. She feels her heart burning with love for her son, for his wishful thinking in spite of everything she has done, for the fact that he is sitting here now, in her bathroom, and he still believes she has a chance. How she wishes she could simply agree, throw her arms around his neck and thank him, and tell him that yes, it will all be okay and it's a wonderful plan. But she can't do this because she knows it's too late. It wouldn't work.

There is a video recording of her confession, and there would have to be a trial. She would have to stand in court and deny everything in the face of so much evidence. She would have to commit perjury, and so would Nick. He would probably be able to claim in his defence that he thought everything he said was true, but she cannot ask him to do that. She will not allow him to do this for her. She must protect him now, as she has always done.

She lifts her eyes to look at him, and she sees in him all the hopefulness of those early years in Australia, so much happiness distilled so perfectly into his person. She feels a sudden burst of sorrow at the memory of leaving her own mother in the way she did, guilt at the terrible hurt she must have caused by running away without saying goodbye properly, and without ever explaining the real reason for her disappearance. She had always justified it to herself by believing that the alternative would have been worse, and that at least her mother had Lally nearby which must have been a comfort to her, but she also knows that this can't have made up for her own seemingly unfathomable decision to leave so inexplicably and abruptly to live in such a faraway place, so soon before Lally's wedding. Not that her mother complained. She made no demands on her, but Joan could always hear the hurt in her voice, the delay on the line on those Sunday evening phone calls made more pronounced by her mother's incomprehension of Joan's decision. Even when she got her cancer diagnosis and Joan still did not come back to visit, even then, she didn't complain, saying only how sad she was that she wouldn't get to meet her darling Nick, but please could they send more photographs of him eating fish and chips on the beach, just as Joan described, so she could put them up in her room in the hospice.

She did not deserve that.

And for herself, Joan isn't convinced she could cope with the wrench of separation all over again, if it should come to that. But she also knows she cannot say what Nick wants her to say, and as the certainty of this realisation dawns on her, she knows that there is another reason for her reluctance other than to prevent Nick's involvement, and she is surprised to find that this reason is so compelling for her. 'I'm sorry, Nick. I can't.'

'Why not?'

'Because it's not true,' she whispers.

'It doesn't matter.'

A pause. Joan looks at him. 'It matters to me.'

A shudder of anger seems to pass through him, and his expression hardens. 'Look, I don't want to be mixed up in this either. It's not good for me, professionally, to be associated—' He stops himself from continuing with this train of thought even though they both accept the truth of it. 'But I'm here, aren't I? I've come up with a plan. And I really don't think you're in any position to get all high and mighty about truth and the difference between right and wrong.'

Joan reaches out to put a hand on his knee. 'I didn't want you to be mixed up in this. All I've ever wanted was to protect you from it. That's why I don't want a trial.'

'Well, you should have thought about that earlier, shouldn't you?' He shakes Joan's hand off, and his lips are drawn and straight. 'You shouldn't have adopted me, after what you'd done. You didn't have the right.'

Joan feels something snap inside her. 'How can you say that?'

'Because it's true. I've been thinking it for the past few days. You can't say you wanted to protect me if you had already done this when you *chose* me, as you always tell me you did. What about me? Where's my choice in that? When do I get to *choose* whether or not I want an atomic bomb spy for a mother?'

'Oh, Nick.'

'I don't know why you can't just say what I've told you to say. What would it cost you to play along, even if you're only doing it for me?'

'But it wouldn't work.'

'Isn't it worth a try?'

Joan's head is in her hands but she shakes it all the same. Her heart is pounding but she knows now that she cannot back down, not just for him, but also for herself, for the person she was back then; for Leo, for Sonya, for William. For her father. 'But it's not true,' she whispers. 'I did it for a reason.'

There is a pause while Nick takes this in. 'So you're telling me you won't even try?'

Joan shakes her head. Her voice is so quiet that he has to lean forwards to hear her. 'I can't.'

Nick stands up and walks to the door. His hand rests on the door handle as he waits for Joan to say something, to change her mind, but there is nothing she can say.

'Well, then,' Nick says eventually, his voice cold and hard. 'Looks like you're on your own.'

372

Friday, 4.43 a.m.

Joan is in bed but she is not asleep. The landing light filters into her darkened bedroom and her thoughts are punctuated by the small red flashes of the surveillance cameras installed at the beginning of the week, reminding her of what they think she might do. There is at least one camera in every room in the house. They do not intend to lose her, as they lost William. Or if they do, they intend to have it on tape.

The sting of Nick's abrupt departure is still raw, twisting in Joan's stomach. His words echo in her mind, and once again she wonders if it might be better if she simply doesn't wake up tomorrow. Better for her. Better for Nick. She imagines for a moment that she might do it. Not with the sleeping pills but with the St Christopher's medal given to her by William as a parting gift, still there in her bedside table drawer. *Just in case*, he had written in the accompanying note, and she had been appalled by the very idea. Even if she had thought about it, she would not have pictured it happening like this. Not after so many years.

But then again, she had never thought William would do it either.

She knows that she needs to order her thoughts in readiness for the press conference later that day. All night she has lain awake, but the piece of paper upon which her statement is supposed to be written remains blank.

She knows that there is only one approach that would be acceptable—an apology, a display of

373

sincere remorse—but the truth is that she has always believed what she did was a brave thing. Yes, if she had been more aware of the horrors perpetrated by the Soviet state at the time she would have had other reservations, but how could she have known? So little was known back then. And it still doesn't really change anything. She didn't do it to save the Revolution. She did it because of Hiroshima, because of the mushroom cloud pictures and the casualty figures and the reports of the terrible clawing heat. She did it because of the feel of her father's hand in hers as he lay in bed recovering from his first heart attack, and because of the memory of him standing on the school stage, imploring his pupils to acknowledge their duty to each other. *We are each responsible ...*

She knows that Nick's plan could work. She can see that there is some truth in his assessment of what MI5 would be willing to accept. She could telephone him now and tell him she has changed her mind. She could tell MI5 that yes, she regrets allowing herself to be manipulated by those around her, that she should have reported her suspicions about Leo and Sonya at the time, that she believes William killed himself to avoid going to trial. Her story could then be amended to implicate him before being presented to the House of Commons. She can see that this would be the best thing to do, from a purely selfish viewpoint.

But every time she goes to write the words, she finds that her hand will not allow her to do it. The pen hovers over the page but it will not touch.

Because it's not true, is it?

Or at least, most of it isn't true, but she will not tell them what she knows of William. He deserves her discretion, after what he did for her. Thankfully, the files seem to be silent over this point, and Joan is relieved that she does not have to confess to how it ended. He covered his tracks well.

She closes her eyes. There is nothing to be done now but wait.

*   *   *

She telephones her mother from the phone box at the end of Sonya's road to ask if she might come to stay for a few days.

She can tell that her mother is smiling at the other end of the line. 'And to what do we owe this unexpected pleasure?'

The soft familiarity of her mother's voice causes a lump to rise at the back of Joan's throat and she has to make an effort to sound normal. 'Oh, no reason,' she says. 'I had a few days' leave so I just thought I'd visit.'

'Of course you can. You don't need to ask.'

Her mother is there to meet her at the station, embracing her as she steps off the train. 'You're wearing your fur!'

Joan grins. 'I thought I'd lost it. And don't we need to return it at some point?' Joan's voice is muffled from being pressed into her mother's shoulder.

'I should think my cousin's forgotten about it by now.'

'Maybe.' She glances at her mother's foot. 'How's your limp?'

'It's not so bad. Don't tell me off for walking to meet you. I wanted to come. I've missed you.' She smiles. 'Not that I'm lonely without your dad. Don't

375

go getting that into your head. I miss him—of course I miss him—but I'm absolutely fine.' She glances at Joan conspiratorially. 'I've joined a choir.'

'But you can't sing.'

'That was just your father's opinion. I always knew I had quite a nice voice, and the choir mistress seems to think so too.' She pauses, and then continues shyly: 'There's a concert next week. You don't have to come, but if you were free . . .' She tails off. 'It'd be nice, that's all.'

Joan feels the faint pulsing of her heart. 'Of course I'll come,' she says, even though she knows that so much might have changed by next week that she cannot say anything for certain. She leans across and kisses her mother's cheek, and inhales the faint lavender smell of her, the smell of childhood, of comfort, of being told that everything can be made better again. They cross the road and a car pulls slowly to a halt beside the kerb. Her mother barely acknowledges it, but when they pass in front of it Joan sees that there are two men sitting behind the dashboard, neither speaking to the other, their unblinking eyes seeming to be fixed on her. She hears the car slip into gear and pull away behind her, the windows dark and impenetrable as it passes.

A butterfly shivers across her heart.

It's just a car, she thinks. It's nothing.

Her mother glances at her. 'I hope you're not working too hard. You look awfully thin.'

Joan raises her eyebrows. Her mother always says she is looking thin when she means something else. 'Am I?' she asks, although this time she wonders if it might be true. She has always been slim, but recently she has noticed her clothes slipping more than usual. 'It must be the rationing,' she says. She glances behind her. The car is nowhere to be seen.

'Yes, I suppose it must.' Her mother pauses. 'I was thinking I ought to fit you for your bridesmaid's dress while you're here.'

'Might as well.'

'You don't mind, do you? The fitting, I mean.'

They turn in through the gate of the school and follow the path around to the lodge. They have had this conversation before: her mother being utterly convinced that Joan minds her younger sister getting married before she does and that this is why she has been acting so strangely. They have discussed it perhaps ten times over the phone and each time Joan has insisted that she doesn't mind. 'No,' she says. 'And before you ask again, I'm very happy that Lally has found someone she wants to marry. I'm delighted for her.'

'But you do mind a little bit, don't you?' her mother insists, aware that something is wrong with her eldest daughter and unable to fathom what else it might be.

'No.' How Joan wishes she could tell her everything, explain everything, and then close her eyes in a lavender-scented embrace and believe, just for a moment, that everything would be all right.

'Just a little bit. I know you do.'

'Really, Mother. I don't. The only situation in which I might mind Lally getting married would be if Jack was the only man in the whole world I thought I could ever love, but I don't. I don't even like him very much.'

377

'Joanie! You mustn't say such things about him. He's going to be family soon.'

'I'm only saying it to you, and I know you think it too.'

'Joanie!' Her expression is one of guilty outrage. 'I don't think I ever did say such a thing. Or if I did, it was a long time ago.' A pause. Her mother nods to herself as she turns away, and her words are muffled by her collar, but Joan can still hear them. 'I knew you minded a little bit.'

And so it goes on, round and round, until they reach the house and her mother bustles off to the kitchen, and Joan can slip upstairs to her old bedroom to put her bags down. There is a letter on the dressing table, postmarked from the previous day. She recognises William's writing on the envelope, but there is no letter inside; just a folded page of newspaper with a red line carefully encircling a short news report at the bottom of the page below an advertisement for domestic bleach.

Tragic Family, the headline reads. A small white Rover with a curved silver bumper and a dent in the passenger door is reported to have been abandoned at the docks in Harwich. There is a note in the glove compartment, and a hat fished from the water a little way down the coast. The hat is identified as having belonged to Mrs Sonya Wilcox of The Warren, Firdene, Norfolk and, a few hours later, an overcoat belonging to Mr Jamie Wilcox is also recovered. Inquest closed with final verdict of suicide, although no bodies have yet been found. No further investigations pending.

Joan feels cold all over. She reads it again and then carefully tucks it into the back of the grate, ready to set alight later. She knows they will not find any bodies. The hat and coat must have been planted to make them so easily traceable. There will have been a dry-cleaning ticket in one of them or an old name tape, something subtle yet obvious to allow ease of reference. It is one of the things Sonya once told her: that you can make anyone think anything you want them to, so long as you also make them think they have figured it out for themselves. Besides, it is too neat, too tidy. Joan remembers how Sonya always said that if she ever had to escape from England she would go back to Switzerland via Italy, first heading south by sea and then north through the mountains. She wonders if William helped them too. Perhaps that was how he knew to look out for the article.

Why had Sonya not had time to say goodbye? Why had she not warned her?

She imagines their car turning into the docks at Harwich, headlights dipped into the dawn and Sonya's dark hair wrapped up in her favourite silk scarf. ('It's far less conspicuous to look beautiful than to look worried,' she had once said when Joan admitted to being anxious before one of their meetings.) What was she thinking as they stepped out of the car and onto the boat? Perhaps she was thinking of Leo. Of Jamie, next to her, carrying their luggage. Of her daughter, Katya, wrapped up in her arms. Of Joan. Of the test bomb in Russia, that breathless burst of atoms, red and gold and almost beautiful from a distance. Or was she thinking of home, of her long-ago mother, of the house by the lake in Leipzig where she had holidayed in summer with Leo and Uncle Boris?

How long would that journey down to Italy take? Three days in a small boat? She imagines the three

379

of them huddled below deck among ropes and tarpaulin and droplets of sea collecting in pools on the wooden boarded floor. Joan shivers. Such an odd idea, to leave like that, with such finality. But also quite dramatic, Joan thinks, and she finds herself suddenly unsurprised that this was how Sonya chose to leave.

But who will be next? Will this be how she has to leave, when it is her turn?

Joan tries to imagine this but she cannot do it. She imagines her mother and sister being called to the scene, her mother's face ashen and wide-eyed. *My child*, she might cry, *my child*. Joan feels the pulsing of blood in her heart, a sense of bursting flesh, as if someone is shining a torch inside her mouth and up towards her brain. No, she thinks. No, no, no.

*   *   *

Her mother does the fitting that evening, wanting to get it out of the way before dinner. The material for the bridesmaid's dress is soft, pink cotton shot through with silk. It is pre-war material, bought up years before, just in case one of the girls should need it. Or both of them, her mother had hoped at one time although she would not admit to this now. Lally's dress is a heavy satin number with a covering of matching lace at the front. It is cut into a tight fishtail, so that it swings around when she tries it on and twirls in front of the mirror. Which she does. Often. Although not while Joan is there.

'Such a lovely colour on you,' Joan's mother says, and for a moment her eyes mist a little, threatening to break out. 'I just wish your father . . .' She shakes her head. 'Listen to me going on.'

'It's fine, Mum. You can talk about him if you want.'

'Oh, I do. I talk to him as well. He's a good listener now, better than when he was alive.' She laughs, and presses the tear that is glistening on her lower eyelash. 'He was so proud of you, Joanie. I wish you could have heard how he spoke about you. He always said you were going to do something marvellous.'

Joan nods. She feels a terrible ache in her chest, as if someone has wrapped their hands around her heart and is pumping it out of time. 'Silly,' she whispers.

But for the first and only time in Joan's life, her mother does not agree with this statement. She shakes her head. 'No, Joanie. Not silly. I was the silly one. Your father was right to be proud of you.' She puts her hand firmly on Joan's back. 'Now stand there and don't move.'

There is a pause, and for a moment Joan considers telling her mother everything.

'Terrible news about that bomb in Russia,' her mother says suddenly. She does not look up but takes a handful of pins out of her tin and then holds each of them by the sharp point between her lips, so that her mouth is a row of spikes. She has always done this. It is one of Joan's earliest memories, being told to stand up straight while her mother pinned linens and cottons under her arms and around her waist, her mouth so full of pins that Joan was scared to move in case she surprised her mother and caused her to swallow them. She thinks of those months before she left for Cambridge, her mother planning and stitching her University

Trousseau in spite of her opposition, plotting ways of finding a fur coat to make her look the part, all of it parcelled up and packed into her trunk for her to open once she had arrived.

'Yes.'

'They thay,' her mother lisps, removing the pins one by one and pulling the fabric out straight so that she can make sure the hem fans evenly around her, 'they think the Ruthians mutht have had a thpy.' She removes the two final pins from her mouth and stands back, surveying her handiwork, and then she pinches the material just below Joan's bosom and pins it symmetrically, more or less, so that the bust is accentuated. 'They think it's a British scientist.'

A pause. Joan's breaths are suddenly shallow.

'It's all nonsense anyway, that's what your father says. Said,' she corrects herself. 'All wars start because of secrets.'

'So if there were no secrets . . .' Joan whispers.

Her mother frowns, considering this, and then shrugs. 'If only everyone would play nicely,' she says airily, and the moment of vindication that had appeared to be hovering above Joan evaporates.

'But they don't have any evidence anyway,' Joan continues. 'They're only saying they've got a suspect to keep the Americans happy, to show they're doing something.'

Her mother looks at her in astonishment. She shakes her head slowly. 'I shouldn't think so. Haven't you heard? It was on the radio this morning. They're holding that Cambridge professor in Brixton Prison until it goes to trial. So there must be something to base the charges on. Now lift your arms.'

382

Joan holds her arms out at the sides so that her mother can pin the waistline of her dress, tugging the joins of material tighter and tighter against her ribs until Joan can hardly breathe. Does this mean they have actually found some evidence? She sees the furrow of her mother's brow as she bends forward to adjust the waistline of the dress, and she feels a shot of panic rising up inside her. She breathes in, out, in again.

Her mother steps back. 'There,' she says. 'Beautiful.' She pauses. 'Joan? Are you all right? You look rather pale.'

Friday, 7.24 a.m.

Brixton Prison
25 September 1949

Dear Joan,
First day over. They say the first of everything is always the worst, although I can think of numerous exceptions to that rule, but let me hold to it on this occasion so that I can assume the worst has now passed. I have not yet begun etching the days into my bedpost but perhaps that will come. Tomorrow, maybe. I can't imagine that it's going to be easy to adjust. It's not the discomfort; in fact, I find that much easier than I had expected. I have a room to myself, and a choice of bunks, so obviously I have taken the top one. Surprising, really, how I still felt a rush of glee at the prospect of a top bunk. But the mattress is hard and the blanket is

coarse; prison-like, you might say.

To be honest, it isn't the loss of freedom which is so difficult. I can stop myself thinking about that if it becomes too bad. The hardest thing is to give any sense to this kind of existence, other than the purely negative sense of punishment for something I have not done.

Of course, I know that I should look on the bright side—justice will prevail, etc—and in the meantime I should try to consider this whole period as an opportunity for learning. I've already signed up for a plumbing course, and I'm going to move on to woodwork after that. And I've been thinking that I should read the Bible or the Qur'an or some other sort of religious text. I've been meaning to read those for years, although there used to always be something better to do. One of the fellows I met here today is ploughing his way through the dictionary, which sounds like a hellish read—no narrative arc, no plot, no romance!—but anyway, the poor chap's conversation now is so alphabetically top-heavy that all this dreary study hasn't made him any more lucid than he was before. It's all 'antagonism' and 'appreciable' and 'belligerence' with him, which is all very well, but he has to translate himself for most of them in here. He's been reading it for almost a year and still hasn't reached C. What new forms of purgatory we find to punish ourselves!

I hope everyone is well at the lab and they don't think too badly of me. How I wish I could convince them all that I am who I say I am, who I have always said I was—just me. I cannot write more as there is the censor to think of, and

I am not allowed to discuss details of the case in my personal correspondence (but this, dear Censor, is only an indirect detail)—I received a terrible letter from Donald the other day, saying that I could not possibly understand the extent of the dismay I had brought to all of them, and how the least I could do would be to confess. They said that treason cannot be mitigated, but if I confessed (to what??! I wouldn't even know how to approach a Russian agent, let alone become a spy! Sorry Censor, no more I promise) at least I would have made a start. Oh Joan. I sat down on my bunk and wept. Better to have remained aloof, they said, than to have befriended us and betrayed us so deeply.

If you see them, speak well of me. I don't expect you to convince them, only it would help me sleep more easily if I knew someone might stick up for me occasionally.

Lights out soon. Must finish so that I can send this in the morning post. If you do want to write—although I completely understand if you don't—regulations about letters are that I can write and receive one letter at indefinite intervals, at present one every two weeks. So it's not much use writing letters, except in answer to a letter from me, unless it is a question of urgency. In that case the Governor would tell me about it though I would not necessarily see the letter myself.

I can have my first visit on Saturday. Please let me know whether you want to come. I have been told that the first visits are a bit dismal, although apparently we can at least be in the same room for a time, and I might have skipped it only I

don't know how long I shall be here. I have
some news which I want to tell you in person.
I'm hoping the trial date will be set not too far in
the future, and then at least I can find out what
they have against me to keep me here.

And please don't hesitate to say if you'd rather
not come.

Yours,
Max

From St Albans, she takes the train to London and
then the tube to Stockwell, from where she will take
a bus to Brixton. Her travel bag is light against her
body. Money, a change of clothes, a sandwich, a
hand towel, a comb, a toothbrush, and a few
packets of cigarettes for Max. Even after thirty
years of living, the essentials amount to so little.
There is nothing else she really needs to take with
her, apart from the three letters which she will post
once she has left: one for her family, one for the
police and one for Max. She had considered one for
Karen too—after all, it was she who forwarded
Max's letter on to her at her mother's house—but
she will send something to her later. An
explanation, an apology. A lie. She thinks of her
dress for Lally's wedding and feels sorry that it will
go unused, but beyond that she refuses to imagine.
She does not think of her mother singing in the
concert next week, or of Lally dicovering that she
would not be there on her wedding day. She will
not torment herself with picturing her mother's face
when she reads the letter. She cannot, as otherwise
she would not be able to do it.

Stepping off the bus, Joan finds that she can
plant one foot in front of the other quite easily as

long as she does not think about what she has to do next. It is like walking along the edge of a cliff, watching how the breeze blows the daisies and buttercups on one side, and knowing that it is fine, it will all be fine; just don't look down. Except in Brixton there are no daisies or buttercups. There are rows of Victorian houses next to piles of rubble, war damage left untouched even though the war ended over four years ago, crowded buses, fruit stalls, bread shops and a lingering smell of uncooked fish.

It is not a long walk from the bus stop, mainly up the hill towards Streatham. She doubles back, stopping to look in the reflections of shop windows as is her habit. Nobody. Nothing. She is on her own and there is still a chance. The prison is on a quiet street, surrounded by a high brick wall. The Victorian architecture of the building has the intended effect: daunting and unassailable. It makes her shiver to look at the small windows, the neatly packed brickwork, the furnace chimneys soaring above the slanting roof. She has read that the footings of the old treadwheels remain visible in the main hall of the prison, and that at night the cells are overrun with rats and mice, although Max made no mention of this in his letter.

He is being brave but she knows it is a front. All week, he has been with her, appearing at the edge of her dreams. He has been tapping at the side of her head, trying to get her attention. She knows he will be lonely and frightened, even though he would hate to admit it.

She walks faster in the hope that her quickened heartbeat might drive these images out of her head. She breathes in and tips her head back so that the sunlight can splash her face with its brightness. Remember this, she thinks.

She goes to the visitors' entrance and is greeted by a man in a peaked cap, dressed rather like a bus conductor and with an air of having seen it all before. Certainly he has seen women like her before at the visitors' entrance, freshly powdered and prettily dressed.

'I'm here to see Professor Max Davis.'

'Old Lord Haw-Haw, eh?'

Joan looks at him sharply, remembering the fuss after the war when Lord Haw-Haw was hanged in Wandsworth Prison. The dark shadow of a hood flits into her mind, being pulled down, down over her face, and she shivers. She must be stronger than this, she thinks. And besides, it's not the same. Britain wasn't actually at war with the Soviet Union as it was with Germany when he was making his radio broadcasts. She lifts her head. 'Whatever happened to the presumption of innocence?'

The man shrugs, concentrating not on Joan but on riffling through his collection of forms.

'Ah-ha,' he says. 'Here you go. Prisoner Davis. First door on the left.'

Joan takes the form he is holding out to her. 'He didn't do it, you know. They'll let him off.'

The man looks at her. He sees the intensity of her gaze, her too-large irises making her eyes appear almost black, hands encased in gloves, hair swept back. He gives a slight frown and then his face seems to change in some small, imperceptible way. 'All right love, I believe you.'

'Thank you,' she says, and this time she says it very politely. She steps through the gateway and proceeds to the next door where she presents her

388

form to another man in a peaked cap who instructs her to follow him, and this time he makes no comment and nor does she. She follows him down one long concrete corridor and then another, until eventually he stops at a heavy door of reinforced metal and pushes it open with his shoulder to allow her through.

'Wait here,' he says.

Joan nods. The door crashes shut behind her but it is not locked. She sits at the table, facing the window. There is a smell of wet dogs and urine, and over the crust of this is another smell; more industrial, bleach perhaps, or some other cleaning fluid which is not quite enough to cancel out the other, stronger odours. She cannot look at the door behind her, at its dull blue wash of paint, at the bars across the viewing slot, at the great lock with its immoveable handle. She takes off her gloves and grips them tightly, uselessly, in her hands.

It is worse than she imagined. Gloomier, smellier. It might be different for women, she thinks. The smell would be different and there would be different discomforts, different sadnesses. She has imagined the feel of the prison clothes on her back, the bucket in the corner of the cell, eating porridge out of a tin bowl with a spoon. Eating everything with a spoon. And how much worse it must be for Max. To be here and to have done nothing. The thought of it torments her, knowing he will be despairing at the injustice of it all, and that they will not be giving him enough to eat, that he will not be sleeping properly.

She closes her eyes. She waits.

The door opens behind her, footsteps, and then a breathless pause. Slowly she stands up, turns around, and there he is. His hair is cut short and he is in a pale grey flannel jacket and trousers. There is a prisoner number on his chest and, when he sees her, his face breaks into a smile. She wants to sink to her knees, to put her head in her hands at the knowledge that she has done this to him, but she knows that this would not help either of them and so she does not. She forces herself to smile while the silence rises almost palpably between them.

He steps towards her, cautious and questioning, and reaches out to take her in his arms. 'You came,' he says. 'I didn't think you would.'

'No touching,' the guard says.

Joan makes a movement with her head which is somewhere between a shake and a nod, and steps obediently away from him. 'Of course I came.'

Max's arms drop to his sides. 'It's so good to see you.'

Joan swallows. 'You too.'

'How's everyone else?'

'Karen sends her love. She forwarded your letter to me.'

'Where?'

'I've been staying at my mother's while this is going on. I'm sure the others will . . . Well, they'll come round. It's just been a bit of a shock.'

Max nods but does not say anything. He looks uncomfortable, vaguely embarrassed. He sits down at the table and Joan goes to sit opposite him. Does he know? she wonders. It seems impossible that he does. Surely she would be able to tell if he did. There would be something different about him, something sharp.

He looks up at her and attempts a grin. 'Terrible service round here, isn't it?'

Joan smiles. She waits. No, she thinks. He doesn't know. 'I brought you some cigarettes,' Joan says, taking them from her bag and placing them on the table.

'Thanks.' A pause. And then Max speaks again. 'So, I said I had some news. I got a letter from my wife.'

'Oh?'

'She's finally agreed to the divorce. She's signed all the papers. It's official.' His face breaks into a grin and he reaches out his hand to her across the table. 'If I'd known that was all I needed to do, I'd have got myself arrested years ago. I'd ask you to marry me right now only this isn't how I want to do it. I want to wait until all this is done with and I've been cleared and then . . .' He stops. 'What is it? Why are you crying?'

Joan is clutching her bag to her chest and there is a slipping, shifting feeling inside her, as if something inside her is breaking in two. There is so much she wants to say. She cannot bear the thought of leaving him and explaining it all in a letter after she has gone. A huge wave of sound is building up and she has to push it down, down, so that when finally she trusts herself to speak, it comes out as a splutter. 'I can't, Max. I can't marry you.'

'Why not? Of course you can. I'll get out of here. I haven't done anything. They say they've got evidence but they haven't. Or if they have, I haven't seen any.'

'I know you haven't done anything.'

'Then what is it? Why are you crying?'

The words stick in her throat. She hears him ask the guard for just a minute alone. There is a pause, and then there is the sound of the door opening and closing as the guard relents and steps outside. It is just the two of them now in the room and she feels his arms slipping around her, lifting her up, stroking her hair, holding her, calming her, until her sobs have softened. She has to tell him now. There may never be another chance. She doesn't feel brave enough for this. She holds him tightly against her, her lips brushing his ear, and she whispers the words oh so gently into his neck. 'It was me.'

Max's arms grow slack around her body. She does not draw away because she does not want to see his face but he puts her down and steps back, holding her shoulders with both of his hands. 'You?'

Joan nods. She looks at the floor. Her whole body is shaking.

'You?' He walks across the room to the window and then to the door. He comes back into the centre of the room and then walks to the window again. Perhaps he will fling the table across the room. Perhaps he will call for the guard, hammering on the door to get her taken away, to set him free, swearing and shouting and telling her to leave.

'I'm going to confess,' she whispers, cringing at how pathetic the words sound.

Still Max says nothing. He is perfectly still now, staring at the bars on the window.

'I'm sorry,' she whispers.

He turns around. 'How could you?' he asks eventually, his voice quiet and angry. 'Why?'

Joan feels her body flush. 'I thought it was the right thing. After Hiroshima . . .'

Max groans.

'. . . after Hiroshima, it looked like the Russians would be next. I thought it would make everything safer.'

Max puts his hand against his forehead. 'All those commie marches when you were a student. They asked me if you were a security risk because of those and I said no, of course you weren't. I vouched for you. Told them it was just a phase. And Leo Galich.' He shakes his head. 'You did see him in Canada, didn't you?'

Joan looks away. She considers lying about this but decides there is no point. Slowly, she nods her head.

He turns away.

'I only saw him briefly, I swear. And I didn't want to, but he found me. But I said no then.'

A pause. 'Until Hiroshima.'

'Yes.' Joan steps towards him. 'Max, I'm sorry. Nobody was supposed to get caught.'

He snorts.

'Especially not you,' she whispers.

Silence.

'I'm going to tell them everything.'

Max doesn't turn around.

What am I expecting? Joan wonders. That he should be grateful to me? That he should thank me? She shakes her head at her own stupidity. 'But will you give me a few more days? I just need . . .' she hesitates, '. . . a bit more time to get away.'

He does not move. It's too late, Joan thinks. This is the end. He's going to make her confess now, or if he doesn't, he is going to inform the authorities as soon as she leaves and she'll be arrested before she even reaches Brixton Hill. She shouldn't have come here. She should have known that it would be too much for him to take in, that it would be impossible for him, for anyone in his position, to be reasonable about it. And why should he do as she asks? Why should he give her a few more days? Why should he not clear his name absolutely, right now?

She goes back to the table and picks up her gloves and bag. Her eyes are blurred with tears. She wants to put her arms around him, tell him that she loves him, that she never meant to hurt him, but she does not want to make it worse for him than it already is.

'Wait,' he says suddenly, spinning around. 'What do you mean, get away?'

'Australia,' she says. 'I'm going to Australia. There's a boat in five days' time. I promise you'll be fine. They'll drop all the charges once I confess.'

'Australia?'

There are footsteps in the corridor outside the door. She sees Max's eyes flick to the doorway, and she knows that this is her only chance. She has to get him to believe her. She reaches out her hand and touches him, and she feels the burn of his skin against hers. 'I promise you can trust me. I will get you out of here.'

Max shakes his head. 'No.' He grabs her hand. 'No.'

She can hardly breathe. 'Just a few days. That's all I need.'

He shakes his head.

'I know it's a shock for you and I'm so sorry.' Her voice is shaking. 'I can't tell you—'

'No, that's not what I meant.'

'Then what?'

'I mean, don't go.'

'But I have to. I have to confess. I have to get you out.' She looks up at the barred window. 'And if I stay here . . .'

'But don't you see? What's the point of that? I don't want you to go to Australia. I love you.'

She looks at him and her heart cracks inside her. 'I love you too,' she whispers.

'Exactly. So I want you to stay here, with me. There's no evidence against me anyway.' He looks at her. 'Why not just let me go to trial?'

Joan stares at him. She shakes her head. 'How could I do that? Even if you're acquitted, everyone will remember this. Your name won't ever be cleared. You won't be able to go back to your old job. Your old life.' She pauses. 'And you won't be able to forgive me.'

He is silent for a moment. 'You don't understand,' he says. 'I don't want my old life. It's all I've been thinking about while I've been in here. I want a new one, with you.'

Joan cannot speak. What does he mean? Surely he will want her to confess in one way or another. Nobody could be that generous. Not even Max. 'But how can you? After what I've done.'

He gives a wry half smile. 'I'm a mathematician, Joanie. As far as I can see this problem has no rigorous solution, based on my initial assessment of it. So the best I can do is find the closest approximation.'

Joan almost grins, in spite of herself. 'Don't tease me. Not now.'

There is a knock on the door. 'Two more minutes.' A gruff voice, deep and croaky.

Max pulls her closer to him. 'I'm not teasing you. You love me, don't you? I know you do. That's why you're here.'

'Of course I do. I had to see you. I had to tell you.'

'Well, there you are then.'

'What do you mean?'

'I mean, wait for me. Let me go to trial. Let me clear my name and then let's get married and never mention this ever again.'

She shakes her head. 'But now you know the truth, you'll have to lie for me. I'll be making you lie to protect me.' She pauses. 'They'll see it as the same level of betrayal.'

Max looks at her. 'Only if they find some evidence,' he whispers.

Her heart seems to stop, and when it starts again it pounds inside her. She cannot allow him to do this. She does not deserve it. It is too risky. There are too many things that could go wrong. A thought suddenly comes to her and she squeezes his body against her own, hurriedly trying to think how it might work. She can hear footsteps along the corridor outside. One more minute, she thinks. Just one more minute.

'There might be another way,' she whispers.

'What?'

'You'd have to be the running type though.'

'I can't run. In case you haven't noticed, I'm incarcerated in a high-security prison.'

'No, I mean, I think I can get you out.'

'How?'

'I have a friend in the Foreign Office. He's . . .' she hesitates. 'He's in the network too.'

Max rolls his eyes. 'There are more of you?'

Joan hesitates but she knows there is not enough time to explain. 'I'm sure he could sort something out for you. But not in England. That's the deal. If we leave now . . .'

'Not Russia,' he says. 'I couldn't live in Russia for the rest of my life.'

Joan shakes her head. 'How about Australia?'

The footsteps have reached the door now; heavy, hobnailed boots on the rough concrete floor indicating that the visit is over. Max steps forward and pulls her towards him so that her shoulder fits in under his arm and her face rests against his neck. She can feel his breath against her skin, short, indecisive bursts of air, his lips almost tickling her with their nearness. He holds her there, as close as he can, not speaking as the door opens and the guard appears in the doorway.

'Time,' he barks, standing aside so that Joan can pass.

Joan feels a terrible dryness in her throat. She knows she is asking too much. She cannot expect him to give up his home, his life, his country, just like that. And would it work, in any case? Would it not just put them both at risk?

She feels her body tremble as Max bends down to kiss her chastely on the lips. It is a farewell kiss, so painful, so definite. She feels tears rising and she has to close her eyes as his finger traces the line of her collarbone for the last time, and then slips around to lift the hair from her left ear so that when he leans forward to kiss her once more on the cheek, it is not a kiss which he delivers, but a murmured 'yes'.

Friday, 9.03 a.m.

The piece of paper in Joan's hand is folded into perfect quarters. She has memorised the address, but she looks at it anyway. She is wearing her fur, no longer wanted by the second cousin and officially hers to keep. It is flung around her shoulders, and when she walks, it falls open at the knee and swings confidently behind her. She arrives at William's office and the receptionist in the lobby directs her towards a settee whose cushions are covered in golden velour. She perches on the edge of it, her knees pressed together. She is holding herself in, tightly, tightly. There is a painting on the wall opposite her, a ship docked at dawn with the phosphorescent light of the city rising behind it. Where is that? she wonders, trying to distract herself from what she is about to do.

'Ah,' William says, striding into the grand foyer with a smile fixed on his face but his eyes questioning, alert. She can smell the sweet staleness of whisky on his breath as he kisses her. 'You got my note then?'

Joan stands up. 'Yes, and I was just passing,' she says, echoing William's words to her the last time they spoke. 'I thought you might be free for lunch.'

William turns to the receptionist who is inspecting Joan's legs, as if assessing the likelihood of this being a romantic lunch. 'I'm afraid you'll have to cover for me again, Cheryl. Tell anyone who asks that I'm out on business. And if it's Alice, mention that I'll be late.'

'Of course, sir.'

398

William waits until they have turned the corner and crossed the street into St James' Park and then he turns to her and takes both of her hands in his. 'I thought I might be seeing you. Why didn't you come to me earlier?'

'I didn't know anything was happening. You said you'd warn me.'

William's eyes are narrowed in confusion. 'Didn't you hear from Sonya?'

Joan shakes her head slowly. 'No.'

'That's strange. She said not to contact you as she wanted to do it herself. But then when I didn't hear from you . . .' He stops, seeing Joan's face crumple slightly. 'Are you in trouble?'

Joan is shivering now, her whole body seeming to ache with the cold in spite of the warmth of her coat. 'Yes,' she whispers. 'Please. Will you help me? I have to get out.'

He lifts his hands and presses them on her shoulders, intending to steady her but the sensation is discomforting. 'Are you sure? You know it will arouse suspicion if you just disappear.'

She nods. 'They've arrested Max. They know there's been a leak from our laboratory.'

William sighs. 'They think there has, you mean.' He looks down at her and she observes that his eyes are pouchy and tired. 'It's falling apart, Jo-jo. Rupert has been posted to the Washington Embassy. Which is an enormous coup for us, of course, but he's becoming a liability. He's falling out of clubs every night, completely gone. Apparently he told some woman he's a Russian spy and it's been passed off as a joke, but he's a time bomb out there. I think the pressure's got to him.' He glances at Joan. 'Sorry. That's not why you're here, is it?'

'This is urgent, William. I need to get out now.' She pauses. 'You promised.'

William frowns. 'All right, all right. I can apply for full defector treatment for you. I know they hold you in extremely high regard. You'll get a good flat, a pension . . .'

'Not Russia,' she interrupts. 'I couldn't.'

'Ah yes,' William says. 'We never quite managed to convince you on that score, did we?' He takes a cigarette case from his jacket pocket and flicks it open. 'Mind you, I'm not sure it would do for me either. I have terrible circulation.' He lifts up his hands and rubs them together before breaking into a hum. '*How cold my toes.*'

Joan does not smile. 'You mentioned Australia before. That's where I want to go.'

'Really? It's a long way.'

'Exactly.'

William frowns. 'That will take a while to sort out. A week. Maybe two.'

Joan shakes her head. She grasps his sleeve, a desperate, childish gesture. 'I can't wait that long.' She pauses. 'And there's something else.'

'What?'

'I need two tickets.'

'Two? Who's the other one for?'

Joan hesitates. 'It's for Max. I need you to get him out of prison and onto that boat.'

William stares at her. 'The professor? Why?'

'He knows everything. I've told him everything.'

His mouth opens and then closes again. His hands move outwards and then hesitate, falling back to his sides. 'But why?' he asks again.

'I had to, William. I couldn't have him going to

400

jail for something I've done. It's not right.' She pauses. 'He doesn't deserve it.'

William slaps a hand to his forehead and makes a small noise, a groan. He remembers something now, something he had barely paid any attention to at the time and which he had dismissed as harmless gossip over a drink between friends. 'You and Professor Davis. I forgot. Sonya told me there was something between the two of you, but she insisted it wasn't serious.' He pauses and looks at Joan, his eyes searching her face. Joan crosses her arms over her chest. William gives a sudden snort of laughter. 'Well, I guess she was wrong about that, wasn't she?'

'But can you get him out?'

'I'm not a magician, Jo-jo.'

'Please, William. Please.'

William looks at her. 'I'm sorry. It's too risky. I don't want to draw any more attention to myself right now than I need to. The Americans have cracked the old KGB codes. There are endless decrypts from foreign KGB operatives back to the Centre. I've told you, it's a time bomb, Jo-jo. I've got to keep my head down.' He looks at her. 'I can get you out but not him as well.'

'But he's innocent.'

'He's in custody. They want a trial. They need to show the Yanks they're doing something.'

'But he knows. I'm a liability too now.'

'Just keep him sweet. Pretend you're getting him out too. By the time he realises what's actually happened, you'll be halfway to Australia with a new passport and papers.'

'I can't do that.'

William shakes his head. 'I'm sorry, you'll just

have to let him take it. I can't do it. I can't take the risk, especially now with Rupert firing off all over the place. He's my main priority. Just sit tight.'

Joan stares at him. 'But you said—'

William waves his hand at her. 'I know, I know. But I didn't say I could do it for every man and his dog.'

Joan turns away from him. There is a bench by the lake and she walks over to it and sits down. She was not expecting this. She thought it would be enough for William that Max knew everything, and that she was in trouble. She still has one more card up her sleeve, but she will have to be convincing. She will have to say the words and mean them.

William follows her and sits down next to her. 'I'll still do it for you though, Jo-jo,' he says, and his tone is gentle, conciliatory.

She takes a deep breath. She does not want to do this, especially not to William. 'Which is it to be then?'

He looks puzzled. 'What do you mean?'

Her voice cracks a little as she speaks. 'Well, as I see it, there are two options.' She holds up a finger and is surprised to see that it is not shaking. 'One, you do as I ask. Or two . . .' she holds up a second finger, '. . . I send a letter to MI5 about you, giving names, dates, details of all your Russian activity. It'll mention Rupert too.'

'They wouldn't believe you.'

Joan raises her eyebrows. 'Wouldn't they?'

'There's nothing to link me to him. Nothing specific. We've always been very careful about that. Different colleges, different war sections. We've barely even lived in the same country for the past ten years.'

There is a pause. 'Well, that's where the photograph comes in.'

'What photograph?'

'The one I found in Sonya's house. It's of you and Rupert kissing. I have one copy for your wife and one for the *Daily Mail.*'

'You wouldn't do that.'

She must not flinch. 'Don't call my bluff, William.'

William's face turns a pale, ashen colour. 'But I thought we were friends.'

She lowers her hand onto his. She can feel the clammy warmth of his skin, the heat of it seeping up into her palm. 'I'm sorry,' she whispers. 'I'm desperate.'

William stands up. He starts to walk away. Don't! she thinks. Don't force me to actually do it. It is almost as if he hears her. He stops, kicks at a thistle in the grass, thrusts his fists deep into his pockets, and spins back towards where Joan is sitting.

'All right,' he says, and his voice is low and resigned. 'We might have one chance. If I can persuade them that it'll compromise the American decrypts of Russian signals too much to use the evidence they've got, then we're in with a chance. I'll have to persuade them that he's better off being sent out to pasture in Oz as I know they're struggling to find anything on him that doesn't give away our sources. All they have is circumstantial evidence at the moment, and some throwaway comment he made to the head of the Chalk River plant in Canada. It'll be a crappy teaching job and transportation for life, at best. Only they don't call it that any more. But it is possible. I know a few cases where it's been done. Hushed up, of course.

403

New identities. New start.'

Joan leans across and takes William's hand. 'Thank you,' she whispers.

He frowns. 'I'll need a day or two.'

She nods. 'There's a fast boat leaving in four days.' She holds out her hand for his and he takes it, slowly, and shakes it. 'I want us to be on it.'

'You drive a hard bargain, Miss Robson.' He leans down and kisses her hand, but it is a hard kiss, and he is holding her too tightly. 'And if you really want to thank me, you can burn that picture of me and Rupert.'

Joan looks at him, and there is a waft of a smile passing between them. 'It's a deal.'

Friday, 11.17 a.m.

The press conference is scheduled for midday. It will take place at Joan's house and she will address the press agents and journalists from her front step. Certain members of MI5 will be present, not just Ms Hart and Mr Adams, and there will be a strong security element. For her own protection, apparently. Her name was officially released in the House of Commons this morning at approximately the same time as William's body disappeared through the curtain at the crematorium to be turned into ash and scattered by his surviving friends and relations, his secret safe in her keeping.

She picks up the telephone and dials Nick's number. It rings out. She tries his mobile next, but it goes straight to the recorded message. She listens to the entire message, her heart pounding, but when the beep comes she does not say anything because she doesn't know what it is she wants to say. Just that she is sorry. And that she loves him. And that she doesn't blame him for the choice he has made. What he said to her yesterday in the bathroom was quite right. It is his turn to choose now. Actions have consequences, she has always known that.

By mid-morning, the police have cordoned off the front and side of the house, and there are cars and bikes jammed together at the end of the cul-de-sac. There are people milling around, setting up cameras and drinking coffee from flasks. Photographs are being taken of the front of the house, unassuming and pebble-dashed with net curtains and ornaments on the windowsill. The front door is made of solid oak and the narrow path cuts through a neat square of frost-covered grass, bordered by shrubs. A recycling bin stands empty at the front of the house and there is a microphone set up on the garden path.

Joan calls Nick's mobile again. Answer phone. She hangs up.

She feels an ache as she thinks of all the people she has loved: Max, her mother, her father, Lally. She imagines Lally's grown-up children, her nieces and nephew, watching the press conference on the television, calling each other afterwards to discuss their odd estranged aunt who never forgot a single birthday throughout their childhood, who always sent extravagant postal orders tucked into cards with koalas and kangaroos on the front, but who didn't come home for her own mother's funeral, and whose sister never forgave her for that. At least now they would know why she had always stayed away, even if it was too late to explain it to Lally. Would any of them call her afterwards? Would any of them forgive her?

No. And why should they?

She dresses carefully, selecting something neutral and smart. She puts on a lilac skirt and a cream blouse, and then ties a dark brown silk scarf around her neck. She slips on her tan-coloured mackintosh and buttons it up to the top. There is a handkerchief tucked into the bottom of her sleeve. Her shoes are black and practical-looking with Velcro straps. She stands in front of the mirror and looks at herself. She breathes out slowly.

She checks her watch. Two minutes. She goes into the hallway again and lifts the telephone receiver. She starts to dial Nick's number once more, but her hand is shaking too much. She puts the receiver down. It is too late now.

She walks to the front door. Behind it she can hear the hum of people talking, jostling, preparing. She unhooks the silver chain and puts her hand on the catch. She thinks that somewhere inside her she has always known that this is how it would end. Just her, alone with her terror.

But she also knows that it is no more than she deserves. She turns the catch and the door clicks open.

Friday, 12 p.m.

There is a strobe effect of all the cameras starting at once, freezing her in time. Joan steps forward and raises her hand to her chest, trying to calm the terrible pounding of her heart. She stands on the front step, and the door closes behind her. She scans the crowd for Nick but cannot see him anywhere. A young man wearing headphones and a brown duffel coat approaches to adjust the volume of the microphone, and then he steps back, grins and gives her a thumbs-up signal.

She lifts her eyes but the sight of so many people makes her feel giddy and she has to look down again. She had not expected such a mass of interest. Perhaps a local newspaper or two, but not this. There are proper news cameras accompanied by live reporters and huge sound receivers as well as journalists and photographers. She recognises an Australian news logo on one of the microphones, and then an American one, and there are many, many more she doesn't recognise. Ms Hart and Mr Adams are poised at the side of the house, ready to intervene if necessary, along with the line of policemen stationed at intervals along the cordon. Her legs are unsteady. If she could just catch a glimpse of Nick's face . . .

An image of Sonya flits into her head, and for a moment she thinks how much better Sonya would be at this than she is. She would be enjoying all the attention. Joan can picture her standing on a doorstep somewhere, dressed in silk and diamonds, holding a cat under her arm and denying everything, and at last Joan's body floods with a terrible blend of anger and hurt at the memory of Sonya's betrayal. But the anger is not with Sonya. The anger is with herself for not seeing it in time, for ignoring the clues, for not warning Leo, for not holding him in her arms and telling him that he mustn't go to Moscow because Sonya was not to be

407

trusted, for believing that Sonya would warn her if she was ever in danger. For not realising that Sonya did understand the rules because they were her rules, and really, they had both known that from the start. She had known it from the day Sonya took her to that woman's house and pushed her forwards, up the stairs, and told her never to tell anyone.

She takes a deep breath and the crowd falls silent, waiting for her to speak. She knows what she wants to say: that she does not agree with the principle of spying against one's country but these were unprecedented times. But when she tries to speak the words will not come. There are small flashes of black behind her eyes, infrequent at first but becoming gradually more regular so that now all she can see is a familiar watery darkness. She feels her heart falter and then her knees buckle beneath her. There is a rush of air as she falls. Is this it? she wonders. Am I dying? Is it really happening here, now, in front of all these people?

The porch step makes a snapping sound under her arm, the cold grey stone causing her to cry out in pain as her arm folds beneath her. There is a sudden burst of noise, a chatter of camera lenses buzzing and clicking as people jostle closer. She hears her name being called, but the noise is distant and irregular. Her head thrums as the waves of blackness swell and recede.

A hand is placed on her back, and a voice calls out for an ambulance. A blanket is laid over her and there is a tapping on her chest and arms. She slips in and out of consciousness, her mind swirling with memories of Leo and Sonya, until eventually she feels her body being rolled onto a stretcher. An oxygen mask is strapped across her face and now all she can think of is Max. Her body feels suddenly light and soft. Someone is holding her wrist and numbers are being called out. She is lifted up and jolted into the ambulance, her wrist still suspended in mid-air and held aloft by the paramedic. Why could she not just have agreed to Nick's plan? Why could she not just have given them what they wanted?

Her eyes flicker. Her heart is jumping in her chest. 'Nick,' she whispers. 'Nick.' She wants to pull the mask off her face but she cannot move her arms. One of them is strapped down and the other is twisted awkwardly across her stomach. There is a loud beeping noise on the monitor next to her. The paramedic sees her panic and lifts the mask a little, bending down so that he can hear her.

'Nick,' she mouths.

The paramedic frowns uncomprehendingly at her. 'Don't try to speak.' He tightens the mask over her face, and she hears the engine ignite. The siren sounds once and then stops, and a door slams somewhere near Joan's head. The ambulance starts to move.

It is over, she thinks. I will never see my son again. He will never know how it ended, or just how much I have loved him.

But then she feels the ambulance jerk to a halt and there is a sudden blast of cold air as the back door is flung open.

'I'm sorry, you can't just open the door like that. We need Home Office consent for anyone to accompany her. Who are you?'

'Nicholas Stanley, QC,' Nick announces, his voice rising above the sound of the engine and the hiss of the oxygen mask, curt and impatient as he steps up onto the platform at the back of the ambulance.

A pause. The paramedic is not expecting this. 'Well, I'm afraid it's not normal practice for a patient's lawyer to . . .'

'No, no, of course not,' Nick says abruptly, but when he speaks again his words fall on Joan like balm on an open wound. 'But she's my mum and I'm going with her.'

* * *

The mink coat was a mistake. In Southampton it stands out like a small red poppy in a sea of green, but it is too heavy to carry along with her suitcase, and besides, at five-thirty in the morning, the streets are still dark enough for the fur to remain dull and coarse-looking. It could be fake fur. In fact, anyone who saw it would think it was. It wouldn't be real, not here among the dockyard warehouses and traffic. The sky is pink, shot through with tiny flares of orange. There is a milk cart weaving its way through the steady stream of dockers and passengers heading down towards the port. A slowly rising smell of fires and bread filters up among the cranes and funnels.

Impossible to think that the hotel room she has just left will be the last place she ever sleeps in her home country, that she will never again see her mother or sister or the house in which she grew up; that this is the end. Impossible to imagine that she is capable of running away like this, slipping off from one life to another. What will they say at the laboratory when they hear the story? Will Karen

410

pretend she knew all along that something was going on, or will they simply be flabbergasted and silent, as they were last week when Max was arrested? No, she thinks, the silence would not last for long. Perhaps, if anything, Karen will be pleased for them both when she hears. Joan will send her a postcard when they settle in, explaining things. Explaining some things, to be precise. Not everything, of course.

She walks on down the hill towards the dockyard from which the boat will depart. William has arranged to transport Max personally from Brixton to Southampton as the official government escort. Her instructions are quite plain: she must meet them at the boarding station at 6 a.m. precisely—no earlier, no later—and then he will see them onto the boat. There can be no deviation from this plan. It is risky enough as it is.

There is a beating in her chest. It is in her heart, in her lungs, in her head. It is not a pounding, even though she can feel the separate bursts of blood, but the beats are too small to be pounds, too regular. It is more of a ticking. Yes, that is what it is. Her whole body is ticking, marking off the seconds.

What if they don't come? She has her passport and enough money to buy a ticket for herself if they don't show up. In fact, if they don't, she would have no option but to go, as the only reason they would not come would be if something had gone wrong, if they had found some last minute evidence to implicate her, or if William had let them down, or if—she can hardly bear to think of the last possibility—Max had changed his mind and decided that he would prefer to tell the truth and clear his

411

name rather than run away like this. And why wouldn't he? Tick, tick, tick.

A church bell rings, slowly, loudly. Six o'clock. She waits, counting the chimes. She feels a trembling along her spine. Nothing happens. She waits a little longer. A dark blue car turns into the wide cobbled street and approaches slowly, its windows opaque. Somewhere close by she hears the sound of a crane hauling a box of cargo up onto the boat. A sudden cough of smoke from one of the funnels. Tick, tick. A bus halts a little way down the road and begins to offload its passengers. The dark blue car pulls up in front of the bus, just a few feet away from Joan. This is it, she thinks. She pictures Max on the other side of the window, his hair prison-short, no longer fluffing up at the sides.

The driver's window opens. William's eyes are tired and bloodshot. He looks as if he has not slept for days. Joan approaches, resplendent in mink, her suitcase clasped in her hand. Her skin is hot, too hot, and her legs are suddenly weak.

'Have you got him?' she asks, bending to look further into the car. Her view is obscured by William but she can see Max's hands resting on his thighs. His stillness unnerves her.

William nods. He hands her an envelope. Her fingers tremble as she opens it and checks the tickets. Two passengers; Southampton to Cairo, Cairo to Singapore and, finally, Singapore to Sydney. She takes out her new passport and runs her finger over the name. Joan Margery Stanley. She opens Max's new passport and checks that too. George Stanley. Not entirely new but a common enough name for some overlap not to matter, and enough of a difference to allow him a fresh start,

412

albeit on the condition that he never again returns to Britain. Birth certificates, marriage certificate, employers' references. It is all there. And at the bottom of the envelope, a St Christopher's medal with a note stapled to the chain. She will look at the note later.

'Thank you,' she whispers. 'How can I ever repay you?'

'Never tell anyone,' he whispers. 'That's all I ask. And burn the photograph.'

Joan shakes her head. She reaches into her pocket and hands the photograph to him. 'I thought you might like to do it,' she says. 'That's the only copy, as far as I know.'

William smiles and slips it into the inside pocket of his jacket. 'Thank you.' He turns to Max, still sitting motionless beside him, and touches him on the arm. 'Time to go, Professor.'

William winds the window up, his job done. The two men shake hands, and then Max gets out of the car and walks around to take his suitcase from the boot. He does not look at Joan as he does so, not even a glance or a nod to give any indication of what he is thinking. Has he changed his mind? Does he want his old life back now after all? Perhaps he will say it once William has gone, hand her over to the authorities at Customs, tell her that he cannot believe she ever thought she'd get away with it. Or . . .

But the next thought does not have time to form itself in Joan's mind, because just at that moment Max closes the car boot and looks straight at her, his blue eyes glittering in the dim glow of the dawn, and he is smiling, grinning even, and in another second his arms are around her waist and he is

413

lifting her, snatching her up like a leaf caught in the wind, and holding her so tightly that she can hardly breathe ('I'm sorry,' she whispers into his neck, 'I'm sorry I'm sorry I'm sorry') and her suitcase and coat must be making her heavy but he doesn't seem to notice because he is laughing, and then suddenly so is she, both of them giddy like children. He puts her down and they begin to walk—it is almost a run— up the wooden steps and onto the boat, turning at the top of the steps to see William flash the car headlamps in farewell and, for a brief moment, Joan lets go of Max's hand so that she can put her fingers to her lips and blow William a kiss.

And it is not just a kiss. It is also a promise.

Author's Note

The inspiration for this book came from a newspaper article published in 1999 in *The Times* (snappily captioned 'The Spy Who Came In From The Co-op') in which Melita Norwood was identified at the age of eighty-seven as having been the most important and longest-serving Soviet spy of the Cold War era. New evidence to identify her became available when Vasili Mitrokhin defected to Britain from the KGB in 1992, bringing with him a huge number of painstakingly copied files previously unseen by the British intelligence services. Norwood was dubbed the 'granny spy', making a televised statement to the press in her garden in which she was, disappointingly if unsurprisingly, rather economical with the truth, and not hugely remorseful. Norwood's case was later considered by Parliament and a decision was made by the Home Secretary not to prosecute on the grounds of age. I was in the middle of a history degree at Cambridge University when I read this story, and subsequently took a paper led by Professor Christopher Andrew, the historian contacted by Vasili Mitrokhin when he first left Russia and the co-author of the various volumes of the Mitrokhin Archive which finally identified Melita Norwood, and it was during that time that *Red Joan* was born.

Apart from having Che Guevara mugs and not wishing to receive any payment for their activities, the only resemblance between Melita Norwood and Joan Stanley is that they both worked as personal assistants to the directors of important metals research facilities during the Cold War (Norwood working at the British Non-Ferrous Metals Association from 1932 to 1972, and Joan working in a fictitious department albeit located for the purposes of the novel in the real-life Cavendish Laboratories at the University of Cambridge), thus giving them access to the highest level documents on atomic research in the project known as Tube Alloys, while also retaining a level of protection from suspicion which came largely from the fact of their gender. The differences between the two women (one real, one not) are varied and multiple, and Joan Stanley is not intended to be a representation of Melita Norwood. Whereas Joan has a university degree in science and a high level of technical knowledge, Melita Norwood had neither of these advantages, and whereas Joan displays a wavering attitude towards communism, Melita Norwood remained a committed communist right until the end, visiting Russia after her retirement and continuing to distribute the *Morning Star* around her neighbourhood in Bexleyheath beyond her eighty-ninth birthday. In many ways her story is quite remarkable, but it is not the story I wanted to tell here.

The character of Sonya is loosely based on Melita Norwood's controller during this time, one of the very few female controllers operating during the Cold War, Ursula Beurton (also known as Ruth and codenamed Sonya) who trained in China and then operated a radio system in a farmhouse near Oxford with her husband. The case of Kierl was inspired by the trial and prosecution of atomic spy Klaus Fuchs in 1949, who was also controlled by

Beurton (whereas Kierl is controlled here by Leo and remains in Canada).

The setting of much of the story is in some ways inevitable, Cambridge being infamous for its cultivation of some of the most famous KGB spies this country has produced and who were all in Cambridge a little before Joan, but their influence is intended to be felt through Leo, Rupert and William. Leo's thesis is largely based on the research interests of Maurice Dobb and Michal Kalecki, both Cambridge Marxist economists who were interested in the theory of Soviet Planning and its practical wartime implications.

Any other resemblances to persons real or imaginary are entirely unintentional.

*   *   *

A large number of books were extremely useful in researching the background to this book and I would like to mention the following which were of particular help:

The Mitrokhin Archive: The KGB in Europe and the West, Christopher Andrew and Vasili Mitrokhin (London, Penguin, 2000)
The Spy Who Came in From the Co-op: Melita Norwood and the ending of the Cold War, Dr David Burke (Woodbridge, Boydell Press, 2008)
Bluestockings: The Remarkable Story of the First Women to Fight for an Education, Jane Robinson (London, Viking, 2009)
My Sister: Rosalind Franklin, Jenifer Glyn (Oxford, Oxford University Press, 2012)
Klaus Fuchs: The Man Who Stole the Atom Bomb,

417

Norman Moss (New York, St Martin's Press, 1987)
The Thirties: An Intimate History, Judith Gardiner (London, Harper Press, 2010)
Soviet Economic Development Since 1917, Maurice Dobb (London, Routledge and Kegan Paul, 1947)

The National Archives at Kew were also an invaluable resource, with all of the interviews and reports being based, in some fashion, on genuine reports, particularly in relation to MI5's pursuit and interrogation of Klaus Fuchs. There is one deliberate anomaly in the dates where I have referred to the Tube Alloys project as being in existence under this name in 1941, when in fact it was not given this name until 1942.

Please visit my website at www.jennierooney.com for further information.

ACKNOWLEDGEMENTS

This novel went through a number of drafts and my unending thanks go to the people who have given their support, advice and encouragement at each stage: my agent, Clare Alexander, for never holding back with suggestions of improvements and nuggets of wisdom, my editors at Chatto & Windus, Juliet Brooke, whose insightful notes on each draft were almost worth publishing in themselves, and Clara Farmer for her enthusiasm and guidance throughout. Further thanks and appreciation also go to everyone at Random House, especially Lisa Gooding and Will Smith. In addition, I'd like to thank Suzanne Dean for her beautiful cover design.

My very grateful thanks also go to those who have generously given their time and assistance to the research of this book: Dr Peter Holmes of the University of Sussex for his general comments and for suggesting the idea for Leo's thesis; Dr Alix McCollam of Radboud University Nijmegen in the Netherlands who corrected my rather shaky understanding of nuclear physics with admirable indulgence (and Dr Richard Samworth for putting us in touch); Dr David Burke for sharing his knowledge of Melita Norwood's political activities with me, as well as elaborating on the fascinating story of his involvement with her at the time of her exposure in the national newspapers. In addition, I am grateful for the assistance of Anne Thomson, archivist at Newnham College, Cambridge for being generous with her time and knowledge, and for the general assistance given to me by staff at the

National Archives in Kew. As ever, any lingering factual mistakes and discrepancies are my own.

I would also like to give special thanks to friends and family who experienced the trauma of being early readers of the manuscript, and whose comments, big and small, were hugely appreciated: particularly my mum, dad and brothers, Tammy Holmes, Peter Holmes, Ann Holmes, Gillian Hardcastle, Sarah Beckett, and the members of my fabulous 'focus group': Frankie Whitelaw, Emma Clancey, Della Fanning, Helen Harper, Emma Whiteford, Sarah Machen, Lucy Stoy and Kate Wilson, whose willingness to critique with reckless abandon was not just admirable, but also hugely helpful. Thanks also to Joan Winter (she knows why) and to my family and friends who kindly continued to ask how the novel was coming on. But most of all, thank you to Mark, without whom it would all have felt like pretty hard work.

CHIVERS
LARGE
PRINT
–direct–

If you have enjoyed this Large Print book and would like to build up your own collection of Large Print books, please contact

Chivers Large Print Direct

Chivers Large Print Direct offers you a full service:

• Prompt mail order service

• Easy-to-read type

• The very best authors

• Special low prices

For further details either call Customer Services on (01225) 336552 or write to us at Chivers Large Print Direct, **FREEPOST**, Bath BA1 3ZZ

Telephone Orders: **FREEPHONE** 08081 72 74 75